Here's what the critics say about this blazing new novel that tells how three men find the meaning of life—and death—in the U.S. Paratroops!

"Character, events and dialogue hold the reader . . . this is a book to be tasted with relish."

Washington Post-Times Herald

"Tart humor here . . . The author's descriptions of what it is like to jump out of an airplane in flight are excellent."

The New York Times Book Review

". . . Good story-telling, good adventure, good characterization . . . A keen insight into the hearts of men."

Baltimore Sun

PATH FOR OUR VALOR

THOMAS DOULIS

AN AVON BOOK

AVON BOOKS
A division of
The Hearst Corporation
959 Eighth Avenue
New York, N. Y. 10019

Single is the race, single
Of men and of gods;
From a single mother we both draw breath.
But a difference of power in everything
Keeps us apart;
For the one is as nothing, but the brazen sky
Stays a fixt habitation for ever.
Yet we can in greatness of mind
Or of body be like the Immortals,
Though we know not to what goal
By day or in the nights
Fate has written that we shall run.

—PINDAR, Nem. VI 1-7

FORT MOSBY, three times as large as the District of Columbia, extends over 135,000 acres and is approximately 29 miles long and 15 miles wide. The 3,421 buildings on the reservation can shelter a maximum of 170,000 men. In population, it easily surpasses Von Steuben, Tennessee, and it can be considered the city's chief source of revenue.

The barracks, administrative buildings, motor pools, and equipment sheds, rising up on regimented, geometrical company streets, are located at the extreme eastern edge of the reservation. The 43rd Airborne Division area, where the front guard of freedom is garrisoned in a formation of 40 three-story barracks buildings, twinkles in the night like a constellation of expensive apartment houses. Three miles to the south of the Division area is a small hill on which is situated a regimental-sized unit, the Special Troops. These men, too, are paratroopers—Fort Mosby has been called the "Home of the Airborne"—but their mission is less orthodox than that of the 43rd. They are commando-guerrillas, trained to destroy the enemy by cunning, division, harassment, and confusion. It is appropriate, therefore, that the Special Troopers do not wear the conventional garrison cap but wear the green beret, on whose left side is a representation of the Trojan horse.

Beyond the garrisons, to the west, the forests grow freely, the drop zones slumber unguarded, and at night the lakes, with preternatural stillness, reflect the lighted universe of the southern sky.

Von Steuben, a neon-lighted and MP-patrolled community, is 15 miles south of the Post. The City Hall stands in the center of the city, at the crossroads of two wide streets. Fort Mosby cannot be seen from its windows, but the presence of the military reservation can be felt throughout the day and night.

PART ONE

Give me an angel for a foe,
Fix now the place and time,
And straight to meet him I will go
Above the starry chime.

—THOREAU

still asleep." He rubbed his eyes. "By the way, Sergeant, what's your name?"

"Damianos. Tell the captain we caught the escaped prisoner who made off with the guard's shotgun. Someone saw him dash across the highway going to Pine Bluff, near the Ranger's station. Took a few shots at us."

Clarke stared at Damianos. "I'll wake Jenkins up."

He snapped the fluorescent lights on in Colonel Simms' office, waited for a second until the random buzz became harsh light, and went to the bunk. "Captain . . . Captain Jenkins." The officer froze momentarily, opened his eyes, and closed them again.

"What's the matter? Is it time already?"

"No, sir. Sergeant of the Guard's outside. His name is Damianos. They've caught the escaped prisoner."

"What goddamn prisoner?" The officer lunged out of his bunk and began dressing. "Tell him to come right in, Clarke."

"Better give him time to pull his pants on," Clarke said when he rejoined Damianos. The sergeant nodded, wiped the water from his face, and got out of his slicker. As the NCO marched into the colonel's room, Clarke heard the measured pace and the halt. During the pause, he imagined a stiff right arm raised to the salute. The deep voice carried clearly into the large office of the Headquarters, and Clarke, walking to the window, looked out at the stormy night to see the blazing light bulbs on the barracks' fire escapes. Fully three hundred yards separated the Headquarters building from the cantonments in which the Troops were billeted. It was dark inside; everyone was asleep.

A light behind him dimmed Clarke's vision of the jeep, but the saw, within the white mask of his face's reflection, the vehicle and, in the rear seat, wrists manacled by shining handcuffs, a young Negro who appeared to slouch in deep slumber, his head bowed and his chin nuzzling his chest. Clarke nodded to the guard, who had been glancing in his direction.

You were stupid, Clarke thought. *You could have kept quiet, done what you were told, and been free when your sentence was up.* And Clarke knew the captive would be severely punished for his escape, not once, for he had tried to free himself from one punishment, but twice: was his escape not a challenge to the military authorities? He should have said yes and yes and yes and pretended to be a model prisoner, and *then* he would have been free. But he had to be contrary; he had to challenge *them*.

Captain Jenkins came out of his room, clothed but unshaven. His paratrooper boots, still unlaced, dragged their black leather strings behind them on the green linoleum floor. Lifting the telephone receiver off its hook, he dialed a number; he rubbed his hands over his beard while he listened to the buzzing in the earpiece. "Hello. . . . Captain Jenkins here. . . . I'm the OD at Special Troops. . . . This the Provost Marshal's? . . . OK. . . ." He waited. "Hello. . . . This is the Special Troops' OD. . . . You Lieutenant Stegman? Well, we got hold of the escaped prisoner. . . . How do I know what the hell his name is? Do you lose that many? A nigger, a bad one."

Clarke glanced at Damianos for an instant but saw only a blank stare.

"How long will you people be?" Jenkins tapped a pencil's tip on the desk. "Fifteen minutes? OK. . . ." He smiled. "If you aren't here in twenty minutes, we'll give him back his razor and turn him loose. How's that?"

After he had hung up, the captain turned to Damianos. "Bring him in here, Sergeant, and set him in the corner so we can keep an eye on him. I'm going to shave for a minute." He glanced at his wristwatch. "I've got 0415. Just my luck. Once a month I pull OD and hell breaks loose. It never fails." Jenkins picked up his electric razor from the desk. "Clarke, hold down the fort while I shear my whiskers."

"Yes, sir."

Damianos' face was expressionless, yet Clarke had the distinct feeling that the sergeant was waiting for the captain to close the latrine door before he spoke.

"You know"—the door slammed—"Lieutenant Stegman . . . at the Provost Marshal's . . . is colored."

Clarke felt the blood rush to his face but immediately checked his response. "I can't . . . we can't be responsible for what other people say."

"Your face just got red."

This was stated as a fact, but Clarke interpreted it as an accusation. "I can't be responsible for what my face does, either."

Damianos chuckled. "That's pretty good."

The laugh was a pleasant one, and since Clarke detected no sarcasm, he permitted his retort to stand without qualifying it.

The sergeant turned to go. "Hey! Did I scare you that much when I woke you?"

"It was nothing. A bad dream, that's all." He ran his fingers through his hair. "I keep falling in my dreams. Into a city."

Damianos nodded. "Those're real bitches. I never had that one. Maybe paratroopers get inoculated against dreams like that." He paused. "Are you a straightleg?"

Clark nodded.

"Maybe if you went airborne, the dreams would stop."

Clarke smiled quickly. "That's an original way of analyzing dreams, but I don't think it's the best."

"You're scared of something, buddy. And it's not parachuting." The sergeant turned abruptly and walked to the door.

Physically, Damianos did not seem to Clarke to be the kind of man who would need a side arm for protection. A little under six feet in height, he appeared to weigh approximately 215 pounds, without any apparent softness. He wore khakis tapered at the waist which, wet as they were, stuck to his body and revealed his muscular sturdiness. The great difference in girth between his shoulders and waist was accentuated by the brief line of black belt at the midsection. Below his garrison belt, the olive-drab pistol belt hung down across the top of his buttocks, giving him an uncharacteristically youthful and casual look. Above the thick, bearish neck, just over the bones of his cranium, a green beret, thoroughly soaked, perched on his head. Clarke saw the backs of Damianos' muddy jump boots a second before the screen door slammed.

At the window now, Clarke heard a murmur of voices near the jeep and saw the guard pull himself out of the vehicle. Then the sergeant's voice lashed out sharply at the prisoner above the roar of the wind. "On your feet!" There was a start, a faint tinkle of the handcuffs' chains against the braces, and the slow, tentative scraping of boot leather against the jeep's side. Within seconds the prisoner was rushed into the office by Damianos and the PFC. They walked him to a corner and sat him on a wheeled office chair, his back against a row of safes containing classified information. The sergeant lighted a cigarette, took several puffs, and placed it between the captive's lips, while the PFC laid a muddy M1 rifle on the Adjutant's desk.

"Sergeant!" Jenkins shouted from the latrine.

"Sir!"

"Is the prisoner secure?"

Damianos frowned. "Yes, sir." He folded his heavy arms across his chest. "What's your job, Clarke?"

"How do you know my name?"

A smile appeared on the sergeant's face. "You must be half asleep yet. Capt'n Jenkins called you Clarke before he went in to shave, and you got your name stenciled all the way across your T-shirt." Damianos snorted. "And you still don't have your pants on."

Clarke looked down. He was still in his shorts. "One minute." He walked to the chair on which he had draped his trousers and put them on. "I'm in psychological warfare, and I just committed a cardinal error in letting you catch me without my pants." He adjusted his belt. "At least psywar is where I've been assigned since I arrived at Mosby. We don't do very much except prepare for inspections, mop and buff floors, wash windows, and drink coffee."

"What did you expect when you were drafted? Did you think they'd of made you a colonel?" The sergeant's eyes were noncommittal. "What were you in civilian life?"

"Not very much of anything. I went to college and did some radio broadcasting."

"Where?" A drop of water hung on Damianos' heavy eyebrow and he flicked it off.

"San Francisco." The sergeant's questions began to irritate Clarke; he decided to ask a few of his own. "You know the town?"

"A little. I bummed around there for about a year. After the war. . . . It's a cold town. . . ." Damianos was about to continue when a quick movement from the prisoner claimed his attention. "Sit still . . . and don't make another move, or I'll drop you."

Clarke watched the long-nosed profile fix on the prisoner. "Why do you say 'cold,' Sergeant?" he asked when Damianos turned to him. "I found everybody there rather friendly."

"I mean *cold*. A guy needs a blanket in that town."

Clarke stared at him. "A . . . blanket?"

"I said bummed, didn't I?"

"Oh . . . I'm sorry."

"Why're *you* sorry?"

Another question, Clarke thought. He shrugged his shoulders. "I guess you can say I bummed around, too, before I was drafted."

"Doing what?"

Clarke was too interested in the answer to realize he had

been questioned again. "Looking around for myself, I imagine."

"That's death. Sudden death." Damianos pulled his beret from his head and squeezed the rainwater out of it into the wastebasket. "It's all right to look. . . . Don't ever find yourself, though." He smiled, but it was more of a grimace. "Make sure what you'll find is pretty before you start looking for it." He threw the beret on a desk. "What d'you come up with?"

"US 56 545 302."

"That's as good an answer as any." Damianos rested his hands on his hips. "So then you started having these dreams."

"Before that." And now, under the sergeant's brief cross-examination, Clarke recalled having the same dream as far back as he could remember. He had dreamed it in Philadelphia as a teen-ager, when he first realized that he somehow did not belong in his parents' Main Line home, that he was not at ease in the illustrious Clarke tradition, which stretched back to the War of Independence. The familiar dream had occurred to him in Europe on the Grand Tour, where he had gone as a reward for a good scholastic record in high school. But he continued falling: at Stanford, when he had broken with his family and refused to enroll at Princeton, and in San Francisco, where he had gone after leaving Stanford in his second year and worked at odd jobs, trying to make up for the money that had stopped coming from the Philadelphia Clarkes. But why did he fall?

"Do you ever hit the ground?" Sergeant Damianos recalled him to the present.

"No. I always wake up in time."

"It's a happy dream, then. . . . How many days you got left? In the Army."

Clarke hesitated before answering. "I don't count them," he said finally.

"Then you're one draftee out of fifty thousand." He hooked his thumbs in his pistol belt. "But you don't like the Army, do you? Even though it doesn't allow you to go around *looking* for yourself."

"I don't like it and I don't dislike it."

The sergeant smiled, a sharp, crooked grin, the dark eyes as inexpressive as ever. "Then why don't you go airborne and find out whether you like it or really hate it?"

Clarke was annoyed. "Simply because I have no desire to go jumping out of airplanes." He brushed his hair back. "Why should I go airborne?"

Damianos smiled again. "I don't know *that*. There're lots of reasons why men go 'all the way.' I don't know you that well to be able to tell why you should go. But maybe if I did, I might be able to say. Maybe then you'd know about that dream."

Clarke flushed in anger at the sergeant's tone. Just as he was about to make a rejoinder, he realized that Damianos and the colored PFC were smiling at each other. *They're making fun of me!* He reddened again as Captain Jenkins closed the door behind him and stamped across the linoleum floor.

"Hello, Jeffries. You on guard tonight, too?"

"How d'you do, sir? Yes, sir, I am."

"What's your name, boy?" Jenkins stood over the prisoner. "And where did you get the cigarette?" he demanded angrily.

"I gave it to him, Captain."

"As you were, then." Jenkins nodded to Damianos. While he looked down at the captive, the jaws in his florid face set, Jenkins appeared to alternate between wrath and gentleness, as if he were apologizing for the role he had to assume as an officer. "What's your name?" he asked quietly.

"Johnny Milton." The answer was sullen.

"Sir!" Damianos snapped. "And stand at attention."

The captive drew himself erect. "PFC Johnny Milton, suh."

Jenkins balanced himself on his toes. "That's a little better," he said curtly. "What were you in for, Private?"

"Salt and batt'ry, suh."

"Who'd you salt and batter?" The voice was teasing but soft again.

"Some girl Ah know."

"And do you know what the penalty is for escaping from a stockade detail?" Captain Jenkins seemed as angry at the circumstances of the case as he was at the offender. "Didn't they tell you what you're liable to get for making off with the guard's shotgun? And what *he's* liable to get for letting you take it?" The prisoner lowered his head, perplexed. "How many offenses you got, boy?"

"Two, suh."

"*Besides* this? You'll get Leavenworth for sure! How old are you?"

"Twenty, suh."

Jenkins shook his head. "It's such a hell of a lot easier to follow the rules. . . . One thing I know definitely, Private. When you get out, you'll be of legal age, long gone."

"Yes, suh."

Clarke saw the prisoner's dark head lower until it reached his chest; an unthinking, organic melancholy seemed to have taken over the man. His boots were caked with mud, his fatigue jacket and trousers were ripped by the probing fingers of limbs and roots, and drops of water flowed from his head down his dark face.

Clarke stared at the captive's manacled wrists, feeling a mixed anger and pity for the prisoner. *Thought you were going to make it to freedom?* The handcuffs glistened. *We don't matter, jailbird. We're all numbers here. It's so much easier to follow their rules.*

"Clarke." Jenkins turned to him.

"Yes, sir." Clarke was startled.

"Is there any water in the coffeepot?"

"Maybe, sir. I'll heat some." He walked to the hot plate and plugged the cord into the wall socket. While the copper coils reddened, he filled the pot with water and washed the cups. Luckily, there were four cups, and a blind spot in his etiquette remained unchallenged. As he re-entered the office, Clarke saw PFC Jeffries guarding the prisoner, while Damianos and Jenkins sat on the Adjutant's desk and carried on a conversation. The captain chuckled occasionally, but the sergeant was as tight-lipped as before, making no condescension to humor, saying his piece and waiting almost stolidly.

"So I said to him, 'Colonel Moser, sir, how d'you like your new job as Exec?' And he says, 'Well, Sergeant, you know how desk jobs are, five of one and a dozen of another.' 'Know what you mean, sir,' I said." Jenkins grinned. " 'To call an ace a spade, Sergeant—to coin a phrase—things are coming along like they should be expected.' "

Clarke began spooning instant coffee into each cup, listening to the sergeant mimic the lieutenant colonel, who was promoted into Headquarters to stop the havoc he was creating in the Troops as a member of the field command team. *Systems,* he thought, *always protect those who are loyal, even if they are incompetent. Hear that, jailbird? Hear that? Just follow the rules . . .* He glanced at the prisoner and saw that the man, shuffling his feet, was glancing toward the door. The captive raised his manacled hands and wiped the water from his face, but his eyes remained fixed on the door, his body tense.

PFC Jeffries leaned over to him. "Listen, black man," he muttered. "Don't go getting no ideas. You try for that door, and I'll stomp your ass. Hear?"

They paid no attention to Clarke; an unexpected, mutual hatred occupied their minds. The captive stared at Jeffries, his eyes narrowed bitterly, his face arrogant. "Thas right, PFC Uncle Tom. You a *good* niggah. You do what you're tole." He leaned back, slouching in his chair, to get a better look at Jeffries. "Lemme tell you this. . . . Don' lemme catch you downtown. I'll slash you to bits."

"You ain't gonna slash *nobody* to bits, field nigger, 'cause when you get out, I'll be retired, long gone." Then Jeffries glanced toward Damianos and the officer. Clarke pretended to be absorbed in watching the water boil, but he heard Jeffries' comment behind him. "It's your kind that keeps our race back."

"Shee-ut."

Clarke heard a roar, then a screech, and, glancing up quickly, saw a military police sedan halt at the curb. The doors opened and four MPs ran into the office.

"There's your man," Jenkins said.

"Right, sir." A sergeant saluted the captain. He turned to the prisoner. "You come along with us, Sunshine."

Clarke noticed what might have been tears running down the captive's face.

The black MP brassards of the police cut a swath across the men's arms, and the Negro's imprisoned hands hung limply over their elbows. He had collapsed. "No . . . no . . ." he muttered. "Ah . . . diden mean to . . . honest . . . Ah'll be a good . . ." They dragged him across the linoleum and bounced him down the concrete stairs of the building. The screen door slammed. Clarke was unable to see clearly what was occurring in the crowd that had formed at the sedan's door, but, hearing a groan, he assumed that the captive was being hit. Excited shouts came from the sedan. An MP was flattened on the lawn, his face contorted, his chest heaving for air. *Go . . . Go!* Clarke thought. *You've nothing to lose!*

The prisoner was at the median line of the highway with an MP sprinting behind him when he sagged to the surface of the road. Clarke saw the club on the follow-through switch near the MP's knee. The policeman bent over, took the captive by the boots, and dragged him to the waiting sedan. *Too bad, jailbird. You didn't make it.* The MPs threw the prisoner, unconscious as he was, into the back seat, and the man who had been hit in the chest entered with him. The lights from the Headquarters building caught a thick fist as it punched into the darkness.

"Dumb bastard." Jenkins spoke. He and Damianos stood next to Clarke at the window as the sedan drove off to the stockade. "You mean to tell me he wasn't taught the penalties involved?" He blew on his coffee. "Ah, what the hell, no matter how many character guidance lectures you give these guys, some of them never do what they're told." He looked at PFC Jeffries sharply.

"Where's your coffee?"

"I don't drink coffee, sir."

"The hell you don't. Clarke, give this man some coffee."

"His cup is on the desk, sir. I made four cups."

"There's your coffee, Jeffries. We don't want you falling asleep at your post and winding up in trouble. You're too good a man to lose to the Provost Marshal."

Clarke winced at the obviousness of the remark, but Jeffries smiled shyly and raised the cup. "Hot," he said.

"Well, Sergeant Damianos, how's the sky diving coming along? You and the man from the Forty-third, I hear, have been doing some extraordinary things."

"You mean Sergeant Jacks, sir. Yeah, well . . . we've been . . . fooling around a bit. He and I are gonna try something different soon. Can't talk about it till we do it, but we'll be happy guys if we succeed."

"I'd like to go up with you this Saturday, if it's OK. I did a little free falling last summer. Will you have room for me?"

"I think so." Damianos raised the cup to his lips. "Major Zoltan's pilot. I'm sure it'll be OK with him."

Clarke sipped the cup of coffee at his bunk. This, the sky diving, is what happened to him in every dream, but in his nightmares he was not provided with an unopened parachute strapped to his back. The voices continued, droning on about twenty-second delays, about figure 8s, about barrel rolls, with Damianos complaining about the fact that even civilians were taking up the sport. *Somewhere I've lost my footing.* Clarke pursued his thought. *Somewhere I've lost mastery over myself . . . and I'm plunging . . .*

A burst of laughter from the three men startled him. Glancing up, he saw Damianos and Jeffries readying themselves to leave. The sergeant set his cup on the desk top. "Let's go, Jeffries. We don't want to join our friend in the stockade." He put the beret on his head, tilted it rakishly, then slipped into his slicker. "Well, Captain. Sorry we had to wake you up. See you around."

"Right, Sergeant. Take care. See you tomorrow, Jeffries."

"Night, sir."

After the jeep drove off, Jenkins unbuttoned his khaki shirt and loosened his belt. "Ever meet Damianos before?"

Clarke shook his head.

"Quite a guy. Wish I could make him my first soldier, but I already got a good one, and I'm not sure Damianos wants a desk job." He rubbed his eyes. "One of the best NCOs in the Troops . . . and that means the Army." Then, in an offhand manner, he said, "I was his lieutenant in Korea, when the Special Troops were just a gleam in someone's eye."

The thunder had stopped, and only gusts of wind, bringing with them sheets of rain, persisted outside to remind Clarke that an hour before a storm had raged.

"I'm going to get some more shut-eye, Clarke. Make sure I'm up at five-thirty."

"Yes, sir." Clarke heard the bunk in the other room squeak when Jenkins lay down on it. He went to the latrine to shave. Turning on the light above the mirror, Clarke looked at his face briefly. *What are you afraid of, Clarke? Why are you always falling in your dreams? Why don't you go airborne?* He smiled as if, against his will, he parodied himself. *Why don't you go . . . all the way?* Mimicking Damianos, he lathered his face.

Covered with the white mask of lather, his face was blank. *PFC Barrett Clarke,* he thought. *US 56 545 302. . . . During the day I am unhappy. I argue with my wife, I accept orders, I "yes, sir" and salute, and at night, in my dreams, I fall, screaming, into a city. . . .*

He placed and adjusted the blade in the safety razor. Leaning toward the mirror above the sink—the overhead light was inadequate—Clarke began to shave himself, clearing the white mask of his face, strip by strip, of both lather and beard stubble.

After drying himself, he slammed the latrine door shut. Captain Jenkins grunted and turned over. The sky toward the east was graying; an occasional breeze stirred the tall, slender pines; and in the midst of the morning, now that the rain had lessened, Clarke could hear the muffled thud of a pinecone as it struck the wet turf. The water roared into the gutters. He felt tired, but it was too late for sleep; he would wake Jenkins for reveille in ten minutes. There was little to do but pour water into the pot and plug in the hot plate again. Within several minutes, he sat on the desk facing Stuart Road with a hot cup of coffee in his hand.

A dull grayness filtered between him and the trees beyond the window. Clarke looked across the firebreak to the cantonments, their firelights glaring into the dawn. The series of barracks buildings, like piers at a beach, were lighted one by one by the company CQs. First the downstairs, then the upstairs, were shocked into the world of morning by the deep shouts of the cadremen. The firelights were extinguished.

Clarke walked to the OD's side and took his arm. "Captain . . . Captain Jenkins . . . it's time. . . ." Jenkins sat up, blinked, then stood abruptly. He reached for his pistol belt, took his beret from where he had set it the night before, and walked swiftly out of the building.

What kind of dreams does he have? Clarke wondered.

The day grew lighter, the dirty gray dissolved into the blemished white, and finally, in the new-washed blue heavens, the towering, sun-speckled cumuli scudded across the virgin sky. A bugle blew. Clarke saw the ranks of men marching to the large firebreak that separated the Headquarters building from the barracks of the Special Troops and assigned units. They formed themselves on the soaked grass—six provisional companies, each company containing twenty teams of eight men, and the propaganda unit, Clarke's outfit, in which all the men with political, linguistic, and communication backgrounds were grouped and whose duty it was to wage psychological warfare. The top sergeant of each company ordered the men to "Dress right. . . . Dress!" They turned their heads sharply to the right and placed their left hands on their hips. Clarke heard the "Ready . . . front!" of the sergeants, and the men stood at attention.

The bugle sounded again, and from his position at the window Clarke could see the flag being raised on the pole. Crystalline drops formed at the tips of the pine needles and slowly fell to the earth. The men, at attention all this time, saluted the colors; the flag reached the top and fluttered in the crisp morning breeze; and at that moment the sun, a glowing red-orange sphere, surmounted the horizon and shimmered over the soaked earth of Fort Mosby.

"*Re*-port!"

"Fust Provisional Company all present an' accounted fooowr!"

"Secon' Provisional Company two men absent, sir!"

Company by company, the roll call was completed. Then, with a final salute, Captain Jenkins dismissed the formation, and the men ran to the mess halls shouting. The day had begun.

But there was something Clarke had forgotten to do. Hurriedly, he began straightening up: he broke down the bunks, rolled up the sheets and blankets, and carried the bunk frames and mattresses to the latrine closet. Then he emptied the ashtrays and washed the cups. There was mud on the floor where Damianos, Jeffries, and the prisoner had stood, and Clarke quickly swept it up. He glanced at his watch. It was 5:55. Not having time to buff the floor once more, he threw the broom into the utility closet and decided to take his chances on leaving the floor unfinished.

Jenkins came in after his breakfast and told Clarke he was free to go. When he had crossed Stuart Road, now full of incoming traffic, Clarke pulled out his wallet. In the midst of his cards of identity he had a special place for the most important: a small calendar. It was full of check marks, but of open spaces, also. Taking his pen, he crossed off another day.

Only 419 more to go.

CHAPTER 2

Captain Kinnard J. McIlhenny wiped his boots on a rubber mat in front of the orderly room. "Has the mail come in yet, Sergeant Dobbin?" he asked, succeeding admirably, he thought, in hiding the tension in his voice.

"Yes, sir. It's on your desk."

Since he would be revealing too much if he went to his office immediately, McIlhenny glanced through several magazines that lay on the filing cabinet. He selected one—most of his morning's chores were completed—and tarried at the door. "By the way, Sergeant. Has anyone gone to the mess hall for coffee?"

"Battaglia's coming back right now with it, sir. He was bugging out of personnel again, so I thought I'd put him to work."

"Good idea. That little snoop is the closest thing the propaganda unit has to a gossip. Don't let him hang around here."

He walked to his desk and set the magazine near the

telephone. After he had pulled off his green beret, McIlhenny smoothed down the thinning brown hair at the back of his head, frowning briefly as his fingertips encountered the baldness that stretched from his forehead to his ears.

The letters were placed neatly on the top of the desk, facing his swivel chair. One was official, but McIlhenny defeated the urge of his mixed curiosity and impatience, slitting two other envelopes carefully with his plastic opener, reading the advertising circulars, and then dropping them neatly in his wastebasket. *I'm beginning to need this,* he realized, and, as a disciplinary measure, forced himself to read an almost illiterate note from the wife of a man who had served under him—and had subsequently been transferred to another unit—in which the woman complained that she was not receiving her allowance check. The official envelope was next, but he postponed opening it because Specialist Battaglia had entered the orderly room with a pitcher of coffee.

"I'll have a cup of that in here, Battaglia."

"Yes, *sir.*"

When the specialist set a cup on the desk, McIlhenny stared at him. "I don't know why you have so much time on your hands, Battaglia. Sergeant Dobbin told me that you've been hanging around the orderly room again." The captain's thin lips, now colorless because he was angry, appeared grotesque in his round, childlike face.

"Sir . . . I . . ."

"I'm not through yet." McIlhenny's voice was stern. "The United States Army did not draft you so that you'd have the time to wander from office to office as a one-man grapevine." The little man straightened up gradually, put his heels together, and—at attention now—raised his chin. "I won't make a crusade of this, mind you, but I don't want to repeat it, either. This is a warning. *Don't hang around here.*"

"Yes, sir." Battaglia pushed his glasses in place on the bridge of his nose with his index finger, then saluted.

"Was that *your* version of a salute?" He rose quickly and walked to the specialist, glaring down at him from a superior elevation of three inches, which was augmented somewhat by the fact that McIlhenny had specially thick heels on his boots.

"No, sir!"

"Salute properly, then. . . . Again . . . again. . . . That's better." McIlhenny nodded, dismissing him.

When Battaglia had closed the door, the captain returned to the desk, leaned back in his chair, and slit open the envelope. It was a mimeographed bulletin from the Officers' Club: a buffet dinner was planned for the following weekend; after he had paid $2.50, the captain could consider himself cordially invited.

McIlhenny felt curiously relieved—happy that the important news would somehow be delayed. Official letters were too much of a gamble for him now, because he did not consider himself strong enough to bear a possible disaster: his career, perhaps even his sanity, depended on the right letter, and if, in its place, the wrong one came . . . ? If, instead of congratulations that he was to be Major McIlhenny, another letter came—a third and, therefore, a final notice—saying that his promotion had been denied, that he would . . . ?

But he refused to anticipate; he was a captain and would perform the duties of his captaincy as long as he remained a commissioned officer. And his duties for that day were outlined; he, himself—maintaining a lifelong habit—had planned the day's events the previous night.

McIlhenny opened the top drawer of his desk and pulled out the sheet of bond paper where, meticulously and chronologically listed, were the hour-by-hour demands he had made on himself. He checked off the first seven entries:

(1) wake up at 5:30
(2) do calisthenics
(3) take troops out to reveille
(4) eat breakfast (cut down on calories)
(5) check orderly room for neatness—Sgt. Vukovich, CQ
(6) have Dobbin make out morning report
(7) open mail

There was no actual need to detail these everyday affairs, but years of habit and discipline had made him dependent on such a framework to provide him with the comfort and security of a pre-charted day.

The phone rang. *What is it now?* he wondered, annoyed that he would be interrupted before performing his eighth chore.

"Captain McIlhenny, here." He fixed his sight on the acetate cover that protected his desk's surface; under the clear plastic, a religious picture of an auburn-haired, manly Christ looked off to the right in profile. "Follow Me," read the military legend.

"Yes, sir!" It was Lieutenant Colonel Moser, a man whose incompetence in high grade vaguely perplexed the captain but who—as a field-grade officer—deserved his utmost respect. "Yes, sir. I'll attend to that immediately. Of course . . . the CQ's duties are clearly outlined. If Clarke had read his orders carefully, he'd have known he was to buff the floor." McIlhenny paused; he was doing too much talking. "Colonel Simms remarked about the condition of the floors? Yes, sir, I agree. It's inexcusable." He waited again, nodding vigorously. "I'm having the other man, Winters, in for a dressing down in forty-five minutes. I'll handle both of them at the same time, sir. Yes, sir." He set the receiver down.

"Sergeant Dobbin!"

"Sir!"

"Call the radio unit. Have PFC Clarke standing tall in my office in forty-five minutes. I'll take Winters and Clarke on together."

McIlhenny, referring to his schedule again, left the orderly room to complete item (8), the barracks inspection. When the door slammed behind him, the captain strode along the concrete path leading to the cantonments, his brisk, military pace out of keeping with the midmorning quiet. He kept to the rigid confines of the narrow walk, for the neatly trimmed lawns were still wet from last night's storm. *The grass needs mowing*, he realized. *Something for Clarke and Winters to do.*

McIlhenny stopped abruptly, the swagger stick he held in his hand pressing against his trouser leg. A crumpled cigarette pack lay discarded on the ground. He stepped on the wet lawn carefully and speared the pack with the pointed tip of his stick. Opening the crumpled package, he glanced at the brand name; unfortunately, it was a common cigarette. Had it been a Fatima, Players, or Sobranie, something could be done; how could he possibly trace the man who discarded this pack, if forty men in the company, and possibly two hundred in the Troops, smoked the same brand? He walked to the Dempster Dumpster, a square, metallic trash disposal, and dislodged the paper from his swagger stick.

Beyond the Dumpster, the barracks were well kept; McIlhenny had seen to that. When a company commander has such an effective weapon for keeping things in order as the Article 15, and when men in his unit forget things they should not and are punished with extra details, how can a company area be anything but clean and neat? He paused on the path and glanced toward the sharp boundary between the clipped lawn and the sandy underportion of the barracks.

The rainwater, gushing from the billets' roofs, had dug viciously into the earth, which should have appeared, according to McIlhenny, rather light and fluffy. *Well*—he frowned —*this will soon be remedied.*

He opened the door to the barracks and began his latrine inspection. The deep basin was clean, except for a few evident black marks around the rim. *Someone's been polishing his boots here.* The urinals were spotless, as were the commodes. Leaning over, he tore a square of tissue from an almost-expended roll, wiped the tip of his swagger stick, dropped the paper into the bowl, and flushed the toilet. Next came the windows, which, although clean, did not pass inspection because someone, sitting on the commode adjacent to the wall, had used the open window as an ashtray and had succeeded in scattering cigarette ash between the cracks in the wood of the sill.

The four washbasins were clean and *dry*, a very important point in an inspection conducted by a man who knew, and intended to maintain, his standards; the four stopper chains were symmetrically stretched from their hooks, at points equidistant from the hot and cold faucets, to the rim of the basin, and each plug dangled exactly two inches from the rim. The basins, however, were gigged, because there was a puddle of water under each.

McIlhenny hesitated slightly on realizing that each puddle had the same length, width, and general shape as the others and that the water was clean; moreover, there was a pleasing regimentation in the four puddles: they seemed, for a moment, to be standing in rank. But the captain shook such fanciful thoughts out of his mind: *Water on the floor of a latrine is unauthorized!* He gigged the basins, walked into the shower room, glanced at the soap dishes, and found them to be dry and free of any soap.

The cadre rooms, where the detachment cooks slept, were clean. Captain McIlhenny checked the barracks bag at the foot of each bunk by tapping at the denim sack with his swagger stick. Hearing a tinkle, he opened the bag, estimated the liquor drunk since the day before, and—satisfied that it was not disproportionate to that of the previous day's —proceeded into the squad room. The cooks were too good to punish for having an occasional, innocent nip, as long as it did not interere with their work in the mess hall; besides, in the Baptist South, he felt a pleasant sense of being broad-minded when he tolerated the drinking of liquor.

In the squad room, ten bunks were ranked on each side

of the center aisle. There were five windows in each wall: five bunks directly in front of the windows and five between them made up the ten on each side. The first windows on both sides were opened six inches from the bottom; the second, six from the top; and so on down the barracks to the fire escape. Under the bunks to the captain's right, each soldier had placed his boots, his army low quarters, his civilian and sport shoes, his sneakers, and his shower sandals, in that order. McIlhenny, walking through unhurriedly, studied the footwear for shine and maintenance. Most of the bunks were tight; one, however, always looked as if the soldier who used it was still under the blankets. Battaglia would never learn how to make a bunk properly; every day, therefore, when the clerk returned from the personnel office, he knew he would find his blankets pulled loose and thrown on his bunk. Today was no exception.

The captain was surprised to observe that Winters' area did not deserve to be gigged. The bunk was tight; the footwear was clean, well maintained, and straight; the footlocker was not dusty. After walking over to the bunk, however, McIlhenny slapped the blankets with his swagger stick and watched a cloud of dust rise to the ceiling. One gig. He ran the swagger stick up and down his thigh, dusting it off on his trousers, and turned to the bulletin board.

Numerous antimilitary cartoons were tacked on the board, culled from every newspaper and magazine that could be purchased or stolen on Post. A tradition had built up around these caricatures. The men would put them up in the evening and McIlhenny would throw them in the trash can during his inspection. There were a few anniversary greeting cards from men who had fulfilled their military obligations and corresponded, not with the men—for the company roster had made frequent changes in personnel—but with the specific barracks building, hoping to maintain some contact with an existence they had once considered intolerable. The cards were signed in the same way: "Yours with *F*raternal, *T*ender *A*ffection."

I should have realized what was going on and stopped it. But no . . . I waited until Colonel Simms discovered the plot . . . with me expecting my promotion any day. . . . But it had never entered his mind that such an organization could exist in the very unit he considered so well policed by him, a plot discovered by—of all people—Colonel Simms when he was glancing over one of Winters' leaflets. *It's unheard of!* he thought.

Curiously, McIlhenny was hurt, not angry, for he had failed to instill in these citizen-soldiers the necessary feeling of value, of *esprit*, in serving their country in these times. *In these . . . troubled times* . . . He should have caught the Phi Tau Alpha fraternity before it got out of hand, before, that is, it was discovered by the commander of the Special Troops. But . . . he was also perplexed—hurt that these civilians who had served in his company wrote, not to him who knew them well, but to other enlisted men whose lives had briefly crossed or would never cross theirs. He, their commanding officer, should have had their admiration and affection, tender and fraternal though it might be; instead, he had their contempt. And why? Awkwardly, Captain McIlhenny began taking down the cards and caricatures. Because they had been assigned to his unit and their backgrounds, years of coddling and good living, had made them feel that the chasm between officer and enlisted personnel was somehow fantastic, un-American. And now they wrote, on the anniversary of their termination of service, from all parts of the United States and the world, wherever their careers had taken them, not to him, the man whom they knew and saluted, but to men in like circumstances, men with whom they would not exchange nods in a restaurant or an elevator.

He glanced at his wristwatch. Time for item (9).

Winters, in the orderly room when McIlhenny arrived, rose to his feet; the captain, however, swept past him into his office and closed the door. After going to his desk, McIlhenny checked off item (8); then, glancing to the path between the barracks, he saw that PFC Clarke was approaching the orderly room. *Does he smoke?* the captain wondered, but then dismissed the suspicion that Clarke might be responsible for discarding the cigarette pack on his lawn.

There was nothing to do until the two men were announced by Sergeant Dobbin, nothing between items (8) and (9), and so McIlhenny took the heavy *Manual of Courts-Martial* from his bookcase and set it on the desk for its shock value. *I'll show them psychological warfare.* Opening the lower drawer, he skimmed through a portfolio of art photos in the magazine he had taken from the filing cabinet. *The Women of South America,* he read. His sight fixed on a deep-breasted half-breed from Cuba, but quickly, in an almost embarrassed manner, he turned the page. There was a knock.

"Yes?"

Dobbin entered, closing the door behind him.

"Clarke and Winters are outside, sir."

"Tell them to come in."

He browsed through the *Manual* as the men entered the office quietly and stood at attention before his desk. Pretending to be interested in the contents of a paragraph, McIlhenny read it thoroughly, ignoring the heavy silence and delaying his recognition of their presence. Then he glanced up angrily at the two enlisted men who had encroached on the privacy of his office.

"Specialist Winters and PFC Clarke reporting to the captain as requested, sir." They saluted.

"As *ordered,* Winters. I didn't *request* your presence. I demanded it."

"Yes, sir. I'm sorry, sir."

McIlhenny sat back in his chair and laced his fingers over his abdomen. Staring at the men through eyes that appeared frosted, he used the heavy silence that settled in the office as a weapon in his arsenal.

"Winters," he barked. The man stiffened. "What was the meaning of your actions?"

"Sir, I . . ."

"You what?" He reached into the center drawer and pulled out a manila folder. After withdrawing three leaflets, McIlhenny spread them out on the desk and jabbed the tip of his swagger stick at areas he had earlier encircled with a red pencil. "What do you see there, Specialist Winters?"

"Red circles, sir."

"Here." He tapped a leaflet. "Specialist Winters, kindly look at that tree, to the left of the mound, and tell me what you see engraved on its bark."

"There's a heart, sir. With an arrow through it."

McIlhenny was displeased with himself. He was not approaching the problem logically. He still had not established the fact that Winters had been responsible for the leaflet.

"Is this your work, Winters?"

"Yes, sir."

McIlhenny nodded. "Now, to get back. What else is in the heart?"

"Three initials, sir."

"What are the initials, Specialist Winters?"

"FTA, sir."

"And what does FTA stand for, Specialist?"

McIlhenny noticed that Winters glanced briefly at Clarke, but the PFC looked straight ahead. *Two different types,* the captain considered. *One rebels weakly . . . and the other is passive; neither is a man . . . both are cream puffs . . . only one more so than the other.* Winters was looking down at his shoes. *"Well . . . ?"*

"Sir . . . excuse me . . ." He seemed embarrassed. The initials stand for 'Fuck the Army.' "

McIlhenny regarded him coldly. "And why did you draw that on the bark of the tree?"

"I don't know, sir. I guess . . ."

"You don't like the Army?"

There was a pause.

"No, sir. I don't."

"Then why did you become a soldier?"

Winters appeared to be surprised. "I was drafted, sir."

"You have *free choice.* You could have refused to serve. You could have become a conscientious objector."

"I don't believe in that, sir."

"Then what *do* you believe in, Winters? Petty rebellions? Small FTA fraternities? Safe underground cliques? The camaraderie of the coffee gang?" These were rhetorical questions, and McIlhenny, glancing at both men, knew they realized this. He permitted his sight to rest on the *Manual of Courts-Martial* and maintained a moment's silence. "I have a choice, also, Winters. I can put you up for a court-martial. I'm sure you'll lose the rank you have and forfeit a great deal of future pay. Or . . . I can give you an Article 15. This is my decision." He paused. Winters' face was tense. "I'm going to give you an Article 15. If I hear of any more FTAs on your leaflets, I'm going to throw this rather heavy book at you. Am I understood?"

"Yes, sir!"

"Clarke!"

"Yes, sir!"

"You were on CQ last night?"

"Yes, sir."

"You forgot something, didn't you?"

"I buffed the floor once, sir. But then . . ."

"But then *what?* A prisoner was captured. Was that it? He was brought into Headquarters. He had mud on his boots. Am I correct? You chose to ignore this. Your duty was to have the floor buffed by morning and you completed your chore the night before. The fact that a storm was on did not matter to you, did it? The floor was not buffed in the morning. There were scuffs on the floor. And you ignored this. Isn't that so?"

Clarke mumbled something.

"Speak up! I can't hear you!"

"Yes, sir."

"You don't like the Army, either, do you?"

"No, sir." The PFC mumbled something again.

"What was *that?* I didn't hear you. Sound off as a man would!"

"I . . . I . . ."

"Come out with it!"

"I wasn't . . . drafted to be . . . a janitor, sir."

McIlhenny's head shook briefly, as if he had been slapped. "You weren't drafted . . . to be . . . a janitor, is it? What were you drafted for?" He realized the stupidity of what he had asked as soon as the question left his lips.

"To be a soldier." The boy paused. "To defend my country."

This was unexpected. For a moment Captain McIlhenny did not know how to respond. He had evidently not known Clarke well enough. "How can you defend *your country* if your country is not being threatened?"

"If the United States is not threatened . . . sir . . . then why . . . why was I drafted?"

McIlhenny's eyes drifted to the *Manual,* but he realized immediately that he was merely stalling for time. "You were drafted to keep the Army up to strength. Certain duties must be performed in any Army, at any time. Being Charge of Quarters is one duty. Buffing the floor is a responsibility of a CQ. You failed to perform that duty."

He glanced up at Clarke. The PFC was silent. "I'm going to give you an Article 15, also, Clarke—for your lack of proper appreciation of a military duty *and* for your attitude." The PFC stared ahead. "Both of you are to report to Sergeant Dobbin at the end of the day for a detail. He will tell you how long you will work, what you will do, and appraise you of the duration of your punishment. Is that clear?"

"Yes, sir." The two men saluted.

"You're dismissed."

Clarke and Winters about-faced to the door. McIlhenny pulled out the drawer and checked off item (9). When the two enlisted men had left the orderly room and were returning to their sections, McIlhenny stood up and paced the floor, uncomfortable until he realized his right hand was empty. He retrieved his swagger stick.

They don't know they have free will, he thought. *They're helpless . . . like children . . . and they shun responsibility. What are we coming to here? We're losing our moral strength!* He glanced at the picture of Christ on his desk, then went to the door.

"Sergeant Dobbin."

"Yes, sir?"

"Give them two weeks. Call up their sections and determine if they're busy. If not, give them KP every other day and fatigue duty after work on the days they're in their sections. The lawns need work and I suppose something in the Detachment needs painting." He paused. "Keep them working, at any rate."

The sergeant looked at McIlhenny briefly. "Right, sir. I'll call their sections and adjust the KP roster before chow."

Since it was time for the day's news, McIlhenny turned on the radio. The events of the world seemed to be more depressing each month. With every step of technical progress, the globe grew smaller, and with every riot and revolution, the number of independent nations grew larger. And daily the vacuum of the uncommitted nations separating the giant powers of the earth invited one or the other to assume leadership and risk an all-out war. McIlhenny did not smile at his amusing insight: the daily news, therefore, interrupted by the necessary quota of headache remedies, made the use of the sponsor's pills and powders a virtual necessity.

But we have free will, McIlhenny emphasized to himself; *we can determine our own destinies.* But the world vacuum remained, a constant threat to world peace; each man, with his own free will, should have felt a moral imperative to act out the role forced on him by the daily outline of history which blared at him over his radio between commercials. *But we must do something.* There seemed to be riots everywhere. Africa, Asia, the South, Europe, Latin America: every human being appeared to be in a state of emotional and intellectual ferment. *Our original sin.* He repeated the paradoxically comforting doctrine. *No one seems to be happy.* At that moment, when the unwelcome news had been recited, he realized he had not turned off the radio, for a love song—repeating the words "happiness," "love," and "eternity"—roared in his ears. He reached over and silenced the noise.

McIlhenny had always believed that the error of the century—he called it a "heresy"—was that it had drifted away from God, that human beings had lost their moorings and were now "ship-wrecked" as a result of this heresy. But God had survived, and all that men needed to do was reach for

Him again. The system was still intact. A certain order ruled this world, and human beings reflected it and yearned for it without knowing what it was or what it meant. And thus, the chichés that the songwriters, in their benighted condition, continued to use from a bygone day—when happiness, eternity, and heaven were actual, virtually provable realities—had a real truth which could not be obscured.

In his vaguely troubled state, Captain McIlhenny glanced at his day's roster. Item (10) was "chow," but it was fifty minutes away. He opened the drawer, took the magazine, and leafed through the pages of advertising until he came to the photo essay, *The Women of South America.* He justified his more than curious interest in these portraits by citing his layman's fascination in photography, inspecting the women—all of whom were unrealistically beautiful—with what he hoped would soon be a professional eye. But as he studied one page after another, he became increasingly interested in the objects, rather than the lights and shadows, the techniques, the speeds, and the perspectives; he stared at the women themselves. First he glanced abstractedly at a white-skinned woman of Ecuador. With her thin, regal nose, her chilly blue eyes, her blond hair swept into a pompadour, the tiny earrings dangling from her earlobes, the slight, taunting smile, she was obviously sure of herself, confident of her proud, matronly beauty. Sitting in a high-ceilinged salon, she reflected the ease, the graciousness of her aristocratic life, her Hispanic lineage, her traditional European upbring, her childhood of musicales, of chaperoned adolescence, of opulent Catholicism, of virginity before marriage. She did not appeal to him.

He flicked the page to see a Cuban mulatto, a fiery Havana prostitute, with shameless, protuberant breasts—a deep, womanly cleavage—with gaudy necklaces, earrings, and bracelets. McIlhenny frowned and looked around the office for his swagger stick, afraid for a moment that he had forgotten it at the barracks. It was on the desk. He returned to the magazine. *With these . . . one spends long evenings* . . . And he imagined the woman's tawny body as it trembled ecstatically under him, her face contorting, her fingernails digging wildly into his shoulders. . . .

He came to his senses, threw the magazine on the desk, and began pacing the floor. *I should be ashamed of myself. Just a photograph . . . and I'm close to losing my . . . my discipline* . . . He looked hatefully at the magazine. *This . . . this pablum, this pornography is going too far!* What had happened to civilization could be seen in the popular songs and the lowered standards of its printed and photographed matter. *We're becoming degenerate. . . . Something . . . something is happening to our culture when these . . . primitive rhythms . . . these lyrics . . . these shameless pictures are considered unobjectionable. Something serious . . .*

Could all the amassed knowledge, all the philosophy, the wisdom, available in the West about the nature of man . . . could all this be inadequate? Could a man become what no other man had foreseen? *Discipline . . . certainly discipline is necessary,* he realized. But were there caverns and depths that neither religion nor the military could probe into and thus order or defeat?

He glanced at his watch: it was not time for chow. Looking at his wall calendar, McIlhenny saw that he was to be present at Post Theater #5 this afternoon to view a film and listen to a lecture on nuclear warfare. That was item (11). His eyes strayed to a crossed square on a lower level of the calendar: the following week he would parachute at night, if the weather permitted. And tonight? *What will I do tonight?* The Officers' Club? *No.* He shook his head vigorously. He had had enough of that. He would read, as usual, in his room at the Bachelor Officers' Quarters; that was item (14) on his list.

He walked to his desk quickly and sat down. After taking out a clean sheet of paper, he wrote "Saturday" at the top.

(1) wake up at 0500 hours
(2) do calisthenics
(3) eat breakfast (cut down on calories)
(4) inspect the Troops

He paused for a moment, realizing that a curious feeling was coming over him, a depression that threatened to smother his equanimity. As he tried to think what the fifth item for Saturday was, he said, in a whisper, but nevertheless aloud: "I must get away."

He paused, startled. *What did I say?* A smile, poised between humorous disbelief and fear, hesitated on his lips. He stared at the wall. *What did I mean?* Then, as always, he began with the statement that had unaccountably left his lips and worked back to what might have called it forth. *Things must be brought into the open . . . into sunlight.* And he groped into the labyrinth of his mind, searching for the trigger to his statement; began with his awakening and followed, item by item, the passing of the day: the barracks inspection, the mail . . . *That might be it,* he allowed. *I'm undergoing a lot of tension because of that letter.* He smiled. *Why don't I say "promotion"? Am I that superstititious?* Item (9) was the punishment of Clarke and Winters. He dismissed this immediately. *The magazine?* Perhaps it was the woman? Perhaps he did not go out as often as he should. *But women bore me. Particularly those who go to the Officers' Club.* What could he talk to them about? NATO? Philosophy? The threats facing the West? U.S. Army history?

But what does this have to do with "I must get away"? Nothing, he realized. *Away? What did I mean by that? Nonsense . . . it's nonsense. Where is away?*

He had led a monklike existence all his life, knowing only two masters—God and the United States Army. Admittedly, it was difficult getting a definite command from the former, for even theologians encountered problems with that; the Army, however, had an admirable chain of command, and a quasi-hermit like himself could always feel confident in pursuing a course of action as long as precedent could be found in the manuals. Of course, the company of women was necessary to a man, but not so important that he need swerve from his goal. *When I become a major . . . things will be different.* He would be a relatively new man, then; he would have confidence in himself. But now, as captain, he would be content to enrich his mind and become a worthy soldier. After all, to be a captain in the Army of the United States in these troubled times was a great responsibility.

I must get away! Had he said that? From what unknown crevice in his mind had that idea come? Slowly, Captain McIlhenny brought all the idiocies man is capable of conceiving into the "sunlight" of his mind and disposed of them one by one. When he had completed his analysis of the "escape" episode, he smiled briefly, stirred slightly in his swivel chair, shook his head in wonderment, and wrote in an entry for item (5): chow.

(6) get clothes from dry cleaners
(7) buy shoe polish
(8) read
(9) get to bed early

He opened the drawer and placed the sheet in it. Then, after taking the magazine from the desk top, he threw it on

Sergeant Dobbin's filing cabinet and walked out of the orderly room, the swagger stick in his right hand tapping his thigh rhythmically.

CHAPTER 3

White, billowing clouds towered above the quonsets and airstrips of Kelly Field. The hangars were drawn shut, the runways were cleared, and Damianos, standing calmly near an equipment shed, felt the heavy autumnal sun on his starched white coveralls. He glanced to the flagpole at the north end of the field to see that the red banner hung limp against its staff. The wind velocity, he estimated, was less than six miles per hour, almost nonexistent.

Saturday mornings were the spice of Army life; soldiers hesitated in the silence before inspection, preparing themselves, their weapons, and their dress, hardly realizing that the beauty of the ritual was rooted in the fact that it had been patterned and perfected over the centuries, like a primitive dance whose origin was obscure. The nameless, institutional tension Damianos had lived with since waking had left him when the ranks were dismissed, and second by second an agreeable tranquillity had taken its place as he drank his mess-hall coffee with the other NCOs. Another cycle had been consummated, another week had ended, and the sergeant—having observed the ceremonial rite—had been awarded his weekend liberation; in his freedom, he chose to wait at Kelly Field under a fleecy stratocumulus.

Aside from the hum the automobiles made as they accelerated along the gradual loop of the airfield, the only sounds he had heard since parking his car were the piercing screams of isolated jet fighters from the nearby Air Force Base as they rocketed above the sun-ridged clouds. *I'll be up there in a while . . . weightless. . . .* Soon he would be above the earth, serene, gliding through a tranquil sky; soon he would be godlike. He therefore consented to the tight embrace of his sports parachute, bore the added weight of the reserve strapped to his pectoral harness, and accepted the stiff, imprisoning paratroop boots into which he had tucked the pantlegs of his coveralls. What were added weight and temporary bondage when he would soar above the earth? What was discomfort when through it he would gain serenity?

With nothing to do until the plane arrived, Damianos put the red-striped football helmet on his head and adjusted the airborne chin strap. *Forty-four hours to do what I want to do,* he thought; *forty-four hours till Monday!* The irony did not escape him; leaping from an airplane was his soldierly duty, but sky diving was altogether different. *I jump when I want to. . . . I'm free.* Damianos surveyed the empty sky, permitting his eyes to trace the shifting outlines of the fickle clouds.

A drab-colored aircraft, its high wings taut above the fuselage, sped over Damianos, skimmed the trees surrounding the field, and disappeared beyond the forest to the south. The sergeant glanced at his watch; Major Zoltan was on time. The single-prop Beaver, now returning and growing larger with each passing second, dipped gracefully toward the concrete runway. *Down to earth,* he thought. *Down from the clouds.* The utility plane bounced once, twice, raced along the strip, then slowed. The sergeant waited until Zoltan, a tall, round-faced man, jumped from the Beaver before saluting.

"Hi, Gus. What about Jacks?"

"It's still early, sir. He'll be around."

"How long have you been trussed up? Half hour?" Damianos nodded. "Cant wait, huh? Know how you feel." The sergeant accepted a cigarette. "Are you going to do it today?"

Damianos shook his head in the affirmative. "I got a feeling in my bones." He grinned. "We'll do it." He leaned over for a light.

"I certainly hope so. A lot of troopers have come close these past few months. It'd be nice if Mosby could take the credit for being first in exchanging the baton."

Damianos stepped back, drawing on his cigarette in silence. He did not like the turn the conversation had taken. What did Fort Mosby have to do with his free hours? Was he being crowded again, forced to succeed in what he had chosen as recreation by people who brought their own ambitions into what was his pleasure? "I saw Captain Jenkins the other day. On OD." Zoltan did not remark on the change in conversation. "He's coming, too."

The major nodded. "Here he is now."

Damianos turned. "Afternoon, sir."

"Hello, men." Jenkins was smiling. "I think congratulations are in order."

Damianos, waiting for Zoltan to make the obvious response, studied Jenkins. The major seemed to have ignored the statement. "What happened, sir?"

"I got my promotion. I'm *Major* Jenkins now."

Damianos grinned and held out his hand. "Nice going, sir. Sweating that one out, weren't you? I didn't want to ask you Thursday night 'cause I figured things were pretty tight."

"The letter just came this morning and ol' Colonel Moser gave me his gold leaf. If you men hear of any First John who's about to become captain, just let me know. My bars are available."

"Don't know of any offhand, sir." Damianos paused. "I heard a couple NCOs after inspection talking about a *captain* that's sweating his promotion."

"There is?" Zoltan was surprised.

Jenkins nodded. "CO of the propaganda unit. A Captain McIlhenny."

"I know *him,*" Zoltan muttered. "A real martinet-type bastard. Almost Old Army, except he came in with most of us. During the war. He isn't a very popular man at the Club."

"Mac's not bad," Jenkins said. "Sort of tight, that's all. He doesn't mean any harm. Just very shy, particularly around women." He chuckled. "Rumor's got it he's still a virgin."

A yellow dot to his right attracted Damianos' attention. It was Jacks, wearing yellow coveralls, walking on an airstrip. A car was making a U-turn on the highway, ready to drive back to the drop zone. A few long, quick strides brought him to the gathering, where he saluted the officers. "Sorry Ah'm late. Hadda wait aroun' for a ride from Normandy DZ. Mah car's out there." He winked at Damianos.

"Right on time, Sergeant," Zoltan said. "May as well pile in. You giving the jumpmaster's check?"

"Yes, sir." Damianos tested the canvas webbing on Jenkins' chute carefully, waiting for Jacks to strap on his helmet. When the taller sergeant was ready, Damianos began his check, pulling hard on his partner's harness. Jacks grunted. "Gettin' hefty there, Slim." Damianos mimicked a southern accent. "Been eatin' too many *e*clairs." As he performed his inspection, Damianos glanced occasionally at the NCO's lean, rugged frame, a rangy, wiry body that seemed built for endurance. Pushing his heavy fingers through his partner's chin strap and jerking it briefly, Damianos managed to get the square-jawed sergeant to smile.

"You feelin' guilty there, boy? Ah'm in better shape than you'll ever be in that sudden-death outfit on the Hill." Jenkins had followed Zoltan to the Beaver. "You may not know it,

Yankee Boy," Jacks whispered, "but Ah got *status*. Ah'm Jump School cadre now."

"Since when?" Damianos asked quickly.

"Since Ah had a few words with mah CO 'bout too many a mah men bein' put on *de*tails."

"What's he doing—sucking up to the colonel?"

"Like a vacuum cleaner." Jacks' jaw muscles tightened.

Damianos was about to speak but thought better of it. Instead, he slapped his partner on the buttocks, signifying that the inspection was complete. "OK, Cougar, let's get up in the sky and fly!" Walking toward the snub-nosed aircraft, Damianos turned to Jacks. "You got the baton?"

His partner nodded.

The Beaver's sole propeller, vertical at the moment, was motionless. Zoltan sank into the pilot's seat. Damianos, after crawling through the three-foot-square cargo opening, sat on the floor, wedged between the right window and the copilot's seat, facing Jacks, who leaned against the rear compartment's separator. Jenkins sat beside Damianos, next to the opening. The three men fastened their safety belts with difficulty over the bulk of their reserve chutes.

"Set?" Zoltan asked.

"Right, sir. Any time."

Its engine coughed, its propeller twirled into a silvery haze, and the Beaver dashed down the broad runway. The toylike wheels spun as they rolled on the concrete path and stopped abruptly as the Beaver climbed into the sky. It attained pine-top level, then soon debased the ordered rows of barracks buildings rising between the level, equidistant stretches of their firebreaks. Geometrical, macadamized roads, outlining the cantonments, framed the inhabited area of the military reservation and dully reflected the glare of the September sun. To the right of the water tower's crimson wafer lay a yellow, sun-ravished field, quilt-square, and beyond that the green pine forests stretched, rolling deeply, like an ocean's swell. Looming at the horizon's rim, the stratocumuli reared up into the blueness of the sky, aloof yet mutable, shading troughs of forest from the sun. As the great clouds shifted westward, the liberated pine tracts were sun-bathed and random specks within the forest's density—wavering creeks, swollen from the recent storm—reflected the sun's blaze.

Abruptly, the forest thinned, and in place of the pines' thick carpet, isolated tree wedges stood, lapped by the red earth of open terrain. The small craft, droning above the pine thickets, finally cast its shadow on the gray sand of Normandy Drop Zone. A fluorescent golden cross, two panels quatrefoiled, shone up at Damianos with a glare. Major Zoltan, having attained the altitude of 7,000 feet, leveled the Beaver off and turned at the drop zone's border.

"OK, sir." Damianos patted Jenkins on the knee. "You first."

The officer loosened his safety belt and—clutching the wing struts—worked himself outside the Beaver, bracing his feet against a metal step welded to the aircraft's floor. As the golden quatrefoil slowly drifted a mile and a third below his helmet, Jenkins freed himself from the craft and, locking his limbs in the spread-eagle position, fell through the sky.

Damianos leaned out to observe Jenkins' descent. Between the aircraft's tail and the sky depths, the white form coasted gradually toward the drop-zone sand, like a sea gull in its glide. Jenkins, doll-like from this vantage, brought his guide arm to his side, attempting to swerve for a figure 8; lost his body stabilization; pivoted wildly in the air; rolled helplessly toward the barren earth below; then—with the panic of a neophyte—pulled his ripcord. The chute blossomed.

Sergeant Damianos pushed his upper body into the compartment, not interested to see where Jenkins landed. Something much more important awaited him. He fingered his chin strap and nodded to his partner. It was time. Sergeant Jacks, unzipping the thigh pocket of his coveralls, brought out a twelve-inch ruler that he had wrapped in a T-shirt and taped with adhesive.

The two men huddled on the Beaver's floor as Damianos made his final considerations. The elevation of the DZ above sea level was approximately 300 feet, which—added to the distance a human being fell in 20 seconds—gave him a total of 6,700 feet. Added to this sum was the 2,000 feet of blanket, the buffer zone, so that when he and Jacks pulled their ripcords, they would be a comfortable distance from the earth's surface. Exit altitude was, therefore, at a minimum of 8,700 feet.

Both men peered out of the cargo door. The golden cross, stretched on the drop-zone sand, glared at the sky. Beyond the crossed fluorescent panels, a small dot appeared on the flatness: the commo man with his PRC 10 radio. A medical truck was parked near him. Minute cars, mere specks of color from the aircraft's height, spotted the brush pines flanking the drop zone.

Damianos asked the major to climb to 9,000 feet and turn so that he could check his final wind adjustments. The breeze was coming from a northerly direction at nine miles an hour; since they were to dive into the wind, they must exit beyond the cross. Damianos shouted his calculations to Jacks, who—nodding agreement—reached down to grasp the wing struts. Zoltan completed the lazy turn and was pointed toward the gleaming target.

The pilot, anticipating Damianos' request, slowed over the silent, glowing panels and coasted above the flatness of Normandy. Jacks dropped from the craft, his arms and legs locked in the spread-eagle position. He seemed attached to the plane for an instant, but in a heartbeat his fall was evident. His body taut, his abdomen nearer the earth than his chin or boots, he glided over the DZ's platform. The baton was clutched in his hand. Within a second, Damianos fell, arms and legs angled in the delta position, and hurled his body earthward faster than his partner's. In the first second, Jacks had fallen 16 feet; in the second, 64 feet; by the fifth, 400 feet; and by the seventh, 904 feet. By the eighth, Damianos, weightless and free now, glided southward to Jacks at the same altitude, like an enormous predatory bird scanning a still landscape.

He saw the yellow helmet approaching him from the north and, to its right, the baton. As they sped toward each other, Damianos made an agonized attempt to grasp the stick, and with the contortion and excitement, both men lost their stability and tumbled in the sky.

Damianos muttered a curse, succeeded in righting himself, and swerved in the air, his body arched, his arm grasping desperately at his side to turn himself leftward. The altimeter showed 4,800 feet above the earth. Jacks' helmet was approaching him from the west. As his partner neared, Damianos realized that too much lateral distance separated them.

The second attempt to pass the baton had failed.

The situation was becoming desperate. Only ten seconds remained for a last attempt. They glided toward each other again, he from the north, Jacks from the south. His mind, like the lower strata of the sky, was blank. Only one object, the baton in another's hand, was important to him as he coasted 2,000 feet above the flatness of Normandy DZ. Damianos stretched again, his eyes unblinking, his muscles and nerves taut, and, as Jacks swooped near him, he reached out, clutching for the baton.

I'm free, Damianos thought, wrapping his powerful fingers around the stick. He passed it to his left hand and pulled the ripcord, flinging his right fist to the horizon in a mute challenge. The sleeve of his parachute deployed, sucked in the air he had just passed, and—for an eye blink—hovered above him at a forty-five-degree angle, pointed cloudward. When the canopy heaved out in a blossom, it caught the sergeant short, bouncing him a thousand feet above the sand. He tucked the baton between the reserve and his chest and reached his heavy hands up to the risers, glancing about in triumph to see Jacks' chute flare out with a pocket of air.

Exultant now, he checked the mounting emotion at its source and muttered, sighing. This is what freedom was—an eye-blink in a week, a heartbeat in a fall, an acrobatic glide between the clouds and sand, a minute's exultation poised between the rituals of duty and his body's limitations, but worth it all, worth the discipline, the manacles, the bugles, the salutes. Too brief, this freedom: it would end, for the human body could not bear it. He slammed his boots together in the sky, above the golden cross, as if bored with his life.

The vast flatness of the earth, on the horizon's hinge, swung up to meet his boots. Toes were pointed for it, awaiting the shock of impact; within a second they touched hard-packed sand. He rolled on the earth and, like an acrobat, stood up immediately.

As Damianos stuffed his canopy into his kit he saw Jacks walking toward him. "That wazzen good enough, Gus." Jacks grinned. "Let's do it ag'in."

"Well." Damianos paused, his face expressionless. He must be himself again; he must be sardonic. "I did my best. Only you didn't pass the baton like you was supposed to."

"Ah don' know 'bout that. Ah had the feelin' you was tryin' to *avoid* me up there." Jacks broke off, glancing peevishly over Damianos' shoulder. "Here they come."

Damianos knew who "they" were. "Let's take off."

"They're jest gonna congratulate us an' take our pitchers."

Damianos shrugged. He disliked reporters and photographers, not personally, but as a type; they pried into everyone's affairs, hoping that what they discovered would be of interest to people who had little interest in anything. He disliked spectators, also, for they were interested mildly in anything that seemed to be of interest and, by their very numbers, threatened to change and corrupt what had been his only escape from regimentation into another form of discipline.

"Hi, fellows." Damianos turned. A man with a camera slung over his shoulder approached them. "I wonder if you would sort of face the camera while I take a couple of shots."

Damianos did not move. Jacks turned slightly, and the photographer walked around in a semicircle until he faced the paratroopers.

"How about a smile?"

"Get fucked," Damianos muttered.

"That's good." The photographer grinned. "That was funny." Damianos heard a click. "I wonder if you guys would tell me just how you did it, what happened up there, what you were thinking about. You know? The works. They're lots of people in the country who'd be interested in reading about it and I'm sure some of the big magazines'd want these shots."

Jacks glanced to his partner. "Ah guess . . . sure . . ." He paused. "You live aroun' here or do you gotta go back?"

"No . . . I'm living in Von Steuben now. I work for the paper."

"Well . . . supposen you come aroun' next Saterdy and we'll tell you all 'bout sky divin'. Right now, Sergeant Damianos an' Ah gotta see a couple friends."

"I get you." The man laughed. "Sure . . . I understand." He smiled conspiratorially at Damianos but, getting no response from him, turned to Jacks again. "I'll be around next week, then. I don't want to interfere with your Saturday night."

"Rotten sons of bitches." Damianos stared at the photographer as he walked back to the gathering. "Can't do anything without *them* coming around and asking questions."

"What's the matter, Gus? He diden mean no harm. Jest wanted to get some pitchers."

"They're crowdin' me." Damianos' jaw was set. "I don't ask *him* to smile." The sergeants picked up their parachute kits and began hiking toward Jacks' car. Damianos was irritated that his partner had promised to tell the photographer about sky diving, certain that next Saturday he would share a Beaver with a tape recorder and a movie camera and be requested to grin like an ape at a lens and answer questions for people who would forget the answers as soon as they had heard them. "Candy-asses," he muttered. "All of them." Jacks was smiling, he knew, and to protect himself from his partner's teasing, Damianos adopted a pose of objective sarcasm. "You best get yourself a secretary, Sergeant Jacks, 'cause before you know it, you're gonna be president of the sky divers and you're gonna need a book on bylaws and a treasurer for the dues you're gonna need."

Jacks laughed. "So what? That'd be fine. The more sky

divers we have, the better. It's a good sport. Ah like it fine. Ah don' wanna keep it secret."

They're crowdin' me, Damianos thought. Walking past a group of teen-agers, he heard one of them—a thin, stoop-shouldered boy—talking knowledgeably about figure 8s and barrel rolls.

"You comin' with me to see *Do*rene?" Jacks asked when they sat in his car.

"Who's gonna be there?"

"That Puerto Rican ginch is free now."

Damianos was silent.

"She was askin' 'bout you. Guy she was livin' with jest got transferred to Gemany an' she's gotta have someone to help her with the rent."

"Not interested. I got a woman."

"Not interested in tonight or in her rent problems?"

"Her problems."

"What about tonight, then?" The car rolled awkwardly until Jacks turned it into a sandy road.

Damianos nodded. "You got booze?"

"Ah figured we'd buy some at the Club."

By the time the two men had driven to Kelly Field—where Damianos left his car—returned to their respective barracks to shower and dress, and met again at the NCO Club to purchase the bourbon, Damianos had decided that today's event was to be his last free fall. The sport was being perverted into a science. Before next summer he would be asked to explain the jargon he, Jacks, and other troopers had created to the nonparticipants, who would analyze, discuss, evaluate, and award trophies. He wanted no part of it. *They're crowdin' me,* he thought bitterly. For a minute today he was free and weightless; the day was approaching, he was certain, when even *free* falls would be regimented, and when this day arrived, he would ignore Saturday afternoons and begin a search for another means of escaping his patterned life. Only sex appeared to have been left unsystematized; on his last trip to the PX, however, he was surprised to see a few books that seemed to have been written to prove that sexual love, contrary to what the supposed reader had assumed, could be enjoyable. This was not very promising. *Candy-asses,* he thought. *Gonna try and crowd me out of that, too.*

But Damianos knew himself too well. When he could laugh at his anger, he knew his mood was changing, mellowing. As he followed Jacks' automobile out of Fort Mosby to

Mosby Boulevard and the trailer camp on the outskirts of Von Steuben, Damianos began to think about the woman Jacks had mentioned. He was not as interested in meeting a new woman as he thought he should be. Was he getting old? *I'll leave early,* he thought; *haven't seen Sophie for a while . . . help her out with the books, maybe.*

The two cars turned into an unpaved driveway that led to a row of cabins and trailers. They slammed the doors simultaneously and waited for Jacks' friend to answer his knock.

"Hi, *Do*rene."

She appeared to be no older than eighteen, with vaguely blond hair hanging to her shoulders.

"C'mon in, Duane." Dorene, stepping back as Jacks entered the cabin, smiled briefly at Damianos. "Didja bring any liquor? Ah'm all out of the stuff."

Jacks set the two bottles on a narrow table. "Mah frien', Gus." He nodded in the girl's direction. "*Do*rene."

"Pleased to meet y'all."

"Hi."

"Where's your girl frien'?"

"Ah'll call her." Dorene went to the door and shouted. " 'Sper*an*za!"

The sergeants glanced at each other. Damianos winked. "Nice and warm in here." He felt oppressed; the walls were no closer than those of his cadre room in the barracks, but the cabin was cluttered with chairs, a long narrow table, a radio console, a rather empty cupboard, and a double bed covered by an Army blanket with the U.S. emblem off to the right, slightly below center. "Think maybe we can open a couple windows?"

"There ain't but two." Jacks raised the windowpane of one and, walking to the other, bumped into Dorene, who was near the cupboard, rinsing glasses in the sink.

"Didja bring any sodas?" She ignored Jacks' clumsiness.

Damianos fought a smile when he saw that Jacks was irritated.

"Figured you'd have *them*. Gus an' Ah don' mix ours."

Dorene did not reply. She opened the refrigerator, brought out a large bottle of ginger ale, pried the cap off, and dropped ice cubes into two glasses.

Damianos appraised her carefully. She was bovine, he considered—not at all his type. What did Jacks see in her, other than the obvious, which he could get from any woman? Washed-out levis stretched over heavy, blocklike thighs; great sloping breasts pushed out her peppermint-striped man's shirt;

freckled hands worked peasantlike over the ice tray. *A real cow,* he thought. *Gotta fix him up with something better.*

He lighted a cigarette. "I can't stay too late."

Dorene did not look up. " 'Speranza'll be here in a minute." The answer was peevish.

Damianos made a face at Jacks as the door opened. He was not enthusiastic about what he saw. The woman was slender and dark, with black hair combed into a high pompadour. Her full lips were painted the same color as her long fingernails—a pastel red. As she entered the cabin, Esperanza managed to make her pouting mouth smile, betraying brownish, childlike teeth with wide spaces between them. Cheap earrings hung down to her shoulders, almost touching the magenta blouse, whose color clashed violently with her general brownness. Her tan skirt was wrinkled at the middle. One saving feature: her abdomen was a soft, plump one, slightly protuberant. *What the hell,* Damianos considered. *A man's gotta relax sometime.*

Jacks introduced them and distributed the drinks. "Well . . . we passed the baton today." He turned to Dorene. "Gus an' me. Took us three tries."

"That's good," she said, evidently uncertain how to respond. "What'd they give y'all for it?"

Damianos, turning to Esperanza, fell into a pidgin English. "You have cabin here, too?"

"Yes. I have cabin next door. Nice place."

"How long been here?" He pointed to the floor.

"Two year. Divorced last May."

Damianos nodded significantly, inspecting her again as she leaned forward slightly in her chair to sip her drink. He wanted to get this over with, confident this would be the last time he would see her. One woman at a time was enough for any man; only continent men overestimated their sexual endurance. Besides, his salary would not support two, particularly since the tavern he had recently opened was not earning as much as he had hoped. *Still,* he allowed, *there's no telling how good this ginch is.* But Sophie was a better woman. *Too good . . . too good for the likes of me.* For the first time since the end of the inspection, he perceived a feeling of restlessness coming over him; he forced himslf to continue the conversation, however, for he realized immediately that—in a moment of weakness—a sense of being unfaithful to Sophie was beginning to worry him. *I'm free,* he maintained, quickly stifling a whisper of commitment.

He glanced at Esperanza. "Let's see your cabin."

She had not been prepared for the demand. Her dull, brown eyes opened in surprise, but she nodded her head. "OK."

Damianos stood up and took the opened bottle. "I'm going next door for a second," he said, leaving before Jacks could comment. When they entered the cabin, he saw that it was as cluttered as Dorene's, only Esperanza's room was slightly larger, her bed was unmade, and luridly covered Spanish magazines littered the table and bureau top.

"You want to dance Spahnish music?" She looked at him timidly, as if afraid of him, his size, his audacity, the strange intensity of his eyes.

"Nothing too fast." Even his statements carried the timbre of command.

She kneeled for a moment—a delicious agitation in her movements obvious to him—and pulled out an album of Argentine tangos, showing a wedge of smooth, tawny knee skin through the slit in her skirt. Damianos considered this briefly and observed her nervous, expectant gait as she walked to the record player. Her hips were good, but the insides of her calves seemed flat. *Thin legs.* He frowned. But these inadequacies were unimportant to him; she found him attractive, and that was enough to provide him with a welcome feeling of mastery. He was glad he had accompanied Jacks. Liberation was good, particularly when—simultaneously with his freedom—a man could win dominion over a partner.

Esperanza returned to Damianos purposefully. *"Quieres bailar?* You want to dance?"

It had been years since he had involved himself in anything as frivolous as dancing, but, responding to a quick change of decision, he took her waist in his large, calloused hands and danced with a competence he had long ago forgotten he possessed, smoothly toe-stepping on the floor to the sensuous but vibrant beat. A curious dance, this tango: unexpected and thrilling.

The woman's heavy perfume assaulted his nostrils, but he did not criticize as he would have if another woman, Sophie, had used the scent on herself. After all, this was casual; it was not his prerogative to tell her how to dress and what perfume to choose. When he would know her better—if that was his decision—he would give her the necessary guidance. Now he merely danced, a ritual before the other—the ceremony whose sacredness he had long ago discredited.

Turning on the cabin's linoleum floor, he listened to the

disciplined abandonment of the tango and yielded to its rhythm, knowing that an occasional submission was inevitable.

The woman danced well, intuiting every step he took, compensating for his every error. She cupped his elbows with her small hands because of his height, and instead of dancing away from him as she had done previously, Esperanza retreated into his embrace. Joined now, they moved as one to the steady beat. He pulled her closer to him, sensed her warm breath on his open chest, and felt his thigh—with every forward step—push tightly between her legs. As the strings of the orchestra whimpered to a close, she raised her mouth to him languorously. He kissed her, allowing his hands to shape the curve of her back to her hips.

Freeing Esperanza from his embrace, Damianos took off his jacket. She pulled down the shades, for the sun was still shining. A glowing light now poured through the opaqueness of the windows. He refilled the glasses and joined her on the bed.

"What are you going to do when you run out of money?"

"Maybe stay. . . . Maybe go Neuva York." Unbuttoning his shirt, she held the open collar lightly. "You?"

Damianos thought he detected an implication in her question. "I stay." Even this statement, with all its brusqueness, carried with it a hint of apprehension. He drank the remaining liquor as he felt the warmth of her hand caress his hairy chest. When he turned to her, after setting their glasses on the nearby table, Damianos saw that she lay on the bed, her eyes fixed on the ceiling. He unbuttoned her blouse and cupped her small, warm breasts.

"Now," he said. They undressed, she turning away from him, unfastening her skirt and permitting it to fall to the floor. Her tawny skin gleamed. Damianos embraced her as she faced the wall, cupping her trembling abdomen in his hands, and nipped her dark shoulder flesh. After their kiss, he raised her aloft and laid her gently on the bed.

Her heavy eyelids fluttered as he mounted her, and in an instant he felt weightless, as if in the sky, hurtling through sun-ridged clouds, released.

It was dusk when Damianos opened his eyes. Immobile for a moment, he stared at the ceiling, trying to recall what he had dreamed. Barefoot, he seemed to have been walking on the damp earth of a great, treeless plain. A deer, its neck bent gracefully to the turf, had munched on wet grass. Something had kept him from it. Then he remembered. He had been weighted down with a heavy rucksack full of strange, half-familiar objects: old clothes, a Palm Sunday cross, work boots, a photo of his parents' village wedding, an ax handle, an icon of Saints Constantine and Helen. As he had set the rucksack down, he had felt free, like the deer that had gazed at him with curiosity. He had stepped over his heritage of burdens. The deer had taken fright and bolted, watching him from a distance. He had been rooted to the spot, glancing first at the rucksack, then at the deer. It had wandered off eventually. Then he had awakened.

Damianos dressed quietly, not to wake her, took a ten-dollar bill from his wallet, and placed it on the magazine-cluttered bureau top. *Yo te amo por la eternidad:* a guady cover promised the true story inside. Above the dresser, to the left of its small mirror, a glossy painting of the Holy Virgin, standing on fleecy clouds and attended by pink angels, hung on the wall.

Esperanza's body stirred, and a dark hand drew the sheet over her bare knees. "You are nice," she said. "Do you like me?"

But Damianos closed the door without answering. Within minutes he had driven into Von Steuben and made an abrupt turn at the City Hall into Combat Alley. Fortunate enough to find parking near the Green Light, he backed his car into a space and rolled up the windows. There might be rain. Sophie was at the register, facing the television set at the rear of the bar.

"Hello, Sophie." His eyes rested on her briefly, then focused on the flaming match tip as he lighted a cigarette. *Can't look at her. What's the matter?*

She smiled warmly. "I had a feeling you would come today." A delicate fragrance of soap drifted to him. Her glowing blond hair was held neatly by a ribbon whose blueness matched the color of her pleated skirt. "Do you want something to eat?" She touched the collar button of her white, lacy blouse, as if attempting to disguise a nervousness.

"OK." Damianos nodded self-consciously, then forced himself to confront her eyes. "How's everything been?" The question was forced; he would have to do better immediately. "I mean with you. Sorry I couldn't stop around more often. My team had to go through a lot of exercises for the maneuver."

"Oh . . . I guess you could say . . . all right." She folded her arms across a full bosom. "Business picked up last week. Don't look now . . ." Only several men were at the bar. "We've been getting good crowds after nine o'clock. It's only . . ." She gazed blankly at the wall opposite her, then quickly looked to her wrist. She wore no watch. "It's no more than . . . seven-thirty, now."

Damianos turned to the large clock. "Eight," he corrected.

"Here . . ." Sophie pointed to a booth. "Sit down. Do you want a beer?"

Sophie left him briefly to enter the kitchen. The hem of her skirt swayed as she walked down the aisle past the empty booths. *Fine woman,* he thought. *What in the hell does she see in me?* Yet he was reasonably free of responsibilities. He owed her nothing. The surprise, however, was that he felt vaguely dissatisfied in being uncommitted, being free of inhibiting duties. *I didn't want her.* He remembered Esperanza. *What am I trying to do . . . prove something?*

Sophie returned with a bowl of salad, vinegar, olive oil, and a lemon half. Her face seemed flushed; the blue-gray eyes glanced quickly over his face. "Well?" She smiled expectantly as she slid into the bench opposite him. "Did you pass the baton?"

"How'd you know we was gonna try that?"

"Sergeant Jacks was here last night. We talked for about an hour; then he left because of this morning's inspection."

Damianos felt a twinge of jealousy. "Yeah." He nodded. "We passed it . . . but it took us three tries." After a pause, he said, "I'm not sky diving any more, Sophie."

"Why?" She touched her hair quickly.

"They're crowdin' me. Bunch of candy-asses are coming in and taking over. Pretty soon even civilians will be jumping, acting like it ain't nothing to be a paratrooper." He ignored her smile.

"Are you staying here tonight?"

Damianos was busy chewing and delayed his answer. "Yeah, I guess so." He looked down to spear a tomato slice with his fork. "Maybe we can drive to the shore tomorrow." It was more of a suggestion than a statement, and when Sophie responded happily that she would love to, that the beach would be splendid this time of the year, he pushed the empty bowl away and grinned. "I could go for a steak right now. How 'bout one?"

"I've put one on the fire."

Damianos leaned back in the booth. "Aren't you gonna eat?" he asked tenderly, hardly realizing he betrayed an affection he had long ago determined to repress.

CHAPTER 4

"The jump is on tonight, isn't it?" Winters reached into a large pot filled with brown water and extracted a potato.

Clarke, digging out a final eye, paused until Winters sat back in his chair before dropping his potato into the clean tub. The two men were removing the potatoes' eyes, an act that eluded the otherwise efficient peeling machine in the corner of the mess hall, and transferring the cleaned potatoes to the pot filled with cold water.

"I imagine they'll be parachuting. The weather's been mild."

Making conversation had become an effort of the will for Clarke. Winters, he had to admit, was a pleasant companion, full of wisecracks against the numerous people who irritated him, but his unending store of gossip had exhausted Clarke, particularly since the two men had shared the KP detail four times in the past week.

"I wonder what those clowns see in jumping." There was a pause. "Barrett!"

Clarke looked up. "Yes?"

"I said, 'I wonder what those duds see in parachuting.' To listen to them talk, it's a cross between bullfighting and sex. Do you think they get their kicks like that?"

"Don't ask me. I don't know a thing about falling through space. Why don't you get one of the troopers to tell you?"

"Are you serious? Those duds can't think for one minute without getting a headache. You think they'll be able to explain anything?"

"Why don't you go airborne and learn for yourself, then?"

Winters laughed quickly. "What're you . . . a comedian? What's a guy with a near-genius IQ like me got to do with jumping out of airplanes? That nonsense is for retarded juvenile delinquents."

"I don't know, Harvey. I wouldn't mind trying it." Clarke noticed the other's shocked expression. "No, really, I *would*. Don't you think there's something . . . you know? . . ." He was embarrassed to say what he thought.

"Something epic and grand?" Winters laughed.

"Yes, damn it. Something different."

"You're out of your mind. What d'you want to do? Prove something?"

"I'm tired of what I've been doing." Clarke leaned over and rested his elbows on his thighs. "I don't want to prove anything. I just want to change, to do something, something different, something exciting."

"With a wife like Nikki . . . you don't think life is exciting? No offense, Barrett," he added quickly.

Clarke shrugged. "We're in the Army and what do we do? When we're not on KP, that is. We do the same things we did in civilian life. I'm fed up. I'm tired of the Army. Tired of psychological warfare. Tired of Voice of America and Radio Moscow. I'm tired of me!" Clarke stopped. It was improper to confess everything. There were some thoughts a man had to keep to himself, hidden from his friends, even his wife.

Winters tried to keep the conversation going, but Clarke answered in monosyllables, attempting to halt the dialogue without hurting his partner's feelings. He was bored with himself, bored with Barrett Clarke and the life he led—a routine of waking; dull, mechanical labor; eating; arguing occasionally with his wife; and then sleeping. And then dreaming. Nothing ever changed. He was a prisoner within himself. All that occurred was that he grew duller each day, weighted down by the virtual certainty that tomorrow would be as similar to today as today was similar to yesterday.

Sergeant Lucas, a powerful Negro, walked into the rations room for a number ten can of peas. A mild, good-natured man, he was less concerned with keeping KPs busy at all times than in maintaining the plaque awarded the propaganda unit for the cleanest and best mess hall on the Hill. A large-size T-shirt stretched across, but could not cover, his enormous shoulders and chest, and he was forced to pull at the short sleeves occasionally to keep them from biting into his armpits. Clarke and Winters had recently learned that it was difficult to fool him; he knew when the tray machine had not been scoured, when the grease trap had not been cleaned, and when the floors had not been thoroughly scrubbed. Except for one weakness, Lucas was invulnerable: he liked to hear the KPs compliment him on his questionable ability to speak French and German like a native.

"When you philosophus finish yore analization of life, you jest maght scrub down the garbage cans outside." He expressed a mock concern. "That is, if you don' mind."

Clarke smiled. "Not at all, Sarge. Be glad to. Anything else?"

"That's all for now." Lucas returned to the far end of the dining room to tack a notice on the bulletin board.

"You know"—Winters plucked out a potato eye—"the political theorists keep talking about an eventual war between the white race and the Chinese."

"So?"

"Well, when that day comes . . . I want to be on Sergeant Lucas' side."

Clarke smiled. "I've got enough problems right now without worrying about a race war." Since his hands were stiff from the cold water in the pots, Clarke stopped briefly, lighted a cigarette, and rested in his chair. "I need a break. Look at my hands." He showed Winters his palms. The skin was puckered and colorless.

"What's the matter?" Winters imitated the harsh voice of a drill sergeant. "Don't you like to soljer?"

A horn blared. Clarke, standing up to glance out of the kitchen window, saw a Deuce-and-a-Half parked on the company street. It was the provisions truck.

"Hey, KPs," Sergeant Lucas called from the dining room. "Git out there an' see what he's got for us."

"Right, Sarge." While Winters dried his hands on his fatigue trousers, Clarke looked for a dry, safe place to set his cigarette and chose the top of a cardboard box. The food-distribution men had placed the company's provisions on the concrete path that skirted between the whitewashed coal bin and the garbage-can platform. Not waiting for the unloading to end, Clarke and Winters began carrying the boxes and bags into the rations room, where Sergeant Lucas checked the goods on his tally sheet.

When the chore had been completed, the men took their seats again and began eyeing the remaining potatoes. Winters asked if Clarke had read about the Negro's trial in Alabama.

"The one up for life imprisonment for stealing $1.79 from an old lady?"

"That's not all. The prosecuting attorney claims the man tried to rape her."

Clarke was not interested. He had heard too much about the case; had read the factual, embarrassed articles in the American newspapers; and had monitored the equally factual but interpreted broadcasts from Radio Moscow. "She must have been rather attractive," he commented. "Some women of eight-five are well preserved."

Winters grunted. "Well, I can't say. I, personally, haven't seen too many attractive women at that age, but since I consider myself a cautious, scientific person, I can't ignore the theory that occasional women may keep their beauty past the age of seventy." He pulled out another potato. "Hey, Barrett? What's Radio Moscow been saying? Anything interesting?"

"Just the facts. But the facts still make us look like savages."

Winters showed his irritation. "Can't they understand it's just the goddamn South?"

"Why should they? The South is part of America, isn't it? Why should they make allowances for us? Voice of America isn't soft on them when something goes wrong in Russia, is it?"

"I don't know," Winters mumbled. "I've had my fill of psycho-warfare. FTA, that's what I say. FTA, demobilization, and the U.N.: the three hopes of salvation." He dropped a clean potato into the clear tub. "Why don't they leave me alone? I want to lead my own life." He groped in the brownish water. "It's these small ones I hate. Jesus, you eye ten small potatoes, and what's it worth to you? Not even two big ones. If I were in charge of food procurement, I'd make damn certain the Army got nothing but big potatoes. Small ones are a waste of the taxpayers' money."

"At ease!"

"What was that?" Clarke glanced at Winters.

"That was Sergeant Lucas. I imagine McIlhenny just walked in."

From where he sat, Clarke could see beyond the kitchen stoves and tables to the dining room. The short, slender form of the captain passed from the coffee urn to the silverware table, on which Sergeant Lucas had set the cream dispenser and a sugar bowl. The long swagger stick, covered with unit crests, was tucked under McIlhenny's arm. What was remarkable to Clarke was that the captain's face seemed boyish and soft, hardly what he expected in a company commander's appearance. His head, pink and bald to the ears, made him appear almost sensual; but Clarke knew too well how wrong a first impression of McIlhenny would be, for his seemingly pampered exterior disguised a keen, puritanical mind. The captain walked swiftly, as if, even on a fifteen-minute coffee break, he felt a compulsion to relax in a military manner.

"Well?" Winters could not see into the dining room. "Is that Ignatius Loyola himself?"

Clarke nodded. "He's in for his nine hundred seconds of rest and recuperation."

"I wonder how the inspection went today."

"Two to one says Battaglia's bunk is a mess."

Winters grinned. "Do you call those reasonable odds?" Leaning over the pot of potatoes, he whispered in Clarke's ear. "You know what I've been thinking? I'll bet everything I have that McIlhenny's queer. Battaglia looked at his personal file the other day. Something very suspicious there. He's almost forty. Never been married. Doesn't drink or smoke. No one sees him with a woman, much less take one out." Winters lowered his voice even more. "That guy has no vices, man. He *must* be queer!"

"You're going too far, Harvey." Clarke bent over for another potato. "If that were true, he wouldn't last too long in the Army." He paused, smiling as if in possession of a great secret. "We don't know anything about ourselves. . . . How can we presume to know anything about others?"

"I'm not saying he is. I'm saying he's inclined to be. Like he's latent."

Clarke grinned good-naturedly.

"What I mean is . . ." Winters' attitude became even less dogmatic. "What I mean is he fits into all the categories."

"Which categories? Whose categories? Look, Harvey . . . how old are you?"

"Twenty-three. Why?"

"Are you married?" Clarke answered his own question. "No. Do you have any vices? Not really. You don't make enough money to drink and smoke heavily. With your salary and the few available *and* eligible women in the Von Steuben area, you can't possibly average more than two or three rather dull dates a month. What do you do when you're off? You go to the Post movies and the library. With whom? Certainly not with girls. With male friends, am I right?" Winters was fighting a shamefaced grin. "When you take leave, where do you go? New York. That's home, isn't it? And who's at home? Mother, that's who. OK, Oedipus, I rest my case."

"You got it all wrong, Barrett." Winters shrugged his shoulders and groped in the brown water. "All I meant was that it's unnatural for a guy like him to lead this kind of life. He's too bound up about something. Like he's compulsive. That goddamn swagger stick, for example. Notice sometime how he handles it."

"I know, I know. Look . . . I don't like him any more

than you do. It's just that . . . well . . . it's pleasant to know that at least one man is sure of something in this world. I'm not judging his principles—merely the way he lives up to them. He's happy. He has his duty and his duty has meaning for him."

Clarke pulled back. There was little possibility of convincing such a partisan as Winters that McIlhenny was not as despicable as he thought. The very fact that the captain would have said the unexpected—"You have free choice"—was enough to persuade Clarke that he was no ordinary company commander. The man *believed* what he said. How many military minds could conceive of such a revolutionary idea?

"I wonder how Ignatius is taking the jump tension?" Winters began whispering again. "Believe me, he makes on like he's a real hero, but I'll bet anything he shivers when he's up there."

"Maybe he has a near-genius IQ?"

"That was unfair, Barrett. I expected better from you."

Clarke heard voices approaching the kitchen. McIlhenny, followed by Sergeant Lucas, walked past the counter and headed directly for the KPs. Clarke stood up.

"Good morning, sir."

McIlhenny nodded. "How are they doing, Sergeant?"

"Fine, sir. They're workin' perty good."

"Just keep them busy." The captain glanced at both men quickly. As he was about to stride to the kitchen door, his eyes sighted something. "What is this?"

Clarke realized he had forgotten his cigarette on the cardboard box. McIlhenny picked the butt up carefully; it had gone out, but two inches of it remained intact.

"That's mine, sir."

"Do you make a habit of leaving cigarette butts and wrappers lying about, Clarke?"

"No, sir. I set it there when the provisions truck arrived."

McIlhenny looked at the trademark on the cigarette paper. He nodded his head. Whatever he looked for did not seem to exist on Clarke's cigarette. "Be more careful next time. Lighted cigarettes can be very dangerous."

"Yes, sir." There was not much else for him to say. If Clarke had stated that he agreed lighted cigarettes were dangerous, McIlhenny might have responded quickly that Clarke evidently did not practice what he knew so well. All he could do was wait hopefully until the matter was closed.

McIlhenny nodded abruptly to Sergeant Lucas. "Good

day," he said. Head tilted back, shoulders and back straight, the captain walked out of the kitchen. The screen door slammed.

Glancing out the window, Clarke saw McIlhenny marching toward the orderly room, his swagger stick gripped tightly in his right hand. He walked as if, any moment, an attempt would be made to wrest the stick from his grasp. At approximately every four steps the white-tipped baton struck his right thigh and bounced off into another period of immobility.

"You mens should know bettah than that. Christ, man, he's a hard nut. You nevah should have butts aroun' where he kin find 'em."

"I forgot. I'm sorry."

When Sergeant Lucas had returned to the dining room, Winters glanced at Clarke. "What did I tell you? That man is a real bastard. Look at him!"

McIlhenny's figure was quite small by now. "One of these days that man is going to snap, and I want to be around when it happens. I'd give anything to see him crack." Winters' lips were tight. "Look at that obscene swagger stick of his."

"He's tough," Clarke murmured. "I wish I were that tough. He'll never break." When McIlhenny turned off the path, Clarke sat down in his chair. *At least he knows what he is and what he believes,* he thought. *What do I believe? I deserve to be pushed around. How can I deserve any better if I don't know where I stand?*

"You going to be home tonight?"

"I think so. Are you thinking of stopping by?"

"I'd like to. I've got to get out of these goddamn barracks. If you and Nikki are planning to go anywhere, just tell me. I don't want to interfere."

"Well . . . how about a beer in town? She's been staying at home since we got the Article 15."

"OK. Tonight, then."

Clarke nodded. "Stop around any time."

CHAPTER 5

The evening had settled calmly over the marshaling area. The clouds slowly lost their whiteness and became gaudy in the final moments of daylight as the westering sun dipped toward the earth's curvature.

The marshaling area of Rickenbacker Air Force Base gradually darkened as a pair of Deuce-and-a-Halves drove toward a C-124 Globemaster standing idly on a runway's skirt. By the time Damianos had released the tail gate and watched the paratroopers leap to earth, twilight had descended over the forests and airstrips.

The darkened bulk of the Globemaster dominated the background; its enormous, whalelike fuselage lay poised a few feet above the concrete. The round snout increased in circumference, drooped in its belly until it virtually scraped the concrete runway, and hardly tapered until it rose to the towering, spankerlike tail. The wings, like outstretched arms that never tired, parelleled the flatness of the field with their sweep. Inert and cold, the Globemaster seemed to brood, waiting for its fuselage to fill with men so that it would achieve a human meaning. Its four engines, much larger than jeeps, waited patiently to transport the human cargo into the darkened, now star-swept and moon-crested sky.

A conventional tension worried into Damianos. By now, after fifteen years of parachuting, the sergeant had accustomed himself to the recurring dread. A military jump at night was not a sports event, for too many imponderables lurked between a dark sky and the earth's obscurity. It was chilly. To warm himself, he double-timed in place.

Between the Globemaster and the gradually augmented group of paratroopers, two trucks were parked, one loaded down with heavy T-10 parachutes and the other, a half-ton trailer, filled with reserve chest chutes. Several men leaned against the trucks and spoke in the darkness, the red coals of their cigarette tips flaring on the drag to spotlight a chin strap, a hand, a pair of tape-secured glasses. The smoke drifted into the quiet heavens.

At precisely 8:45 the headlights of the Deuce-and-a-Halves that had brought the troopers were turned on, and the rush of light glare froze the gathered soldiers in poses resembling those of figures in wax museums. Damianos walked to the wooden "A" frame he had set up earlier, placed a chart on the horizontal ledge, and cleared his throat. As jumpmaster tonight, he would find it important to know the latest weather and wind information from the radio that popped and hummed nearby, its antenna tip impaling the nascent moon. All seemed to be well. An occasional gust of wind blew on the surface of Sicily North DZ, not at all threatening.

Damianos, glancing at the men he had known for years, played his usual game: *Which one tonight?* All the troopers seemed relaxed. *Me?* he wondered, and quickly dismissed the taunt. For a man like Damianos who had jumped five hundred times from an airplane, three times in combat, a peacetime drop was tame only when viewed from the prospective of the blood-soaked North Africa, Sicily, Normandy, and Holland drops, where thousands of men, their canopies spotting the black skies like clouds of dandelion fluffs, drifted earthward into red flak. Every jump had its own terrors, however, for a next drop was inevitable, and each safe mass jump raised the odds for injuries and death on a subsequent drop.

"Hey, Corporal!" The commo man turned to Damianos. "Come over here for a second." He waited. "Don't look right away. Over next to Captain Trombeaux and Major Jenkins. There's a little guy. Got his arms folded. Do you know him?"

The corporal looked over his shoulder carefully. "McIlhenny. Captain McIlhenny. CO of Psywar. Why?"

"Just askin'." Damianos shrugged his shoulders. The captain looked nervous. *If he gives me any trouble at the door,* he thought, *McIlhenny's gonna get my boot.* There was something troubling to Damianos about the captain, an intensity of concentration, a virtually glassy-eyed stare.

He picked up the microphone, blew into it, heard the result, and began calling the names of the men listed on the jump manifest. Forty men responded.

The paratroopers, in the order they were called, lined up and walked between the truck and the half-ton trailer, receiving a main and a reserve from the men of the parachute rigging detachment. After lugging their bulky harnesses to to the lighted area, the jumpers strapped themselves into their chutes and, using the buddy system, tightened each other's waistband.

Damianos, with two other NCOs, inspected each trooper to see that he wore the dog tags which would identify his body in the event of the perpetually expected disaster. They checked the helmet, the airborne chin strap, the shoulder adjusters, the breast straps, the quick-release mechanism, and the waistband attaching the reserve to the main chute. They made certain that the reserve's rip cord faced to the right and that its rigger seal was intact. Then, surveying the ranked paratroopers from the rear, they inspected the static lines, the risers, the folded canopies' break cords, and the canvas packs, checking to see if any nylon was showing.

When the personnel inspection was over, the two NCOs went to the Globemaster to check it while Damianos returned to the lighted area for the final briefing.

"As you can see," he began, "we'll be using the pregnant whale for the drop. Speed at jump-off will be about 120 miles per hour at 1,250 feet. Direction of flight will be south by southwest, right down the long corridor of the DZ. The weather's pretty good, but the atmosphere's dry, which means the landing will be hard. So be careful to make a good parachute landing fall. Can't take any chances today on a bad PLF. There's a little wind on Sicily North—not much, though; about ten knots—but it's sorta spotty, with gusts going up to eighteen knots."

It was awkward speaking to a group made up of both enlisted men and officers. Colonel Simms was in the foreground, to Damianos' left. *Look straight ahead,* he cautioned himself, *and pretend like no one's there.*

"When the Globemaster is airborne and we're six minutes from the DZ, the pilot will flash the red light. At that point I'll begin the eight jump commands, which are Get Ready, Stand Up, Hook Up, Check Static Lines, Check Equipment, Count Down for Equipment Check, Stand in the Door, and Go. The green light will indicate that the aircraft is over the DZ."

Damianos scanned the assembled men's faces. McIlhenny was still nervous. The right side of his mouth seemed to bother him, for he constantly worried it with his thumb. *Looks like he's gonna get my boot,* the sergeant thought.

"A few days ago," he continued, "a man in the Division was killed 'cause he and the man behind him on the stick didn't check to see if his static line was clear. He hooked the damn thing under a riser, so when he jumped from the door the break cord didn't break and he just hung there ten feet under the tail till the jumpmaster—a friend of mine—went to pull in the packs of the troopers that just dropped. This guy was dangling there, and my buddy didn't know if he should cut him loose, 'cause he wasn't sure the guy was conscious." Damianos paused. "I know most of you have heard this by rumor, but I'd like to give you the exact truth." He glanced sharply at McIlhenny to see his expression. The captain appeared uncomfortable, as if he wanted to leave but was held back by his self-respect.

"So the jumpmaster radioed the Base and had 'em cover

the runway with chemical foam. The plane circled around till the strip was carpeted with the stuff. When the plane landed, it was too late. The guy was dead. He couldn't breathe up there and his body was black and blue from being slammed against the tail."

Damianos squared his shoulders. "Now here's what's been decided for the future. If a man is caught outside, he will put his hands on his helmet to show the jumpmaster that he's conscious. If he's OK, he'll be cut free and will activate his reserve. If he doesn't put his hands on his helmet, I got to assume he's out cold and begin, with some of the Air Force personnel, to pull him in, if I can. All care will be taken to bring him in quickly and safely, but he will be pulled in, *dead or alive!* Any questions?"

There were no raised hands. "Now don't worry about the rigging detachment, 'cause they got a new man in there who's pretty good with parachutes." He paused briefly, then delivered the punch line without a smile. "Name is Mortis, but the guys call him Rigger Mortis, so go on over and shake his hand after the jump. He'll be glad to meet you."

The reception of the pun was slow, but when most of the paratroopers had understood it, they burst into excited, nervous laughter. Major Jenkins shook his head in bogus disbelief, burst into laughter again, and finally controlled himself. "Sergeant . . . that was bad . . . very bad."

"Is everybody gonna jump?" Damianos shouted the ritual question.

"Yes, Sergeant!" The officers and men formed a file, did a right face, and marched toward the Globemaster.

«««««»»»»

Captain McIlhenny felt the urgent need to urinate. Seated as he was on a canvas bucket seat welded to an airplane that had just leveled off at 1,300 feet, however, crowded on both sides by fellow paratroopers, and burdened with 50 pounds of equipment, he knew that relieving himself was out of the question. The gum he always chewed on jump nights had lost its flavor an hour before, but he masticated automatically, hoping merely to relax his slowly mounting tension.

McIlhenny stared at the window directly across from him to view the white haze of the lighted Post below; when the aircraft banked to its left, he saw that the thousand sparkling lights of the officers' homes, the barracks, the service clubs, and the streets formed a terrestrial galaxy in the night's midst that seemed to mimic that of the heavens above. The roaring engines shook the Globemaster, and the open doors invited the chilling wind. His neighbor, Major Jenkins, leaned over to tell McIlhenny something; he had to repeat it, shouting, before the captain understood.

"Want to go for a beer after the jump?"

McIlhenny replied "Yes!" before considering the question. For a moment he experienced a feeling of loss; after all, he preferred to spend the night reading. But then, recalling that he had not gone into society for weeks, McIlhenny decided that an evening of conversation, dull though it would prove, might help him defeat a growing sense of depression. He leaned toward Jenkins and shouted: "Thanks for the invitation!"

The major waved deprecatingly and stared ahead, his gentle features relaxing in the permanent half-smile McIlhenny had known for years. The two men had been lieutenants together years before, had met again briefly in Korea, and had been COs of neighboring units at Fort Mosby for three years before the past weekend, when Jenkins had received his promotion.

It was much better to talk than to stare into the darkened cavern of the Globemaster, McIlhenny decided. "Pain in the neck!" he shouted. "Been up a half hour already!"

Jenkins asked him to repeat.

"Been up a half hour!"

"Fly-boys gotta log in time!"

McIlhenny nodded. It was better to talk but not worth the effort. He and Jenkins would have enough time this evening to say all they wanted to say. McIlhenny hoped he would be able to restrain the bitterness he felt about the delay in his promotion. It was embarrassing to congratulate men with less time in grade than he and call them "sir" when he had been a soldier while they were still in high school. *Why are they holding it up?* the captain wondered. *No . . . no . . .* He stifled his thoughts. *I'll think about something else.* McIlhenny settled back into the bucket seat. *We'll be jumping soon!* he realized. *Got to think of something else.*

It was possible to sing without being heard in the roar of the engines and the howl of the open door, and he had developed a workable pattern for crowding the jump thoughts out of his mind. First he hummed a few Gregorian chants; then he progressed to the vaguely remembered lyrics of the IRA songs his father had sung to him and, from these—quieted now—to recollections of his childhood and youth.

Where would I be today if there wasn't a Second World War? He answered his own question. *In the priesthood, maybe. Or a monastery.* He had passed the stage, however, where he concerned himself with the workings of destiny! God was deep; moment by moment He appeared ready to reveal Himself, only to cloud man's understanding, at times almost teasing him into doubt and despair. The questions man plagued himself with were answered in riddles, and he who possessed eyes was blinded, he who kept faith was perplexed, and he who deserved not was rewarded.

"Get ready!"

He groped through the bulky equipment for his safety belt.

"Stand up!"

He lurched to his feet, desperately trying to maintain balance on the aircraft's bucking floor, and grasped the static line's metal fastener. This cord, attached to the canvas pack in which his chute was stored, would break open the seal when he jumped, filling his canopy with air.

"Hook up!"

Reaching with his left hand to the wire that ran from one end of the fuselage to the other, he hooked the snap on the line and tried to pass the safety wire through the fastener's small hole to lock the catch. The lurching of the aircraft precluded this.

"Check static lines!"

The stretched wire was pulled and released by the men on the stick as they tested their lines, and McIlhenny found it impossible to lock his fastener. "Oh, God," he pleaded, praying to the Doubtful, beseeching the Crafty, begging mercy from the Devious.

"Check equipment!"

While the others were checking their equipment, he tried again and again to lock his fastener.

"Count down for equipment check!"

"Twelve OK!"

"Eleven OK!"

"Ten OK!"

"Nine OK!"

The soft wire slipped to one side and then to the other. "Oh, God! Oh, God!"

"Eight OK!"

"Seven OK!"

Then he realized what he had been doing wrong. He pushed the catch up violently and pierced the hole.

"Seven OK!"

The countdown had stopped for him. He disciplined himself quickly and slapped the buttocks of the man in front of him.

"Six OK!"

The count resumed and the line moved forward, nearing the open door. McIlhenny could now feel the cold prop blast strike him in the face and pull his trousers taut against his legs.

"Stand in the door!"

His heart beat faster; his hands and arms felt as if they needed the support of his side. He leaned against the wall of the fuselage. The light was still red. The aircraft had not flown over the drop zone yet. "Holy Mary, Mother of God . . ." No more. He could remember no more: a fitting punishment for having doubted. "Pray . . . pray for us sinners . . ." The jumpmaster leaned out of the door. ". . . us sinners now . . . and in . . ." The sergeant pulled himself into the cavern again. ". . . now and in the moment of our . . ." The green light flashed.

"Go!"

The line rushed ahead, one second per man at the door, and before McIlhenny knew it, he was at the opening, his boots scraping the threshold, his trembling hands grasping the cold metallic jambs. He leaped into the sky, was caught in the vicious, frigid prop blast, and, for three seconds, crashed toward the darkened earth with only the umbilical cord of his static line attaching him to the aircraft. The pathfinders' blinker lights on the drop zone winked at him knowingly.

«««»»»

Falling in the dark silence from the star-flickering heavens, suspended under the gray mushrooms of their canopies, the paratroopers descended like murky snowflakes, with only the humming prayer of the wind convincing them that their eardrums functioned. On the drop-zone sand a jolt awaited them, yet they had other matters to consider before the impact came, knowing that they should not worry, else their limbs might tighten and break on impact. Moments of danger must be labored through calmly; man's concentration must limit his fluttering mind to the present, making that certain, before rushing on to new problems, new concerns.

Where are the trees, the rigid, flesh-loving, bone-shattering trees? Beyond the silent, moonlit rectangle of the drop zone. How strong is the wind? Too strong, uneven, blowing in gusts. Where is the wind taking them? Into the trees. *If Ah die on the old drop zone . . .* To the left; must pull to the left. *Box me up an' send me home . . .* Grasping their left-front and left-rear risers, the paratroopers pulled themselves up, hand over hand, until they reached the shroud lines. *Lay my head upon my chest . . .* The descending canopies tilted dangerously to the left, sending men earthward diagonally, slicing the darkened sky with taut, vibrating nylon. *Tell the girls Ah've gone to rest . . .*

Upon leaping from the Globemaster, the paratroopers could span the width of the drop zone with their spread jumpboots; but now, falling twenty-two feet a second, they saw themselves as playthings descending toward an earth in whose clay their aspirations were imprisoned and in whose vastness their transient exultation would be stilled. There, on the outer fringes of the ghostly sand, they would relearn their true proportions. There, near the sky-piercing trees, they would recall their triviality. The moment had come to know themselves.

In the shadows lurked the trenches where gushing creeks had roared after torrential rains, where the probing fingers of water had leaped across the drop zone to the soft forest turf, where tree stumps, glaring at the rootless sky with empty eye sockets and frazzled rims, lay in wait. *Tambo, Tambo, it's been said . . .* The earth swung up to meet the dangling boots. *What's fifty dollars if you're dead? . . .*

Toes jolting on the hard-packed sand, the troopers fell immediately to their left, rolled on their calves, their thighs, their buttocks, twisted on their backs, and leaped to their feet again, mere men, shaking sand from their clothes: this was their native land. They struck their quick-release to feel the leg and shoulder straps fall limp. As they stuffed the parachutes into the kit bags, they glanced once more to the heavens to see the Globemaster roaring over again to spawn another stick of men.

«««««»»»»

Sergeant Damianos wandered through the forest with a flashlight for two hours before he located Major Jenkins. The officer had landed in a tree and dangled toward the earth like a boy on a playground swing. His face had been scraped off by a scaly limb which projected quietly and secretively from the trunk, as if the tree had yearned to end its isolation. A few teeth, a handful of flesh, and about a cup of blood had oozed over his reserve parachute and dripped, like mucus, to the dry-grass- and pine-needle-covered turf below. Both arms had shattered when he crossed them to protect his face, and they dangled like puppets' limbs from the pulpy mass of his shoulders. The bridge of his nose, crushed back to the forehead, made his nostrils appear like two black holes which bored directly through his skull. He swayed there gently, almost irresponsibly, in the forest, in the night, carried effortlessly back and forth by the caressing breeze.

CHAPTER 6

"It's only a block away. You can see the sign from here." Nikki pointed. "See it?"

"Well, I hope Harvey finds the place."

"It just opened a few months ago, I hear, and thank God for that. The Green Light seems to be the only decent bar in town."

With his wife quick-stepping at his side, Clarke walked toward the tavern, annoyed that he had agreed to meet Winters there. As if twelve hours a day was not enough to spend with the specialist, he must pass an evening with him, too, listening to the perpetual Army gossip. Clarke had originally believed that he did this as a favor to Nikki, but a secretive desire for honesty with himself forced him to unearth a more complex motive: tonight Winter's would share the burden he bore every day; tonight they would both talk to Nikki.

"Oh, look!" She halted at a dress shop. "Isn't that lovely? I like a puffed sleeve!"

Nikki leaned against the windowpane to view the price, while Clarke, glancing at the fashionably dressed mannequins, rested his eyes briefly on his wife. Nikki wore black leotards under a tartan skirt, a heavy black pullover, and a smart beret over short-cropped auburn hair. A small girl, slender and intense, she obviously accepted, and even capitalized on, her gaminlike appearance.

"How long are you going to stay there?"

Nikki turned quickly, a hurt look on her face. They walked

again, Clarke realizing that he had not rid his voice of its edge before speaking to her. *I'll have to make it up,* he thought. *I'm spending half my life apologizing for the bitterness I can't control in the other half.*

"Do you need any clothes?" His voice was soft.

"No, I don't!"

They walked past several storefronts before she spoke again. "I just like to look at the clothes we can't afford, that's all. I'm sorry I bore you."

Clarke did not respond. She opened the tavern door without waiting for him and walked into the Green Light. Winters and Battaglia were sitting in a booth near the left wall. *Oh, fine,* Clarke thought. *Battaglia, too. We're all here, then. All we need is McIlhenny and we can muster the unit.*

"Hello, Harvey. How've you been?"

Clarke experienced a twinge of irrational jealousy on hearing Nikki's happy greeting. He nodded casually to the two men and sat across from Battaglia. Winters introduced the personnel clerk to Nikki.

After shaking her hand vigorously, Battaglia turned to Clarke. "What d'ya say, smart money? I hear you and Harvey are planning to elope." Battaglia's small eyes blinked rapidly behind the thick lenses of his glasses. "You know"—he glanced at Nikki—"I got to hand it to these guys. They see each other just about twelve hours a day and they haven't had an argument yet."

"Don't speak too quickly." Nikki turned a blank, expressionless face to Clarke. "They've got another week to go."

After bringing his cigarettes out and placing the pack on the table, Clarke realized he had made an error.

"*Hey* . . . just my brand!" Battaglia speared a cigarette with the dexterity of an accomplished borrower and waited politely to light his own and Clarke's cigarette. "Well . . ." He blew out a cloud of smoke and spat a few grains of tobacco in Clarke's direction. "I've been keeping pretty good tabs on our exalted leader, Von McIlhenny, and he still didn't get his promotion. I think our boy's had it."

"Isn't anyone going to take our order?" Clarke made a point of inspecting the bar. "So far I haven't seen a waitress or a cashier."

"The woman who runs the place left about twenty minutes ago. She got a phone call. The guy in the kitchen isn't too fast." Harvey reached to the ashtray. "She won't be long, I guess."

"You mean she just left? Like that?" Clarke, although more

interested in changing the conversation, found himself genuinely curious that a manager would leave a bar untended.

"She's got a good head. A real looker," Battaglia contributed.

"Who?"

"The woman who runs the place." Nikki glanced at Clarke. "I walk past every now and then coming from the market. She seems very pleasant."

The conversation had become deadening. "Is she married?" Clarke asked Battaglia, hopeful that the small man—notorious for his ability to notice a wedding ring at great distances—would enliven the dialogue.

"She don't look married. Why?"

"How can you go wrong?" Clarke smiled at Winters. "She's good-looking *and* manages a bar."

"Give me time," Winters cautioned. "After all, I just got here."

Four men in civilian clothes came in and took a booth on the right side of the tavern, near the cash register. One, before taking a seat, walked to the Wurlitzer and selected a few records. A guitar twanged, and a man, whose voice identified him as a Southerner, sang of a woman's infidelity.

"I knew it was too good to last," said Battaglia. "These meatheads don't know *one* about music."

The new arrivals began shouting for a waitress. When, after five minutes, no one had come to take their order, they walked to the rear and demanded service, making a great deal of what Clarke considered unwarranted noise. He wanted to tell them to keep quiet, but practical considerations forced him into silence: there were four of them, and neither Battaglia nor Winters was capable of defending himself very well. Nikki, moreover, would consider any outburst of his as immature and impractical. Having made a decision to ignore the noise, Clarke felt unable to participate in the conversation, for every shout from the opposite booth irritated him more than it should have, reminding him as it did of his timidity.

"Bunch of airborne clowns," Winters muttered. "A guy jumps out of an airplane and automatically he figures he's a hero."

"It's a paratroopers' town," Clarke answered. "Nothing strange about their behavior. They feel that straightlegs just don't belong at Fort Mosby."

"They don't have to be so goddamn loud about it," Battaglia said. "Pardon the French. Like we're defending our country, too . . . in a way. Sure, I don't make a big deal about it, but, *man,* if them records are ever wrong, the whole Army becomes a mess in no time flat."

"Atta boy, Battaglia." Winters smiled. "You tell 'em, boy."

"Hey!" Battaglia evidently decided to change the subject. "You know what I saw?"

"No." Clarke and Winters answered simultaneously. For a brief moment Clarke had forgotten the newcomers in the other booth and developed an interest in the conversation.

"Well, a new field manual came into Headquarters the other day, full of FTAs, which means that the guys on the other posts are doing a hell of a lot more than we are. We're dropping the ball here at the 'Home of the Airborne.' "

"Who's dropping the ball?" Winters snapped. "I don't see *you* sticking your scaly neck out! I'm the only one who rebelled against the brass and got caught. When you sneak a few FTAs into some of the *Daily Bulletins,* then you can talk."

The front door opened and a blond woman entered, followed by a powerfully built man. Clarke had never seen the woman, but the dark man, walking with his hands deep in his pockets, a preoccupied expression on his face, seemed familiar.

"Hey, *you!* How about some service here!" one of the four men at the booth shouted at her.

The woman's companion, ready to sit down on a barstool, paused for a moment, walked to the booth, and stared at the heaviest man.

"Shut up, candy-ass. Are you looking for a knuckle sandwich?

"I sure am," the paratrooper said. He stood up. "You ain't gonna give me one, though."

The dark man backhanded the soldier across the face and threw him against the wall, wedging him between the booth separator and the record selector. "It's closing time," he said. "Everybody *get out*. We're closing up."

The other three at the booth rose slowly, muttering at the stranger, and stopped their companion from continuing the fight. The dark man, walking past Clarke's booth, told them they could stay if they made no noise. He returned to his barstool and raised a tumbler of straight whiskey to his lips. When the four men had left, the blonde locked the door and turned off the outside lights.

"Who's he?" Nikki turned to her husband.

"He's very familiar. I can't place him, though. I've seen him somewhere. Harvey, do you know that man?"

"Yeah. He's been around. Probably some airborne dud."

"I think he's in the Special Troops. Wait . . . wait . . . He's a sergeant." Clarke was certain now.

"What else can he be?" Battaglia asked. "He's got that ol' NCO smell."

"Damianos, that's his name." He stared at the man for a moment. "Remember the night I was on CQ . . . when I forgot to buff the floor?" He spoke to Nikki. "Well, he was the Sergeant of the Guard that night. Brought in the colored prisoner and woke me up. You know, the night of the storm? I told you about that, didn't I?"

"Yes." Nikki recalled the incident. "It's a shame the way they pick on Negroes, even in the Army."

Clarke did not wonder what his statement had to do with Nikki's response, for by now he had accustomed himself to his wife's habit of misinterpreting everything he said.

"That's not the point, Nikki," he reminded her softly. "The man was a prisoner because he beat up a woman—assault and battery, it's called in legal terms. He was placed in the stockade and assigned to certain details. He escaped with the guard's shotgun."

"It's a wonder the Von Steuben police even bothered to book him. The way I heard things like that—I mean fights, stabbings, and murder among Negroes—are handled is that they aren't handled at all. At least they cared enough to arrest him."

"I'm sure we all agree with your liberal sentiments." Clarke stopped himself. He seemed to recall being even more violently disposed in the prisoner's behalf but quickly ignored the recollection. It was better left unsaid, for it would appear conciliatory.

Conversations between him and Nikki always took this turn. They agreed substantially on every question; she, however, voiced her opinions in a way that made him feel—because he tried to speak objectively—that he appeared less humane than he actually was.

"Well, I'm glad you agree. Why is it you didn't speak out against his treatment that night?"

"I had no business to speak out. It wasn't *my* problem. What treatment?" He flushed. "He was a prisoner, wasn't he?"

"Then you sided with *them,* didn't you?"

"Look, Nikki. As long as I'm in the Army, my personal

beliefs are meaningless. I told you how I felt that night. It wasn't my affair."

"They didn't bother *you,* did they?"

"The *system* bothers me. Officers and NCOs are part of the system. I have more cause to dislike it than you do. I'm a soldier, Nikki. Remember that. You don't know anything about the Army. Your universe is limited to Von Steuben. I'd appreciate it if you didn't involve me in any of your crusades, because I'd like to leave the Army without a court-martial."

"You'll have to make a stand somewhere, Barrett."

"When I do, it'll be *my* stand, not yours."

This was awkward. Each exchange of dialogue brought them closer to a serious argument. That the tense relationship they had had with one another for the past few months made the possibility of an argument inevitable, and virtually desirable, was understood by Clarke, but the time and the place of the quarrel would be selected by him, far away from friends, in their own apartment. And she was much more perceptive than he liked to admit; he *would* need to make a stand somewhere. Their marriage had been deteriorating steadily since the wedding, and it was just as much his fault as it was hers. He was to blame because he had not taken a stand. How could she know what kind of wife to be if he had not decided what kind of wife he wanted? It was all his fault, granted, but if she wanted him to take a stand, she would be surprised, he knew, when he chose to take it.

Throughout the disagreement, Battaglia and Winters had maintained their silence. It was up to Clarke to salvage the evening, if at all possible. As he was thinking of changing the conversation, Nikki spoke.

"Have you finished scolding me?"

Clarke stifled his anger. He would disregard everything until they returned to their apartment, and if she continued this course, he would be obliged to make his stand tonight. "I'm sorry. I didn't mean to speak that way." He spoke these words dully. "I just wanted to . . ." She had him at a disadvantage, and he knew her well enough to realize that she was determined to make a scene in front of Winters and Battaglia. He waited helplessly for her to continue.

"Why is everything I say or do always wrong?" The question was asked calmly, as if Nikki were addressing a panel of marriage counselors. "Why is it that you think you can attack anything and anyone, and when *I* do it you feel that

I'm trying to be superior or trying to take over your *critic's* role?"

There was more to come, Clarke knew, but he would restrain himself. He would make no more outbursts in front of the two men from his unit.

"Do you feel threatened somehow, Barrett?" Nikki's voice was surprisingly mild.

"No . . . you don't threaten me. You embarrass me. I'd rather not continue this conversation. I'm sure Harvey hasn't come down to Von Steuben to hear us squabbling." But, just as he was about to conclude, he understood the hopelessness of salvaging the evening. He wanted to get up, to leave, but etiquette demanded small talk, demanded goodbyes and promises to meet the following day.

He stood up. "Excuse me. I'm going over to speak to the sergeant. I'll be right back." He walked angrily toward Damianos, making a point of not turning to the booth until he paused before the seated man. "Hello," Clarke said, attempting a friendliness that immediately struck him as false. "I wonder if you remember me? I'm Clarke, the fellow on CQ the night you brought in the prisoner." Nikki, Clarke saw, was getting up from the booth.

"Oh, yeah . . . Clarke. How the hell are you? Have a drink."

Having run, crying, to the door, Nikki opened it quickly and, as she was about to rush out, bumped into a man who stood at the entry, evidently wondering if the Green Light was closed for the night.

Clarke was committed. He resumed the conversation, hoping to find a proper moment to excuse himself and try to overtake her before she arrived at their apartment.

"Have a drink," Damianos repeated. "On the house." He called the blond woman, who had just entered from the kitchen. "Sophie, bring my friend here a drink."

She neared them, glancing apprehensively at Damianos. The sergeant had evidently been drinking too much, for his movements gave Clarke the impression of a studied disorganization. Sophie smiled at Clarke, but the smile, he realized, was the embarrassed reflex of a woman who was faced with someone's unruly and potentially violent behavior. She brought a glass for Clarke and poured bourbon into it. There was no ice, and Clarke did not want to ask for any.

"Gus . . . please," she whispered. "You're drinking too much. Go upstairs and sleep. You'll feel better tomorrow."

As if in answer, Damianos snatched the bottle out of her

hand and refilled his glass, licking his fingers where some liquor had spilled. "I feel good. As good as possible. What the hell? A man's entitled to get drunk once in a while." He held his glass at eye level. "Here's to ya, Clarke. Go airborne is my advice." After gulping down the bourbon, he tapped his glass on the bar.

"Gus . . . you've been drinking like that for an hour. If I didn't get you at the Club, you'd be in the stockade now."

"Dark clouds floatin' in the sky . . ." Damianos ignored her, chanting a Jody rhyme that was suspiciously off-key. *"I wonder, Lord, when will I die . . ."*

Sophie motioned to Clarke. "Look, mister. You're his friend. Can you get him to stop drinking and go upstairs to bed? Me, he doesn't listen to."

"You see," Clarke began, "I don't know him that well. I've only met him once before. Is he . . . I mean, are you married?" He understood the irrelevance of his question as soon as it had left his lips.

"No, not married." She did not lower her eyes. "He's had bad luck today. He was jumpmaster a few hours ago and a man, a good friend, was killed. It's not his fault, I tell him; it's not his fault . . . but he won't listen."

"Who was killed?" For a brief, insane moment Clarke knew that Captain McIlhenny was dead. It would be so; in one second she would tell him. This was the way death came: in the third person, somewhere—miles away—when Clarke was occupied with other matters.

"A man from the Special Troops. An officer."

Clarke's hands trembled.

"You don't know him."

His mind fluttered: *Yes, yes, I do, I do,* he thought.

"Major Jenkins."

Clarke recovered. "Major Jenkins! I *know* him!" But men died this way. In the third person. Far away. "Killed? How? I was . . ."

"Can you make him stop drinking, please?"

"Hey, woman! What are you two saying over there?" Damianos laughed. "Making a date behind my back, eh, hussy?"

"Gus . . . please go upstairs."

"Let's get away from here, Clarke." He waved his hand in front of his face as if trying to shoo away a persistent fly. "Women talk too much. Talk, talk, talk. Bunch of candyasses." He lurched off the stool but caught hold of the bar's ridged edge. "Let's go over t'your table!" He paused, weaving. "Candy-asses over there, too, huh? Straightlegs all over the place."

Clarke was uncomfortable.

"You're a straightleg, too, ain't you? Goddamn 'em." Damianos became conspiratorial. "C'mon over here." His thick index finger wagged him closer. "I'll tell you what, Clarke. You go airborne . . . an' I'll fix you up with a fine, a *fine* woman."

Clarke was about to tell him he was married; instead, he asked: "Who?"

"Sophie, there. The blonde. *Fine* woman."

"I'm already married."

"That's bad . . . bad. What got into you?" He laughed. "If a man's got brains"—he tapped his forehead, swaying gently—"he gets into them, not vice versa. Know what I mean?"

"Yes."

"Ffft." Damianos frowned. "You know what I mean . . . but it's . . . too . . . damn . . . late." He shook his head. "Where's your wife if you're married?"

Clarke did not want to admit that his wife had left him, but since he had witnessed a few of the sergeant's problems, he felt obliged to be frank with Damianos, particularly since the man was so obviously drunk that he would not remember a thing.

"Had an argument. She walked out on me."

"You mean the little broad with the long black underwear?"

Clarke nodded.

"Typical, typical." He shook his head wisely. "Know the type well. Run off, eh? Typical." He made a massive fist. *"Discipline!"* He jabbed at his nose with a heavy, square thumb. "Break heads . . . that's the answer." He closed his eyes briefly, then glanced up with a secret smile. "Now if you wasn't married, I'd fix you up real well. Good woman, too. Not the kind that runs off." He pointed to Sophie. She was gazing at Damianos, obviously worried and tired. "The blonde," he whispered. "Good in bed, too. Bites." Damianos cleared his throat. "But you probably don't like that, eh? Too common, eh?" He laughed. "Fine woman. Not my type, though. Make a good wife. Want me to fix it up?"

"Thank you for asking," Clarke said uncomfortably. "I . . . I can't accept your offer. I'm already married. But if I weren't . . ."

"Shit!"

That, evidently, put an end to the negotiations.

"Hey, Sophie, come on the hell over here. I want to talk to you."

She ducked under the bar passage and walked to the booth, where Damianos had staggered and fallen.

"Sit down, honey. I want you to meet a good friend of mine. Clarke, this is Sophie." Damianos winked secretly.

"Yes, Gus," she pleaded. "I've met him before. Please, Gus, don't drink so much and go to bed."

"Ah . . . you're old friends, eh? Good, good." He nodded his head. "You're a fine woman, Sophie. A *fine woman.*" He paused. *"Sophie* . . . I want you and Clarke, here, to get married . . ."

"He hasn't asked me," she snapped. "But," she paused, evidently annoyed, "Sergeant Jacks did."

Damianos' head shook. "Why, that no-good, sneaky, mother-humpin' rebel. He . . . he . . . you mean he *asked you* . . . ? Without asking *me* . . . ?"

Sophie, her lips pursed, nodded her head vigorously.

"What'd you say?" Damianos' eyes narrowed.

"I said no."

"A damn good thing, too. I'd of killed the bastard."

"Come to bed, Gus. Please. You need sleep. It wasn't your fault."

"I won't go to bed, it wasn't my fault, and I don't need sleep. I want to get drunk. Do you mind?" Damianos grew sullen. "Jenkins don't need my sympathy. He knows the score." The sergeant slammed his glass on the table. *"Clarke* . . . front and center. Do you know what death is?"

"No."

It was the easier answer.

"Hung up on a tree, see. His boots're about ten feet off the ground . . . swaying like a kid on a swing . . ." Damianos' heavy voice had softened, in respect to the major's memory, and his deep-set brown eyes, ordinarily harsh and probing, stared at Clarke with a drugged intensity. "Can't get him down, though. . . . I'm all alone there. . . . Other guys're far away. . . . So I get my flashlight and point it at him. . . . He's got no face. . . . It's scraped off, see." A nervous smile appeared on Damianos' swarthy face and—possibly sensing how hideous it seemed to Clarke—he covered his mouth briefly. "Nothin' . . . nothin'. . . . I know it's him by his name tape, that's all. Ol' Jenkins . . ." He shook his head. "Ol' Jenkins . . . I *gotta* get him down." Damianos shrugged his shoulders. "So . . . I climb up the goddamn tree. I get my knife and cut the risers." With his elbows leaning on the table, the sergeant cradled his face in his calloused palms. "But the ground's hard. He hits like a bag full of stones. An' do you know what?" The eyes fixed on Clarke again. "You know what?" He paused. "I got a feeling that next is gonna be me. . . ."

It seemed to Clarke that, as if on cue, no one stirred. The silence was full, brimming. Across from him, the sergeant gazed off to the wall in a stupor.

"I sit down next to him and chant a dirge. Like in a church. Death, I think, you mother-humper. Death . . . you got another one of us. Come on out, I think; come on out an' fight like a goddamn man!" Damianos' face hardened; his hands fisted. *"Come on out, Death! Come on out an' fight!"*

Clarke, staring at the sergeant, felt the blood throbbing in his temples. He was mysteriously thrilled. Even this vulgar man, he thought, sodden with drink, had within him a vibrant spark. Clarke stared in wonder at the sergeant.

Damianos shook his head and lifted his glass again. "Why're you a straightleg, Clarke?"

The vibrant spark had evidently been extinguished. Too soon, a man's grandeur was too soon debased and forgotten. "I don't know," he said, bored now. "I don't know why I am." The bar and the sergeant were beginning to oppress him. For a moment he had been stirred; now the deadening feeling returned to him.

"You ain't scared of jumping, are you?"

"I don't think so. But . . ." Clarke was unable to fight his irritation. "But why should I jump?"

"To find out what death is, maybe. Get to know him as much as he knows you. How old're you? Twenty-four, twenty-five? You been ignoring Father Death too long."

Clarke was silent. Why should he worry about death when there were so few things he knew about life?

"Why don't you go airborne?"

"I will," Clarke replied, realizing the moment he said it that he had answered without duress, calmly. He was shocked. *Would he go?* His eyes narrowed. *He had said yes!*

"Please, Gus," Sophie begged. "Go upstairs to bed."

Unexpectedly, the sergeant gripped the tabletop and pulled himself erect. "Going upstairs . . . get a little sleep . . . wake me early . . . we got a reprise jump tomorrow. . . ." He lurched across the floor, caught the lip of the bar, steadied himself, and swayed into the kitchen.

Sophie looked at Clarke. "I'm sorry. I told you why he's like this. He was with the man who died today. In Korea.

His commanding officer. You understand; you're in the Army."

"Yes, I understand." He lied. A temporary pity would be all he would feel if McIlhenny was killed—a pity, then a transient feeling of relief, then nothing.

"Come in again sometime." Sophie retrieved the sergeant's glass. "When Gus isn't feeling so bad."

"I will. And . . . don't feel embarrassed. I understand what happened." He shrugged. "I've already forgotten what he said."

"Thank you." Sophie smiled. "I hope your wife is waiting for you at home."

"So do I." When Clarke turned to walk to the door, he realized that Winters and Battaglia had gone. They had probably left when he and Damianos sat at the booth.

CHAPTER 7

When McIlhenny had closed the door of his room at the BOQ, he sensed an oppressive finality in that simple act, as if an epoch had passed into dead history and a new age, one with frightening and unknown possibilities, had begun. Going through the routine of undressing, lifting the helmet off his head, undoing the laces of his paratroop boots, and stepping out of his sandy fatigues, the captain felt a curious sense of disengagement from himself, as if he were looking over his own shoulder at a man, himself, taking off the clothes of mock combat. Something peculiar was happening: he felt strange in his own room. Even the bookcases lining the walls seemed odd to him, odd to a man who spent virtually every evening in his room, reading.

I must get away, he thought. *This evening,* he added quickly. *I must get away this evening.* Yes. He would go out after showering. Reading might prove difficult tonight, for he knew his mind would wander back to the same scene. He would hear the jumpmaster's shout and—with five others who combed the forest surrounding the DZ—would jog fearfully toward the sergeant, burst through the underbrush, and halt abruptly, looking down to see a faceless man who stared blindly at the darkened sky. *Poor man.* He frowned. *Just got his promotion, too.* No one knew what Providence had in store for him. Jenkins became a major and, within a week, was dead; McIlhenny, still a captain, was now stepping into his shower stall and bathing under the warm, kindly water. Everything occurred for a purpose; man's duty was to learn what that purpose was.

If this had happened several years before, McIlhenny would have been thrown into a spiritual turmoil. Jenkins was a Protestant, not very religious—it went without saying—but a worthy man in his own way. The precise location of his soul in the various anterooms of the other world would have puzzled McIlhenny for days. Now, however, he was less concerned with the heavenly accommodations than he was with more earthly matters. Was Jenkins' wife notified as yet? How would the children be taught to understand the meaning of death?

Drying himself, McIlhenny was again impressed with the strangeness of the world. Life was such a paradox! Thanks be to Him Who created it that some coherence could occasionally be discovered in the midst of such confusion. *If I didn't have my faith,* he realized, *If I—for one moment—doubted . . . I might go mad.* It was a chilling thought, and he did his best to forget it. For a moment, the mere possibility of his being threatened by an intellectual chaos probed subtly into his defenses and, as quickly, retreated again.

He stepped into his pajamas, put on his robe, and sat in the overstuffed chair near the bookcase. It was better that he stay in tonight and read. Where was he? Oh, yes. Aquinas. He had determined, last month, to reread the great theologian and now—strangely—found himself reliving his youth, the time he spent in sacred study, preparing himself for his vocation. What an odd instrument the human mind was! In scanning the five proofs for the existence of God, he recalled the surroundings in which he had studied them: the house he lived in was resurrected as he read of the "argument from motion"; the "efficient cause" reminded him of an old leather jacket he wore as he walked to school, stepping on the fallen, red-orange leaves; the "argument from possibility and necessity" called back the fragrance of his mother's cooking and the warm nights he spent in the kitchen, listening to the radio after preparing his Latin homework; the "gradation to be found in things" reminded him of the makeshift desk in his room and the crucifix at eye level on the wall; and, reading and rereading the fifth proof, "the governance of the world," he recalled his Sunday-afternoon walks, alone—for he was always a lonely boy—to the double-feature movies which carried him into the Europe of empires, of cloaks, of sword-play, and of dungeons.

But it was impossible to concentrate. A strange thought worked into his mind: *All men are faceless when they die.* The captain frowned. *I must discipline myself.* Why force himself to read, though? Why not take the evening off, as he had planned? A few hours more or less would not bring him any closer to an understanding of the complexities of God and man.

He stopped reading and looked up. The room was small—small and stifling. His bed, set in the corner, waited for him, its newly starched pillow ready to cradle his shampooed head. A portrait of his late mother stood on the bureau top, and above it an auburn-haired Christ looked to the right, away from man, His side pierced. The stolid bookcase, colorful with thick volumes, appeared to hold back the wall. Plato, Aristotle, Augustine, Aquinas, Loyola, Dante, À Kempis, Papini, Chesterton—he would reread them all. But, curiously, the thought depressed him. Good books, they were; fine books—learned books. All said what he knew, however; repeated the truths he had learned years before; evaded the same questions; tolerated—as if in a conspiracy—the same euphemisms; assumed the validity of the same myths. Wedged against one another, the books seemed to form a phalanx against man's despair and his fear of meaninglessness.

I must get away. There was the sinister thought again. It was coming more often, though. The feeling of depression was accelerating. But what a curious instrument the human mind was! If there was joy in faith and certitude, might there not also be a certain pleasure in doubt? Could one not wallow in the destruction, not solely of heathen gods, but of one's own as well? *I must get away . . . from these books . . . this chair . . . this room.* He stared fiercely at the wall. *I must get away from myself . . . my life.*

When he finished the *Summa,* would he *know?* When he finished the *Dialogues,* would he *know?* When he had reread *Spiritual Exercises,* would he know more than he did now, or would all the philosophical truths merely lie sluggishly in his memory, unrelated to the danger and death around him, remaining what they were, the well-articulated fantasies of men in states of despair equal only to his own?

He looked at his clock. The second hand, swinging in its prescribed orbit, victoriously checked off the moments of his equally limited life. Then, as if hearing a command, he rose to his feet, threw off his slippers, his robe, and his pajamas. He dressed quickly—stepped into a pair of blue slacks, put on a gray button-down sport shirt, a pair of black loafers, and a tweed jacket. He fumbled with his wristwatch, scooped up the coins from the bureau top and dropped them into the right pocket of his jacket. His keys went into the left. Suspended on a nail in the wall was his rosary. He ignored it. At the door, when he had turned to survey his room for the last time, McIlhenny confronted the mirror. The light above him made his balding head glisten. His eyes, fierce now, committed, stared back at him. *I don't care,* he thought. *I don't care. . . . I'll get away. . . .* The red second hand was turning irresistibly; his life was swirling away in a steady blur. Within five seconds he had snapped off the light, shut the door, and walked down the hall of the BOQ.

The captain wandered through Von Steuben for a half hour before he found a tavern that interested him. Was it closed so early? As he was about to push at the door, he felt the knob swing inward and was struck by an attractive, dark-haired girl who was at that moment evidently angry about something. Her softness and vitality captivated him, and as they jockeyed back and forth in the vestibule, both going right at the same time, both going left, he grinned awkwardly —he had never made a habit of smiling—and grasped her by the arms. "Excuse me, there," he said in what he hoped was a properly cavalier manner, and saw her glance at him with moist eyes which appeared blue in the muted lights of the bar's exterior.

"Excuse *yourself!*" she snapped, quick-stepping to the sidewalk.

Captain McIlhenny viewed her as she ran crying down the street toward the lot where he had parked his car. Should he follow her? The possibilities that existed in the world were infinite. He decided against it, for the girl was obviously leaving someone she loved or hated too intensely to permit the advances of a third party. Might he not catch her on ricochet, though? He rushed to the parking lot and, breathing heavily, caught a glimpse of the girl's swaying skirt as she turned a corner. He reconsidered his badly conceived plan and returned to the Green Light.

It was now out of the question that he enter the bar, for he saw Winters and Battaglia sitting in a booth and, to the rear, Damianos and another man in conversation. Hands in pockets, the captain strolled toward the parking lot, debating whether or not he should drive to the Officers' Club. That would be not only frustrating but also stultifying, he realized, for there he would see the same people, feel his perpetual alienation from them, and involve himself in the inevitable conversation. Postmortems did not appeal to him.

A poster for an agricultural fair being held on the outskirts of Von Steuben was tacked to a telephone pole. Glancing at his wristwatch, McIlhenny realized that the fair would close in an hour.

It took him ten minutes to drive to the tented area, and, locking the car door, he felt his heart leap as it did when he was a child and went with his parents to a carnival. *City of Man,* he thought; *City of God.* The captain followed a dirt road leading to a large tent in which, through an open flap, he saw the handicrafts and farm produce of the region.

Because it was late, there were few people near the stands. Raising the collar of his jacket, for the night was chilly, he strolled into the great tent and gazed at the visitors and hawkers. The latter were slowly taking down their wares. A Ferris wheel, the only mechanical amusement, stood now, its lighted rim encircling the darkened sky, immobile until the following day. To his right, great ears of Indian corn lay in bins next to pumpkins, cotton, squash, and large tobacco leaves.

As he neared the section where wooden handicrafts and old-fashioned samplers competed for a visitor's attention with the more recent ceramic and earthenware exhibits, McIlhenny noticed a small, slender girl at a railing, viewing a heavy, grotesque vase of the type he had often seen in lobbies of neighborhood theaters. At that moment the girl, obviously Puerto Rican, turned to him and smiled, exhibiting brownish, widely spaced teeth.

He swerved abruptly, unthinkingly, with heart racing, walked out of the large tent, and entered a smaller enclosure, where a bingo game was in progress. Only three figures moved, yet the tent was crowded with unshaven men, all silent and intense, who leaned against the tables and followed the letter-number count. He stared at the three change girls with a feeling of revulsion. They resembled clowns, with their silvery-white hair; their thin lips, pale by design; and their faces, which, under the naked, overhead bulbs, appeared harsh and overpainted.

Oh, God, he thought, *is this what I wanted to find?* But, after all, this was a carnival; the masks that people wore in life were merely exaggerated under tents, and the goals for which they strived were here explicit and unashamedly tawdry. Dressed in black leather jackets, the girls prowled through the aisles, their reddened hands jingling coins in their change aprons. He glanced at the prizes: stuffed dolls; flashlights; blankets; brush, mirror, and comb sets; silverware; beribboned pillows.

Bingo! The game was over. Someone had won. Most had lost: this was the theory of games. After the girls scooped the dimes and quarters into their aprons, the next game began.

The scene was disquieting to the captain, and after returning to the larger tent, he began an active search for the dark girl who had smiled at him, sighting her finally at a refreshment stand. He ordered a cone of popcorn and a bottle of root beer, turning to her gradually. *No,* he thought, and stopped. *This is not what I want.* But he could not leave; he had spent money; he must consume what he had purchased.

"You like this place?"

McIlhenny did not turn. "Yes." He became conscious of his pulse. For a moment his left hand appeared to be trembling, but, glancing at it quickly, he saw the girl helping herself to his popcorn.

"You afraid to look at me?"

Obediently, McIlhenny turned.

She was smiling. The captain realized how silly he must have appeared: the girl was at least twelve years his junior. Her skirt, a cocoa brown, barely covered her knees, and a tan sweater, fitting tightly across the breasts, rewarded her with more girth than she deserved. Looking in the girl's brown eyes, he felt again the sense that he was outside himself, viewing the entire tableau at a remove, a mere actor in the scene. *Is this "away"?* he wondered.

"Do you live here in Von Steuben?" a voice inquired. Was it his voice?

"Yes. On highway. In cabin." She took a napkin from the dispenser and wiped the butter from her fingertips. "You?"

"I live on Post."

"A soldier boy?"

"Yes," the hollow voice replied, "a soldier boy."

"You have car?"

He nodded. "I could . . . drive you to your cabin . . . if you don't have a ride . . ."

She smiled again. "I'm hungry, first."

I'm hungry, first, McIlhenny considered idly. *I'm hungry, first!* What a curious syllogism erotic love was: an illogical premise led inevitably to the sole conclusion.

"I have my car," he repeated. "We'll drive to a restaurant."

Walking toward the parking lot, the captain could see her next to him, and as he thought of her brown skin and her slightly protuberant abdomen, he quickened his pace. But people had names to go with their faces and bodies. He turned to her, shocked to see that her impudent and confident eyes were regarding him coquettishly. "What is your name?"

"Esperanza. Esperanza Feliciano."

"That's a lovely name." The stupid words had left his lips. *Is this me?* he wondered. *Am I mouthing these inanities?* As he walked on the dirt road, the fair at his back, its lights gradually darkening for the night, McIlhenny felt her hand slip around his arm and her body lean against his. "My name is Kinnard." She had not asked.

Fumbling for his key, he wondered if she expected to be kissed. What was he to do? Open the door and then kiss her, or kiss her and then open the door? *What an idiot! I'm botching this!* He straightened up quickly and put his arms around Esperanza's waist, pulling her toward him abruptly and pressing his lips to her averted face. Chastened—he had kissed her ear—the captain opened the door.

"Ah . . . you have radio!" Esperanza seemed pleased. "Kin I play?"

McIlhenny nodded, for in speaking he might communicate to her only the humiliation he felt.

A hesitant, sensuous alto promised the listening audience that her love would last "till the end of time," and before McIlhenny could become aware of his ironic predicament, he realized that Esperanza had brought herself nearer and sat next to him, her legs spread and her hands cupped in the folds of her skirt. *"You are my destiny . . . my life . . . my love . . ."*

The promise was everlasting, but the song was brief; it was time for a commercial.

"Is a beautiful song." She turned to him. "I have beautiful records, too. At my home. Spahnish records."

The captain hesitated. "I'd like to hear them sometime."

"Tonight," she said. "Tonight, no?"

"Yes." McIlhenny, stopping himself as he was about to thank her, turned into a drive-in restaurant and parked in a service stall. An old woman dressed in red slacks and a white jacket waited for him to lower his window.

"Do you want a hamburger?" Esperanza was close to him now.

"Yes . . . and coffee."

"The same for me," he told the waitress. When she left, McIlhenny felt Esperanza lean against him and place her hand on his knee.

"Do you love me, Kinny?"

"Yes." It was an awkward moment for him. "I love you."

"Do you love me much?"

McIlhenny hesitated. "Yes . . . I love you very much."

"I'm glad. After we eat," she whispered, "we go to my home."

He doubted that this was what he wanted to get *away* to but perhaps it was not a change of scene he needed, merely a woman. He turned to her, feeling a helpless anger, hurt that this vulgar woman was capable of making him nervous and expectant. *Is this what people consider love?* The irony was overpowering. This was not a defeat of principle, he defended himself; it was merely a short-term compromise with a force he had stifled all his life. Nevertheless, his pulse quickened when she pulled off her shoes.

«««««»»»»

The cabin was permeated with an exotic combination of heavy perfume and stale cooking odors. When Esperanza turned on the small lamp next to her unmade bed and walked to the record player, McIlhenny glanced about timidly, amazed that a woman's room could be so slovenly by accident. A week's dishes were stacked on the table, full of gravy and tomato sauce and spotted with a mosaic of cigarette butts snuffed out at random. While closing the door, he heard muffled laughter from the darkened cabin next to Esperanza's.

A metallic blast of trumpets and trombones startled him. Wild, throbbing drums, with the tenor thud of bongos rapping through the heavier beat, rumbled an Afro-Cuban rhythm, paused briefly, then rumbled again; cowbells clanged, stopped, then clanged once more. The brasses screamed as Esperanza, in her bare feet, stepped back several paces and swayed her lithe body sensuously. Her mass of black hair followed the abrupt movements of her head by a beat. Mouth slightly open, she leaned back briefly; her half-closed eyelids shot open in mock surprise when the trumpets blared and closed again slowly when the horns were silenced by the throbbing drums.

She raised her arms and beckoned him.

"I . . . I can't dance. Not that!"

Evidently she had not heard, for her hands waved him closer. McIlhenny did not know the difference between a fox-trot and a tango, and, approaching Esperanza, who was now trembling in what appeared to be ecstasy, he placed his right arm around her waist and glanced to the floor, expecting to be taught the dance step.

Esperanza had stopped moving. McIlhenny, perplexed, looked up briefly to see that she smiled at him with her teasing, petulant lips. Small hands caressed the back of his neck. Her abdomen touched his. As he bent to kiss her, his eager hands exploring the soft, yielding flesh under her sweater, a final, defiant trumpet blast sounded, the quieting drum throbs merged into the quickening beat of his pulse, and the final *clang, clang, clang* of the cowbell predicted the inevitable silence.

CHAPTER 8

Barrett Clarke had been sitting in the orderly room for twenty minutes. Ordinarily, this would not be surprising to him, for company commanders evidently believe that the longer an enlisted man waited to be called into an office, the more respect he gained for his superior. What was remarkable, however, was that Captain McIlhenny had not arrived at the orderly room on the very morning he had commanded Clarke, by way of the bulletin board, to be standing tall before him promptly at eight o'clock. Could the captain possibly be late for anything? According to the clerk, the top sergeant had taken over in McIlhenny's absence and was now performing the daily barracks check. When the captain finally opened the orderly-room door, he was forty-five minutes late.

Sergeant Dobbin, returning from the barracks inspection, took the morning's mail and several pages of distribution into the captain's office. When he came out, the first sergeant nodded, signifying that the commander was ready to receive Clarke.

"Sir, PFC Clarke reporting to the captain as ordered, sir." He repeated the formula and saluted. McIlhenny leaned back in his swivel chair and laced his hands in front of his abdomen. *Another long wait,* Clarke thought. *He'll let me sweat it out for a few minutes.* But the *Manual of Courts-Martial* was not on the desk.

"At ease, Clarke." The captain's voice was soft. "Pull up a chair."

This was unexpected. Clarke sat down carefully and rested his fatigue cap on his knees. Since the punishment for his Article 15 had terminated a week before, his order to appear before the captain could have nothing to do with not buffing the Headquarters' floor or not performing his KP details properly. Had he done something wrong this week?

"As you know, a large-scale maneuver will begin in a little more than two months. Possibly you've seen evidences of Operation Razor Blade in the various bulletins on Post. Now"—he paused, tapping at an unopened official envelope with his plastic opener—"the Special Troops will be an important element in the war play, and, as such, our progaganda unit must supply five men to be attached to the Guerrilla Headquarters when the Troops go to the field. Of course, you will be one of them. I *have* called you in for something else, though."

"Yes, sir." This was unfortunate. Being assigned to Maneuver Headquarters meant a stay of at least three weeks in western North Carolina. But the "something else" that McIlhenny threatened was even more disheartening.

"I find your attitude, aside from the obvious lack of discipline you showed on CQ several weeks ago, rather favorable. Clarke . . . to be frank . . . I feel you have the makings of a good soldier. I know that to be a good soldier is something that might not appeal to you, taking into consideration your rather obvious civilian orientation"—a thin, frosty smile appeared on the captain's face—"but I also think that you are prepared to take advantage of your two years in the Army. There are some experiences, after all, that can't be duplicated anywhere else, and certain men are more liable to take advantage of all life offers them."

"Yes, sir." Clarke wondered what the captain meant. And, now that he recognized an obvious relaxation of the coldness that had seemed to him to be an integral part of the captain's character, he realized that McIlhenny was leaning back, actually *leaning back,* in his swivel chair.

"Many of us go through life blind to the countless adventures it offers us, only to realize, probably when it is too late, that we could have learned much more and involved ourselves more fully in a life that is now closed to us. Sometimes, though, we learn before it is too late."

"Yes, sir." McIlhenny seemed to be enjoying the conversation. Clarke felt ill at ease, sitting as he was, but debated whether he should cross his legs. It might be unmilitary, but he was uncertain, for he had not read his field manuals as carefully as he should have. Impulsively, he crossed his legs.

McIlhenny took no notice. "To get to the point. I'll need a man in the field a few days before the others get there to prepare the propaganda effort with me. The detail sounds more forbidding than it actually is. All that's involved is a few hours' work per day. The others will be required to load and unload the Deuce-and-a-Halves and prepare the presses. I want you to come along."

"Yes, sir." It was obvious to Clarke that he was not being asked to volunteer. "Yes, sir. I'll be glad to." The captain continued to lean back in his chair; evidently the interview was not over. "Sir?"

"Yes?"

Possibly this would be the ideal moment for him to speak. Ordinarily, the company commander is the last person an enlisted man wants to talk to about his personal affairs, but this short conversation with McIlhenny had changed their relationship, Clarke thought, and now he felt less inhibited. "Sir . . . if you've finished with me . . . I wonder if I may speak to you about a personal matter?"

"Certainly." McIlhenny nodded quickly. "One moment, though." He took the envelope quickly and slit it open. After scanning its contents, he crumpled it and the letter and threw them into the wastebasket. "Go right ahead."

"Sir . . . I find myself in a bind. As I said . . . it's personal." He uncrossed his legs. "I don't pretend that my case is unique in the Army, and I don't want any special treatment. My wife has been having . . . well . . . spells of anxiety. I'm to blame for this, I guess. She becomes disturbed over the slightest matters—things she used to ignore or shrug her shoulders at. It may be because she is a highly strung woman. I don't know. But I've noticed this condition becoming more pronounced until it's almost a nightly thing."

The captain motioned for Clarke to close the door.

"I don't think," he said when he returned to his seat, "that a few weeks in the field will aggravate the situation, so I don't want to appear as if I'm asking for any favors. My being away might help, even." McIlhenny remained impassive. Clarke paused, looking down at his boots. "I don't want to go into it more thoroughly, sir, but I think she's rapidly approaching a crisis of some sort—maybe even a breakdown." His hands were damp.

McIlhenny straightened up and faced Clarke. "Your wife evidently needs a rest—a rest which, I imagine, is difficult to get here in Von Steuben. Tensions just build up in people. Possibly she needs"—he hesitated—"possibly she needs to get away briefly. Why not have her visit her family for a period of time? Being home with her parents might do her a lot of good while you're out in the field. It would be better than being alone in Von Steuben. You *are* childless, aren't you?"

"Yes, sir."

"Why not send her home for a few weeks, then?"

"Her father is dead, sir. Her mother and he were divorced, and she remarried a few years before I met my wife."

McIlhenny thought for a moment. "Obviously, that's no solution at all." He leaned back again. "Still . . . she needs a change of scene, a different environment. What about your family? Can she visit them while you're in the field?"

Clarke hesitated, then decided to reveal more of his life. "My family rejected me when I married her."

"Oh . . . I'm sorry." McIlhenny shifted his gaze momentarily. "You *are* in a bind. You're in more of a predicament than I thought at first." He played with the letter opener. "I'm sorry. I've run out of advice. Do you have any leave time accrued?"

"Yes, sir. About two weeks."

"The maneuver doesn't start for another two months. I can easily spare you for a couple of weeks. There's a great deal of preparation, but I can have Winters and the new man work a little harder. What about a leave?"

"Thank you, sir. I'm sure you're doing more than you need to." He studied his boots. "The fact is, sir . . . I'm broke." Clarke did not look at the captain. "I've found it impossible to save here." He prepared himself to lie. "What little money I had saved up from civilian life has gone to"—he did not say "placate my wife"—"to buy furniture and repair my car. As I said before, the relations between my family and me are strained—severed, actually—and I won't ask them. I don't want to borrow money, either."

"You don't leave yourself much hope, then, do you?"

"There is none, sir."

"Don't say that. Never say that, Clarke. Remember, despair is a great sin. It implies that one has given up searching for a solution, a meaning." The captain's voice, though admonitory, was mild. "How much time do you have left in the Army?"

"About fourteen months, sir."

"There's a way you can earn a little extra money while in the Army. I don't suppose you've given this the slightest thought, but don't reject it without some consideration. Mind you, don't construe this as pressure from me at all. I realize that certain events occur in a man's life that almost forbid his asking relatives and friends for aid, even though at times they may be prepared to offer it. But there's a way you can help yourself out of your problems. Have you ever thought about going to Jump School and becoming a paratrooper?" He paused briefly. "Now I'm not the type to give you a pep talk about how much of a man it will make you. I think most of those arguments are weak. What I *am* saying is that you, as an enlisted man, will find your salary increased by fifty-five dollars per month. You'll work hard for it, of course. You'll be trained. And, I admit, it does sound like the last sort of advice to a man in despair." He hesitated at the word. "But the money will be enough to help you out of your difficulty."

"To be honest with you, sir, I've been thinking about going to Jump School. It seems ludicrous to admit this, but I didn't see it as a solution for my worries about money. Parachuting has been mentioned to me several times . . . and I was intrigued. I'll give it some thought, sir."

"If you decide . . . let me know. I could have Sergeant Dobbin type up the orders and make the necessary arrangements. The money will come in handy. And, I might add, this time and spring are about the ideal training periods. Not too hot, you know, or too cold."

"Sir." Clarke stood up and came to attention. "I want to thank you very much for all you've done for me. You've been a great help." He saluted.

McIlhenny returned the salute. "If you decide to go, you'll just manage to enroll in the final training cycle and have a week to yourself before the maneuver preparations begin."

"Yes, sir. Thank you, sir." Clarke about-faced to the door.

Walking toward the firebreak on his return to the propaganda building, Clarke thought about his interview with McIlhenny. What an unbelievable change had occurred in the man! *He's become human!* What could have happened to alter his strictness, his harsh self-discipline, so completely in the past few weeks? For some reason, McIlhenny was a finer, gentler man than Clarke remembered his being.

It was curious, moreover, how everything that perplexed Clarke had achieved a relevance in the conversation with McIlhenny. His own fascination with parachuting, Sergeant Damianos' badgering the two times he had seen him, and—Clarke could not forget—his strange, terrifying dream of falling through space, had all held a solution to his problems which he did not recognize until it was discovered for him. Of course, there *was* an alternative to poverty and what he had feared: the eventual breakup of his marriage. It was not hopeless. Clarke wondered why McIlhenny was obviously chary of the word. Then he realized: *Maybe that was my initial fault. In thinking my situation was hopeless . . . I had neglected to look for a solution.*

Walking past the mess hall, Clarke heard argumentaitve voices in the dining room. It was time for coffee call. Sergeant Lucas was busily checking the ovens, making certain they were clean, when Clarke entered.

"Hey, Clarke. Ah miss you back here!"

Clarke laughed. "I'm about to goof up again, Sarge. I'll be back soon."

In the dining room he saw Winters, Battaglia, and the new arrival, Private Martin, discussing something heatedly. As he approached their table the conversation quieted somewhat until Winters turned to him.

"Sit down, laddie, and tell us all about it. When you're through, we'll sympathize and give you the *really good* news."

"It wasn't too bad. I mean, we're all going on the maneuver. He just wants me to go out a few days before you guys to help set up the propaganda unit, that's all."

"You're taking it like a man, there, Blue Eyes." Battaglia pushed his glasses against his forehead. "Now get yourself a cup of coffee and relax."

"I'm fine as I am. What's the big news?"

"How about a cigarette, then?"

"Lay off, Battaglia." Winters smiled. "You got a new pack on you. I saw you opening it this morning after reveille."

"Screw you, Judas. A guy can't make a living anymore." Battaglia probed into his pocket for a cigarette. "Now all this info can't be bandied around, man. We gotta be, like they say, discreet. If they find out all the EM know about this before certain parties do, my bushy tail has had it. Right?"

"OK, OK," Winters agreed. "It won't get any further than Barrett here. We promise."

Clarke waited for the discussion to quiet before making a comment. "Well, if this is secret information, you can be sure I'll keep it to myself."

"No, no, it's nothing classified, smart money. It's just that . . . well . . . Sergeant Hopper, my beloved personnel sergeant, the pride of the baboons, is beginning to suspect me. So far, I've been in personnel for fifteen months and everything that's supposed to be quiet has been known in every mess hall on Post in four hours. He's beginning to suspect me, like I said. After fifteen months, this is a record for Hopper; but, man, don't forget, he can arrange for things to be very tough for this wop. Meaning myself."

"Well, if you don't want to tell me, don't tell me. If you think you can trust me, go right ahead. You're perfectly safe as far as I'm concerned. I won't say a thing."

But Battaglia could not withhold the information any longer. "Well, it's like this, see." Leaning over, his elbows resting on the table, Battaglia glanced about conspiratorially. "McIlhenny's been passed over for promotion twice already, see."

Clarke had been aware of this. "So what? I don't understand?"

"Marron!" Battaglia struck his forehead, dislodged his glasses, and then pushed them back in place with his index finger. "Look, every officer has a category, right? Now, there's a list of the officers in the U. S. Army and their ranks. Only the West Pointers are sacred. The other duds—guys who went to OCS, et cetera, et cetera—gotta wait for their promotions. Like if they're lieutenants, they sweat out the lists for their captaincy; if they're captains, they wait around for majority; if they're majors . . ."

"OK, Battaglia. I'm with you. I understand."

"Well, if a guy has been passed over by the Pentagon once, he's sweating out the next list. Right? If he isn't promoted the second time, he's got one chance to go. After that, he's had the meat."

"Would you get to the point? All of us know this."

"The point is *this!"* Battaglia banged on the table. *"Captain McIlhenny is being reduced."*

"Shhhhh." Winters looked around. Fortunately, Sergeant Lucas had stepped out of the kitchen.

"When?"

"He'll know soon. He keeps talking about enemies or something, so I figure even the officers hate him. This was his last chance and they passed him over. Now he'll come under the Reduction in Force the Army's putting through and be *riffed* down to his highest enlisted grade."

"I don't believe it." Clarke managed to disguise his feeling of shock.

"Don't believe what?"

"He won't stay in. McIlhenny's too proud to stay in the service after being kicked from captain to EM. I've got just as many gripes against him as any of you, but I've got to say he's a proud man. He'll resign before he's kicked out."

"OK, Blue Eyes. How much will you put up says he's gonna stay in this dud's Army four more years?"

"I say he'll resign his commission."

Winters turned to Clarke. "How many years do you think he's put in? How many before he retires?"

"I don't know." Clarke shrugged. "How many?"

"Captain McIlhenny"—Battaglia lowered his voice—"has sixteen years in the service. He's got four more before he gets his pension. You think he's gonna give that up? He'll swallow his pride and take the reduction and like it."

Clarke held his breath. "What was his highest enlisted grade?"

Battaglia smiled. "I knew you was going to ask that any minute." The personnel clerk took a sip of coffee and a slow, teasing drag on his cigarette. Evidently the others had not heard all the information, for they appeared as eager as Clarke. Finally, as a stream of smoke cascaded from his nostrils, Battaglia spoke: "Corporal." He smiled. "And that's not all. He'll be a lot more uncomfortable before everything's over. He's not married and probably will sleep in the barracks with the other EM."

Clarke was silent. A montage of images rushed through his mind, all involving the captain: McIlhenny walking, swagger stick slapping at his thigh; standing in front of the men in ranks for inspection, balancing on his toes, the green beret pulled down to an inch above his eyes; sitting at a desk in the dayroom, counting out the money for the troops during pay call; saluting the flag at retreat, his slender, tight body proud and straight, as if America were only his country, no one else's.

Clarke controlled his temper when he heard Winters saying that "it couldn't happen to a nicer guy." He felt oppressed.

He was pitying a man he thought he would never pity, a man who was too proud to need anyone's sympathy. But here he was, Barrett Clarke, PFC, with troubles of his own, retreating from a conversation he would have enjoyed an hour before. He felt no malice toward the captain now. McIlhenny, he had just learned, was a fellow human being. His pity grew stronger. The man had given sixteen years of his active life to an organization, had fought in two wars, had been given a battlefield commission, had tried to improve the service by putting the fear of the system into citizen-soldiers, had maintained military discipline seriously and conscientiously (had enjoyed punishing a little too much, perhaps, but had done it, nevertheless, to the best of his ability), and now, after serving for sixteen unblemished years, was to be released four years prior to receiving his pension, whether by design of a few men or by the unfeeling dictates of an automaton system.

What else could McIlhenny do? He would remain a soldier; he had no choice. What trade could he have learned in the Army? How could a man who had spent his entire adult life defending his country find a suitable job as a civilian? Clarke was now certain that McIlhenny would accept his EM status. And, depending on the type of unit to which he was assigned, he would perform details with the other soldiers, live in barracks with men who would have saluted him previously, find his name on Charge of Quarters rosters, buff the floors every morning, be on guard mount and on KP when his turn came, and go on police calls, picking up discarded cigarette packs, candy-bar wrappers, and old, wet scraps of paper.

Clarke wanted to leave, to get away from his friends as quickly as possible, so that he might think about the fall of McIlhenny in solitude.

"When is he going to know for sure?"

Clarke glanced up at Winters' question.

"Couple of days. Maybe a week. Who knows?"

"Just think . . ." Private Martin, fresh from basic training, made his first contribution. "In about a month he'll have four years to go. He'll have as much time as two draftees."

Battaglia lost control of himself and laughed uproariously. Winters clutched at his sides. The laughter was general, but too exaggerated to be good-natured, and Clarke felt himself withdrawing from them, as if they had become involved in scandalous behavior. He excused himself and left the table, opening the door quickly to the clean air outside.

CHAPTER 9

"What's the matter, Gus? You seem depressed." Sophie turned to him from her chore of putting away the dishes she had just washed. "You haven't said anything since we sat down to eat. Is it . . . is it about the reconnaissance mission you were ordered on?"

"Naw. I don't feel like talking, that's all." He spiked his elbows on the table and stared at the curtained window, from which the sun streamed in and shone on the lineoleum floor.

Sophie closed the cupboard door, took a dishrag from the sink, and wiped off the tabletop. "Did something happen during inspection today?"

"Everything went all right."

"But you didn't go sky diving again, right?" She hesitated. "You know . . . Sergeant Jacks called last night and wanted to talk to you."

Damianos angered briefly. "I told him I wasn't gonna sky dive anymore. What the hell does he want from me?"

She sat across from him and opened a book of crossword puzzles, flicking the pages aimlessly and glancing down the word columns to determine whether the puzzles interested her or not. "What are you going to do with yourself on Saturdays?"

"I can do a lot of things on Saturday. I don't have to be up in some goddamn airplane grinning like a baboon for every candy-assed son of a bitch that has a camera."

Sophie chose a puzzle and began filling in the squares, seeming to ignore Damianos' conversation, but possibly pleased that he had decided to speak.

"Do you know what that wise-guy photographer *said* to me?" Sophie did not look up. " 'How 'bout a smile,' he said. 'How 'bout a smile.' The nerve of that bastard. You wanna know what I said to him?" The room was silent for a moment. "I told him to get off my back," he said finally. "That's what I told him. Treating me like I'm some trained bear. Let them go to hell. I don't need them and their sky diving. Not when I gotta grin like a baboon to get up in an airplane."

Damianos did not look at Sophie, but he knew she was

listening to every word he said, even though the pencil she held in her right hand never stopped filling in the empty squares.

"It's getting so you can't do anything without them rushing after you and asking questions. Mark my words, Sophie." His voice grew stern. "The next time I see that camera-degenerate, I'm gonna smash him right in the chops. For nothing. What d'you think of that, huh?" He waited for her reaction, but she kept looking down at the puzzle book. "He won't know who I am, see, and he'll be confused as hell. And I'll stand right over him and say, 'That's for nothing, Flash. Wait'll you do something.' "

"I'm going to have a cup of coffee, Gus. Will you join me?"

"Naw." He waved his hand angrily. "I don't want coffee. I got work to do."

"The cellar?"

"Yeah, I'll go down and clean it up. I got too many things lying around there. Stuff I should of throwed away years ago."

"Have some coffee before you go down."

When he did not refuse again, Sophie started the coffee and placed clean cups and saucers on the table.

Damianos' brief anger had subsided. He watched her move about the kitchen in her graceful way and thought she looked pretty this afternoon; it may have been the new apron, a blue one with fluffy white lace at the borders. But the feeling of being domesticated did not comfort the sergeant today, and the reasons were evident to him. In less than half an hour, he would walk down two flights of stairs to the cellar, where he would begin the long, dirty process of sorting out the accumulated possessions of a lifetime. This would require many decisions, for—no matter what he said—he was still not convinced that he wanted to throw his boxes away.

Rather than anticipate his dilemma on confronting an old object, he glanced at the calendar on the wall. Less than two months remained before the Division and the Troops would go on maneuver. Within three days, Damianos and his team would perform a short reconnaissance mission in western North Carolina. There would be plenty of time out there to lose the anger and hostility that had been building up in the past weeks. He was, in fact, looking forward to the mission and, after that, the maneuver, for they would provide him with opportunities to get away from whatever discontented him.

Sophie poured steaming coffee into their cups.

"Is this the same brand we use downstairs?"

She nodded.

He leaned over to take a sip, slurping the coffee noisily and burning himself. "Pretty good." He crossed his legs and jiggled a cigarette out of his pack. "Where'd you put the matches? I can't find my lighter."

After setting the pot on the kitchen range, Sophie brought him a book of matches from the shelf above the stove.

"Some guy is gonna stop around later tonight. I'm thinking of buying some more insurance."

She did not look up. "What for? You have enough."

"I figured I'll buy another $10,000 worth." He sipped some more coffee, intently watching the reaction on her face. "Can't do any harm . . . what the hell? I'm putting you down as my beneficiary."

"Thanks, Gus." She did not react. "You don't have to, you know."

"I know. I know I don't *have* to, but I want to."

"Keep this up, Gus, and you'll be worth more to me dead than you are alive."

"Yeah. That's no joke." He grinned. "This way, though, I can guarantee some woman coming to my grave now and then with a bunch of flowers."

"Don't talk like that, Gus." She stared at him. "I prefer what little I have of you alive than nothing dead." She paused, then—embarrassed—and added quickly, "I'm sorry. I wasn't complaining. You don't owe me anything is all I wanted to say."

"That's right." He spoke slowly. This sort of talk was dangerous, probing as it did for some commitment. "I don't owe you anything. I just want to make you my beneficiary, that's all. No more, no less." He paused. "And neither of us is holding any strings, right?"

Damianos knew he had hurt her, but knew as well that he had wanted to, without cause, merely on principle, to emphasize his lack of commitment.

He was about to continue, but Sophie interrupted him. "I never asked for any strings, Gus. Remember that. I never . . ." She stopped. While staring at the crossword book for several moments, she held the pencil with both hands, but she failed to stop its trembling. She looked up at him. "You might want to go down to the cellar now. I'd rather not have the insurance man see the mess it's in."

"Yeah. That's a good idea." He stood up and drank the remaining coffee in one gulp. "Well, I guess I'll be going downstairs." She did not respond. He paused over her briefly, wanting to say something pleasant, cheerful, but could think of nothing. "I'll see you later, Sophie."

"I'll be in the tavern when you come up."

As Damianos walked down to the cellar, he raged at himself for hurting Sophie. What had gotten into him? *I just wanted to tell her something nice.* He was making her his beneficiary, he should have said, because he had no close relatives and wanted her to have the money. Instead, he had defended himself fiercely from her disinterested love.

I'm just an idiot, he thought as he opened the cellar door and switched on the light. The basement was uglier and damper than he had remembered its being. A twenty-five-watt bulb shed its inadequate light on his heaped possessions. Wet, grayish walls, the acrid odor of wet canvas, and an unreal, isolated quiet served to divorce the gloomy cellar from what the sergeant would normally associate with the neatness and color of anything that belonged to Sophie. But this was *his* storehouse. In this damp, darkened cellar Damianos had stuffed all the salvage of his past.

After shedding his sweater, he rolled up his shirt sleeves. It was chilly here, but no matter. He would soon be warm. He had been aimless too long, carrying his entire past with him in cardboard boxes, crates, trunks, and suitcases, which followed him from post to Army post and grew in number as his life developed and its course was altered. Postponing the decision of what was burdensome and what vital was a sentimentality he could not afford.

Damianos began at the beginning. But how could he jettison his youth? Three heavy trunks contained his childhood and the memory of his parents. The day he had placed them in storage was stenciled on the tops: December 6, 1941.

Opening a trunk, he picked up an ax handle and felt its balanced weight, knowing that with this piece of wood, when he was a young man in western Pennsylvania, during a steel-mill strike in the thirties, he had involved himself in a process that had become a part of his life. He glanced at the heavy stock and spun it, watching it wobble in the air. But this was the first time he studied the handle unemotionally, as if, in trying to be objective, he would understand the secret it contained. With this beautifully curved and polished piece of wood he had killed his first human being. By crushing his skull. After all—he thought ironically, his eyelids narrowing as he defended the coldness that came over him when he gazed at the instrument of a man's death—after all, the small man, with an impudent, Slavic nose, was only the first man who died at Damianos' hand. And he was a traitor to his class, a scab.

But that was long ago, when if he had killed anyone, it was because he hated him, although he had never seen him before. The scabs, the Pinkertons, and the National Guard had killed Old Man Damianos on a previous strike, and the sergeant was only avenging his father's death. He had his ideals then, too, kept pure and inviolate in the proletarian songs the strikers sang as they patrolled the besieged steel mill, keeping watch on the banks of the Monongahela River and the cyclone fences barring Donner Avenue from the area of the open hearths.

All his life, Damianos now realized, he had groped for answers to the questions that perplexed him, and though everyone he asked pretended a lack of interest in the answers, he realized eventually that it was because they had grown tired. Why did the strikers begin to desert the besieged factory? Why all the violence in his life when, in Pittsburgh, thirty miles north of the mill around whose gates he had paced, discussions in an almost civilized manner had been occurring that would determine whether he could leave the mill in peace or be forced to withstand another attack? Why did the destiny of some men allow mediation as a solution to problems, while his demanded the guilt of bloodshed? What were violence, wars, and strikes for, if not to test men, ignorant men like himself, and to separate the heroes from the cowards, the deserters—from all the men who could be bought, not only by money, but by comfort and good food and warmth and love and lies?

Desertion had never come to him at that time as a solution to the danger of the siege. Had he left his friends—as other strikers had done—and gone home, he would have felt imprisoned by his guilt. Outside, in "freedom," he would have been the prisoner of his conscience, castigating himself with the realization of his own inadequacy as a man. Besieged, he was free of his own imprisonment: his position was fixed, his duty unrelenting. As long as he remained a willing prisoner within the besieged steel mill, he had realized, as long as he looked about him to the steel tusks of the cyclone fence, as long as he could not walk in the streets and sleep in a bed and drink what he craved and eat more than a dry hunk of bread, only so long was he free.

And the reward for his perseverance had come to liberate him. First the automobile industry in Detroit accepted the demands of the workers, and then, one by one, the steel mills in western Pennsylvania capitulated. But, as young Damianos walked out of the mill—the wintry sun warming his face and the cheering women and children lining the soot-covered, cobblestone streets—he felt dissatisfied. He was missing something. It seemed he had left some vague, shadowy happiness back in the mill with his imprisonment.

"Gus! . . . Gus!" A woman's voice called him from the cellar door.

He stopped himself before answering in Greek. For a moment, now that he was thinking of his steel-town youth, the woman's voice reminded him of his mother's. There were some memories, evidently, that a man could not efface.

"What is it?"

"We've run out of change. Do you have any?"

The cellar was quiet until he remembered where he was and what he had been asked. "What do you need, Sophie?"

"Quarters and dimes."

"In my coat pocket. I'll go across the street later and get some more."

"Which coat?"

"The overcoat. The green one. In the closet upstairs."

The cellar grew quiet again. He sat down on a trunk. *I gotta throw this stuff away. It's cluttering up my life.*

He threw the ax handle, his work boots, the clothes he had folded carefully, union buttons, and envelopes full of keys to long-forgotten locks back into the crate and pushed it into a corner.

In the next trunk he saw the icon of Saints Constantine and Helen. This he must keep. His mother had prayed before it at dawn and at dusk, and even now, years later, the icon carried the fragrance of incense in its wood.

Since the only photograph he had of her was the old, brown-tinted picture of his parents' village wedding, he did not remember what she looked like during the years he matured. In fact, now, as he studied the icon, he realized that Saint Helen and his mother had fused themselves in his memory and that he had visualized his mother all these years wearing a black gown, staring straight ahead of herself, and holding a piece of the True Cross in her hand.

Coming as she did from a different culture, the woman

never understood the confusions, the hostilities, the almost traditional rebelliousness that grew in her son when his father was killed. And—Damianos winced at the memory—he had ignored her, hardly saying a word to her during the breakfasts she prepared for him, giving her his paycheck as if what she needed for their upkeep was an unjust levy, coming in any hour of the night without telling her where he had been and what he had done. He had made her life a torment.

I'm gonna pay for this, he realized. And nothing could be undone.

His mother had died one spring, a few weeks before Easter. A foreman, he remembered, had tapped him on the shoulder as he sandbagged the levees on the flooded Monongahela after a regular shift at the open hearths. The doctor, when the boy ran home, told him to get the priest, for his mother had hemorrhaged internally and wanted extreme unction.

The sprint to church brought the enormity of what was happening to Damianos, and while he waited for the priest to get ready, three drunken men told him that the river was threatening the open hearths. When he refused to follow, they seized him. As he fought, pounding their faces with heavy fists, his pent-up guilt and frustration at last finding targets he could hurt, cripple, Damianos' eyes filled with tears. "Leave me alone," he moaned. "I'm free. I can do anything I want." And when the drunks left and the old priest emerged, Damianos (a free man) reeled from his bruises and staggered behind the bearded priest's black, windswept cassock.

Seated on a trunk in the cold cellar, Damianos clenched his fists and forced himself to remember all.

The lamp of the icon at which he now stared had flickered out when he and the priest arrived in his mother's bedroom, and Damianos, the apostate, filled and lighted its cup again. The priest worked the censer, and the blue-white clouds of incense smoke fluttered into the room. The liturgical murmuring of the priest lulled and hypnotized Damianos as he knelt on the floor. His mother kissed the Holy Bible the old man offered her. She was ready for death now, for the Great Eagle, for Christos Pantocrator, for the Byzantine God. As Damianos shouted the words he had kept from her all his life—*"holy woman . . . holy mother . . ."*—she drifted from a life of turmoil and unhappiness to a black, secretive death.

After her death, he had begun packing the trunks. The rooms near the steel mill, the only home he had known, were almost bare of furniture. He had sold everything but the bed, a table, two chairs, and a heater, ridding himself slowly of old memories, old needs, freeing himself week by week of his past, so that when the apartment was empty, the floorboards visible and strange-looking, and the trunks stored, he would leave quietly, without goodbyes, jettisoning the cocoon of muddy boots, work clothes, union buttons, icons, and memories.

But then the bells of Saint Vladimir's clanged one afternoon. The world seemed peaceful; the strikes had been settled; the river was placid. What could it be? It was merely a Sunday in December. The Monongahela Valley looked forward to Christmas, the Birth; but the bells rang loudly, telling of death and war, unwelcome news from the outside, far away from the now serene Monongahela.

I owe them nothing, he had thought. *I owe them nothing. They can shove their billy clubs.* He would leave as he had planned. Disappear. He was a free man. Who cared if the Pacific fleet had been sunk? Hadn't the National Guard killed his father? *I owe them nothing.*

He packed a bag and walked to the train station, passing the storage building to which he had taken his trunks the day before. Germany and Italy, he learned, were expected to declare war on America, also. *What do they think we are?* he had wondered. A line of men waited at the post office. It was closed on Sunday, he told them. But they were joining up. For what? he asked. The Army, they said. *The Army!* He had never known anyone in the Army! He knew only of the National Guard. They were like scabs, always against people like him, always armed. And these steelworkers were *joining?* What was Pearl Harbor—some kind of dock? No one knew.

Damianos was silent. He waited in the train station's lobby all night, smoking cigarette after cigarette. Then, hours after dawn, he drank a cup of coffee at a nearby luncheonette, went to the post office, waited in line, and joined the Army.

He had stuffed the war in another trunk: trophies, bayonets, decorations, snapshots of smiling buddies whom he could not remember, everything but the blood he had shed and the fear that had become a companion. This was a new life, a new portrait. But only to himself, alone, in the cellar with his trunks, would he ever admit that those four years, for all their hatefulness, had given him a freedom that, otherwise, he would never have known. In the battlefields of the European War, in the midst of fear, of stench, of brutality, of imprisoning discipline, of exhaustion, he had caught glimpses of an unexpected liberation. He was a member of a unit again. He was a paratrooper, and they were men let loose in North Africa, in Sicily, in Normandy, in Holland; let loose as wild animals are let loose, leaping and shouting from the sky, hung up on wires, killed in the air, impaled on steeples, crucified on glass-covered walls, entombed in wells, but—though wounded or exhausted—always assembling and moving on to their targets with the same grin, saying to themselves in a proud, lunatic glee: "Man, there ain't *ever* been such a fucked-up operation!"

And the bitterness after the war was in the same trunk: the return to the steel mill, the rubbled spot that told him the building he had lived in was torn down, the new people with war money and "E for Efficiency" buttons in their lapels, the beers he was treated to, the slaps on the back, the whorehouses near the Monongahela, the quick marriage to a neighborhood slut, the equally quick divorce, and, finally, the long-postponed thumb-ride to the West—to Chicago, to Denver, to Las Vegas (where he lost everything at craps), then to California, to the Mission District of San Francisco, where he found himself one evening, lying in a doorway, and realized what he had become.

On a Saturday morning, without enough money in his pockets to buy a cup of coffee and two slices of toast, with all his possessions in his pockets and all his clothes on his back—except the objects stored in the trunks in western Pennsylvania—he walked into a recruiting office and re-enlisted in the United States Army.

Why should he kill these memories? They were part of him; when he would die, they would perish with him. Gathered and stored, they made up the face he bared to the world. To destroy the past would be to destroy an image of himself, an image he needed to remind him of what he was.

Damianos closed the final trunk and pushed it to the wall, next to the others. No. They would stay intact. This, he knew, was not a postponement of decision; it was a decision *not* to destroy.

"Gus! Gus!"

He prepared himself. "What is it, Sophie?"

"The insurance man is here."

"OK. I'll be right up."

He had changed his mind about the trunks, but his decision concerning Sophie was immutable. He must make some provision for her, because he was to die soon. It was his turn. Marrying her was out of the question. She would have the Green Light; why would she want his name as well? Besides, he should leave her free to marry. Sophie would be a good catch, particularly with the tavern as her property and the insurance policies. He brushed the dust from his trousers, put on his sweater, and walked up the stairs to the first floor.

As soon as he entered the tavern from the kitchen area, Damianos realized that he had forgotten himself and the time while in the cellar, for the tavern was filled with men. Most of the booths were occupied. He hurried the interview with the insurance agent, looking upon their discussion as more of a game of chance than a business deal, since Damianos was betting that he would soon die and the insurance man was betting that the sergeant would live long enough to pay a sufficient number of monthly premiums to make the insurance company's loss not such a great one. He finally purchased a $15,000 policy and made Sophie his beneficiary. When the insurance salesman left, Damianos went behind the bar to help Sophie draw the beers and wash the glasses.

It was only toward the end of the day that they had the opportunity to talk.

Sophie was at the register, tallying up the day's receipts. "Are you all packed?"

Damianos went to the door to make sure that it was locked. "I decided not to throw anything away."

"I knew you would." Sophie laughed. "Are you ready for your mission is what I meant." She broke open a roll of nickels and poured the coins into the register drawer. "When are you leaving . . . ?" Her voice was mild, for he had told her often that he did not like being questioned about his affairs. "How long will you be gone?"

"About a week." He turned the outside lights off and cleared a few tables of empty beer bottles. "We should be taking off about dawn on Tuesday." He paused at the register. "Are you going to be long?"

"I'm finished."

They went upstairs. Damianos said nothing while Sophie was in the kitchenette heating a pot of coffee. As she took two cups and saucers from the overhead cupboard, he put down the magazine he was thumbing through. "Sophie . . ."

"Yes?" She turned off the fire. "What is it?"

"You know . . ." It was difficult speaking. "You know . . . Sophie. . . . You're a good-looking woman."

"Thank you." She smiled. "That's the nicest thing you've said to me all week."

"I mean . . . I don't know what you see in me."

She did not look up. "I like my freedom just as much as you like yours." The sergeant's statement was one that he had made before, and Sophie needed no time to formulate an answer. "You're a good man, Gus. I'm satisfied with things as they are. I made a bad marriage . . . just like you. I don't want to take another chance."

Damianos was irritated. He did not want to hear women talking like this; it was shameless. "You know"—he controlled his temper—"you're free to marry another man if you want to."

"I don't want to."

"But if you want to, you know you're free."

"Even Sergeant Jacks?"

Damianos' jaw muscle twitched. "Even him," he muttered.

"Why are you talking like this, Gus? You're depressed about something. I don't remember you being this way since we met. What's the matter? What's happened?"

He shrugged his shoulders. When Sophie brought the tray to the divan and placed it on the coffee table, he motioned for her to sit down with him. "How much money do you have in the bank?"

"Do you need some?"

"No. I just want to know."

"I have enough. I don't want any more." She looked at him quizzically.

"I'll tell you what, Sophie." Damianos stared at his cup. "When I come back, next week sometime, you and me will go down to the bank and put the Green Light in both our names. OK?"

"What are you *talking* about?" She was angry. The cup of coffee in her hand wobbled and she set it on the table. "You talk as if you're getting ready to die!"

He put his finger gently to her lips. "Shhhhh. We'll do as I say. Sophie . . . as a favor to me . . . we'll be partners. OK?"

She sat near him. "What is it, Gus? What's the matter?"

"I like you, Sophie." Damianos hesitated. He leaned against the backrest of the divan, staring at the ceiling. "Do as I say."

CHAPTER 10

The curve of a woman's hips as she slumbered at his side; the small, pointed breasts—supportless—gradually softening in her effortless sleep; the sweet, tawny body stretched in faith and quieted loving against the whiteness of a sheet: was all this love? McIlhenny did not wonder what he meant by the word—whether *eros* or *agape*. These qualifications were all forgotten, swept into the dustbin of his past like dry, yellowed newspapers thrown out for rubbish men to collect. Previously, he had treasured words, using them sparingly, never saying *perhaps* when he meant *yes* or *no, forever* when he meant *temporarily*.

But all this had passed. Now words had lost their value, for they were imprecise. How can emotions that caused his blood to throb in his temples, that shook his once steady hands like regimental banners in a gale, that alternately chilled and heated his body be termed transient, ephemeral, fleeting?

He caressed her shoulder, feeling the soft, warm flesh mold to his grip, seeing the skin ripple over her small bones, the delicate, tender breasts stir like living things in his hands.

How could he have faced the past two weeks without her?

A steady pour of rain washed off the gabled roof, and the windowpanes shook to the nudges of the wind. It was the tail end of one of the autumnal hurricanes that were born in the Caribbean and roared up the Eastern Seaboard to New England. But it was warm and dry inside, and, in his pagan nakedness, he leaned against her sleeping body. *Life is good*, he thought. *I've ignored it, attacked it too long*. Why was the world created, after all; why were men placed on it, if the only purpose of their existence was to test their ability to deny themselves the pleasures it could give?

Day by day, the captain had lost his hostility, the tension he had thought to be an integral part of his character. At the end of every Army day, after retreat had sounded, he would ignore his books, those documents of human pathos, and drive to Esperanza's cabin, where, until the morning, he would forget his almost permanent dread.

Why had his promotion not arrived yet? He could not

understand how the Pentagon operated. Such a monstrous edifice, built to house the best military and administrative minds in the nation, and they constantly made important mistakes. *A labyrinth,* he thought; *a modern labyrinth.* Certainly he had doubts about his status: his efficiency reports were couched, as every officer's were, in the stilted, meaningless phraseology of commendation. Was a *superb* officer any better than an *excellent* one? Words had lost their meaning. Was one man's *military bearing* equivalent to another's *puppetlike efficiency?* And McIlhenny could not discount this: he had been the company commander of a Headquarters unit for three years, and in order to be promoted to major, he should be transferred to a major's slot, to a duty that demanded the higher rank. As yet, however, he had not been notified of any transfer.

But he had enemies who would seize on the fact that he was not a college graduate. The Second War had come as he was about to commit himself to a monastic existence; following the Korean crisis, when he had returned Stateside and learned of the emphasis on college-trained officers, he had dutifully taken courses at nearby accredited colleges. Then, realizing that it was just busy-work, that he was not *learning* anything, he had stopped. That was a mistake; his enemies would not ignore that. Possibly they had even found desks in the Pentagon and were holding up his promotion. But, he cautioned himself, he was relatively insignificant; he was not even Regular Army! This comforted him, paradoxically, for if he was too insignificant to have important and powerful friends, might he not also be too insignificant to have powerful enemies?

The fact remained that he had made one mistake: he had not played up to Colonel Simms as he should have, as the other officers had done. He was a soldier, however, not a politician, not a salesman. This was not a mistake in his actions but a weakness in his character, and since this personal passivity was rooted deep in himself, he could not change it without altering his self and thus committing a much greater error.

The promotion will come, he thought. *It must come.* Life did not contain the violence a man's fears led him to expect. Life was good. The wind blew and rain fell, but people, after all, managed to keep warm and dry. *Major McIlhenny.* He considered the phrase, and it sounded good to him. *Major McIlhenny.*

Esperanza stirred. As she turned to face him, her soft

shoulder caressed his chest. "It still rains?" She nestled close to him, pressing her lips to his neck.

"Yes, it still rains." McIlhenny adjusted the blanket over their bodies. "Are you hungry?"

"Hmmmmm."

He felt her breath caress his skin.

"I have hunger . . . but I'm too tired."

"I'll make dinner, then." He patted her shoulder.

"Not yet, not yet . . . stay . . ."

He luxuriated in the present, the moment of the here and now, which he had ignored all his life. For the first time in his existence, McIlhenny actually *lived* the present. And it was not love that did this; it was pleasure, no more, no less. He used the girl and she used him, and occasionally, when they both felt affectionate, they mentioned the word "love."

After the first week of their intimacy, McIlhenny had wondered why he was spending so much time—and money—on Esperanza; why, now that he had liberated himself somewhat, he did not frequent the Officers' Club and have more to do with the women who went there often. Certainly they were as available as Esperanza. They made him feel on edge, though. American women expected equality in conversation, but they so desperately lacked anything that approached McIlhenny's demands in a conversational partner. They either would think him mad when he spoke of politics or philosophy or would nod politely and tell him that their next dance was promised to someone else. They knew how to dress only because they studied the fashion pages of the local newspapers and conformed like puppets to the dictates of New York and Paris.

Certainly Esperanza was not much of a conversationalist; nor did she care about fashions, wearing only what he had purchased for her. But she had a warmth, a vivacity, which the other women did not have. And, as she changed certain unfortunate mannerisms she had picked up in her youth, she became much more presentable. Though far from a lady, she was learning to take care of her clothes, to groom herself properly, to stand erect, to keep her abdomen in. Perhaps, McIlhenny wondered . . . perhaps the very fact that she was pliant to him, that she adopted his every suggestion—perhaps all this pleased him. Perhaps it was the Pygmalion instinct in him that was gratified because he had found a pliable, willing-to-be-manipulated piece of clay. Perhaps he did not like American women—McIlhenny probed his motives—because they did not allow him to tamper with their personalities, puny and insignificant though they were. At any rate—he stopped dissecting himself—he had found what he wanted: a woman who made him feel at ease with the world, content to be what he was, an Army officer, and content to strive for what really mattered to him now—a comfortable feeling of attaining some sort of truth, of relieving his acute tension as he waited for the Department of the Army letter, and of providing him with something to do in the evenings when he had surfeited with reading.

Raindrops washed steadily on the roof's shingles. It was dark now, and only the occasional automobiles driving past the trailer camp lighted the cabin, briefly drawing the reflection of their headlights across the walls and ceiling. McIlhenny knew he could not fool himself: he had come, in this series of presents he had discovered on her bed, as near as he ever would to attaining an earthly contentment. He may have been destined for many things, but joy and happiness, he felt certain, were not included in the history of his life. Pain—certainly. Doubt—definitely. Introspection—doubtlessly. But—and here he hesitated—*nothing more, nothing more presumptuous, nothing more . . . tragic.*

He knew that by continuing to see her his status had changed from that of a devout Christian to that of a nominal one. He did not attend mass as regularly and dropped confession. It was undignified to appear before the chaplain, a major, and confess his systematic derelictions, sins he did not intend to do without. They were therapy. How could he have maintained his equilibrium otherwise? He had come too near madness before he met her, had been balanced too precariously on the boundary that separated rigid discipline and the compulsive behavior of a man who existed in his own universe.

"Kinny?"

"Yes?" He brushed the hair away from her eyes. "You want dinner, don't you?" Pushing the blankets aside, he got out of bed and dressed himself slowly. He stumbled over a shoe in the darkness on his way to the lamp.

Within a few moments he had lighted the oven fire and put two steaks in to broil. The refrigerator was full of food, his own purchases, and with the attitude of a proprietor he chose the vegetables for a salad. Lettuce, tomatoes, cucumber, onion; yes, yes, he must not forget the anchovies. As he prepared the salad, he stopped abruptly. Were the beers sufficiently chilled? Into the refrigerator again. Fine; they were fine. Enough Italian bread? Plenty. He must remember to warm the bread when he turned the steaks over.

Why not listen to the small radio he had given her? In a few moments, the tubes had warmed and McIlhenny sang along with the music; it was a love song, of course. Only the songs of love are considered worthy of beautiful melodies. A blaring commercial followed immediately, forcing him to turn off the radio.

Esperanza got out of bed and watched McIlhenny closely as he put a loaf of Italian bread in the oven.

"How do you want your steak? Rare, medium, well-done?"

"Like yours."

"Medium, then." He did not look at her nakedness, trying to ignore her as much as possible as she set the table. There was one thing about himself he could not understand. Why was it, when he was surfeited with her body, when the bond of their physical intimacy had been severed, he could not bear to look closely at the body he had used until he wanted her again? Why should he struggle against a feeling of revulsion? The human mind was a curious instrument. At times it seemed to be the least adequate tool man could have developed to answer the questions he asked himslf. It may have been his ascetic background, McIlhenny allowed. Possibly with time he would be able to confront the universe with undiminished enthusiasm, whether it was in the state of dress or undress, whether he was surfeited or aroused.

"Kinney?"

"Yes?" He concentrated on tossing the salad.

"What are you thinking about?"

"I'm thinking about you."

"That's good, Kinny. It means you love me."

CHAPTER 11

McIlhenny woke up to hear the steady shower of rain on his windows. He thought it curious, though it was autumn, that the heavy rainfall communicated to him a contentment, a warm feeling of regeneration—not distant, not coming the following spring, but immediate. A regeneration promising him that he, too, would participate in what had been spoken and sung about and made into poetry for as long as man existed and needed woman. He faced the winter now with more secretive pleasure than he had faced his every spring.

As he walked to the bathroom, towel and toilet kit in hand, he stopped momentarily at the window and looked down at the lawn and the wet-dark macadamized street that ran past the BOQ. McIlhenny opened the window, caught some rainwater with his free hand, and bathed his face with it.

He smiled, realizing that the key to human existence was paradox, not discipline, suffering, or denial. Did not three hours with Esperanza appear more vivid to him than the years he had spent alone, dissecting his brittle soul, oozing deeper into error, and separating himself from the real world? This was his great mistake: to reject the evidence of his senses and confront a congenial world with suspicion and hostility.

With Esperanza, whom he did not *love*—he smiled at his whimsy—he had found that love could exist, though he might not attain it. In realizing that pleasure existed for a purpose, and that this purpose was to soften the forbidding universe he himself had created, he had discovered one of the multitudinous truths, and even this had set him free.

Love, however, was running into money—and this was the problem. As the days passed, the "little things" he had purchased for Esperanza were becoming slightly larger and more numerous than he had anticipated. Not that he was disturbed; it was just that occasionally he found himself recommending that they stay at her cabin for the evening or get along on what food and drink she had in her refrigerator rather than go out and spend more money.

After attending to his toilet, he frowned for the first time this morning. Approaching the closet where he kept his clothes, civilian and military, he found that only one of his khaki suits was wearable; the others were wrinkled or had been splashed by gutter water and could not be worn again. Luckily, however, this would be the last week the Post was on the summer clothing schedule. The following Monday everyone would change to the winter uniform. The days were getting chilly and the clothing change would be inexpensive, for ODs rarely showed they were soiled and required only a quick pressing to look fresh and military.

When he arrived at his office, McIlhenny was spoken to in the third person by the company clerk, who mentioned that "the captain" had what seemed to be an important letter on his desk. Setting the swagger stick in the in-box, he felt a tremor pass through his body; the letter had been posted from the Department of the Army. He sat down and attempted, with trembling hands, to plunge the plastic opener into the envelope. *This is it,* he realized. He felt shame at his failure, for neither the letter nor the blade remained still.

He had succeeded admirably in forcing the great fear of the letter's contents so deeply into his mind that he had disguised it even from himself. His daily calls on Esperanza, McIlhenny realized, had saved him from a crisis. He set the opener and the letter on the desk. Waiting until his hands had stopped quivering and until he gained confidence in his voice, he called the clerk.

"Have you brought any coffee from the mess hall yet?"

"Yes, sir. Top just came back with a pitcher." The clerk spent some time in the latrine washing a cup out for McIlhenny. When he came into the office, the captain was in the same position he was in when he stopped cutting into the letter. His hands rested awkwardly on the desk.

He went through the business of preparing himself for the first sip. A dash of cream, two spoonfuls of sugar—he coddled himself—and stir; stir longer than necessary. Another luxury. Then he took the first sip. It was bitter. He sat on the edge of his swivel chair and stabbed at the envelope with the tip of the opener. The letter was light, flat. One sheet.

Because his hands shook, McIlhenny had difficulty reading the text. He did not read slowly, attempting to understand every sentence; he read frantically, the words overtaking his cognition, his eyes skimming the lines to determine whether this was the threat or the blissful mistake he had expected. He read phrases merely: *In accordance with . . .* his quaking hands were cold . . . *I must inform you of your release from active duty. . . .* They were withdrawing his commission? Was he wrong? Had he misinterpreted?

He began at the beginning, reading slowly now, trying to understand every sentence before reading the next, teasing himself with the hope that the following sentence, the one at which he had stopped reading, would say something else. *In this connection, your attention is invited to. . . .* There was a meaningless series of numbers preceded by an Army regulation. . . . *If you decide to re-enlist in an enlisted status, your application must be submitted so as to arrive in Headquarters, Department of the Army, not later than 10 days prior to termination date.*

He was being riffed, then. This was it—what he had feared. And only now, to be honest with himself, did he realize that it could have happened no other way. He was destined to be terminated. But he could reapply to the Army for his enlisted grade. He had been a corporal! The shock—the jolt of going into the EM class after having been an officer for so long—would be brutal, but he could still manage to last out the four years he needed for his pension. Then he would retire with captain's pay. He read further.

> This release does not, in any way, detract from the record of meritorious service you have established. I assure you that the Army is cognizant and appreciative of your record of devoted service and the important contribution you have made to the Army and our country.
>
> I hope you will accept from me, in the name of the United States Army, which you have so well and faithfully served, sincere best wishes for your future hapiness and success.

The letter was signed by the Adjutant General. McIlhenny read and reread it. His mind was a jumble. All he could think of was: *They misspelled "happiness."* He took another sip of coffee and picked up his swagger stick. Striding back and forth in the little room, he tried to control his raging, fluttering mind. *Sixteen years! Sixteen years!* The swagger stick felt as if it were part of him, as if it quite naturally belonged, an unfleshy appendage, in his hand. His patternless walk aroused the interest of the company clerk, who glanced at him in surprise; McIlhenny quickly closed the door.

In the well of his mind, covered over by layers of doubt, fear, and hope, the truth he had tried to conceal glimmered eternally. It could have happened no other way. It was written in his character that he would be bypassed and released. For he needed the Army too much: discipline, faith, subservience, and position were essential to his being.

And the Army had known that thousands of good officers would be riffed, that somehow, with the reduced budget, the service would need to rid itself of all but the superior officers. And the superior officers were those who received favorable efficiency reports from their commanders; and to receive good reports, the officers found it necessary to agree in thought and in action with the predilections, the whims, the thoughts, and the doctrines of their commanders. And Simms had his own brand of consistency. With him consistency was the hobgoblin of small minds; reality, for

Simms, changed not when various factors in life changed but when he tired of things as they were.

And McIlhenny had done all he could. He remembered countless times when Simms had praised the condition of his barracks, the well-kept company area, the excellence of his mess hall. Yet, in the next moment, he would come out with something as unexpected as "Life in a guerrilla camp is not as neat and as orderly as this!" What did one have to do with the other? When an army was in garrison, the cleanliness of the latrines was just as valuable as the cleanliness of a unit's rifle bores when in combat. These incidents had completely unnerved McIlhenny. *What does he want from me?* he had wondered. And, searching about for a clue to Colonel Simms' personality, the captain was forced to accept the unwelcome fact that all that mattered was that the colonel simply disliked him as a person.

Where would he go? He was not going to allow himself to be coaxed out of the service because he was to drop down into the EM ranks. Not with four years remaining before going on retirement. He would stand on his head for four years, if necessary. He would be transferred to another unit, to another post, would go back to being a squad leader in an infantry company, anything. But he would stay in the Army for four years. He would get his retirement. The government owed him that much.

Then he would be forty-two. But what could he do? How could he start life again, on the outside? There was no one in charge out there. How does one go about applying for a job? Even the thought of walking meekly, reverently, up to a personnel manager and stating his qualifications aroused a feeling in him that he had soiled his dignity. And what were his qualifications? He could jump out of an airplane; he could tear down and reassemble an M1 and a carbine blindfolded; he could blow up a bridge. But, somehow, these abilities were considered laboring on the outside, while in the Army they were considered the craft of a military man. And he would be shorn of the illusion that he was defending his country. He would never walk behind the Stars and Stripes and his unit colors in a parade and salute the reviewing stand; he would never again feel the urgency, the importance of being a member of a proud organization, with a chain of command that reached up to the President of the United States. And not only that: America, through fate and the wisdom of God, had become the leader of the Free World, and therefore this chain reached above the President, thus involving America with the forces of war and peace, of freedom and slavery, of truth and falsehood, and of light and darkness. He would no longer be even a minor, insignificant cog in an important wheel, a holy enterprise. He would be a shoe clerk, a digit in a labor pool, a statistic on a commercial report, a consumer.

I must get away, he thought. *I'll go for a drive.* He took his raincoat from the clothes stand, put on his green beret, and opened the door. The first sergeant looked at him steadily.

"Good morning, sir."

McIlhenny nodded absentmindedly and walked out. In his car again, he drove recklessly on Mosby Boulevard, looking at the trailer camps, the service stations, and the drive-in theaters speeding past his windshield. When he arrived in Von Steuben, he parked diagonally across from a bar, empty now because few troopers were in town. A light drizzle sprayed his windshield.

He had gone wrong, he realized, when he had believed in his own religion of discipline, when he had twisted the world into what he wanted to think it was. He had erred when he considered worth having only those things that required discipline and virtue, determination and altruism. He should have taken the comfortable way so often that it would have become easy for him to think in terms of chicanery and cunning. He should have returned to civilian life after the war, somehow relieving himself of further military obligations. He should not have glibly accepted his illusion that the rigorous military life was more virtuous or patriotic.

That was his first error—confusing boredom, conformity, and altruism with duty to his country.

And even if he had made that first error, he could still have sidestepped this Department of the Army letter. He could have gone to the Officers' Club every night, courted the favors of the proper people, forced his way into the necessary groups in order to be introduced to the important guests, smirked with the best of them, rehearsed the appropriate jokes to tell to his colleagues and superiors wherever and whenever he could in order to be considered the pleasant man he was not. He should have made it a point to be invited to cocktail parties where he could have met women—daughters and relatives of senior officers—whom everyone ignored, and teased them, danced with them, behaved in a way all promising men should, the only way to rise in status. His calendar, and even his thoughts, should have been full of the unimportant, the trifling, the superficial. Not the groping questions on what created national greatness . . . not philosophical questions on what was valuable and meaningful . . . but what will the fashions be next year? Should an automobile's motor be in the front or in the rear? Who will win the World Series? What are the top ten records this week? He had failed because he was not a man to whom success came; defeat was imprinted on him by his nervousness at social gatherings, by his musings on dilemmas and problems that were not his personal responsibility, by his hesitation and dislike of currying favors with his superiors on matters that were the responsibility of every company commander.

Waves of rain now riddled the hood of his car and rainwater dripped on his floor mats from somewhere behind the dashboard.

He should have purchased a newer car, of foreign make, and worn paisley ascots and gone horseback riding with Mrs. Simms and told smutty jokes and fornicated, not with women who attracted him, but with influential women who attracted no one.

He embraced the steering wheel and rested his forehead on his wrists. He felt an overwhelming pity for himself; his eyes burning, he tried to cry, to release himself. His eyebrows wrinkled, his chest contracted, but the tears did not come to cleanse him. Dry, hacking sobs racked his body, but he sat there, gasping bitterly, helplessly, with the rain plunging out of the heavens and cascading on the roof of his car. "God, God, God," he sobbed. "Oh, God." He gripped the steering wheel. In his mind he saw himself saluting a young second lieutenant just out of ROTC, or, even worse, forgetting to salute one and being reprimanded by him: "Corporal, don't you know what these bars on my shoulders mean?" His upper body shook again, and his eyelids felt hot and prickly.

The rain did not stop until dusk. When the neon lights were turned on in Von Steuben, he drove back to the Post on the wet roads, went directly to his room in the BOQ, and lay in bed until dawn.

CHAPTER 12

Clarke shut the front door and saw that there were no letters for him or Nikki on the vestibule table. For the first time since he and his wife had moved into the house, the cooking odors from the kitchen of the old ladies from whom he rented his own apartment did not strike him disagreeably, possibly because he had his own worries today. He had made an important decision this afternoon, one that could have a lasting significance on his life. Perhaps he was maturing: he had never really been aware of the dynamics of compulsion and free choice as he was now. The step he had taken two hours before—because *he* had made a conscious decision to take it—was irrevocable. Now, after freely choosing, he knew he was compelled to see the decision through.

The door to their apartment was open. Nikki, he saw, was sitting on the couch, reading a book.

"Hi." She did not look up.

Clarke did not answer. He went to their bedroom, threw the manila folder on the bed, took off his khakis, hung them in the closet, and dressed in more comfortable clothes. When he returned to the parlor and sat on a leather chair near the bookcase, he began leafing through the various forms he had signed. Nikki glanced up from her book briefly but quickly returned to her reading.

"Are you going to make dinner?"

"I suppose I have to. Are you hungry?"

"I suppose I am."

She glanced up angrily, but Clarke ignored her. It was impossible to put off telling her any longer. Sometime this evening he would need to explain his decision to her. In order for him to do this, the two of them would need to be on relatively good speaking terms.

"What are you reading?"

"A book."

"Is it a good book?" To his surprise, Clarke realized he was smiling.

"So-so."

"It's amazing to me how you can lead such a miserable,

unhappy life, Nikki, and still retain your great enthusiasm." He covered his grin.

"Oh, I manage. I give as good as I get."

Clarke struggled to maintain his bantering tone. "What I don't understand is the fact that you're always here when I get back. Do you know what I always expect?"

"No." She turned a page. "Why don't you tell me?"

"I always expect to return one evening to find all the furniture gone and a note on the door saying you've sold everything and taken a plane to San Francisco."

"Not on your life. That would gratify you too much."

"Your old flame is probably wandering around North Beach looking for you. You said you'd wait for him while he was in Yucatan, didn't you?"

"I don't recall. Possibly I did."

"And there he is, with dysentery, and no one to care for him."

Nikki fought a smile. "I don't know very much about dysentery. Anyhow, curing men isn't my line."

"What about destroying them?"

"That's more my style."

"How many men to your credit so far?"

"I'm working on one now. I'll let you know in a few months."

His intestines rumbled. "If you don't fix dinner soon, you'll know in an hour or two."

Nikki closed her book and exaggerated a smile. "Well, *dar-ling,* tell me all about your day at the office."

"Nothing much happened. We lynched three Negroes and burned all of Ezra Pound's books."

"That's not funny, Barrett."

"Aha! Since when are we on a first-name basis?"

She walked into the kitchen quickly and opened the refrigerator.

"I've been looking forward to your cold cuts all day. I said to myself—"

"We're having meat loaf," she interrupted. "Meat loaf, soup, string beans, and coffee."

"I can't wait."

"Well . . ." There was a pause. "I do as well as I can on what we can afford."

"Interpret that." He did not hide his irritation. "I don't follow you."

"Read *Das Kapital.* It's in the book."

Clarke picked up the folder and went into the kitchen. "I

think I've found a way—talking about capital—to earn a little more money."

"What are you going to do? Sell all the psychological warfare secrets?" She made more noise banging pots and pans than Clarke thought necessary.

"No. Let's stop the sarcasm. I'd like to have a serious discussion, if you don't mind."

"I can see the headlines. 'Young GI confesses. Worked for Commies during two-year enlistment. Lean, rapacious, blue-eyed scion of a Philadelphia fortune today admitted being the ringleader of a vicious, underground, antimilitary organization—code name: FTA—in direct pay of the Red Octopus.' "

"Nikki, *please*. I'm not in the mood for that."

"OK . . . I'm sorry. Now"—she turned to him and smiled cheerily—"what were you saying?"

He found it impossible to speak. There was no way he could reply to her. The longer he waited, the more violent he grew. Nikki continued to smile. He slapped her across the face.

Her head was shaken and red marks appeared on her cheek. For a moment she did not reply; she merely blinked her eyes in incomprehension.

Clarke put his hand behind him in embarrassment. "I'm sorry. I didn't . . . I couldn't control . . ."

She turned to the gas range, and then, after a few seconds of aimlessly adjusting the flame under the soup, she broke down and sobbed.

He put his hands gently on her shoulders. "Please, Nikki, I'm sorry. I didn't mean . . ."

She shook off his hands.

"I wanted to tell you that I've volunteered to go to Jump School and become a paratrooper. It means fifty-five dollars a month."

Her sobbing quieted somewhat. After a few moments, the soup began to hiss and bubble around the rim of the pot, but Nikki and Clarke ignored it. She turned to him slowly. "Jump School! What do you mean?" Her face was streaked with tears.

"I've got to do something, Nikki. It's the only way we can keep out of debt." He reached and pulled her to him, cradling her forehead on his shoulder. "This has been no life for you. At least, if we had a little more money, I'd be able to take a three-day pass and we could go somewhere, not stay around the house doing what we do every day."

The soup bubbled even more violently now, but Clarke retained his hand on Nikki's back: it would have been inappropriate to reach over to turn off the flame.

"I want to buy you new clothes. I'd like to be able to afford a steak every now and then. As it stands, the guys in the barracks eat better than we do. This is why we fight all the time—not because we've stopped loving each other." He wondered: *Why bring that up?* "Not because we've changed our minds about each other. We don't have enough money! And we won't have enough money unless I do something about it."

Evidently Nikki had been waiting for him to release her from his embrace, because when he dropped his hands she wiped her face with her sleeve and turned off the gas jet under the pot.

"I don't like it, Barrett." She took the handkerchief he offered and dried her cheeks. "It's too dangerous. The money isn't worth the risks." Her eyes were still brimming. "I can go out to work."

"Doing what? Working at the five-and-ten?"

"Anything. You don't have to go to Jump School! We're not *that* desperate!"

"Don't use that word."

"Why not?"

"I don't know. I don't like it. It's too strong." He shrugged his shoulders. She was, he knew, going to tell him that she had always offered to find work but that jobs were not plentiful in Von Steuben, particularly for a woman who could not type. Teaching at the Post schools was out of the question for her because she did not have a sufficient number of college credits to receive a degree, having withdrawn from school in her second year to continue art studies.

"The money isn't worth the risks you'll take."

"Other men have done it. I don't see why I can't."

"But you're not other men. You're my husband. I don't want you getting killed or injured."

"You're exaggerating the risks, I think."

"No, I'm not. I read the local paper. I know what happens. Every week a man gets injured or killed. I don't like it, Barrett. I don't like it at all."

"And I don't like the life we've been leading. The life *I've* been leading."

Nikki stared at him. "What . . . what do you mean?"

His statement had been too blatant, too obvious. He looked down to the floor. "There's no getting away from it,

Nikki. A man's got to feel that he can support his wife. That he can buy the things she wants. If he can't . . . he begins doubting himself . . . his manhood. I know"—he shrugged his shoulders—"I know it's silly, but it's the truth. Since we've been married . . . I've felt . . . insecure." He would go on. He would tell her everything. "I've lost hold somewhere. I've lost the feeling of mastery a man should have."

Nikki stared at him, her eyes welling. "Oh, I'm sorry, Barrett. I'm sorry. I did this to you. . . . You didn't feel this way before we met."

"No, no." He caressed her hair. "You didn't do it. This was a weakness in me as far back as I can remember. All you did was bring it out. All you did was help me see it." They went to the table and sat across from each other. "I guess, Nikki, this is something I had to do. All my life I've been easing along, never making any important decisions. Just trying to get away from my background. And when I broke with my parents . . . don't you see? . . . it was typical. I had to find an excuse: you. Everything . . . I've done everything the easy way. Everything except this." He tapped the manila envelope. "This is one decision I made on my own. And there's no backing away from it. I've got to succeed. I've got to become a paratrooper. If I don't, I'll be a failure all my life. I know. This is it."

Nikki remained silent, staring at her husband fearfully, her hand occasionally straying to her face to dry it with his handkerchief.

"All these fights we've been having." His voice was low. "All these arguments. They were just evasions, Nikki. You know? Sometimes I actually hated you, wishing we hadn't married." He bent over, resting his elbows on his knees. "And then it dawned on me. I was beginning to feel impotent. Everything—movies we saw together, books I read, jokes I heard—everything reminded me of my weakness."

Clarke raised his eyes and confronted her. "So . . . it's not only the fifty-five dollars, you see." He suppressed a nervous smile. "That should be obvious. I've got to do something. Not have it done to me. I want to stop being passive." He paused. "That's what I wanted to say. You were right that evening in the tavern. I *did* feel threatened. And I'm not going to be intimidated anymore. I'm not going to be intimidated by you, Nikki, or by anyone else. My father tried to do it, and I left. I had to. A son has too many handicaps. A father has too many advantages. So . . . I've been drifting all my life. But I've stopped. *I'm* making the decisions now. Three years ago I was twenty-one, and I'm still not a man. I guess I'm silly telling you this. You already know it. I guess I'm really telling myself. I'm going to become a man. Whatever that means. Whatever it takes. I'm telling you this now, Nikki, so you'll know. You won't like it; I don't think you will, anyhow. But I've got to come into my birthright."

"And what's that, Barrett? What's your birthright?" She had stopped crying. Her face was serious, her eyes immobile.

"I don't know what it is. All I know is that I'm tired and disgusted with myself as I am."

"I'm not. I married *you,* not some god."

"I know. I'm sorry, but I'm tired of being what I am."

"Suppose . . ." Nikki took her time in phrasing her statement. "Suppose the *you* that you discover and the *me* that you've married are incompatible? What then, Barrett? Or suppose I want to change? What am I to do while you're becoming yourself? You know"—she placed his handkerchief on the table—"a woman has a personality, too. Why do we exist if all we're to do is wait around until you create your faces? Our only function can't be to be impregnated and to cook your food."

"I don't know. But you know where I stand, Nikki. I'm wrestling my angel . . . and I've got to win. If I don't . . . it would have been better for us if we hadn't met."

"Maybe . . . maybe . . . that's true now, Barrett?"

Clarke shrugged his shoulders.

"What am I to do while you're wrestling your angel? Stay here?"

"I hope you will."

"You know, Barrett: this is something you should have done before you married. Life may be a masquerade . . . but a husband and wife should know each other's face."

"Nikki, please. Human beings change. I don't want to be a different person. I want to be myself. I have your interests in mind just as much as I have mine." He paused. "Let's stop talking, Nikki. Let's just say I'm going to Jump School to earn fifty-five dollars a month. We'll leave it at that. That's simple enough. Money is important. We'll take it . . . we'll take my actions at their"—he hesitated—"at their face value." He looked at her. "Will you wait, Nikki?"

He stopped himself from saying any more. Someone else had asked her to wait for him, and she had said she would. But she had married Clarke instead. That was a year ago. Could he trust her? The actor she had been going with steadily had trusted her before agreeing to go to Yucatan to make a low-budget film, and in the interval she had met Clarke, gone with him from party to party, and eventually shared his apartment. Could he trust this woman? Could he trust her when she had felt no particular need to marry him and had had to be convinced that she should be his wife since she had lived with him for several months?

Without answering, Nikki went to the cupboard and reached for two soup bowls. Clarke was motionless as she set the table. When Nikki sat down again and opened her napkin, she looked up at him. "I'll stay. I'm just as interested as you are. I won't sell the furniture. I won't go to San Francisco. I'll stay right here."

They began on the soup.

CHAPTER 13

Damianos and his team, to fulfill a premaneuver phase, had parachuted, with their rucksacks dangling below their boots, into a clearing in the Pisgah forests of western North Carolina. The helicopter from which they had dropped had hovered above them until they hit the hard-packed earth, then, after swooping down to see if anyone had been injured, had disappeared over the pine trees, swaying their tops gently with its swirling rotor blast.

Seeing that all the team members were present, Damianos began the march to the northwest, where, according to his orders, he would encounter and inspect a vast, flat area—referred to as Crossroads Drop Zone—and determine over a period of one week whether or not the immediate region could logistically support approximately one thousand guerrillas. It was a certain ten-hour trek, and Damianos hoped the team would penetrate the perimeter of Crossroads in time to make camp by dusk.

There was little general conversation among the team members. Being in each other's company for a year, they had learned the mannerisms, habits, and attitudes of each individual thoroughly. When the actions and comments of the men had shown that the brief, warm comradeship they had initially felt on being assigned to the team had disappeared, Damianos, as leader, had made it clear that if he sensed any conflicts among the members he would either transfer the troublemaker to another team or break his jaw. After that day, the relations had improved; each man had selected close friends within the team, excluding the others from the intimacy of jokes, gossip, and drinking, and had performed his job without acrimony. Sergeant Damianos, not wanting to take sides, had managed as best he could without conversation.

He was just as happy, as he marched with the heavy rucksack on his back, to remain placid in the integrity of his own thoughts. This maneuver, regardless of what he had told Sophie, had come to him as a godsend. Too quickly he would tire of what little civilization Von Steuben had to offer. Garrison life, with its constant routine, its roster system of details and busywork, its spit and polish, oppressed him; and when he was oppressed, he constantly thought of death. A patterned existence made him gloomy. Adventure, violence, the outdoors, fresh air—even danger—revivified him: when his body is exhausted, when his mind is occupied with stratagems and tactics, when his very life is endangered, who has time to think of death?

As first in the file, Damianos came upon an approach to a long hill. A path, worn by both feet and running water, gradually wound between rocks and trees, exposing in its gash a tan, pebble-flecked earth. He leaned slightly and stretched his legs to the challenge of the moderate climb. At a loop in the path he turned to check on his men as they followed him up the incline. Breathing deeply of the pine-scented air, he began the ascent again. *How can I die?* he wondered, feeling the bracing air fill his chest. His heart was strong, confident, hardly responding to the exertion. He was alert; his eyes, never resting, passed over the rugged terrain lovingly, paused briefly to see a hopping, frightened rabbit, and followed the quiet, ascending stateliness of a protected pine. Autumn was the earth's death, he knew; but why were men never truly persuaded of their immortality even in a region where the trees were ever green? Death was unfair—an individual blackness when the earth would continue to resurrect itself, a deafness while the wind would continue to stir the trees, and a final slumber without a hope that man would waken to see the daily sun.

When he came to the top of the hill, he glanced about quickly, marked the area he was to recon, and took out his binoculars. A vast platform was stretched before him, flanked on the east and west by mist-enshrouded mountain ranges.

At its north, a great pine forest stood wedged against the rectangle of the plateau; its south end was open, and scraggy pines grew helter-skelter until the brown earth was covered by the vague greenness of another forested tract.

This was to be Stage Three of Operation Razor Blade. This was to be Crossroads Drop Zone. In Indian times two paths had intersected on this great tableland, two foot trails dwarfed by the fearful, mist-enveloped mountain ranges. Crossroads. And within weeks this forgotten platform, this secret plateau, would be the time and place in the maneuver where the planning staffs would know if Razor Blade was a success or not.

The name appealed to Damianos. There was the anticipation of the glory of a mass jump, certainly. But "crossroads" also meant chance encounters with strangers, with the unknown, which man confronts whenever he breaks from the routine of his existence. Looking through his binoculars at the vast canvas of what was to be a drop zone, bordered as it was by great carpets of forest and dominated by two mist-filled mountain ranges, Damianos felt a curious sense of distortion. Crossroads Drop Zone had a mystery about it that had no place in this brisk, wintry, sun-filled day. The breeze from the Appalachian ranges stirred the coniferous trees gently, and the comforting *plop, plop* of the pinecones amid the general rustling of the forest seemed inappropriate to the vision he witnessed through his binoculars.

Damianos checked his exhilaration. He raised his hand, and the team, single file, followed him down the path into the forest that would eventually open into the tableland of Crossroads Drop Zone.

«««««»»»»

It was dusk. The vastness of the plateau, now that the farthest reaches of the drop zone were shrouded in twilight, appeared exaggerated. It was a windswept plain, open to the north, where the two mountain ranges seemed to converge like rims of a funnel. Damianos, after sliding out of his rucksack, assigned two men to search for firewood, a third to dig a hole and line it with stones, and the remaining four to chop down slender trees to make a communal lean-to in case of rain.

He walked away from the gathering and glanced at the forests, the mountains, the sky. It was an awesome moment. Toward the east, as far as the mountain crags permitted him to see, the sky was darkening. At the west, the blood-red sun was dropping behind a spur, and, as it disappeared, the violent sunset colors were muted by the advancing gray. A northerly wind rearranged the grains of sandy earth under his boots. *All this time,* he considered, *all this time . . . Crossroads was here . . . and I didn't know it.* He felt chilled, although it was not cold.

As he returned to the camp, he saw that a fire was blazing and that the lean-to was almost completed. The sergeant helped his men pack the rucksacks against the lower back end and stretch the sleeping bags out under the slender trunks of the pines.

Damianos did not select a guard. He was usually lax about such things when they were unimportant, primarily because he feared his team would think him ridiculous. Instead of choosing a guard, he elected to sleep between the fire and the lean-to with his .45, loaded but locked, near his side to ward off any prowling animals that might wander into the camp. Bears were common in the area, and Damianos did not want to be gouged or mauled by one of them. Before getting into his bag, he made note of the wildlife the team had seen on the hike, the number of brooks, and the possible routes of escape and evasion the guerrilla bands might find useful during Operation Razor Blade.

He stretched out under the night sky. The pungent pine fragrance drifting to him was pleasantly clean and antiseptic. Whippoorwills, which had made themselves heard from the time dusk had approached, became more noisy now, and their cries kept the men on edge, not because of any terror they aroused, but because no sooner would the men accustom themselves to hearing the birds' *reep-oo-wee, reep-oo-wee* from one area than the birds would secretly fly to trees nearer the campfire and break an almost total, preternatural silence with their calls.

Towering above him, totally blacked out by the night, the peaks of the mountain ranges, he imagined, reached humpbacked into the sky. Their presence was unmistakable, partitioning the broad, flat plateau of Crossroads, as if God had collaborated with the General Staff to create an ideal laboratory for the experiment that was Operation Razor Blade. An occasional bolt of lightning slithered its vibrant, broken back across the ranges, but the deep serenity of the night was not disturbed.

«««««»»»»

Something had startled him. A dream. All he could remember was a fight, himself and another man, fighting in the snow. Just a fight. But why so much emotion? Why did the dreaming Damianos sob? His eyes shot open to a grayness that dominated his vision. Crossroads was shrouded in an eerie mist. Above him, the mountains were completely obscured by fluffs of vapor. The plain of Crossroads was in utter silence, a silence so profound that Damianos' eardrums hummed from the lack of anything to register. As he pulled on his boots and laced them, the hard strings struck against the leather of his boots in only muffled slaps. He walked about as if hypnotized, his heels twisting into the soil, which seemed to have the consistency of powder. Pouring water from the canteen into his cup, he purposely struck the two, but heard only a dull ring, which was silenced as soon as it had sounded. He turned quickly toward the lean-to, where his men still slept, but saw only pockets of clarity within a totality of grayness. The wall of trees behind the camp, present the night before, was gone, and in its place a curtain of grayness separated the lean-to from the forest.

Damianos became conscious of his breathing and the beating of his heart. *Death must be like this,* he thought. A silence, a gray blindness, the curious sensation of being disembodied. On a mysterious impulse he began walking toward the center of Crossroads, telling himself he wanted to inspect the secretiveness of the shrouded field but really not knowing where he went or why. Fifty feet away from camp he turned to see that the lean-to was completely lost in the mist. His hand touched the .45 on his hip and strayed back to its swinging, as if it operated on a vagrant, unreasoning impulse. He stopped suddenly, feeling the excited blood throb through his body.

Ahead of him, her graceful neck bent to the turf, a doe munched on a tuft of grass. She raised her head, looked at him inquisitively, and went back to her eating. So quickly had Damianos stopped his movement that his boots now felt frozen to the earth. His glazed eyes were fixed on her beautiful, quivering body. *I've been here before!* he perceived. *I know this place!* But his mind was dull. He could not remember. *In another life?* he wondered.

The doe moved on, sniffing the earth as if she owned it, as if she were the beloved beast of a local deity, and stood confidently over another dew-drenched tuft of grass.

Damianos' heart pounded fiercely. That an *animal* should live in godlike freedom while he, a man, was oppressed. That it should be graceful and lithe while he, a man, was rooted to the earth by heavy boots. *I remember you,* he thought. *I don't know where I've seen you, but I know you.* He seemed to recall that they had been enemies. The doe ignored him.

The sergeant snapped open the pistol case, unlocked the .45, raised it, pulled the trigger, and caught the deer in the shoulder. The entire valley resounded with the roar. Damianos charged ahead, every control removed from him, blindly, his lust and hatred overpowering his reason, to where the doe had been thrown. She attempted to get up, but her shoulder and foreleg were shattered, and she collapsed again to the earth. *This I don't remember,* he realized. *I've never done this before.* He stood over her and pulled the trigger. The doe leaped from the bullet's force, shuddered for the last time, and froze in death, the red blood caking the brown skin of her coat.

What have I done? He tried to rationalize his actions. He had killed men, after all; and to feel qualms about killing a doe, a mere animal, while having killed men (How many? Ten? Fifteen?) was ridiculous, was scrupulousness carried to the point of insanity. Still . . . the doe lay at his feet, lifeless. It was not merely the act of shooting the doe with a .45. No, it was not only that. It was the context of the killing: the mist-shrouded plain, the terrible silence, the echo of the shots, the vague recollection that this had all happened before, and the innocence and trust of her whom he killed. What time was it? He could not judge. It was half light, half darkness; it was a gray timelessness, when he and the doe, killer and victim, had been involved in an eternal act whose end product was always death.

The first rays of the sun shafted over the eastern range and pierced the heavy mists of dawn. The blood on the doe's coat was beginning to harden. Damianos' boots had not stirred, but his head turned constantly, as if he expected a divine revenge for his irrational desecration. On edge, he stood with his hand resting on the holster when above him he heard a horrendous scream. An eagle, gliding from the heavens, circled over the sergeant's head and then, as if having the killer's features firmly memorized, slapped its giant wingspread and flew to the protection of the clouds.

Damianos fumbled for his .45, pulled it out of its holster again, and *shot, shot, shot* at the great bird as it winged its way into the brilliant glare of the rising sun.

PART TWO

Now the Lord is that Spirit, and where the Spirit of the Lord is, there is Liberty. But we all, with open face beholding as in a glass the glory of the Lord, are changed into the same image from glory to glory even as by the Spirit of the Lord.

—PAUL, II Corinthians, 3:17-18

CHAPTER 14

The Airborne Trainees' billets were old but well-kept wooden buildings, constructed prior to the Second World War, with pavements separating the landscaped lawn of one barracks area from that of another. The walls seemed newly painted, the windowpanes were clean, the sand under the barracks was freshly raked, and the grass was trimmed. There was a feeling of quiet anticipation in the cantonment area, as if a great deal was expected to happen, but no one had arrived yet.

Clarke, approaching the orderly room, knocked on the door, wiped his boots, and took off his fatigue cap. When he heard a "Come in" and opened the door, he saw a rugged sergeant sitting behind a desk reading an adventure magazine. The man's name tape read "Jacks," and over his left breast, above the black-and-gold U. S. Army plate, he wore a master parachutist's badge.

"You a trainee?"

"Yes, Sergeant."

"Where you from?"

"Special Troops . . . psychological warfare."

The sergeant's eyes narrowed. "So you're gonna be a *real* killer from the skies now! What's the matter—you tired of bein' a straightlaig?"

Clarke glanced at the sergeant for a moment. "Yes, I'm tired of being a straightleg."

"Well," Sergeant Jacks said, "you're gonna be tired of bein' a trainee soon, but Ah'll wait aroun' before tryin' to explain *that* to you." He looked at Clarke's name tape and then studied a sheet of paper on which was listed a column of names and ranks. "Well, it looks like Ah'm gonna be in charge of your trainin', so Ah might as well check an' see if you got ever'thin' you need." Jacks closed his eyes and considered. "You got your *dis*play?" He waited for Clarke's nod. "You got five sets of fatigues, cleaned an' starched?" Nod. "You got three sets of boots, two laig an' one jumper's? . . . You got a suit of Class A's, with the n'essary brass? . . . You got your shoe-polishin' equipment, combat pack with mess kit, a set of long johns, five sets of summer underwear, five pair of OD socks, steel helmet, helmet liner, airborne chin strap, roll of *ad*hesive tape, poncho . . . ?" Clarke nodded to all of these. "You got yourself a copy of the New Testament?"

Clarke smiled. "Yes . . . I have the one issued me, but I didn't think the Army demanded that I read—"

"That's jest for your *dis*play. The Army don' demand you read it . . . but you look like the kind that might like to start readin' it sorta careful these next three weeks."

"I don't know why you say that, Sergeant."

Jacks shrugged his shoulders. "Guess Ah'm wrong. Well, Clarke, you seem like you're in perty good shape so far. We'll see what you look like when the course starts tomorrow." The sergeant pushed his chair back and walked to the orderly-room door. "That's your barracks over there." He pointed to a corner building. "Take your gear an' stay on the first floor. The other trainees'll be comin' in any hour now, so Ah suggest you try an' shape yourself up a bit before they start showin' up."

"Thank you, Sergeant. I'll do that."

"You married, Clarke?"

"Yes, Sergeant."

"Where's your wife?"

"In Von Steuben."

Jacks considered for a moment. "Well, mebbe, if you shape up, Ah might jest let you off sometime on Sundays. If you don' goof up oncet! If you do, Ah guess Ah'll hafta restrict you till you either wash up or graduate."

"Thank you, Sergeant. That's very fair of you."

"That ain't fair. Ah'm jest tellin' you what Ah'm 'bout to do. Fair or not don' enter into it. Jest goof, though, jest one time, an' you've had it."

Clarke walked to his car, picked up his duffel bag and boots, and returned to the building pointed out by Sergeant Jacks. He climbed up the three concrete steps of the barracks' stoop and, with his arms full, struggled to open the door. There were a few men on the first floor, cleaning their areas, preparing their displays, or lying on their bunks, resting, readying themselves for the great onslaught of the cadre, who would appear in an hour, when all the trainees were to be present.

Clarke quickly set about making his display. He dusted the footlocker, inside and out, and laid a white towel on the tray of the locker, folding and stretching it so that it looked taut and neat. To the left of the center divider, flush against the top of the tray, he placed a can of tooth powder, a brush, and a shaving stick. Below the center piece—the brush—he set, in descending order, a safety razor, a packet of razor blades, a toothbrush, a black comb, and, finally, a bar of soap, still wrapped, one inch from the bottom of the tray.

To the divider's right, Clarke placed a clean, squared handkerchief and, next to it, a pack of unopened cigarettes. A round can of shoe polish was set under the handkerchief, and below that was a small Army copy of the New Testament and then a large shoe brush. Between the shoe brush and a file of rolled woolen socks on the right, Clarke placed an OD flashlight, 7-shaped, with the window facing left. A major chore had been completed. The tray was finished.

As Clarke was storing his extra towels in the bottom of the footlocker, a busload of trainees disembarked and filed through the barracks. A sergeant directed most of the men upstairs; the remaining few were routed into the first floor to take the empty bunks. Clarke hung up his fatigue suits and Class A uniform, made his bunk, and set his boots, a pair of low quarters, and sandals under the left side of the bunk, near the center aisle. Now that he was prepared, he lay down and watched the others establishing themselves.

After a whistle shrieked in the area, Clarke heard Sergeant Jacks' voice shouting that "everybody inside" should make his way "outside" as quickly as possible.

Clarke leaped out of his bunk and ran into formation outside the barracks. The men stood at attention while Sergeant Jacks inspected them, making what Clarke considered uncalled-for remarks; the NCO doubted their masculinity, marveled at their ignorance of the ferocity necessary to a paratrooper, and finally attacked the blissful overconfidence with which they stood at attention when it should have been obvious that the likes of what he saw should not have been standing at attention like any group of "pathetic straightlaigs" to enter Jump School but should have been in line for sick call or, more precisely, for the Post "sickiatrix," to get out of "this man's Army on a Section 8."

Jacks neared Clarke slowly and leaned to within an inch of his face. "How old er you, Private?"

"Twenty-four, Sergeant."

"Ah can't hear you! Sound off like you got a pair of balls!"

"Twenty-four, Sergeant!"

"That's better!" Jacks smiled coldly. "You been evadin' the draft perty long, ain't you, Private?"

"No, Sergeant! I've been going to school!"

"That's evadin'!" Jacks leaned back and balanced on his toes. "What's your excuse, Private?"

"No excuse, Sergeant." Clarke did not shout this time, because Jacks' voice had softened somewhat.

"Sound off! Ah can't hear you!"

"No excuse, Sergeant!"

Jacks stepped back and pointed to the ground. "Git down an' give me ten good push-ups, Private, an' when you do ten good push-ups, give me one more for the airborne."

"Yes, Sergeant!" Clarke shouted, and leaped to the ground for ten push-ups.

"Count 'em out! Ah can't hear you! Start over ag'in!"

"One, two, three . . ."

"Can't hear you!"

"Seven, eight, nine, ten, airborne . . ."

Jacks walked down the rank and began exhorting the other trainees. "We don' want no mamma's boys here. If you can't sound off like you got a pair, then you're gonna go back to your unit and ast a real man to lend you his. *Am Ah understood?*"

"Yes, Sergeant!"

"All right, now, ever'body. Git down an' give me ten."

Clarke had just finished doing his eleven push-ups when Jacks gave the order for the entire platoon to "do ten," and he stood awkwardly at attention. Jacks turned abruptly to see Clarke standing straight and waiting anxiously, surrounded by the rising and lowering shoulders and buttocks of the trainees.

"Hey, you! Ain't you in this here platoon?" Jacks strode toward Clarke. "Er you in Jump School or er you jest gatherin' material for *re*search?"

"No, Sergeant . . ." Clarke saw that Jacks was about to say something. "No, Sergeant. I just finished doing the push-ups and I didn't think you wanted me to—"

"You diden *think!* Git down an' give me ten! You ain't *suppose* to think!"

When Clarke had finished his eleven push-ups, he stood up with the rest and listened to Sergeant Jacks explain what he wanted from them.

"The important thing in Jump School is mental alertness. 'Cause if you ain't got mental alertness, you've had the course. Somethin' can happen up there in the sky, an' if you ain't prepared for it . . . well, it's jest goodbye. Ah can't go into too much today. You'll git the works tomorrow. All Ah'm gonna do is tell you what we emphasize here at the

School, give you your numbers, an' make a few points." He looked at the men assembled before him and stepped back. "First of all, if we find anyone here not interested in what we're sayin', out he goes." He stopped abruptly and stared at someone. "Hey, *you;* what you twitchin' your *be*hind for?" He glared at the man. "You—Ah'm talkin' to you. What're you doin'—the hootchy-kootchy? You got a wild hair up your ass?"

"No, Sergeant!"

Jacks yelled: "Well, then, what're you twitchin' your *be*hind for?"

"I got ringworm, Sergeant!"

Jacks' jaw sagged. "You got *what?*"

"Got it sitting down on a YMCA bench." Jacks, exaggerating his shock, approached the man as if hypnotized. "It's like athlete's foot, Sergeant."

"An' you wanna be a paratrooper? With athlete's foot up your ass?"

"Yes, Sergeant," the man answered, for the lack of a better rejoinder.

"How'd you git past the doctor?"

"He said it was OK, Sergeant. It just itches."

Jacks, after staring at the man in disbelief, triumphed over his shock. "Well, don' lemme see you scratch yourself. *Do you hear?*"

"Yes, Sergeant!"

Jacks composed himself for a moment, then continued his lecture. "If Ah find anyone here not interested in what we're sayin', out he goes. You got to pay attention to what the instructor is sayin' ever' minute, 'cause one minute he can be sayin' somethin' that's important and you can be thinkin' 'bout poon and not hear it, an' your first or second or third jump somethin' can happen while you're comin' down an' there ain't no one around for you to ast. That's why when we tell you somethin', we always ast somebody we don' think is listenin', an' if he can't tell us what's jest been said . . . well . . . he does a few *co*rrectional push-ups. *Am Ah understood?"*

"Yes, Sergeant!"

"Now in this here School," Jacks continued, "we don't touch the men. There's some that needs it, but we ain't allowed to touch the trainees, and we ain't allowed to blas*pheme*. That is, say bad words. What we *can* do is drop you from the course, an' if you wanna go airborne bad enough, you gotta start all over ag'in. We demand instant obedience to all our commands. We will not tolerate any insubordination, an', soljers, insubordination can be a mean-assed look. When Ah want somethin' done, Ah want you to do it immediately, an' if it ain't done, you will do *co*rrectional push-ups. *Am Ah understood?"*

"Yes, Sergeant!"

"Startin' right now, we, the instructors, er not interested in your names. In a few minutes Ah'll give each of you a number. That's what your name is gonna be for these next three weeks. You better not forget it even oncet, 'cause if you do, you'll do *cor*rectional push-ups. Your rank don' matter to us. You can be master sergeant, an' if you goof up, we'll ride you so hard you'll think your ass was grass and the airborne was a lawn mower." Jacks' eyes shot to his left. "You! With the ringworm!"

"Yes, Sergeant?"

"Git down an' give me ten. You was twitchin'."

"Yes, Sergeant!"

Jacks waited until the push-ups were completed. "You er all alike," he continued, "from PFCs to majors, an' you'll see that we're gonna have a few majors, a few captains, an' about ten second lootenants in this here company by tomorrow. The officers er bein' briefed right now by the CO of the School. Each person does their own work. If a major asts you to help him do somethin' an' you do it . . . you'll both do *co*rrectional push-ups. *Am Ah understood?"*

"Yes, Sergeant!"

"In Jump School all the trainees er equal. They're equally *un*important. From privates to majors. What Ah say goes. Follow mah orders an' you'll have no problems. An' remember: Ah say things only oncet. It's up to you to understand an' know what Ah mean. If you goof up, it means *co*rrectional push-ups. In the three weeks you're gonna be here, you're allowed no more than three major gigs. As soon as you git your fourth, you know that you had the course an' you hafta start all over ag'in. A major gig . . ." Jacks paused. Someone had raised his hand. "What is it?" he asked testily.

"I was going to ask you, Sarge, what a major gig was."

"Git down an' give me ten!" The man started counting. "Ah can't hear you! *Sound off!"* When the man had completed his eleven push-ups and leaped to attention, Jacks resumed. "Ah don' wanna be interrupted. Ah ain't gonna be made a nervous wreck 'cause some of you want somethin' cleared up in one second flat. Ah'm gonna tell you all you need to know. So don' crowd me. *Am Ah understood?"*

"Yes, Sergeant!"

"Well, ever'body, git down an' give me ten." He waited in silence until the men had completed their punishment. "A major gig is when you fall out of a mornin' run or when the instructors think you're not in sufficient shape to continue the physical trainin'. You can't make up a major gig, but you can suffer for it by havin' to do extra PT in the evenin' before bein' sent back to the barracks. A major gig is when Ah think you're thinkin' 'bout bein' insubordinate. Ah got a little black book and Ah write the major gigs down. Ah don't *ever* forget who had 'em." Sergeant Jacks reached into the back pocket of his fatigue trousers and pulled out a black memo pad.

"Three minor gigs make one major gig." He scanned the platoon. "Ain't no one gonna interrupt me an' ast what a minor gig is?" He waited.

Clarke did not know whether Sergeant Jacks wanted his question answered or whether it was merely rhetorical. When Jacks remained silent, Clarke was certain the NCO wanted the question answered. *"No, Sergeant!"* he shouted.

"Who said that?"

Clarke, fearful, hesitated. "I did, Sergeant!"

"An' who er you?"

"Private First Class Clarke, Sergeant!"

"Well, Private, you're the only one here that's mentally alert. OK . . . ever'body but Mr. Mental Alertness . . . git down an' give me ten!"

When the group had completed the push-ups, Sergeant Jacks continued. "A minor gig is when you don' accomplish somethin' *co*rrectly after bein' tole what to do. A minor gig is when your area is not military, when a button is missin' on your fatigues, when you ain't mended a tear in your clothes, when your military bearin' is not sufficiently"—Jacks paused, evidently searching for the proper word—"sufficiently . . . *military*. When your hair is not cut in a military manner. An' pay attention to this, gentlemen: *we love haircuts here!* We got a *git*tar in the orderly room for anyone who don't wanna git himself a haircut. An' when we give that man that *git*tar, he better play it good. *Am Ah understood?"*

"Yes, Sergeant!"

"Abbott!"

"Here, Sergeant!"

"Number 181! . . . Acorn!"

"Here, Sergeant!"

Jacks looked up and smiled. "Number 182; don' lemme catch you scratchin' your ass."

"Yes, Sergeant!"

Jacks shouted off the list of men under his control and, when they responded, gave them the numbers by which they would be known. Clarke's number was 227. Jacks stopped at 240. There were sixty men in his platoon. That evening they would take their rolls of adhesive and tape their numbers on the fronts of their steel helmets, their helmet liners, and the backs of their combat packs. They were to be ready for inspection the following morning, clean-shaven, wearing fresh underclothing and clean and starched fatigues; their boots were to be spit-shined, their fingernails cleaned and clipped, their hair cut short. They were to be "alert, bright-eyed an' bushy-tailed!" *"Am Ah understood?"*

"Yes, Sergeant!"

Jacks dismissed them. Clarke ran toward him and asked the sergeant, who was walking toward the orderly room, if he could possibly have permission to call his wife.

"Who er you?"

"PFC Clarke, Sergeant!"

"Git down an' give me ten!"

When he had completed his eleven push-ups, Clarke stood up.

"Who er you?"

"Number 227, Sergeant!"

"What was it you wanted, Number 227?"

"I wanted to know if it would be all right for me to call my wife on the orderly-room phone."

"Nope." Jacks continued walking. "You goofed up today, Number 227. Ast me tomorrow."

«««»»»

"Mary, Mary, quite contrary . . .
How does your garden grow? . . ."

The steady clip-clop of the paratrooper boots on the macadamized road began to lose its precise rhythm and, particularly in the last platoon, became more perceptibly a disorganized thudding of leather on the hard surface than the machinelike regularity of an airborne jog.

"How does your garden grow? . . ."

Open hands at the trainees' sides pumped mechanically, and the whitish steam from the men's nostrils and mouths merged with the grayness of the morning's mist. Since Clarke was not permitted to move his head while jogging, he found his sight limited to the file of heads and torsos ahead of him and caught glimpses of a blurred world of pines—their tips lost in the early fog—that pointed toward the blanketed sun.

"Mary, Mary, sweet contrary . . .
Pudgy-like and sorta hairy . . ."

The sergeants sang, drawing from the inexhaustible warehouse of marching and jogging chants; the trainees, instructed to sound off when the moment arrived for the response, shouted in choral unison: *"How does your garden grow? . . ."*

Since the last platoon was again losing the rhythmic pattern of its jog, the sergeant in charge began clapping his hands each time a boot of his thudded to the macadamized surface; within three beats, his sound was drowned out by the claps of the five platoons. *Clip-clap, clip-clap, clip-clap . . .*

"Two-mouth Mary, known for sin . . ."

The chant was unfamiliar to the trainees; they followed the chant immediately with a repetition as their response.

"Two-mouth Mary, known for sin . . ."

The pattern of the perfect rhythm had still not been achieved by the five platoons, and for a few seconds, a pause between chants, the trainees clip-clapped until the sergeant who had begun the couplet was satisfied enough to complete the second line.

"One mouth's for Jody an' the other's for gin . . ."

Although feeling the effects of the day's exercise, Barrett Clarke was forced to smile in surprise at the number of songs the sergeants knew. But no sooner had the Jody rhyme been swallowed up by the morning mist than Clarke felt the tentative, sadistic tug of a stitch in his side.

When the sergeants sang a chant, Clarke responded only with the movement of his lips, saving his breath for the long climb on the platoons' return to Jump School. Exhausted as he was by the merciless run—his arms and legs pumping frantically—Clarke coaxed his mind and will to maintain control over a body that was being taxed beyond its limits. But now he wondered if his body had as many restrictions as he had assumed, particularly since the limitations it possessed had been imposed on it by the mind and will, faculties which now struggled as much with themselves as with the body to continue the run.

This is what he had never experienced before: a pain administered by others. It seemed to Clarke that to inflict pain and discipline on oneself was much easier, for a man knew, deep in his will, that he would never hurt himself; but to have pain and discipline inflicted on him by others was unbearable. The man in agony did not know when the pain would end, if it ever would. Pain created its own present. When the terrain was unfamiliar, when he did not know the time the whistle calling for a halt was to be blown, when the pain he felt in his side became more insistent every time a boot hit the ground, then a man seriously considered dropping out of the run and lying on the side of the road, holding his side and pretending he was seriously ill to the five or six sergeants who ran up to him and shouted at him to "stand up like you got a pair an' git down an' give me ten!"

"Ah don't know but it's been said . . ."

The response came loud and clear from the platoon, and Clarke moved his lips as if he were singing along with them. But he felt the intensity of a sergeant's stare, saw the booted feet not involved in platoon ranks, and realized that the training sergeant had been watching him for some time and had not seen breath coming from his mouth.

"Jody's had your wife in bed."

Clarke sang-shouted this time, but it was too late. The NCO, Sergeant Thornhill, yelled at him.

"Git out here, Number 227! Git out here!"

The men on Clarke's right made way for him to leave the moving columns; he extricated himself from the juggernaut as skillfully as possible and stood before the tall sergeant.

"What's the matter, Yankee boy—you think you're too bright for us?"

"No, Sergeant!"

"Sound off like you got a pair!"

"No, Sergeant!"

"Well, Number 227, you *ain't* too bright for us. We're too bright for you. Now lissen to me . . ." The sergeant leaned over to Clarke's ear, and his face became savage. "When Ah stamp mah foot, Ah want you to leap down—*an' Ah said leap*—an' give me ten as fast as you ken. An' Ah want you to sound off after ever'one. An' when you give me one more for the airborne, Ah'm gonna stamp mah foot ag'in, an' Ah want you to leap up—*an' Ah said leap*—an' stand at attention. *Do you hear?"*

"Yes, Sergeant!"

The sergeant stamped his foot. Clarke dropped to the ground, his boots still in the air when his hands were firmly braced on the off-road turf, and began doing push-ups. He got to the sixth when he heard the sergeant's voice booming over him.

"That wazzen fast enough! Start over ag'in!"

He started at one and got to nine before he was stopped. On the third try he got to seven. On the fourth he got to nine again. On the fifth he slowly oozed to the turf after his sixth push-up and struggled on the ground. But his arms would not respond.

"What's the matter, Number 227? Er you tired?"

"No, Sergeant!"

Clarke bounced himself off the ground and precariously attained the starting position for the push-up, but his arms promptly caved in and he landed on the turf again, his stomach and chest by now wet with the dew on the grass.

"On your feet, Number 227!"

Clarke rested his weight on his knees and slowly rose from the ground. His arms were shaking from exhaustion; his shoulders felt numb.

"Stand at attention! Catch up to your platoon!"

Clarke turned to see that the trainees had run about one-third of a mile since he had been pulled out of ranks, and he tried to catch up; but since his recent punishment had left him depleted, all he could do was maintain a pace equal to the platoons'.

Sergeant Thornhill was behind him. "Git movin'," Clarke heard at his back, "git movin'." His heart pounded wildly in his breast. His arms and legs felt drained of all their strength. He had experienced a difficult enough time keeping to the pace the sergeants had set for the platoons while he was in the group, running shoulder to shoulder and boot to boot with the other trainees. Now he was required not only to maintain the established, killing pace but to improve upon it, to surmount what he had considered impossible to equal. *"Git movin'!"*

Clarke's legs moved out uncontrollably. "Move your ass, Yankee boy." And his boots shot out, his arms flailed at his sides, and—no longer thinking about his heart or his lungs or feeling the sadistic pinch at his side—he ran toward the running mass, ran with his eyes focused on the wall of shoulders and hips, on the soles and heels of alternately lifted boots. And in agony and hatred, without one small feeling of gratitude or joy, he caught up to the runners; ran past the ultimate platoon; passed row on row of struggling, agonized trainees; shot beyond the lead row of the last group; covered the ten empty yards that separated his platoon from the final one, the one he had just passed; and eased his pace down to the one he had found impossible to maintain at the beginning of the morning's run.

As he approached the row he had been pulled out of earlier, two men dropped out of the run. They collapsed on the side of the road and rolled on the turf, sucking in air, their faces grimacing at the sky. Clarke stepped into one of the vacant slots and shortstepped for several paces until he assumed the boot patterns of the man ahead of him. He was exhausted, but he had passed the point where exhaustion is reckoned in degrees. He felt no different now, after taxing his body to the point of collapse and frenzy, than he did before being pulled out of the run by the sergeant. But he was too tired to understand the significance of his insight.

The whistle blew for the cessation of double time. The ranks slowed gradually to a march step. There was no time to rest, for the mind knew it would be taxed again. All there was time for was a hiatus in the straining of the will. In a few moments, the mind knew, it would be called upon to resume its agony—not the body's agony, for the body was a tool of the mind, but an agony of the will, which was master of the mind. A will that was not his own but a tool of the sergeants.

Clarke could not think. It appeared that in this moment of agony, of *suffering,* a few curtains had been pulled aside, a vision of something had been presented to him—something frightening, occult, irrational. In agony, in travail: was there, in these states, a secret to be discovered? Before he could pursue his thought, the whistles sounded and the right fists of the sergeants were raised. When they were brought sharply down to the NCOs sides, the run began again.

The first platoon made a right turn to a steep hill, and the other trainees and sergeants followed, bending their upper bodies to help them in managing the climb. The singing stopped. All that Clarke could hear was the disorganized slap of leather on the macadam, the occasional snorts of men behind him, and the short, guttural commands of the sergeants, who never seemed to tire.

Clarke had been told that, on hills, one should never look up to see how much more of a climb there is—particularly when in doing so he would move his head (and that might earn him a few sets of correctional push-ups), he would tire himself by moving his head, and, finally, he would groan with the realization that much more distance remained to be covered than he had anticipated. One foot thrown out at a time: this was all a man in pain could expect from himself. One foot thrown out, and the other, until boot by boot he conquered the hill.

"Ah don't know if this is true . . ."

If the men had not been afraid to be given push-ups, they would have groaned in unison. They responded to the sergeants' chant.

"But Jody's had your sister, too."

The curiosity that Clarke had been fighting grew too powerful for him; he lost control. Pretending to have slipped to the right, struggling to regain the balance he had not lost, he looked avidly up the long, straight column to what his grateful eyes told him was the top of the hill. When he reestablished himself in the column and saw no sergeant bearing down on him, he was doubly pleased.

A whistle blew; the jog was halted. Platoon by platoon, the trainees stopped double-timing and marched until they had all negotiated the narrow U-turn on the road. With the platoons in line again, the inevitable whistles sounded again, the sergeants began shouting again, and the trainees advanced again from a march to the double time, made inhuman now because the platoons were covering a long downhill stretch, because they were on their way back to the Jump School and the promised twenty minutes' break, and because the sergeants were displeased by the conduct of the trainees: quite a few men had dropped out of the run momentarily but had continued the first day's training. This made, according to the NCOs, "ever'thin' sorta sloppy," because many of those who dropped out did not stay out and, therefore, leave the Jump School but remained to take up their time and, conceivably, to fail some other day. The homestretch half would be more punishing, the sergeants' angry voices seemed to threaten.

When all the platoons had made the left turn at the bottom of the hill, the sergeants began the familiar clapping of hands. To Clarke's nervous imagination, however, something ominous sounded in the frantic clip-clap. The place had been raised; they were going to sprint back!

From somewhere in his body he would need to draw reserves. Luckily, the stitch in his side had been worked out by the push-ups the sergeant had made him perform on the turf. But he had no strength; he was now exhausted, from his shoulders down to his toes. The pace the NCOs were demanding of him now, on the return, was one he would not have been able to maintain when they started out in the morning. A man in the platoon's first rank collapsed. One moment his head was bobbing up and down in the column, and the next he was gone, swallowed up by the boots and the scissoring legs of the runners. Agonized to make an extra leap, Barrett Clarke jumped over the man's body as he lay on the macadam. Behind him, Clarke knew, the first-aid jeeps would spurt in and the medics would place him on a stretcher, take him to the hospital, and give him the bad, or good, news: he was out of Jump School.

The breathing lost its steadiness, lost the ease, the machine-like quality, and gained something else—the panicked, disorganized gasping of men who were digging within themselves to find the necessary strength and energy to keep up to the pace demanded of them.

I can't. . . . I can't. . . . . The fleeting words slithered through Clarke's mind, his determination at once faltering, dropping to the point where he thought he could not manage another boot's advance, and then strengthening miraculously, as if whatever forces arrayed within him, which acceded to his requests for more power, teased him before supplying him with what he had asked for. But the pace he followed never faltered, and neither did he, no matter how much he thought he weakened or gained strength. His body was a willing tool, his mind was horrified at what was happening to him—for his will was will-less, having abdicated in favor of the will of the sergeants who led the pace—and Clarke ran on, too busy fighting the desire to stop, too busy fighting the desire not to stop. He had become confused, not remembering at that moment whether he actually wanted to stop or to continue running, so he suspended any abrupt change of policy until his mind cleared for him to make his decision. He ran on, therefore, because he did not remember whether or not he should stop, and his mind took the easier decision to perform the more grueling chore.

A powerfully developed Negro fell out from the third platoon, the platoon ahead of Clarke's. Barrett had met him the previous night—a good-natured man, full of rippling muscles, with a ridged, washboard abdomen. He glanced wild-eyed at the Negro, and then, with a confusion that was soon washed away by pain and exhaustion, went back to deciding whether or not he should drop out of the run. For running at an impossible pace was not a physical exercise, he now understood; it was an exercise of the will. Running, when it passed a certain point in space and time, became a spiritual struggle, not an athletic one, for beyond a certain distance that was covered at a fixed punishing pace, physical activity transcended its material basis and soared into the realm of pain; and at that point powerful and weak men, small and large men, lean and fat men—all were equal, all were equally punished, and only will and determination kept them in the treadmill. This Clarke realized at the point where the small incline rounded off into a quarter mile of plateau and where the short-legged sprint up the gradual incline changed perceptibly to a long-legged sprint across flatland. Two more men dropped out, one next to Clarke, on his right.

"Close it up!" he heard behind him, from a sergeant. *"Close it up!"* And the trainee behind the man who had dropped out at Clarke's right moved up to take his place.

Since the platoons were becoming mobs of men running toward an identical goal, the clip-clap of the sergeants' hands sounded again, forcing the trainees into the unbearable confines of the pace and of their ranks and columns.

"Women. . . ."

This meant they had a quarter-mile sprint to go, a fact that at the beginning of the run would have been pleasing to Clarke but that was now meaningless, because it was not a matter of stopping within a quarter of a mile: it was a question of stopping or not stopping now, here, on this square foot of macadamized surface, on this grease spot on the road—of collapsing near this braked-tire mark.

"Women. . . ."

Over the bobbing shoulders and heads of the runners, Clarke could see the red-white-and-blue military signs of the Airborne School outlined against the neatly landscaped lawns. But in his agony he did not see a clear picture of anything: he saw merely disjointed images that he had seen the day before, that he remembered, but that at this time he did not have the interest in or energy for organizing to resemble what they were, merely what they were to him, to Clarke, who at this moment thought of them simply as the place where he would stop.

A man on the extreme left end, near the curb, collapsed and rolled on the ground. It was comic. Clarke felt like laughing at how the pathetic man had flopped on the turf, not knowing whether to register sexual release or the most severe form of agony, and, as if uncertain what to do, alternated between one and the other.

"Wine. . . ."

"Wine. . . ."

"Whiskey. . . ."

"Whiskey. . . ."

It appeared that they would all make it back to the gates of the School, that those who had continued all this way, at least outwardly showing no more agony than anyone else, would make it safely, in ranks, in step, to the dirt road that led to the Airborne School. But at that moment the sergeants called for an increase in the pace of the run, and four men dropped out, even before the pace was raised. It was as if they had promised themselves, secretly, in the recesses of their own minds, that they would easily manage the run to the School, that they could make the required effort; but then, when they heard that the pace would be raised, they surrendered, as if a nonexistent contract had been violated. At that point, they gave in, not because they were more tired physically, but because they felt that if they continued running, they would violate a trust they had signed with themselves, within themselves, just recently, perhaps at the moment they broke it.

As the platoons galloped toward the dirt road of the Jump School, Clarke could not be certain he was running, because all he felt was a general oppression and not a local one. He may have been dreaming; there was no specific pain in his legs, in his chest, in his shoulder blades. The sergeants were tight-lipped, also, feeling at last the killing pace they had set. They ran alongside the columns, hardly looking at the men to see if anything was wrong, to see if anyone was out of step.

Clarke disciplined his sight. He was not going to look. This was the only way to stop thinking while he ran. Otherwise, he would say to himself, *120 more steps to go; 114 more steps to go; 100 more steps.* And then, when he got to 92, or 84, or 76 more steps to go, he might decide that he thought it was ridiculous to go further, that he did not care if they kicked him out of Jump School, that he was too tired and that was all there was to it. Rather than live through the agony of panicked indecision, he decided not to think, not to decide.

The first platoon had passed the white marker and turned into the road that led to the School—still running, for the fifth platoon had not reached the marker yet. The second platoon passed the white pole. Then the third platoon. Then the fourth. Sergeant Jacks blew on his whistle, and the platoon sergeants gave their men "march" as the fifth platoon passed the white marker. The trainees walked unsteadily into the area of the Airborne School.

The morning had been chilly, but this had been forgotten long ago by Clarke, and at this moment, marching toward the assembly area, he was overheated, the perspiration pouring off him as it would have done in the summer. The sun was high and had dissolved the mist and the excess moisture in the air. The trainees' backs glistened beneath their T-shirts, and, reddened from the cold of the morning, their skins glowed. Clarke stumbled along the dirt road, too tired to make sure he was walking on flat ground, occasionally stubbing his boot toe on a stone; but he continued with the group, recalling how close he had come to dropping out of the run. This would have made one major gig, and he would be permitted two more before being released.

But he was amazed at himself. Why had he continued running? He was not as strong and as physically fit as the Negro and the five to ten other teen-agers in his platoon. Why did they drop out and he stay in? It was inadequate, explaining things the easy way, the logical way, discussing muscle tone, fat, condition of heart, weight in relation to height. If these objective, pragmatic "facts" were brought up, then surely he, Barrett Clarke, would prove to be inferior. But today showed him to be superior (perhaps only for today). At any rate, he had not fallen out; he had continued running when others had collapsed. Something irrational, Clarke decided, occurred in the moment of pain, of stress. What if the application of pain, of suffering, were like the opening of Pandora's box . . . ?

The trainees marched to the area where they had left their neatly folded fatigue jackets, their pistol belts, their combat packs, and their numbered steel helmets. Column by column, the men advanced between the mounds of equipment until the places were taken, except for those of the men who had dropped out and were being given "additional individual attention" on the side of the road. Sergeant Jacks ordered them to put on their fatigue jackets; when they had finished dressing, they were called to attention. Jacks was disturbed at the showing his platoon had made on the run, at the number of men who had dropped out. As is usual in military affairs, the failures of the few were taken out on the successful many. He berated them.

"At least ten men dropped out. *Lemme tell you*"—Jacks' lips were thin and unsmiling—"this here better not happen ag'in, 'cause Ah'll git ever'one of you so-called soljers an' work you down to the bone."

He walked through the platoon rank by rank, and when

he got to Clarke he stopped momentarily. "Well, Number 227, Ah see you dropped your ass out today."

"No, sir!"

"Don't call me *sir!*" Jacks leaned toward Clarke and muttered. "Ah *work* for a livin'!"

"I did not drop out of the run, Sergeant! I was taken out by Sergeant Thornhill, who thought I wasn't singing loud enough."

"Was you singin' loud enough?"

"No, Sergeant!"

Jacks walked down the rank. When he had finished berating the trainees, he had them stand at parade rest until the others, the men who had dropped out of the run, returned to their places. Then he gave them a left face and marched them to the PT pit, where they were to do their exercises, starting with pull-ups on the chinning bars. After that, they filed into the large sawdust-filled area and went through their grueling daily dozen calisthenics: two sergeants carried a large wooden platform into the foreground, and a rugged Negro sergeant climbed to the top of the platform and led the trainees in their exercises.

By this time Clarke and every man in the pit was fighting the second-by-second battle against his wish to stop, second by second defeating the voice that became more insistent with every punishing repetition. When they had finished the half-hour period, they were led back to their equipment; they stood at attention for five minutes, then were released on their twenty-minute break.

CHAPTER 15

Corporal McIlhenny felt dizzy. He had gone to the dispensary on early-morning sick call and stood in line, certain that at any moment he would lose his balance and fall to the floor. A young, rosy-cheeked sergeant in his middle twenties spoke to McIlhenny, but the exhausted corporal could not maintain his part of the conversation and replied with "Yes," "No, really?" and "Well, that's life"; the sergeant misinterpreted this as indifference toward him, turned his back to McIlhenny, and faced the front.

The NCO in charge of the dispensary looked through his

files for McIlhenny's health records, found them, opened the brown folder, glanced to see the examination-date entry, and handed the folder to the corporal.

McIlhenny held the records in his left hand and stared ahead at a patriotic poster which showed a group of ragged colonial soldiers in front of bonfires at Valley Forge. A typewriter clicked away at one of the counters, a group of enlisted Puerto Rican medics stood in one of the doorways talking quietly—white intern jackets covering the small, boyish bodies—and signs on the walls ordered the gazer to THINK or apologized that THIS IS A NONPROFIT ORGANIZATION. WE DIDN'T PLAN IT THAT WAY BUT IT IS.

The line had moved, and McIlhenny stepped up a few paces. When someone tapped him on the shoulder, he turned to see a youthful PFC staring at him with what appeared to be contempt and disbelief. "You dropped your records, buddy," he said, and pointed to the floor. The brown folder had fallen, exposing the white recorded pages, and had been trampled underfoot by men walking through the building. Heel marks were imprinted on the sheets.

McIlhenny looked down to his hand to see that it remained in the same position in which he had left it: the four fingers, bent slightly, met the straightened thumb and formed a triangle. A quarter of an inch separated the flesh of the thumb from that of the index finger. Unnoticed, the brown folder had slipped out of his grip.

McIlhenny stared at his hand for quite some time, then bent over; picked up the folder; dusted it off in an absorbed, listless manner; and placed it under his left arm. He faced the head of the line, neglecting to thank the young man.

"I don't know what's wrong with me, Captain, sir," McIlhenny said when his time came to speak to the doctor. "I've been getting dizzy spells too often lately. I lose my balance and find I must lean against a wall or sit down, my sense of feeling has deteriorated, and sometimes I'm so nervous and shaky that I'm afraid to shave. Of course, I shave, but . . . but . . ." He paused for a moment and looked out of the window at the Division drill team practicing on the parade field. The men's silver helmets appeared flat in the dull morning.

"But *what*, Corporal?" the doctor asked testily.

"But"—McIlhenny replied as if hypnotized—"but, of course . . . I've got to shave." His interest was resumed as he described his symptoms, and McIlhenny began talking about the peculiar things that had happened to him recently. "Take, for example, right now. I was standing in line with my medical records in my left hand when—"

"These records are filthy," the doctor interrupted. "My God, have you no respect for government property? Or, for that matter, for your own health?"

"I was trying to explain that, sir. I was standing in line when a young lad, a good-looking PFC, tapped me on the shoulder . . ."

The doctor stopped listening to McIlhenny and wrote out a slip for the corporal. He opened a few drawers of his desk and brought out a small bottle of green liquid and two plastic vials of pills, one red and the other white. "Take one of these every three hours," the doctor said, pointing to the white pills, "one of these after waking and before going to bed"—he referred to the red pills—"and sip a teaspoon of this"—he picked up the bottle—"before every meal. Present this note to the first sergeant to be taken off details for this week."

The corporal took the medicines and walked out of the building. Alternately, he felt chilled and overheated. He placed the vials of pills in his pocket and carried the bottle in his left hand, concerned that if he approached an officer he would be too long in saluting the gentleman. For reasons like this, he was often on the verge of tears, but he fought these states successfully for most of the day. Whenever possible, he would find an excuse to get away from what he was doing and walk purposefully to the building in which his company was housed; he would stride up the stairs to the platoon bay on the second floor, walk aggressively into the latrine, and, if it was empty, go to his bunk and lie down until he heard footsteps or sounds of conversation and laughter. Then he would stand up quickly and pretend to be clearing out his wall locker.

As he walked along the company streets his eyes traveled to certain objects: the Division Museum, with an airplane used in the Normandy drops outside on the lawn; the unit PX sign, stripped of the allure it gathers when the day begins to ebb; the spire of the Protestant chapel. His gaze fixed on these objects, and it took an exhausting effort of the will to get them unfocused, to get them to view something else. *Perhaps my eyes are tired,* he wondered. *Yes, that must be it.* If he remembered correctly, this always happened when one's eyes were tired. *But why are my eyes tired?* He had been getting much more than his share of sleep, for many times he would return from the mess hall, lie on his bunk, and wake up in a silent barracks, the light still on but all the troopers gone. He would stare at his wristwatch for fully a minute—until he comprehended that it was nine o'clock—rush to dress, and drive to see Esperanza. True, he would return at about midnight, but the hours he had slept in the evening were restful, and he should not be so tired.

No, he realized, the exhaustion was caused by other factors. In the incredible silence of the past weeks, McIlhenny had begun diagnosing his own ills; it was obvious to him that he would know more about himself than any other man, even a doctor, for a physician would know only about drugs, germs, and what he could see under a microscope. He was tired, McIlhenny reasoned, because for the first time in his life his mind had become disorganized and undisciplined. He had fallen abruptly from captain to corporal, and no one could sympathize with him, not even Esperanza, for he had not told her what had happened. Like a meteor, he had fallen silently, and no one had witnessed the glow.

McIlhenny glanced at his wristwatch. Eleven o'clock. He had an hour before chow, and in that hour he could lie down and close his eyes. But he was not hungry. He would sleep. If no one disturbed him, he would sleep until it was time for supper. If one of the NCOs or officers woke him, he would have the note from the doctor to excuse him. He walked into the mess hall, stood in front of the menu chart, and read that they were having steaks that evening. On his way to the stairs he passed through the game room and the reading room into a hall. In a preoccupied manner —as if he had a mission to accomplish—he walked past the orderly room, the company commander's office, up the stairs, into the latrine for a moment (it was empty), and finally into the platoon bay. McIlhenny eased himself into his bunk.

He was committed. Something was happening to him, happening quickly, hardly giving him time to think. It was obviously beyond him, working within the structure of religion, of the Army, and it was something, moreover, that he could not understand. Was there something about the nature of man that neither the Army nor religion could discipline, neither the *Manual of Courts-Martial* nor the Dogmas of the Church expose, give battle to? McIlhenny closed his eyes. A force seemed to impel him toward self-knowledge and destruction. Were these two terms synonymous? He would await this joyless revelation with what approximated joy.

Someone nudged him. He woke up. "Time for chow." It was PFC Lennox, the blond boy who slept in the next bunk. "They're still feeding downstairs if you hurry." McIlhenny stared at the ceiling, motionless. The PFC was undressing for the shower. "We had steaks, but the bastards ruined them." He got his sandals, picked up his towel and toilet kit from the bunk, and began walking toward the latrine. He paused. "Hey, Mac! You up? Chow time!"

"Yes, yes," Corporal McIlhenny said. "I'll just lie here for a moment." His jaw muscle twitched, but his eyes remained focused on the ceiling, almost hypnotized by the glare of the overhead lights. Then he lurched out of his bunk, squeezed into and began lacing his paratroop boots. He spent five aimless minutes searching for his fatigue cap until he found it under the dust cover of his bunk.

He walked slowly toward the PX after dinner, not rushing because by running he would get there sooner and have more time to waste. He walked slowly, consciously, feeling the cold night gradually seeping down his back, chilling his chest; his hands shuddered with the cold, but he took his time crossing the street.

The sign of the PX flickered in the darkness, and when McIlhenny opened the door, the warm blast of air struck him agreeably. Two pinball machines were tinkling away, the jukebox was playing a song concerning eternal love, and the salesgirls were trying to serve the soldiers who wanted to inspect the toasters, the cameras, the radios, and the electric razors. In a darkened corner McIlhenny saw a trooper glancing at the revolving bookstand and decided that he would fritter away an hour or two by thumbing through the pocketbooks, then purchase a magazine or a book to read in the study room of the barracks.

The evening would have to be spent wisely. He must apportion time carefully so that at the moment he accomplished what he wanted to do, it would be time for sleep. If he completed too soon the regime he was now establishing, the temptation would arise for him to visit Esperanza, and once he found himself in her cabin, he would be involved again in what he wanted to terminate. Too often he had felt committed to go to her cabin because he knew that if he spent an evening alone he would feel vaguely uneasy, guilty of some stupid reserve. But now he realized that she could offer him nothing, that she could, in fact, take away what he treasured most: his loneliness and the integrity of his thoughts. He wanted no more intrusions, for what he was thinking and where he was going were more important and interesting to him than anything she could say or do.

The pocketbooks were stacked six deep in their wire stalls; after looking at the titles on his side, he gave the revolving rack a spin. A book that had been dislodged from its wire stall fell to the floor, and McIlhenny stooped to pick it up. When he straightened, he saw Barrett Clarke looking at him. McIlhenny flushed and turned abruptly, his hand shaking so violently that he dropped the book again.

Where could he go to hide? The PX was as well lighted and open as an amphitheater. It would not do for him to run away. He stared at a sign above the cigarette counter which promised that one would be happy if he smoked a certain cigarette and, behind him, heard the squeaking of the rack. He would pretend that he had noticed no one, turn to the rack, replace the fallen book, and walk to the counter for a pack of razor blades. Then, slowly, inconspicuously, he would walk out of the PX and . . . where? Where? Back to the barracks to lie on his bunk and stare at the ceiling? To Esperanza's, where he would perform erotic motions that day by day were becoming mechanical? And afterward stare at *her* ceiling?

"Sir," McIlhenny heard behind him. "Sir, I wonder . . ."

"Don't call me sir. I'm not an officer anymore." McIlhenny, staring at the tobacco counter, had not turned.

"I know that. We all know that back at the company. I wonder if I might talk to you for a moment?"

A great pain seemed to grasp McIlhenny at the shoulder blades and travel toward the back of his head; his nerve edges were raw, throbbing with the tension he was undergoing. "I'm not the man I was, Clarke. I'm not well."

"Would you like to sit down, sir? I'll get two beers."

McIlhenny said nothing. He turned gradually and looked at Clarke. He accepted the inevitable. "Yes," he said. "Thank you. I think I will."

He sat at a table that was full of beer cans piled up in a pyramid. Since the top of the table was wet, he rested his elbows in his lap. The world was on a string for someone in the jukebox, and the tinkling of the pinball machine counterpointed the joy in life felt by the singer. A few troopers at the next table burst out in laughter at something a sergeant said, and beyond them an old NCO was sitting hunched over a table talking to three colored PFCs. Clarke brought two cans of beer and set one in front of McIlhenny.

"I'm glad I saw you, sir. There are a few things I want to tell you—things I've wanted to tell you all along."

McIlhenny's heart beat faster. He knew what was coming: the insults, the personal attacks, the EM bitchings. He could not bear to listen, for his sanity was at stake.

"I'd rather not hear, Clarke. If you don't mind. I've got quite a few things to do this evening."

"I want to tell you, sir, that I've always respected you, as a man and as a soldier. That, as far as I was concerned, you were one of the few men in the United States Army I respected. At first I may have disliked you, but later I saw you as a man true to your principles. I may not have agreed with those principles, but I respected the way you lived and the way you fulfilled those principles."

McIlhenny said nothing for a moment. He found it difficult to concentrate with the noise in the PX. He felt a twitch across his eyebrow and raised his hand to rub it. "Clarke . . . I don't believe in my principles any longer." He paused, as if he had something to add, but did not continue.

"If that's the case, what you believe in now," Clarke continued, "is truer than what you believed in then."

McIlhenny felt his eyes burn and tried to crush a sob that roared through him. "Is it?" he managed to ask. "Is it more true—or is it more reasonable to me in my predicament?"

"Only you would be man enough to ask that question."

McIlhenny stared at the wet tabletop; the pyramid of beer cans rose to its pinnacle beside him.

"And I want to tell you something else, sir. What they have done to you I'll never forget. It was cruel. It was everything we in America are supposed to be against. In knowing you and in learning of your past weeks, I've found out where I stand." There was a pause. "I don't believe in my principles any longer, either. And what I don't believe in now is truer than what I believed in then. My life, too, is a shambles, sir. But I'm only twenty-four years old. My marriage is breaking up. I've been calling my wife for three evenings and there's been no answer. I can't return to my family. Three years ago I had everything and now I have nothing. Nothing. But I'm closer to what might be considered truth now—at least a personal truth, about myself—than I was then."

McIlhenny's head was stooped, but as he spoke he raised it gradually until he faced Clarke. "You're a young man yet. Young men always think their personalities are sacred and important. Be careful that life does not mangle you. Be careful not to weaken. Keep your enthusiasm for as long as you can, because it will soon be eroded. It will soon be destroyed." He paused, then shook his head angrily. "No . . . no . . . I was about to weaken and depend on folk wisdom by saying that life is a mess. But it isn't. Our lives are messes because we don't search for truth as much as we think we do. We think we're making the decisions and never realize they're made for us." He sipped his beer. "I'm an unhappy man, Clarke—unhappy because I can see something else coming, something frightening, something I've feared all my life. And I'm too old to fight it. I should be young now. I should be fearless. I should have my faith now. But"—he squinted at Clarke and raised his hands in frustration—"but when I need all my weapons, I'm naked. I've nothing."

He frowned and stared at his beer can. "And it's not only in my mind. It's outside, too. I've feared it as long as I've been old enough to think consistently. I don't know what it is. All I know is that I'm not strong enough to fight it. I see an Armageddon. And whatever this Armageddon is, it is something horrible and frightening." He did not add that it was, also, somehow reassuring.

"I've lost my faith, Clarke. I've lost it completely. And yet, the peculiar thing is that I've begun thinking almost constantly in Biblical terms. Armageddon, for instance. My faith blew up in my face, and, blinded, I find myself groping around on my hands and knees trying to salvage something, trying to locate a few of the pieces. I can't go back. I'm through forever. But the strange thing is"—he laughed weakly—"the strange thing is . . . I'm always thinking about Christ."

McIlhenny paused for a moment and sipped his beer. "I do nothing now but what I'm ordered to do. I am the ideal soldier. I never initiate anything. There is something like a mist about me. The only things that break through it are sounds coming from officers and NCOs of a higher rank. I do what these sounds say, and then the mist gathers again." He glanced at Clarke quickly, fixed him with a deep stare, then lowered his eyes again. "I had been standing on sand all my life, thinking it was rock, substantial and broad. But it was sand. A few large waves came and shook my foundations. I imagine those waves were the waves of truth, but, whatever they were, they leveled me." He took the can and emptied it. "But I rarely think back. I think of myself—pityingly, I guess—and then I think of the future. Something is coming, Clarke; something more. I see anguish, dark nights, terror, flares, death. It's not pretty, but I can't convince myself that it won't happen. I can't convince myself that I'm going mad, because it would be good to know that it won't happen that way, that I'm just sick, and that nothing horrible will happen to other people." But he disguised the fact that he looked forward to it, for it would mean the end.

McIlhenny stood up. "I must go now. I'm sorry to hear that things aren't going too well with you and your wife. Have you separated?"

"No, sir." Clarke paused. "I'm here in the Division for a few weeks . . . going to Jump School." He mumbled the next sentence quickly. "We spoke about that a while back. . . . A year ago, sir, I would not have understood what you meant by sand and rock, but now I do. So much in life, sir, appears to be rock but turns out sand when you lean against it, when you need it. It looks substantial and solid from a distance, but all you have to do is test it to learn that it's papier-mâché rock."

"And it would be too much to ask"—McIlhenny continued Clarke's thought—"that these rocks remain untested. But they never are. Sooner or later, something happens. Someone decides to test them, and when you need them most, they crumble. It's too much to ask that life be livable. We should expect the worst all the time."

The two men began walking toward the PX door, passing pyramids of beer cans, garbage cans full of napkins, crushed cigarette packs, and empty soda bottles. On the walk leading to the company street, Clarke paused.

"I hope to see you again, sir, and I hope your fears of the future don't materialize." He held his hand out.

McIlhenny took the outstretched hand. "Thank you. Good luck to you." A slight smile played upon his lips. "Do you know—I've just had the first whimsical thought in weeks." His smile grew wider, and that moment a twitch crossed his eyebrow. He lifted a hand to rub it. "Don't take any papier-mâché rocks," he said, and walked off.

CHAPTER 16

Damianos was bareheaded. A car coat, tightly belted at the waist, stretched around his great bulk as he cruised along the darkened streets of Von Steuben. It was midnight; the bell of the City Hall struck twelve times as he paused briefly at a men's clothing store. He pretended an interest in winter fashions, while actually trying to determine—in the windowpane's reflection—the precise door the woman he had been following would open. There was something familiar about her, from the extraordinary black stockings and the plaid skirt to the quick, nervous step. No decent girl would be out alone on a night like this—not on payday night. She was too pretty to be unattached. If married, where was her husband? And if he was at home, what kind of man would let his wife walk in the streets tonight, or any night?

Ordinarily, Von Steuben was not a stroller's town. People walked to get somewhere, not for the pleasure of walking. There was nothing to see. Not even women. The shapely legs one usually saw belonged to overweight or underweight bodies. When, by the miracle of immigration or native American mobility, the legs seemed interesting to a man of Damianos' taste and the bodies appeared attractively lithe or buxom or well-proportioned or languidly slender, then the faces were overly painted or hatchetlike or covered with small pimples of suspect origin. Besides, since he had somewhere to go, the interest he took in women who walked through the Von Steuben streets, waited placidly for traffic lights to change, or swung their closed knees outward prior to stepping out of a parked car—betraying in the process a one-inch strip of flesh above the knees—was academic, a series of fragmented, beguiling tableaux reminding him of his basically excitable and acquisitive nature and not necessarily signals that triggered the expensive and time-consuming process of the erotic chase. After all, why did men stroll in cities?

But Damianos was puzzled. Something curious was occurring to him. As he grew older, he found himself reaching the point where he considered women not as casual lovers, conspirators in a game played when the lights were out, but as partners, as companions in a much more significant and disquieting game. He had not reached this stage abruptly; it was a gradual evolution, with him not seeking *the* partner but becoming convinced eventually that the casual women were somehow inadequate. Marriage had quite often appeared to him as the simplest, most obvious conclusion, but very early he had realized that a simple vow, proclaimed with honesty and complete good intention, did not control a man's hidden desires, desires that blossomed like secretive tropical flowers, in the night. He had seen too many couples who knew a great deal about life, who were mature, who loved one another, gradually break up, go their separate ways, leaving two or three children to make a confused and weary adjustment to legal and, occasionally, good-natured orphanage and to the realization that the warmth and love they knew with their parents was diluted when another man took their mother to wife and another woman replaced their mother in their father's home. He also had seen marriage ceremonies performed, to be dissolved later, and had read in newspapers of people marrying one another, explained by phrases like "she for the second, he for the fourth." He had been involved in a wedding he could not remember, a ceremony where he conceivably had said that he would love and honor a woman he did not know, until death did them part.

But something else was involved. Damianos was thirty-four years old: he had seen too many men who remained single develop peculiarities, idiosyncrasies, become eccentric because they lived alone and kept the daily heartaches and frustrations to themselves.

And he loved children, even though he fully realized that they were occasionally stupid, obstinate, and superficial. He had watched many harried mothers beseeching their sons or daughters to stop playing with toys in department stores and follow them; he had seen families eating in restaurants and heard silverware clatter to the floor, heard wails from unreasonable and unreasoning creatures shattering the quiet of a dining room, seen the besmirched faces of infants at the table, and turned to his own plate with a curious feeling of hollowness, of incompleteness, gnawing at him.

His freedom as a single man had begun to seem imprisoning. He had the freedom to read in his cadre room at night when the barracks were empty; he had the freedom to eat with the other NCOs in the mess hall; he had the freedom to wander from tavern to tavern every evening; he had the freedom, in principle, to sleep with any woman he possibly could without helping to support her, without even talking to her for more than half an hour. And yet, for some mysterious, atavistic reason, he felt robbed of something.

The streets were still crowded with troopers, although Damianos was certain that the trailer camps lining Mosby Boulevard, which linked Fort Mosby with Von Steuben, were all occupied by now. What was Esperanza doing? Should he visit her? No, it was too late. Has she found someone to support her yet? It need not be one man, Damianos knew, for she may have decided to involve herself in the sociological pattern of the area, where it was not unknown that a woman, legally unattached, would keep a trailer or cabin, acting, for all purposes, married to not one man but several, with each soldier aiding in her support and spending certain predetermined evenings with her. After all, community living of this sort was necessary in the unnatural conditions of existence on an army base and attested to the American instinct for improvisation and the desire for a temporary permanence.

Fist fights and riots in Combat Alley, the familiar name for the street that ran past the Green Light to the City Hall, were also inevitable, as were the whistles and billy clubs of the MPs. Damianos was on Combat Alley now, having just rounded the City Hall corner. There was, as he expected, a noisy crowd in front of the Green Light. Nothing unusual, though, for as many as two hundred men had fought with bare fists for what had turned out to be a rather obscure reason: a soldier in one battle group had possibly said something offensive about another unit, a fight had begun, and soon the street had been crowded with clusters of battlers. Von Steuben was a paratroopers' town, after all. The soldiers, out in the fields for weeks, were kept from the sweetening influence of the civilization for which they were trained to fight, and it should not have been surprising that at a certain point in a soldier's training, when he had become confused as to who was his enemy, he would soon grasp the truth that any man who was not himself could be a potential threat.

Glancing ahead now, Damianos realized that the crowd was noisier than before. He recognized at once the sounds of a large, well-represented fist fight. Muttering a curse under his breath, he seriously considered using the street parallel to Combat Alley and approaching the Green Light from the rear when he noticed that the mob surged toward his tavern. He hesitated briefly, then lengthened his stride, and took the most direct route—through the fighting mob.

Since there were no flashing red lights on the streets, Damianos reasoned that neither the police nor the MPs had arrived. When he heard the sudden, sharp crash of glass—a large pane had been broken—he began running, and by the time he elbowed several paratroopers out of his way, Damianos saw the swaying billy clubs of the four MPs who had had the misfortune to be where they were supposed to be at the proper time. He stopped jogging when he saw that the windowpane did not belong to the Green Light. After shouldering his way through the mob, the sergeant opened the door to see a couple of troopers fighting near the bar. About five tables had been overturned in the battle. Broken beer bottles and glasses lay about, ground to dust under the shoes of the combatants. Pale from fright, Sophie stared at the fighters from the corner where she stood.

Damianos took off his car coat, folded it neatly, laid it on the bar, and walked over to the men, who were now wrestling on the floor. He studied them for a moment, wondering how to get them to stop without having his clothes torn or soiled. Methodically, he approached the pair and jumped on the one who was on top, landing on the man's back with two heavy knees. The top man twisted around desperately, trying to see who had jumped on him, but Damianos calmed him somewhat by squeezing his face with a calloused hand.

"I'll give you mother-humpers thirty seconds to get out of here. If you ain't out by then, I'll rip your guts out."

He stood up and waited. The top man rose to his feet swinging and went down again promptly, holding his chest in agony with both hands. Since the bottom man had the worst of the battle and could not rise of his own volition, Damianos reached down, helped him to his feet, and threw him out of the tavern. He went over to the other man, now gasping for breath, slapped him a few times in an authoritative manner, dragged him to the sidewalk, and locked the door.

"How's everything otherwise, Sophie?"

A nervous smile appeared on her face as she left the corner and approached him. "I didn't want to use the gun, Gus. I know you told me to, but there'd be too much trouble. They broke a few chairs, and no more than ten glasses, but outside of that, no real damage was done." She stood close to him and looked at Damianos carefully. "You aren't even breathing hard."

"What the hell did I do?" He rested a hand on her shoulder. "Have much trouble yesterday?"

"No, they fought down the street last night. Near the barbecue place." She took off her apron. "There were a few police cars in front . . . and the Provost Marshal's sedan."

"How was business?"

"Pretty good. Want to go over the books?"

"Later on," Damianos said. "Let's get the man in here right now to clean the place up."

Sophie walked back to the kitchen quickly and summoned the dishwasher into the bar. After that, she and Damianos sat together in a booth in the rear of the tavern, turned on an overhead lamp, and began going over the bills they had gathered and the daily receipts. Damianos decided that something would have to be done about the drop in business that became obvious on the third Monday of each month and threatened the tavern's profits a week before the next month's payday.

"What about making those days special days? We can knock five cents off each stein of draft beer and a dime off the cheeseburgers or give them a side order of shoestring French fries with each sandwich—something, anything, just so we get this third and fourth week up enough to pay for the expenses."

"Whatever you want, Gus." She leaned back and looked at him steadily. "If you want the specials, I'll get Harry to make signs for the windows."

"OK," Damianos said; "that's a good idea. Tell him to make cheeseburgers thirty-five cents each with a side order of potatoes, a stein of beer twenty-five cents. Tell him to ignore bottle beer. It'll be the same . . . and . . . and"—he snapped his fingers, trying to remember something he wanted to add—"tell him that the Texas franks are the same, twenty-five cents, but that with an order of two it'll be forty cents, side order of French fries ten cents extra." Sophie was writing these details down, and her lustrous blond hair was tumbling onto the table as she bent over the writing pad. Damianos reached over and touched it. "Watch your hair, Sophie. Keep it away from some of the machines in back." She looked up at him and smiled, then returned to her writing. "What's the matter? Why are you so close to the table? Are you getting eyestrain?"

"I guess so. My eyes water occasionally."

"Maybe you need glasses.'" He pulled a cigarette out of his shirt pocket and groped for his lighter before he realized that he had left it in his car coat. "Why don't you have a doctor give your eyes a checkup?" he shouted from the bar as he lighted his cigarette.

When Damianos returned to the booth, he saw that Sophie was smiling. "What's so funny?"

"I do need glasses, Gus, and I went to the doctor." She reached into the side pocket of her white apron and pulled out a pair of glasses.

"Why in hell ain't you been wearing them? What's the use

of buying a pair of goggles when you never wear them?"

"I wear them, Gus."

"I never *see* you wear them."

She nodded her head and smiled, a smile that would have been tender had it not been mixed with embarrassment. "That's the idea."

"Why don't you want me to see you wearing glasses?" He leaned over the table and rested his elbows on the top. The table creaked. "What kind of game is this?"

"I thought you would think I looked ugly with them on." Her blue eyes seemed to glisten. "You would say to your friends: 'Hell, I don't wanna go to the Green Light. I know a woman there who wears goggles. Let's go somewhere else.' "

Damianos' eyes narrowed. "I would not say 'I know a woman there.' I would say: 'Go where you wanna go; I'm going to *my* place, the Green Light, and see *my* woman, and I don't give a good goddamn what she wears.' That's what I'd say!" He slid out of the booth and stood up. "You wanna beer and a sandwich?"

Sophie nodded. When Damianos returned from the kitchen with the food and drinks, he saw that Sophie was wiping her eyes with a handkerchief.

"Put your glasses on, for Christ's sake," he said wearily. "Let's eat and go upstairs."

Sophie folded the books shut and pushed them out of the way, under the record selector. She faced down, put on her glasses, and raised her head to look at Damianos.

"You look damn good," he said. "They frame your face. They're dark, your hair is blond, and your face is light. You look damn good." He sipped his beer, still looking at her closely. He thought: *What's to become of her?* He cleared his throat. "I don't see why you're ashamed of them. You should wear them all the time."

She smiled again, and the silent tears rolled down her cheeks.

"What the hell are you crying for?"

She shrugged her shoulders.

"Damn it. I'll never understand you! Why should you be crying just 'cause you have to wear glasses? It's so silly." He reached over and covered her hand. Usually he was not so tender with her, but her tears and her gentleness had made him go against his principles. "Come on; eat a little." He poured beer for her. "Come on."

She nibbled at the sandwich while he told her of the pre-maneuver phase from which he had just returned. Something interesting had happened to the team on the return from Crossroads Drop Zone. The men were marching to the assembly area where they were to meet the Deuce-and-a-Half that would return them to Fort Mosby. He consciously ignored the doe he had killed on that misty morning. It seems that while he and his team were marching in a deep pine forest over which towered a great cliff, the wind blowing along the Appalachian range rushed into a small cave hidden among some boulders. It made an eerie, awesome noise, much deeper and steadier than the cry of a wolf or a coyote. The moan—for that is how the soldiers thought of it at first—was a dreadful sound, and everyone in the team agreed that it reminded him of the moans he had heard from men wounded in battle just before they were given needles to quiet them. A lonely, pitiful sound, it chilled them all.

It was peculiar, Damianos said, how, as tired as they were, the men insisted on finding the source of the moan before continuing their trek to the assembly area. Finally, one of the team members scaled an almost vertical wall of the cliff and located the cave. He probed about in the cavern and found a few small bones. The place looked as if it had been used by an animal—a large one if the feces they found on the floor were any indication, perhaps even a mountain lion. Damianos had heard there were a few in the area, although he had never seen one and personally considered that all the large cats were to be found in the west. It was interesting, Damianos said; many interesting things had happened to him on that mission. Peculiar things. He stared at the wall behind Sophie.

After clearing the booth, Sophie checked the register, leaving a hundred dollars in the till for the morning, tallied up the day's receipts, and put the rest in the petty-cash box and locked it. Damianos had come around to her while she was working on the register and, noticing that the tape was running out, had replaced the used spool with a new one. When they had finished the last-minute chores, they checked the bar to see that everything was in place—the door locked, the shades drawn—then left by way of the kitchen and walked up the stairs to Sophie's rooms.

He watched her carefully as she began putting her apartment in order. Evidently she had taken an afternoon nap and overslept. Realizing Sophie's embarrassment at having him witness the disorder of her rooms, Damianos pretended an interest in a photo magazine, glancing at her occasionally as she bent over to pick up a shoe, to give the coffee table a quick dusting, and to straighten up the newspapers she had read and left on a chair.

What will become of her? he wondered. Tomorrow they would see a lawyer. At least she would have the tavern. He would have nothing. Like a vagrant wind, he would have swept over the earth and perished without leaving an image of himself—only the trunks that contained his past.

When Sophie walked into the bedroom and closed the door, he turned on the record player he had bought for her. As he looked through her record collection, the door opened and Sophie emerged quickly, walking into the kitchen to begin the dishes. The bed had been made. She cleared the table and bent over to empty the pail next to the sink.

Nice legs, he thought. Well tapered and sturdy, her limbs moved her body gracefully, and his furtive eyes followed her movements with the same excited interest with which they had studied the women he had seen on his many strolls. There was a strangeness in every woman, a mystery that could never be understood, even by herself. *Did they fear death?* They spoke of it, certainly, but never with the heavy pauses, never with the wonder or the terror that men possessed of death.

Damianos selected a record and placed it on the turntable. He had stopped buying records for her since she let him know that she appreciated the gesture more than the music he chose. His taste, he had learned, was unbelievably bad, for he bought only what he liked and—since what he liked changed when he heard something new, and since he soon became bored with what he had liked, having played it so often—had hundreds of records lying about that had proved to be wastes of money. It was much wiser to give Sophie the money to buy the music she wanted. When the playing arm alighted on the record, Damianos walked into the kitchen to talk to Sophie.

"Don't come in, Gus; the kitchen is a mess."

"So what? You're cleaning it up, ain't you? Can't I watch you dry the dishes?"

"I'll be right out." She turned to him. "I feel embarrassed that the place looks so bad. I overslept and . . ."

"OK, OK, I'll get out of your kitchen. I'll make a couple drinks." He leaned against the doorjamb. "I'm gonna need ice cubes and you won't let me in your kitchen. How am I gonna work that?"

"Here"—Sophie walked to the refrigerator and opened the door—"I'll get you the tray."

As Damianos pried open the divider in the tray and dropped the cubes into an earthenware bowl, he thought he detected a smothered sob, but when he looked he saw that Sophie was rinsing off the dishes and facing the wall. It must have been the rushing of the tap water. He busied himself with his own concerns, getting two old-fashioned glasses, dropping ice cubes in them, and pouring a respectable amount of bourbon in the glasses. He heard another sob. When he turned questioningly toward the sink and Sophie again, he saw her dabbing her eyes with a napkin.

"What's the matter?" He walked up to her quickly and turned her around. "Are you crying again?" Her face was streaked with tears. "What the hell is going on, Sophie? Are you sick? What is it?" He pulled her to him and caressed her soft back. "It ain't healthy to be crying all the time. Are you worried about something?"

"Yes, Gus," she said simply. "I didn't want to tell you. I wanted to keep it from you." She paused. "I'm pregnant, Gus."

And, unthinkingly, Damianos asked: "Me?"

She pulled away from him, her face red with embarrassment and affront. Just as her face was beginning to harden into anger and hatred, she sobbed again. "Since I met you, Gus, I haven't let another man touch me."

"I'm sorry," he said quietly. "I wasn't thinking."

But she kept her distance. "What have you thought of me all this time to ask something like that?"

Damianos, rather than continue mumbling "I'm sorry," said nothing—stared at her, embarrassed more than she was. What she had done she did out of what he knew was love, while what he had asked proved him to be base. *She is proud,* he thought, secretly grateful; *a proud, fine woman.*

"I didn't want to tell you, but I did tell you. I want you to know that you don't owe me anything."

He pointed to the parlor where they would sit and talk. After taking the two glasses in one hand, he turned off the kitchen light with the other and followed Sophie into the carpeted room. She lowered the volume of the record player and they sat down on the divan.

"I could go away and have the baby. Atlanta, Washington, Chicago, Baltimore, New York—it doesn't matter. I can leave when I'm about five or six months gone and come back after everything. I could put the baby up for adoption. That's one solution."

Damianos remained silent, his face cradled in his hands,

his elbows on his knees. He was motionless, listening as Sophie enumerated the paths open to them. Evidently she had given the problem a great deal of thought, for she presented each possibility with the force of a philosopher discussing the alternatives of a dilemma.

"I could have an abortion and solve the problem quickly. There is some risk, but I'm willing to take it if you want it that way." She paused and looked at Damianos, who continued to stare at the wall opposite him. "Finally, I could have the child, with you paying the hospital and doctor's expenses, and keep it while you help me in the support."

She stopped. She had obviously said all she was to say; now it was up to him. Damianos turned to her slowly. "There's another solution that I'm wondering why you didn't bring up. I could marry you."

"That's no solution, Gus."

"What do you mean?" This had come out louder than he expected.

"I'm afraid of you, Gus. You're a good man . . . but . . . but I don't think you are the type to be a husband. You accept responsibilities, but you have a way of not making them very binding on you."

Damianos was staring at her. "What do you mean, Sophie?"

"Well, you gave me the money to run this place, didn't you?" She interlaced her fingers and rested her hands on her abdomen. "The bar is in your name and I run it for you. For some reason, now, you want to be partners in the tavern. I don't understand you. Men are too mysterious for me. I was your friend for a year before you got the idea of doing this. Right? You were paying for my apartment two months after you met me. Yet, in all the time I've known you, you've never come to see me more than three days in a row. It's as if you're afraid of me. Afraid for your freedom. Oh . . . you've got good excuses. You're always doing something different. But I can never expect you any night and be sure you'll come."

"I'm a soldier. My time's never my own, that's all."

"You're not out in the field all the time."

"Yes, but I don't know when I'll get a detail. You can't tell those things ahead of time."

"I don't want to argue, Gus. I just wanted to tell you what I thought. You're independent. That's good. That's why I like you. But you're too independent to be a husband. When people marry, they give up some of their freedom."

"What kind of freedom do people have?" he asked.

Sophie stared at him. "I don't understand."

"Forget it. I was thinking about something else." He paced back and forth across the room. "When did you know about this?"

"Two weeks ago."

"And you're only telling me now?" His hands fisted in anger.

"I haven't seen you in two weeks," Sophie replied quietly.

Damianos continued pacing.

"You don't have to make up your mind now." She touched her abdomen. "We have a few months yet. Then I'll be getting pretty big and I'll have to go away."

What had begun as great freedom with Sophie had turned out to be responsibility, for when he first met her, the possibility of anything serious occurring was not considered. The two of them merely drifted into a peaceful life together—two people who seemed to know rather well what they wanted. Sophie was a waitress at the time, recently divorced from a GI husband who had married her in Germany and she was trying to earn enough money to go to Milwaukee, where she thought she had a relative. Damianos had arrived from the Orient that week, had gone into the restaurant where Sophie worked, and had talked to her. Two months later they were living together. But, somehow, the fact of living together seemed different to Sophie and Damianos, for it was not merely a physical attraction that drew the two together: each had something the other needed. Damianos had strength, and Sophie needed strength; she needed someone who would permit her to feel protected, befriended in a peculiar and occasionally frightening environment. And Sophie provided him with a love and respect which he knew was constant: when the foundations of strength he possessed or thought he possessed would weaken, he could always retreat into her embrace, pretending to himself that he merely wanted her body and the release it offered him, and could find what he really wanted—the love and respect he was certain he did not need.

And life had been good for both. There were no serious disputes; each felt perfectly free toward the other. Damianos, in particular, made a cult of his freedom by not always going to the Green Light, even though he wanted to go, so that Sophie would not learn to expect him. And now this had to happen. A mistake, an oversight, and the world the two had skillfully and carefully built was altered. The child growing in Sophie's womb could not be ignored. *What's to become of her?* he wondered. *What's to become of me?*

Killing the fetus was out of the question; it would be dangerous to Sophie, and any risk for her was to be avoided. The very idea of killing a not-yet-human being in someone's body was repugnant to him. Giving the baby to an orphanage was also out of the question, for the child would be a Damianos, and to grow up under the impersonal care of social workers or nuns was something no Damianos would do. No, he would refuse to think about the first two possibilities. Because he was unfree, Damianos treasured the life of others (though not necessarily his own), and because he was limited, he disliked the idea of limitation for others.

He could pay the hospital expenses for Sophie and then support the child until it was eighteen years old. But that would be quite a jolt to his salary, for he would be getting no allowances from the Army and the child would have to be born in an expensive civilian hospital. Or he could marry Sophie . . .

He drank. If the world was strange and confusing, might a man not attain clarity while senseless?

"I'm going to bed, Gus."

He stood up in his stupor and followed her across a heaving, chaotic room. Evading the door, he crashed into the darkened bedroom, reached out for the swirling bedstead, and collapsed on the mattress. Sophie pulled off his shoes and socks and then unbuttoned his shirt. The night was chilly. A wave threatened to cover his face, but it was merely a blanket, and its softness was tucked under his chin.

"Forget about it tonight, Gus. Think about it tomorrow. In the daylight."

Yes, the sun would rise again tomorrow, obscuring everything. As usual. He would be sober, but uncertain, confused, fearful of death, jealous of the freedom he did not have, encountering a borrowed face, his only for a lifetime, convinced by the deceiving sun that what he saw was himself and not an ancestral mask.

"Marry me, Sophie," he said. "I want the kid."

For the child would be another self.

He placed his hand on her abdomen. "It was something I had to do, anyhow." *Had to do,* he thought; *had to do.* Mysterious world, that a man would fear what he needed, find freedom in necessity, and encounter himself within another.

Her hand covered his.

CHAPTER 17

The terror of the five-mile run had become commonplace, merely the first obstacle to be met in a long day. Other obstacles lurked behind the ten o'clock barrier. Training periods had resolved themselves into two-hour blocks, with the first block composed of the five-mile run and the physical training and the second, after the long break, devoted to one of five lessons. This completed the morning's schedule. Two lesson blocks in the afternoon brought the day's training to a close.

During the midmorning break the trainees were permitted to rest in an area divorced from the apparatus of the school under bare deciduous trees. There the trainees sat on long benches until they saw the senior NCO of the Jump School approach a white line separating the "campus" proper from the rest area. This, the mere approach, was the signal for the trainees to mass on another white line, which separated the rest area from the middle ground—the no-man's-land between campus and rest area.

The men in charge of the trainees, trainees themselves but company-grade officers and NCOs, would see the head NCO walking from the sergeant's building to the white line and call the trainees to get up from the benches and mass at the white line. Following the head NCO, the other instructors would walk to their positions in the open plaza between the apparatus and stand there, waiting. The whistle would blow, shrill in the winter gray, and the trainees would roar "airborne-airborne-airborne-airborne" and sprint the seventy yards from the rest area to their platoon positions.

Occasionally they would perform this important function impressively. More often, however, they would look "lazy an' sloppy." Then, in keeping with Jump School policy, they would be ordered to return to the rest area, stand massed at the white line—the dust kicked up by the two-way stampede circulating through them—and wait for the sergeant to raise the whistle to his lips and blow it. Shouting "airborne-airborne-airborne-airborne" again, they would sprint the seventy yards to their platoon positions, again to learn that they were embarrassing their cadre—and, in particular, the head NCO—with their undisciplined, careless attitude toward the instruction. They would be given correctional push-ups to perform, and many trainees, still stiff from the calisthenics they had struggled through less than thirty minutes before, would turn in a disturbingly poor performance. These men would be assigned additional individual attention until they either collapsed to the hard-packed soil in exhaustion or performed satisfactorily what was asked of them by the cadre.

Such close attention usually came about when—after eight training days—there were still too many trainees. Clarke had arrived at four possible interpretations: the course of instruction was easier in this particular cycle (this did not appear reasonable); the men as a group were much more tenacious and toughened than those in the other cycles (the cadre would unanimously declare this a lie); additional airplanes would need to be ordered from Rickenbacker Air Force Base to be filled by a disconcertingly large graduating class (out of the question now, since the premaneuver phases of Razor Blade were already under way); or, finally, the acme in physical and mental exhaustion had not been reached, the men had not been fully tested, had not been badgered to the point where they lost their ability to control forces within them that were definitely antidiscipline, forces that might erupt at another point, a point where it would be necessary for everyone to be subservient, follow orders, and jump out of an airplane.

To Clarke this was the most logical answer, for the cadre would know that most men can control their tempers, particularly when they have vowed to themselves that they would do so for a variety of "goods": for a parachutist's badge; for a pair of paratroop boots; for an overseas cap emblem, with the fused glider and blossomed canopy; for a manly tattoo reading "airborne," unmistakable at a beach; for fifty-five dollars a month hazardous-duty pay; or for a chance to strut in Von Steuben. The volunteers, all men who had made a conscious decision, could bear punishment, could control their anger to a certain point, to the point at which they could justify "correctional measures" and understand the necessity for seemingly unnecessary discipline. However, when they reached the point at which the sergeants would appear to them as devils enjoying the torture they administered, when it would be important to stop doing push-ups, tell the sergeants to go fuck themselves, try to punch an NCO, fall out of a run, refuse to do an exercise—more important to do these things than it was to wear the paratroop boots, have the tattoo, and spend the fifty-five dollars—then that, Clarke knew, was the point beyond which the Jump School cadre had not pushed the trainees. For a man who could control his temper was valuable in the Army, but more important was the man who did not remember he had a temper when a sergeant spoke to him; when the screaming airborne door was open; when the pockets of white fluffy clouds obscured the vague outlines of a dull, misty earth; and when the hollowness of the open door was to be filled by the darkened bulk of the disciplined soldier.

Clarke stood at attention in platoon formation. The run was acceptable for the other platoons; Sergeant Jacks, however, was dissatisfied with his platoon's performance. When he blew his whistle, the trainees were to run back to the rest area and mass again at the white line. If necessary, Clarke's platoon would run back and forth until sundown; then at dusk, after chow, they would continue the day's instruction under floodlights. The madness of it all offended Clarke. It served no useful purpose to be running back and forth. There was so much instruction to be covered, so many techniques he knew he had not mastered yet. But the sergeant stupidly insisted that the trainees sprint for four hours, if necessary, to stress one point; the men were not as disciplined as they had been the previous day. It was stupid and indefensible.

The whistle blew. Clarke ran to his right, passed a few of the slower runners, stretched his lean legs as soon as he found an opening, sprinted across the seventy yards, stepped on the by-now-brown tape, and swerved abruptly, standing easily, waiting for the rest to gather behind him for the return dash.

Sergeant Jacks stood in the area the platoon had just left. "Number 227!"

"Yes, Sergeant?"

"Git down an' give me ten!"

"Yes, Sergeant!" Clarke hit the ground and began doing the push-ups, not at all angry at the punishment, hardly considering it unjust, observing it merely as if it had been assigned to another man. He sounded off loudly while performing the push-ups, and when he had completed the eleventh one for the airborne, he leaped to his feet and stood at attention.

Jacks afforded him less than a second to recover. The whistle blew again, catching Clarke off guard, permitting an entire wall of moving bodies to pass him, and forcing him to run through the mounting dust. When he arrived at his position in the formation, most of the platoon was motionless, standing tall, staring directly to the front.

"All right, Numbers 227 an' 182, for bein' late, git down an' give me ten! Also, Number 182, for scratchin' yourself when you thought Ah wazzen lookin'—ten more!" All this was said without the hint of a smile, without the threat of a frown, impersonally, as if Clarke were not a man (or Acorn, either), not even an animal that must be trained, but merely a number that must be taught certain activities.

Clarke dropped to the ground again and did the eleven push-ups. When he finished, he leaped up and stared directly ahead of himself, hearing the agonized count of Number 182 as he called out his exercises.

Clarke was too tired to be angry. The twitches in his deltoid muscles and his triceps were too insistent, claimed too much of his attention, and thus did not permit him to realize that he was being harassed, that the others were not being tested as thoroughly. And he was determined. The hatred that gnawed at Clarke was focused on himself and not on the system—or on that other cog in the system, Sergeant Jacks. There was only one enemy: Clarke's proud yet fearful self. This was the only enemy. He had completely ignored the obvious motive which caused him to volunteer for Jump School: the fifty-five dollars. He now comprehended that *he* had not made the decision to become a paratrooper: something within him made the decision unavoidable. Was he not, after all, a paratrooper in his dreams?

Signing up for Jump School was not a reasoned rebellion. It was an eruption. And only now, as he underwent a confusion toward his own actions, did he understand his family's bewilderment when he left home: the act of estrangement from his parents, too strong to be denied, was interpreted by them as the climax to a cunningly disguised, lifelong hatred. And perhaps it was. How could a man know what was going on within him when the turmoils he hid never came to the surface?

The application of pain, of exhaustion, was doing something to him, he knew. That which had always been amorphous within him was slowly beginning to take form. This self, submerged deeply into the more obvious, external self, might never have been reached if it had not been stirred, if something had not prodded it. And perhaps,

Clarke speculated, only suffering, only a pain that confused the external self, that confounded and distracted the mind and will (faculties dependent on senses that were designed to register only other externals)—perhaps suffering was the only force strong enough to uncover the secret self that lurked beneath the mask provided to Clarke by his family, his years of comfortable living, and the daytime world that, by the very dynamism of its forceful logic, had pre-empted the rightful place of the other, truer world.

Was this very insight now occurring to McIlhenny? Or was it madness? Or was every man's insanity covered over by layer upon layer of reason until the secret face was buried? Were sane men only those who ignored or who crushed this caldron of seething, formless impulses and instincts? Then, if this were so, how could a man know himself unless he had uncovered and studied everything about himself, within and without? Unless he was liberated by suffering?

The platoon practiced running back and forth from the rest area five times before Sergeant Jacks was satisfied. Two men had dropped out. One fell to the ground far behind the sprinting mob and did not move when the sergeant called him to get on his feet. Jacks wasted no time. He waved to the ambulance driver who was always nearby, and two medics drove up and placed the trainee on a stretcher.

For the two hours until chow, Sergeant Jacks' platoon was to practice on the thirty-four-foot tower. The men had been jumping from the tower for the past three days, but no one had yet made a satisfactory exit.

The blockhouse of the thirty-four-foot tower rested on great wooden beams, much higher and thicker than telephone poles, which were driven deep into the hard-packed earth. Crossbeams rose diagonally from the ground to each corner of the house, and crossbars, ledge by ledge, climbed the skeletal framework. Flights of wooden stairs within the crisscrossed logs zigzagged to the tower room, where three sergeants waited for the trainees. One NCO was at each door, while a third made certain that each trainee wore his harness properly. Cadremen, sitting on lifeguards' chairs under the mock doors of the tower, looked up as the trainees leaped out of the room and judged their exits.

Clarke entered the tower room gasping for breath after the long climb. Besides the necessary harness, he had strapped on a paratrooper's combat pack—it dangled between his legs—to prepare him for the military jumps. He had walked up the two hundred steps with his feet spread, in an attempt to minimize the irritation of the canvas webbing, which viciously burned his groin and the inside flesh of his thighs.

Clarke hooked his harness rings to the metal clasps that were attached to metal risers. The risers terminated in a pulley whose grooved rim loosely embraced a taut cable, which stretched from the inside of the blockhouse to a mound of hard-packed earth one hundred yards away. Since Clarke was to jump from the right door, he held his make-believe static line with his left hand. His right foot was extended.

The sergeant gave the first man a nod, and Clarke heard a stamping of boots on the wooden floor and a sharp count of "one-two-three," and saw the trainee poised at the open door. The sergeant tapped him on the buttocks. This is all Clarke saw. Within four seconds he heard the sharp whizzing of the pulley on the metal cable, and soon afterward he briefly saw the man swinging across the one hundred yards on an almost invisible wire.

Number two man was given the nod and tap. Number three was called. And then Clarke saw the sergeant nod to him. Probing right foot shot out, left was kept in drag, left hand gripped the static line, and Clarke danced, stamping his way to the open door. "One-two-three." He was poised at the threshold.

To his left, as far as his peripheral view would allow him to see, was the road on which the platoons ran in the early morning. In the background was the wooden building where the trainees were instructed in parachute direction, where they were suspended in harnesses for an agonizing fifteen minutes and taught to land in water, in wires, in trees. To his extreme right was the Swing Landing area, where the men were trussed in harnesses on a platform ten feet above the sawdust-covered earth, told to clear the platform, swung back and forth several times, dropped violently by a sergeant who held on to a rope pulley which kept them aloft, and were expected, upon hitting the ground, to make an acceptable parachute landing fall. In the center of the Jump School was the sawdust pit where the men performed their physical training.

Great activity was going on beneath him, but Clarke had no interest in it, for he was poised at the door, his hands nervously touching the jambs, his knees bent. His chin was now up, divorcing his eye span from the action below him. As he focused his sight at a horizon dominated by the large three-story Division barracks, he felt the tap on his buttocks and the quiet but meaningful "go."

His spread boots kicked out, scissored, and joined in mid-air; his hands left the jambs and embraced the two ends of his reserve parachute, which was attached to his chest harness at a point two inches below the nipples; his head was down; his chin burrowed into his chest; his back was bent; his eyes were open. He fell, motionless, for eight feet and looked at the NCO seated below him. Then, as he was caught on the heavy cable and bounced abruptly, he recalled that he should have counted during his descent. Using the momentum he had gathered on his initial fall, he rushed down the cable, zinging toward the earthen berm. "Four thousand," he shouted, but knew it was too late. He looked up, pretending now, playing the cadremen's game, to where his canopy should have been; pretended he had seen it; reached up and grasped his risers; and rode the one hundred exhilarating yards to the mound of earth.

The trainees who were on details waited for him. Clarke raised his boots as he came to the top of the mound and rushed over it. He was stopped by a wire stretched a few feet behind the berm, parallel to it, and was sent back to the mound, where the trainees awaited him. His harness straps undone, Clarke walked along the top of the mound until he found himself on flat earth, then ran, shouting "airborne-airborne-airborne-airborne," to the line formed on one side of the lifeguard's chair.

He was breathing heavily when he arrived in formation. Above him, he saw men standing in the open door, being tapped out, falling, some making good, some poor, exits; heard the zinging of the wire as they sped toward the earthen berm; and saw other trainees stamp their feet at the threshold. Both doors were operating at full capacity, with two men occasionally leaving the opposite doors within the same second, following each other down the wires like coasting sea gulls.

Clarke was thirsty. His mouth was completely dry. He wanted to spit but knew that it would end in failure if he tried. The men, waiting in formation near the NCO's chair, stood at parade rest, never permitting themselves to gaze, staring straight ahead, ready to respond instantaneously to any command.

"Number 227!"

"Yes, Sergeant?" Clarke snapped to attention.

"That was a good exit. I didn't hear your first three counts, but your feet were together, your head was down, and your eyes were open." There was a pause. The sergeant was probably consulting his clipboard, although Clarke did not permit himself to look. "Go on up and make another jump."

"Yes, Sergeant!"

Clarke ran to another file and presented himself to the NCO, who rechecked him, pulled on various parts of the harness to test its tightness, and loosened the straps that criss-crossed Clarke's groin. "You wanna watch that, Number 227," he said quietly. "You don't wanna ruin the family jewels, do you?"

"No, Sergeant!" Clarke shouted. The NCO tapped him on the buttocks and Clarke ran toward the stairs of the tower again, shouting "airborne-airborne-airborne-airborne." As he climbed the two hundred steps, the straps again tore into his skin. By the time he arrived at the tower room, the training cadre were the only men there; it was Clarke's turn to jump, without having any time to wait, any time to rest. As he struggled to attach the clasps of the cable apparatus to his harness, the sergeant gave him the nod, told him to hurry—he did not have all day. Finally Clarke managed to hook the clasps.

"Stand in the door," the sergeant intoned.

"One-two-three!" Clarke blocked the open door again.

The tap came quickly. He shot out his legs, slammed his boots together, embraced his reserve chute—*"one thousand, two thousand"*—fell motionless into a void, strained to keep his eyes open, saw the sergeant glancing up at him—*"three thousand, four thousand"*—felt the cable take him and swing him toward the earthen berm, looked up to the nonexistent canopy, pretended it existed, arched his back, and grasped the risers.

Back in formation near the NCO's chair, he learned that he had performed another good exit, that he should go up to the tower immediately and try to make another one. He had three more good exits to go.

When the morning's training had been completed, the trainees were told to run back to their platoon formations and wait for further instructions from their sergeants. Jacks told them that the coming Saturday, their last training day, they would go on their long-threatened ten-mile run over sandy earth to Rickenbacker Air Force Base. At the marshaling area they would be familiarized with the airplanes they would jump from the following week. If any man fell out of that run, Jacks warned, he would be dropped from the cycle. No quitters would be permitted to say they were paratroopers.

After chow the trainees were ordered out of the barracks for mail call. Clarke was given a letter, postmarked Philadelphia and rerouted through the Special Troops' Mail Center. From his parents. What was this nonsense, he was asked, about Jump School? There was more shocked surprise than concern in the letter. What did he think he was doing? He was, after all, a Clarke! It was evident to Clarke that his father thought Barrett had had enough of the kind of life he had been living; the fact that he was in Jump School proved his affairs to be in rather desperate circumstances. And Clarke was forced to agree. Anyone who would jump out of an airplane for fifty-five dollars a month was mad when all he needed to do was crawl from Fort Mosby to Philadelphia on his knees, beg forgiveness for his youthful inanities—particularly for marrying the girl he loved. (And what was love? his father had once asked. If it existed at all, love was a type of disease that attacked the system of a person when he was ill, weak in motivation; when his mind was idle!) That was all Clarke would need to do: admit that his father had been right about Nikki and then hold out his hand for money.

Now that Clarke had the possibility of getting back his original *Clarkeness* and everything that went with it, he no longer needed it or thought of it. Now that it seemed his family would accept Nikki as one of themselves merely because Clarke had evidently decided that he loved her, that he wanted her to remain his wife, Clarke was certain he no longer felt the same way about her as he did when he elected to challenge his family for her.

As he tore up the letter and dropped the small pieces into a wastepaper basket in the barracks, Clarke heard the screaming of the NCO whistles. He ran to his place in formation. His hands were shaken by a powerful emotion. *I'm beginning to know myself*, he thought.

"Dress it right an' cover down . . ."

"Dress it right an' cover down . . ."

"Forty inches all aroun' . . ."

"Forty inches all aroun' . . ."

The wind machine stood in an empty field. The dull loam of the earth lay rutted, with occasional specks of glinting silica proving to Clarke that there were much harder properties in the soil than he had originally supposed. Since there had been no rain in the area for a week, the earth was as unyielding as a city pavement.

The wind machine, an enormous fan the size of an airplane propeller, was mounted on the back of a Deuce-and-a-Half; a protective screening shielded the man who would stand before it from the razor-sharp blades, which could be adjusted to rotate at any speed up to fifty miles an hour.

But now the wind machine was motionless, waiting for whatever chore it was to perform. The men were run off from their formations and lined up for their afternoon's instruction. One of the teaching sergeants, a colored man, appointed four volunteers. The first man, Clarke, was to get into a harness that lay stretched on the ground in front of the wind machine. The second man was to hold the apex of the canopy, pulling it taut, while the other two were to grasp the skirts of the parachute, pulling at them so that the canopy would fill with air. The air was to be provided by the machine that was so quiet now. Clarke, in harness, lay on his back, grasping the risers with arms outstretched. The sergeant instructed him to cross his feet.

"It would be neither safe nor practical to train the troop in canopy-collaspin' technique by jumpin' 'em in high winds. This wind machine am a safe and easily control trainin' aid." The sergeant carried a pointer but had evidently just remembered its existence, for as soon as he glanced at it he seemed to realize it was fitted for a variety of uses. The pointer's most important function seemed to be its use as a threatening weapon toward the man who lay on the earth, his feet crossed, waiting for something painful to occur to him.

"When there am no groun' wind, the parachute collasp without assistance. The T-10 chute may not collasp without assistance when the groun' wind am in excess of eight mile an hour. Failure to take immediate step to collasp the parachute resultin' in the jumper bein' dragged an' injured." The lecture continued with countless jabs with the pointer at Clarke, the training aid.

When the sergeant had finished the academic portion of the class, he gave a signal to the sergeant behind the wind machine. There was a pause, a sharp click of the switch, a rush of wind from the whirring fan, an order to the skirt and apex men to open up the blossom of the canopy, and the swift, effortless slide across the hard-packed earth. Clarke was dragged fifteen feet before passing the sergeant who gave him the signal to recover from the wind. He drew his knees up to his chest to form a pivot on the small of his back. With his hands gripping the risers, he curled his left hand into his chest, gave a vigorous tug with his right, pulled his body around in the direction of the parachute, and dug his heels into the ground. He was up now, facing the taut parachute, which had pulled him to his feet. Running toward it, he circled around the canopy and watched it collapse of its own accord.

The sergeant commended him for understanding so quickly; Clarke nodded his head. When he glanced at his hands and wrists, he saw that they were bleeding. A few inches of skin had been rubbed off by the hard-packed earth. As he was about to return to his place in the formation, Clarke was recalled by the sergeant to give another demonstration. He walked to the center of the area, lay on his back in front of the machine, and stretched his arms backward. A whole line of trainees began laughing until Clarke realized that the three canopy men had not returned the parachute to the wind machine and that he, in effect, had merely lain on the ground.

In a bored manner, the sergeant looked down to Clarke and told him to "git down an' give me ten." Which Clarke did. He leaped up after he had completed his eleventh, for the airborne, and strapped himself into the parachute harness.

"The lass time," the sergeant continued, "the trainee, Number 227, recover on his right side. Now Ah want you to see how he am gon' recover to his lef' side. Number 227?" The sergeant raised his pointer; the machine began whirring.

The winter clouds, slender and curved, hung riblike in the cerulean sky, and at the corner of Clarke's new horizon—stretched beyond the soles of his boots—he saw the green crew cut of pine trees. He passed a man who waved an axlike hand at him. This was Clarke's signal. He had traveled fifteen feet.

He drew his knees to his chest again, attempting to form a pivot point at the small of his back. With his right hand he pulled one riser into his chest; he tugged at the other with his left. He threw his boots over to his left side; rose to his feet, facing the blossomed canopy; and felt his left calf muscle freeze painfully as he was about to run after the parachute. He fell forward, struck the ground with his elbows, and was dragged, stomach down, across the pebbles and hard-packed earth.

The sharp stones dug viciously into his arms and into the soft, fleshy part of his thighs. His privates were scratched by the debris on the ground, for he was being dragged at a speed of twenty miles per hour. From the position he found himself in, there was no way he could get up. He decided to roll on his back again and to attempt a quick recovery, for he was nearing the rockier section of the training area. He raised his boots, pulled the left riser into his chest, tugged on the right, and found himself erect, facing the canopy again. He limped toward the inflated chute, catching the hem of the skirt, and collapsed it easily.

The sergeant appeared angry as Clarke returned to the gathering of trainees near the machine. He did not speak until Clarke, who was obviously hurt from the fall, came closer to the group. The fleshy parts of Clarke's body were still stinging from the dragging.

"Number 227 . . . Ah diden see you recover to no *lef'!*"

"I got a cramp, Sergeant! I got a cramp in my leg when I got up. You saw me!"

"Ah saw you all right. Thas no excuse! Why diden you do it the secon' time?"

"The same thing would happen again, Sergeant!"

"Thas no excuse. Git down an' give me ten!"

Clarke stared at him, fighting within himself the desire to shout, to curse, to do something. In the moment he hesitated, the reasons for his going so far in the training did not present themselves to him reasonably. In fact, for the second he paused, his contradictory emotions evaporated; he no longer felt insubordinate. His mind was blank. Falling to the ground, he did ten push-ups (for the man was an NCO) and one extra for the airborne (for he wanted to be a trooper). When he leaped to attention and was told to "git down" again because he seemed to hesitate slightly after being given the first order to "git down," Clarke dropped to the ground and performed his eleven push-ups without a pause, without a murmur.

The sergeant called another trainee to act as training aid, thus giving Barrett Clarke a chance to inspect his sores to see if they were as serious as he thought they were. The tips of his fatigue sleeves were well soaked with blood, but—since he had stopped doing the push-ups—the bleeding had ceased. His fatigue suit was caked with dust, and the cloth at his knees, elbows, and buttocks was ripped by the small barbed stones over which he had been dragged. He bent over, listening all the while to the instruction, so that if and when the time came for him to be challenged to determine if he were listening, he could repeat verbatim what had been said. Bending over, he attempted to massage his left calf muscle without calling the other sergeants' attention to what he was doing. Several moments later, when the switch had been flicked on once and Clarke had heard moans coming from the first rank but preferred to minister to his own needs rather than witness the troubles of someone else, the cramp had been worked out and Clarke stood tall again.

It would be pleasant, he thought, *to go back to Philadelphia for a week or two after Jump School.* But he knew this was out of the question, not because he had a maneuver facing him, a maneuver he was ordered on by a captain who was now a corporal (strange, shifting, formless world!) but because he would return to Philadelphia when he could do so as a man and not merely as a son.

He would ignore every letter, every threat, every promise. He would not be cajoled by Nikki; nor would he be tempted by an end to his pvoerty or by anything the Clarkes of Philadelphia might offer him. Something was gnawing at him, and he knew what it was. Not independence, though this was part of it. No, not only freedom, a personal freedom. But something greater, something freedom was only the first step to: self-definition. And in order to determine what Barrett Clarke was, it was vital that he should have been Number 227. It was all so simple! In order to be found, one had to be lost.

The trainees were formed into two lines; the first was for the men who were to put on parachute harnesses and be dragged while the second was for the canopy men. Each line would participate in five runs, five drags, and then would change positions and duties with the other line, going around the canopy counterclockwise. This was to continue for four hours, two lesson blocks, until the day darkened and the training was halted.

The area was full of activity, a patterned, choreographed activity, presided over by stern, articulate, and capable dance masters whose very existence was to prevent injuries and death by the administration of punishment. In the course of training, injuries but not death became rather common. The enemy that the training was to confound was the one who stalked every airborne unit, wearing various guises, provided with many masks: this enemy was fear, but not mere fear. Fear of death.

Fear, Clarke had learned, was exorcised with every airborne chant, but fear was present in each syllable. Fear made the paratrooper proud of his unit, but fear made him despise, with a badly masked hatred, the straightleg whom he always challenged when he drank too much. It was fear he lived with, because—if fear was ever-present—the challenge to this fear, the act of jumping in spite of fear itself, was forced to be as constant. This was why each paratrooper jumped once a month: to prove to himself and to his unit that he was not afraid, that he did not consider it unnatural for a man to leap out of a flying airplane. Through constant fear came valor—for even rabbits, when desperate, had occasional courage—but constant valor required the constant pose of valor.

Instant obedience, fortified by the constant pose of courage; facilitated by the threat of punishment, which brought dishonor; and motivated likewise by the hatred and ill-concealed envy of those who did not live in fear: this was the path for valor The path for valor was the first step to freedom. The goal of freedom was self-definition. And the climax to the search for self-knowledge was death. The first step on the path for valor, therefore, was instantaneous obedience, the hypocritical pose of constant courage, and the fear of punishment, motivated by hatred and envy and threatened with dishonor. And these were rewarded with freedom? These were the foundations of self-definition?

Barrett Clarke was dragged across the hard-packed field five more times that afternoon, seven times in all. By the final whistle of the day, his arms and legs were full of bruises and his forehead was clotted with dust and blood.

Sergeant Jacks held him up for a few moments after he had dismissed the other trainees in front of the barracks and asked to see his bruises. When he had taken a shower, Jacks instructed him, Number 227 was to come to the orderly room, where the NCO would be as CQ and would determine if 227's bruises were serious enough to require attention.

The shower water felt good on Clarke's body in all the areas except those where he was bruised. And they were few. He was alone in the room, and only two men were in the other section of the latrine. With the warm water bathing his tired body, he thought of Nikki, this time in pleasant circumstances: Nikki and he making love, Nikki and he talking quietly over a cup of coffee.

Things would change once he had accomplished his five novice jumps and was released to his unit. He would have a week to set a new course in their marriage. Then he would be taken again to go on the maneuver. But that would be enough time to establish a new regime, to enjoy each other's company, before he was assigned to the Special Troops' maneuver headquarters. She would receive the first money he would earn as a paratrooper, and on his return from Operation Razor Blade they would have enough to live on comfortably; they would have missed each other enough to want to talk long hours and get along as they had at one time. Perhaps a new life would begin for them.

He dried himself, dressed in olive drabs, and took the torn and dusty fatigue suit he had worn that day to the laundry situated within the PX building. McIlhenny, Clarke assumed, was in his barracks, for he could not see him in the PX. He headed for the orderly room and Sergeant Jacks.

Following the advice of a sign posted on the windowpane, Clarke took off his cap, knocked on the door, and wiped his feet. Jacks was sitting at the desk, his booted feet resting precariously on the desk top.

"C'mon in, Number 227." Jacks smiled and spread a newspaper before Clarke. "What d'you think of that, now?" He pointed to the headline as if he feared it would be missed.

GIANT AIRLINER CRASHES IN CARIBBEAN.
75 KILLED.

"Happens all the time, doesn't it, Sergeant?"

"That's right. Happens all the time. Happened two times lass week. Oncet to an Air France in Africa. Sixty-three went down on that one. Oncet to a Spick plane in South America with forty." He leaned toward Clarke and smiled again. "How does that make you feel, Number 227? Specially since you're gonna be jumpin' next week?"

"You said yourself, Sergeant, that parachuting is a very safe occupation, that there are fewer airborne disasters than there are automobile crashes. You even said that jumping out of an airplane is safer than taking a bath at home."

Jacks snorted. "You don' believe ever'thin' you hear, do you, Number 227?"

"I believe everything you tell me, Sergeant Jacks."

The sergeant decided to change the conversation. "How do you feel?" he asked. "Take off your jacket an' shirt. Ah wanna see what your back looks like. You been takin' a lot of punishment lately, an' there ain't no reason for you to be rippin' the scabs off an' bleedin' ag'in tomorrow."

Clarke peeled off his jacket, zigzagged his necktie off, and unbuttoned his shirt. He threw his clothes on the chair and pulled up his T-shirt. Jacks turned him around to view the long scrape marks on his shoulder blades, bruises with deep-red interiors.

"You got yourself some real scrapes there." He turned Clarke's arms outward to see the raw skin at his elbows and wrists. "Ah suggest you remind me tomorrow that Ah gave you the mornin' off from any trainin'."

"Thank you, Sergeant."

"Now wait a minute. That don' excuse you from the run. Ever'body's gotta make the run if he wants to be a paratrooper. Ah'm jest excusin' you from the trainin', an' you'll agree with me there is some difference there, won't you?"

"Yes, Sergeant."

Jacks motioned Clarke to get dressed again and went back to his seat, taking the newspaper and folding it over to the second section, where news of the airline disaster was continued. "You know"—he spoke as Clarke was tying his necktie—"Ah never go by airplane when Ah travel. Airplanes are the most dangerous things ever invented. Them an' gliders. You can shove gliders. There was more dead asses in gliders than in the Merchant Marines on the *Mur*mansk run. Gliders an' dirigibles—you can shove both of 'em."

"Why don't you like to fly commercially, Sergeant Jacks?"

" 'Cause they don' give you no parachutes, that's why. 'Cause they try an' pretend you're right in your livin' room, givin' you mixed drinks an' astin' er you comfortable an' lettin' you read magazines. Shit! Makin' on like that's a safe way to travel. Now the Army don' give you no crap 'bout parachutin'. They tell you it's tough, it's a man's game; they give you plenty of trainin'; and, finally, they give you extra money. Look!" He straightened up in his swivel chair. "Takin' off is perty dangerous, flyin' in the air ain't so bad, but that's all. If you got seventy people in a craft ready to go, hooked up on a static line an' ever'thin' all set for them when they git into trouble, OK, most of 'em'll be saved. Sure, Ah fly in airplanes . . . for a livin'. But Ah don' land in 'em; Ah jump out! Jumpin' out is safer!"

"Yes, but you can't sell an old lady a ticket for four hundred dollars to get on an airplane and, as soon as she steps on board, get her in a parachute, hook her up, and tell her how to land. She's liable to get a heart attack on the spot."

"Don' mean nothin'. If she's gonna git a heart attack

when you tell her 'bout puttin' on a harness, she ain't got no business bein' on an airplane."

"Well"—Clarke shrugged his shoulders—"everybody's got a right to his own opinions. I, personally, don't think they're too dangerous, and I believe that airline disasters run in some kind of pattern. You get a series of them one week, and then you forget about them, nothing happens for a few months, and then, without warning, they start happening again."

"When you become a paratrooper an' git your master parachutist's wings, you'll have a right to develop your own theories 'bout disasters. Right now you're talkin' like a newspaper reader. Later on you'll be talkin' like a man that jumps outa aircraft while in flight."

Clarke, since he had nothing more to say, did not want to terminate the conversation so abruptly and shrugged his shoulders, hoping that Jacks would take that as a hint that he, at least, had exhausted his store of theories concerning airline disasters.

Jacks glanced up from his paper to see that Clarke had not approached the door. "You'll hafta make the run tomorrow," he repeated.

"Yes, I know." Clarke neared the desk. "I wonder, Sergeant. Do you mind if I use the telephone? I'd like to call my wife."

"Go 'head." Jacks stood up and took his newspaper into the next room, the captain's office.

After dialing, Clarke rested an unbruised portion of his hip against the desk and heard the secretive, metallic clicks sounding in the telephone receiver. The number was finally selected and the buzzing began, a steady *buzzz,* pause, *buzzz* that could not tell him if it sounded in a completely empty room, in a room where an activity too personal or intimate was occurring to be interrupted, or if someone was rushing with unseen feet, bumping into unseen objects, making unheard sounds, in a haste to break the steady, mechanical sound of the buzzer with the tranquillity of human communication. *Buzzz,* pause, *buzzz,* pause, *buzzz.* The telephone rang, and continued to ring, until finally the bored rustling of Sergeant Jacks' newspaper in the next room reminded Clarke that he had held the receiver to his aching ear for approximately three minutes.

Clarke set the receiver on its hook slowly, wondering where Nikki could be. He could feel his pulse throb with the wildness that is hidden whenever restraint has not been provided for in time. He took time, however, to prepare himself and his voice. "OK, Sergeant." He spoke to Jacks in the next room without being able to see him. "There's no answer. I guess she's gone to get the paper. Thanks for letting me use the phone."

He was out of the door before Jacks entered the room.

CHAPTER 18

McIlhenny wrote: "My dear Esperanza." He set his pencil down and tried to massage the twitch over his eyebrow. "During the weeks that we'd been . . ." He stopped there. She would not understand contractions. "During the weeks that we had been friends, I believe I got to know you very well. I doubt, however, that you know very much about me and about what has happened to me recently."

This would be the challenge, McIlhenny realized: to communicate to this ignorant girl, whom he had frankly and brutally used, the fact that he had surmounted his need for her, for the puny flesh that she pathetically believed was all-important. New paragraph. "I have never been a dashing man." Cross that out. Substitute "handsome." "When I decided to become a military man, I did so because I loved the mission, a mission I once considered holy, and not the uniform." *Does she have a dictionary? Why go on?* he wondered. *She probably can't read this and would certainly throw the letter away when she arrived at the end, at the meaning of the letter.*

"In my way," he continued, "I was very simple (*tonto* or *ingenuo* would be better), but I was happy in my ignorance, because my life—as boring and as tiresome as it was—had a meaning to it, a meaning that it can now be said to lack." *Ridiculous. Why go on?* "But I met you one evening and the very boredom of my life was quickened somehow, made alive in a way that, contrary to . . ." Cross that out. "Made alive in a way that, instead of what I had missed in life showing me the path, the only path, to work myself out of my mistakes, what I had missed in life showed me only that I had gone too far, that no woman could show me my mistakes, my errors. They had become too deep, too truthful for a woman, any woman, to combat them."

It was senseless, McIlhenny knew, to continue; even if she

understood the letter, word for word, she could not be expected to understand what it meant to her or to him. Yet it was good to write these thoughts out of his system—good therapy.

McIlhenny rubbed his eyes. The noise from the pool tables in the game room was distracting him slightly, but he fought it, for the turmoil within him was noisier yet. "In a way, though, you did help me escape. Wanting your body as a release, I knew when I had surfeited myself with you that your body was not what I wanted. And this saved me time, for in learning that the escape you offered was not an escape, I ceased thinking of physical relief as an escape. Love, even the pathetic imitation I tried to simulate, was a caricature of what I required. To continue to see you would only waste your time and would add further burdens to a man who must be as unburdened as possible to pursue a goal he can vaguely discern."

His hands were perspiring. When he tried to rub them on his fatigue trousers, he dropped the pencil on the floor. He stooped to retrieve it. "The last time you saw me you remarked that something about me was peculiar, that I was brooding, but when I said it was nothing, you promptly forgot. I have been reduced from captain to corporal. The husband you divorced now possesses a few stripes more than I do and, in fact, is the supply sergeant of my company. When I meet him I must be submissive, must 'Yes, Sergeant' and 'No, Sergeant' him until I can get away by myself to a self that in turn wants to get away from itself."

Never get that. Never get the irony. Won't send the letter at all; just keep it around to read at night. "I have lost my status, my captaincy, through no one's fault. And you served as my first excuse for losing my faith. But I was wrong, and only weeks of constant thought have made me realize that I had lost my faith a long time before. I lost my faith when I began to wear my religion on my shoulder, rolled up like a chip of wood, and challenged others to try to knock it off, for that would mean a fight, an argument, and while I was involved in that, I would not need to think the thoughts that were becoming daily and insistent. I had become a Pharisee. I had lost my faith when I depended on my mind and that lollipop—natural law—and filled myself full of hatred and envy at imagined, secretive, heretical enemies. I had lost my faith at the moment I used it as a weapon."

What I had feared, McIlhenny thought; but his mind was faster than the pencil. "What I had feared, the destructive power of a woman and the feeling of despair, proved to me, when I was riffed, to have been the levers that freed me from what I know now as falsehood, from the lies and hypocrisies of the Pharisee, and have left me as I am, shipwrecked, alone, helpless, despairing. I am now a better man than I was, for I am nothing. I am now a more religious man than I was, for I have lost my pathetic intellectual faith and feel the plucking of divine hands on a harp I did not know existed within me. I am going somewhere. I do not mean physically, but deep within myself. As a shipwrecked man I find my raft nudged along certain streams, and, looking up at the stars, I realize that although my hands are not on the tiller, I am going toward a goal I have always desired. To the Golden Islands, perhaps." His hand shook. McIlhenny rested it for a moment. "Something is about to happen to us, to all of us, and though it seems to be terrifying, I am not afraid. I will submerge myself in my destiny, and when I am washed up on the shore, at the end of our world, on the Armageddon that nears us day by day, I will be satisfied. I do not want death." Cross that out. Substitute "destruction." "But neither do I fear it. Whatever comes, comes as a solution.

"This is why, Esperanza, I will not visit you again. There is only room for one on my raft. You may keep the books and the records I have stored at your cabin or you may sell them. Everything of material value I have is yours. Do not feel you must keep them, that one day I will return to ask for them. Sell them, throw them away, keep them, give them to your friends. I don't care. Goodbye, Esperanza; I have been helped by knowing you. May your destiny keep you as ignorant of the truth of life as it has succeeded in keeping you up to this point. May you never find truth. May you never find God. May your bridegrooms come to you in the darkness, sweetly, and leave you in the morning with nothing more than a feline smile on your surfeited, radiant face. For He is beautiful but deadly."

McIlhenny set his hands in his lap. Then he took out another sheet of paper and, using a fountain pen, wrote:

> My dear Esperanza:
>
> *During the weeks that we had been friends, I believe I got to know you very well. I doubt, however, that you know very much about me and what has happened to me recently. I have become very sick and have gone to the doctor many times. I*

must live quietly and do nothing that taxes my heart.

This is why, Esperanza, I will not visit you again. You may keep the books and the records I stored at your cabin or you may sell them. Everything I have is yours. Do not feel that you must keep them, that one day I will return to ask for them. Sell them, throw them away, keep them, give them to friends. I don't care.

Goodbye, Esperanza.
Kinnard

P.S.: I have been helped by knowing you.

After addressing the envelope and slipping the note inside, he leaned back in his chair. A few young men were slouched in the lounge chairs of the reading room, magazines propped up on their knees, bored, waiting for someone who would drive them to Von Steuben to come by. McIlhenny sealed the envelope. Setting it face down on the table, he pressed it shut. That was finished, thank God. He had done a great deal today. He had written a letter. It had taken him three hours to do it, but, considering his past few weeks' performance schedules, this was rather respectable. And if in one day he could complete one small chore, he might have his affairs in order by the time the 43rd Airborne Division was called out for its participation in Operation Razor Blade.

It would be pleasant, McIlhenny thought, to have all the adjusting completed here at Fort Mosby, to have attended to all the minutiae of existence when it was the most difficult, and then to break off everything, go into the field for a month or five weeks, forget his life and himself, and then return a new man, a man completely at ease with his new environment, a well-integrated Corporal McIlhenny, and maintain this integrated Corporal McIlhennyness for one more enlistment and then retire after twenty years of service and mend mind, for only mind needed repairing, only mind and nerves and God-manipulated heart.

His shaking hands burrowed into his fatigue jacket's pocket and searched for the narrow stamp book. He separated one from the series and stuck it on the envelope.

A good girl, he thought. Perhaps if he had known her earlier, many of his troubles would have been arrested at an early stage . . . perhaps. Perhaps that was all he had needed all his life, a steady woman, and he would never have evolved into the harsh, unkind, austere man he was. Perhaps. But now he felt himself the better man! The irony, the paradox of it all! Everything that had happened to him, everything that was out of his control and at first appeared to be the worst thing for him, what he most feared, had proved to be precisely that which—in his confusion, his error, his timidity—he needed and longed for and would have been incomplete without. His frightful destiny, his unfortunate history—his destruction—had been his unexpressed goal! This proved to him that there was a much more superior God, a much more vast God than even he had anticipated. And it all became somehow absurd—his aspirations, his views of life, his entire past: everything was absurdity. The God he, in his absurd way, still believed in was an absurd God. At least McIlhenny was consistent in that. Absurdity bred absurdity, and McIlhenny believed in it, as absurd as it all was.

That which he feared—chaos—he was undergoing now, and he did not fear it now. That which separated him from others and made him feel uneasy—loneliness—he was reliving again, and he accepted it now as if it were natural. And it was natural for him, for McIlhenny. Absurd, laughable world, that in his degradation a man would occupy himself with dreams and longings and legends, composing wordless panegyrics to an absurd God Who exhibited a dubious love for His creatures by destroying them.

McIlhenny was close to tears. This condition was not infrequent for him. In the past few weeks he had been close to tears many times each day. A story, a melody, a simple word, the silence of a room with only wind and rain stirring outside the windows would fill him with an inexpressible emotion, an exalted mourning, a thankfulness merged with self-pity, a wayward pride in desolation. The heart would pound; the veins would throb; the jumble of words, inchoate, swirling, yet luminous and iridescent, would gurgle within him; his eyelids would burn; and choking sobs would scorch his chest. This, now, was McIlhenny's prayer—not a "neither," not a "nor," not an "on the contrary," not a parrotlike recitation of someone else's rhetoric, but a lava stream of contradictory emotions, of thwarted aspirations, of realized fears, a swollen river of disintegrating images, blobs of memories, meaningless preternatural sounds, and love.

And these moments came to him, not solely at night before sleep, but at all times: standing in line at the mess hall;

at a Post theater, in the darkness of a back row; leaping out of an airplane on a practice jump; marching with his combat pack through countless foot trails in search of mythical guerrillas for a maneuver in which he had no interest. These moments would steal into him unexpectedly, render him shattered, a man whose mind and spirit operated in one world and whose body and reflexes performed in another. Like the flame of an exhausted candle, his soul flickered spasmodically, waiting only for the wick to burn out so that the flame would disappear, if the world was as it seemed to be, or to leap, to ascend, merging its own blaze with that of the greater Fire, if the world were a harsh dream from which, according to the promises, he would waken.

He rose from his chair and, after stumbling momentarily, walked down the hallway to the mailbox. After dropping Esperanza's letter in the slot, he walked up the stairs to his empty platoon bay. When he had hung his clothes on the rack and placed his boots under the bunk, he got into bed and closed his burning eyes.

Whether he slept or not he could not know. Waking and slumber were all one to him now. But sometime that night, when the lights were out, perhaps at midnight, when the stirring of a few bunks told him that some of the young men had returned from Von Steuben, he heard a steady shuffle of feet on the stairs. The shuffle was methodical, not tired or rested, merely methodical, steady, paced: the person ascended step by step, up, up, up to the floor above, to McIlhenny's floor, not hurried, confident that whoever was being searched for would be found. McIlhenny's eyes opened. *One of the troopers,* he thought realistically, and closed his eyes again. But the shuffle continued. McIlhenny began counting now. Five, six, seven, twelve, thirteen, sixteen, seventeen, twenty-five, twenty-six, twenty-seven, thirty, thirty-two, thirty-seven, forty. There were only twenty-seven steps on the stairway. But still the shuffle sounded. Slow, paced, confident, the shuffle-shuffle neared. The lights in the latrine were on, throwing a welcome glare on the highly buffed green linoleum floor.

McIlhenny's bunk was in a corner. The wall to his left obstructed his view of the head of the stairs, but the light coming from the open door of the latrine was unmarred. No one had ascended the stairs and blocked the light. The floor shone comfortingly. McIlhenny tried to reason himself out of his fear, appealing halfheartedly to a mind that had completely discredited itself to him.

And then the light was blocked by a figure and a long shadow was thrown across the floor.

McIlhenny stiffened in his bunk. The figure did not move. The shadow, draped across the linoleum floor, was motionless. As if in respect to the strange caller, no one in the platoon stirred, not one bunk creaked, not one snore escaped a soldier. Only the kettledrums in McIlhenny's head throbbed incessantly, confidently shattering the awed silence beyond his skin. His watering eyes swam, permitting him the obscurity of merging lights and shadows, the pellucidity of a translucent, wavering world.

"Lord . . . ?" a terrified McIlhenny inquired.

The figure moved noiselessly, fluidly, as if its joints were universal, unlimited to the patterned demands of muscle fibers and tendons—a body without a body's limitations, sheathed in a glowing translucence. Stopping at the foot of McIlhenny's bunk, the figure floated an arm upward, and hollow eye sockets transfixed him. "Prepare," it said.

McIlhenny shut his watering eyes tightly and cringed in the bunk—madness, madness, madness pounding into his temples like percussion instruments, a throbbing gone wild, the drummer gone mad, registering chaos by recreating it. He snaked in his bunk, shivered under the GI blankets, drenched them with his perspiration, and then, when the drumming gradually diminished, opened his eyes to see the expected: the unbroken ray of light from the open latrine; the glaring blob of sheen on the green linoleum floor; emptiness devoid of transparency; darkness devoid of pellucidity; nighttime world devoid of demons and gods; silence; tangibility; walls; floor; ceiling; angles and planes searching for a resting place in corners; walls leaning in toward ceiling and floor; floor lying back to back with ceiling, pushing for support against walls; and corners hiding in shadows, providing resting places for angles and planes—the house of cards that is the world, without translucence, without diaphanousness, without occult merging of lights and shadows—platoon bay; bunk; sleeping bodies; creak of springs; shy, hesitant snores.

An instant? Was it an instant? Did anything happen? The snores had never ceased; the men had groaned and turned all night long. *I have dreamed,* he realized. *I have dreamed.*

In time his heartbeat slowed, his tears dried on his face, and McIlhenny drifted into sleep.

He was driving madly down a strange street, over just-rained-on roads that were cluttered with the soggy remains of cardboard boxes, which, like manure, oozed over the macadam. The car was not his. It was old, vague, of uncertain make. The round steering wheel glinted in the slanting rays of the sun like mother-of-pearl, and he twisted and turned the wheel frantically, as if he knew what he was doing and where he was going. The brakes squealed (he had not braked the car) and the dull thud of the closing door sounded in the silence of a shrouded, mist-filled morning. He walked quickly toward a heavy wooden door with arched lintels and large black metal hinges. He glanced down at his feet to see that he wore his old bathroom slippers (the ones he had left in the BOQ), worn down at the heels, oxblood in color, chipped and skinned at the toes. After lifting an enormous brass knocker, he slammed it three times and waited. Farther down in the building a monk ran from one of the doors and began placing slips of paper under the windshield wipers of the parked cars on the street. The brass knocker swung back and to his left; a monk stood before him, motioned him to follow, and waddled down a silent, shiny marble hallway. A series of doors opened before him silently, and McIlhenny found himself staring at the face of an abbot with thin, cunning eyes.

"I want to find Christ!" McIlhenny shouted.

"Fool, dolt, idiot." The abbot grinned sarcastically. *"You want to find Christ, and you don't know how to park your car!"* He laughed and pointed through the window to the street. A monk, wearing a parking attendant's cap, had just placed a ticket between McIlhenny's windshield and the wiper. When McIlhenny turned, he saw the abbot grinning. The abbot reached into a drawer of his desk and pulled out a parking attendant's cap. He put it on. "To get where you are going, you must first learn to park your car properly. We give lessons here. Quite reasonable." He pulled out a large, heavy volume of driving regulations. The book opened to a page full of illustrations: circles, squares, triangles, straight lines, and arrows were separated by thin, dark lines of text. "Study this. . . . And, by the way"—the abbot fingered his crucifix—"before you go . . . you must give us your ignition key. It isn't necessary. We'll book passage for you when we think you're ready."

McIlhenny reached into his pocket to withdraw the key. He smiled. "I don't need a car," he said as he threw the key on the desk. "If it comes to that . . . I can always crawl."

CHAPTER 19

Damianos sat in one of the back booths of the Green Light pouring vinegar and olive oil on a salad that Sophie had made for him. While eating, the sergeant followed a ritual he had long ago established. After stuffing his mouth with greens and wedges of tomatoes, he folded a slice of whole wheat bread into halves, into quarters, and placed it in his mouth, spending a minimum of time in chewing what he had accumulated. The final stage of the ritual was the swilling of the beer, an act which prepared him for the next forkful of salad. When the bowl was empty of salad, Damianos forced a slice of bread into it, soaking the bread with oil and vinegar, and ate the bread, occasionally raising the bowl to his lips to drink the remaining condiments.

"Gus!" Sophie, behind the bar, called to him. "Are you sure you told him to come early? For dinner?"

"What do you think we talked about on the phone—our new dresses? He said he'd be here at seven, and he'll be here. This is his last week out there as cadre, so he ain't too worried about taking off a little early."

After draining his glass of beer, he pushed the wooden bowl away, refilled the glass, lighted a cigarette, and crossed his legs. According to his wristwatch, it was a few minutes before seven o'clock. Sergeant Jacks, since he was not due until seven and was a punctual man, would be sure to arrive within five minutes. Damianos decided to visit the men's room, for he felt a slight pressure in his bladder from the beer he had consumed.

As he stood loose-hipped before the urinal, a slight, customary shiver passing through his body, Damianos repeated to himself the formula he had found difficulty in phrasing before. It was inconceivable to him that of his own volition he would ask someone to marry him. He had been married before, years ago, but could not recall having asked the tramp to be his wife. He had merely wakened one morning to find a woman next to him in bed who would not leave when he told her to. The past was down the drain—Damianos chuckled at the irony—and he was glad of that.

What was peculiar about getting married this time was

that he had asked Sophie after she had told him that he owed her nothing. Of course, the alternatives were unpleasant, unacceptable; but they existed. He had refused to reject her. Moreover, following his initial feeling of being trapped, his initial depression, he felt a great weight being lifted from him and was overcome by a curiously pleasant sensation: Sophie would really be his woman now, and that something that she carried in her soft body was completely his, not something he signed for with a supply sergeant and had to maintain in good condition for an eventual return, but something that would, within a certain number of months, be totally dependent on him, Cosmas Damianos, for support. It would possess soft bones that would harden as he grew; a bald head under whose skin would be stored dreams and memories; a soul—whatever that was; an individuality the child would struggle to complete; a pair of lungs that would gradually come under its control; a face that would resemble the sergeant's own, the one he now scrutinized in a mirror; and a quixotic talent—when it matured—for using words that represented things it would doubt existed—words like love, God, soul, and freedom.

He set his cigarette on the basin's ridge, lighted end facing out, and ran cold water over his hands. While drying himself, he glanced about at the walls and saw the eternal hieroglyphics scratched out with penknives and pencils: *Big Daddy from Scranton. The Wyoming Kid. If you want some real loving, see Jim—likes men.*

Rotten bastards, he thought. *What kind of people write this crap?* He would get the handyman, he decided, to come in some morning and paint over the scratched-out sicknesses of human beings, blot them out, and, if they reappeared, paint over them again. *Can't have Sophie looking at this stuff. She might come in here now and then when the place is closed.* Was the ladies' room like this?

He walked into the tavern, saw that no one had arrived yet, and went to the ladies'-room door. He knocked on it, heard no answer, and walked in. The walls in the washroom were fairly clean, but, entering the booth, he saw that, hand high while seated, a woman would be able to scrawl anything she wanted. And there were many scrawls.

Damianos cursed. *Vulgar ginch!* Women, at least, should be modest, but they seemed to be merely less productive than men. The desire to write on walls, he reasoned, was just as strong, only women did not possess the pornographic discipline of men. As Damianos opened the door and walked into the tavern, he saw Jacks taking off his coat, facing him.

"Jesus McChrist! Is *that* what you wanted to tell me? Ah figured it was important, but not *that* important!"

"Knock it off, Jacks. Goddamn it. I was just checking in there. Stupid broads—they write on the walls, too. Just like men. Go 'head in there; it's disgusting."

"No, thanks. Ah come down here to lissen to somethin' very important." He sat down slowly, as if exhausted, and took out a cigarette. "A frien' of mine tole me to git down here at seven o'clock. Somethin' important he hadda tell me. But he woulden tell me what it was over the phone. So Ah hadda come down here to find out what it was. Then, soon's Ah walk into the Green Light, he comes out of the ladies' room. Ah figured, Ah'm a busy man, what with runnin' mah ass off ever' day in Jump School, but any time a frien' needs me 'bout somethin', Ah come down to find out what it is, even if he can tell me over the phone an' make it easier on both of us."

"Cut it, Duane. I wanted to see you about something important, all right, and joking around don't make it less important."

Jacks looked at Damianos evenly, a thin, teasing smile playing on his lips. His jutting, square jaw was set. He stretched his tired legs. "Ah'll jest git comfortable, if you don't mind."

"I'm getting married," Damianos said. "I figured you should know about it, particularly since I'm gonna ask you to be my best man."

A smile spread on Jacks' face. "Well, Ah'll be dogged." He stared at Damianos. "Why, sure, Gus; anythin' you say." He tapped the ash off his cigarette. "Who you gonna marry?"

Damianos turned abruptly to see if Sophie was nearby. "Jesus, who d'you think I'm gonna be marrying? It's a good thing she didn't hear what you just said."

"You gonna marry Sophie?" Jacks waited for Damianos' nod. "Well, it's 'bout time. Ah wazzen gonna wait much longer for you to ast her. Ah figured to give you 'bout six months more, then Ah'd of asted her mahself. Did she say yes?"

"What do you mean—did she say yes? Of course."

Jacks shook his head knowledgeably. "You got yourself a fine woman there, Gus. A fine woman. Ah'm proud of you."

"Thanks, ol' buddy. You gonna be my best man?"

"Sure will. Hell, that's an honor. Thanks."

Damianos turned and shouted: "Sophie! Duane is here. He says OK."

The swinging doors leading to the kitchen opened, and Sophie came out, drying her hands on an apron. "Hello, Duane. How are you?"

"Fine, Sophie. Ah'm fine. You?"

"I'm fine, too."

"Now that we know that everybody's fine," said Damianos, "let's have a beer." He took Sophie by the arm, inviting her into the booth. "She's got something for us to eat. I know Jacks here. He eats about seven times a day, whenever he can get hold of food. So even if he's had chow, he'll be interested."

"Bring it on," said Jacks. "The cooks gave us fish today, so Ah diden eat too much."

"Is there anything in your religion says you can't eat good red meat today?"

Jacks laughed. "What you got in that kitchen, Gus?"

"Is the food ready yet, honey?" Damianos asked.

"I just looked at it, Gus. It'll take about ten minutes yet. I'll get the plates and silverware." She looked at Sergeant Jacks. "Would you like something to drink, Duane?"

"Yeah, get us some of that wine," said Damianos. "Bring the silverware later." He turned to Jacks. "I got some Greek wine from a friend of mine. How about some of that?"

"Fine, fine . . . that won't ruin my stomach for bourbon later on, will it?"

"No, it won't." He turned to Sophie, who stood near the booth. "Get the wine, would you, Sophie?"

When she had brought the bottle and three glasses, Sophie went into the kitchen briefly to look at the food. Jacks took a sip, but his face remained noncommittal. "Interestin' wine," he said. "You know, Gus, you still ain't tole me when the weddin' will be so's Ah can git mah tuxedo ordered from the supply sergeant."

Damianos smiled. "Cut the tuxedo stuff. I figured on getting married in fatigues. How's that?"

"That's fine. Ah reckon Ah can scrape up a pair. Ah only got 'bout twelve pairs of them."

"How's Jump School, by the way? Anybody I know in this cycle?"

"When'd you start bein' friendly with straightlaigs?"

"I get around."

"Well," said Jacks, "we got one man from somewheres near

your unit. Psychowarfare, or somethin' like that. Barrett Clarke, Ah think his name is. Know him?"

"Name's familiar." He took a sip of wine and thought for a moment. "Good-looking kid; sorta light-colored hair. Good-size chin. Talks like an educated fella? From up North?"

"That's him. He's in mah platoon."

"I'll be damned. He was on CQ one night when I was Sergeant of the Guard. Captain Jenkins—you remember him? He was on OD with the kid." Damianos struggled to recall something else. "I don't know, but I seem to remember him in here one night. I might of been drunk or something and can't be sure about that. So he went to Jump School, huh? How's he doing?"

"Perty good," said Jacks. "Not much of a soljer, but he can take his punishment. Better than most of the dumb ones, anyways."

"You been riding him?"

"Not too much. He does what he's tole and Ah leave it at that. He's perty tough. Ah mean, he keeps on tryin', though you know he's 'bout to go ass over tin cups."

"Rich boy, too," Damianos added. "One of his buddies was telling me he comes from Philadelphia society. I was glad to hear they ain't *all* degenerate. I wondered why he didn't become an officer. You know, you never get guys like that being enlisted men. They got all sorts of family traditions against being swine."

"Well," Jacks said, "he's been takin' ever'thin' we been givin' him without cryin', an' he looks like he ain't worried at all."

Damianos fought a teasing smile. "Maybe you ain't giving him too much to worry about yet. Maybe you're pampering him."

Jacks stared at Damianos briefly. "Mebbe you're right." He took a sip of the wine and set the glass down. "When er you gettin' married, or am Ah gonna hafta come fifteen miles some other night to find out?"

"Tomorrow."

"You don' waste no time!"

"Can't afford to. Tomorrow'll be the civil ceremony, 'cause I gotta get out on the maneuver in a week and won't be back till it's over. We'll have a small church wedding around the middle of January. How's that with you? Tomorrow's the 'Long Run,' ain't it?"

"Yeah, but don' sweat it. Ever'thin's gonna be fine. Ah'm

in perty good shape for it." Jacks put out his cigarette. "You know, Ah'm gonna make the maneuver, too."

"I'm glad you're getting out of Jump School. You won't hafta go back after Razor Blade, will you?"

"Nope. Ah'm gonna be with the Division from then on. Gets sorta tiresome runnin' five miles a day and soundin' off all the time. There's a captain in Division that wants me to be his first soljer, so Ah guess Ah'll sit aroun' for the rest of mah Army time, givin' orders an' not takin' any crap from nobody."

"Except the captain."

"Not much from him, neither. He's a perty good joe."

Sophie came through the swinging doors carrying a plate piled with steaks. Damianos got up quickly and went into the kitchen to bring the potatoes and salad. When he had placed these on the table, he saw that Sophie had set the silverware, plates, and napkins.

Jacks congratulated Sophie on the good news and expressed his happiness that Gus had finally done what was intelligent. Damianos, in the meantime, was buttering his whole wheat bread, silent, saying nothing, merely fighting back a feeling of satisfaction that slowly came over him. It was a good thing, a smart thing, he had done. A wonder he had not thought of it previously, before he learned that he would need to make a decision.

This was the pattern he had followed all his life, he realized. If a decision was not necessary, he did not make it. Only when his hand was forced would he study the alternatives presented to him by life and come to a decision. He could have been just as happy if he had married Sophie two months after he had met her, but the thought of formalizing their relationship had not entered his mind. *If I had any brains,* he considered, *I'd take decisions into my own hands before I am forced to make them.* He would thus have the necessary and comforting feeling of being a free man, not the feeling he usually had—that of being a man tidying up, pretending to be his own master, after destiny had made the decisions for him.

"This is good steak, Sophie." He turned to her. "Nothing like good red meat, baked potatoes, and salad."

"Ah guess Ah'm gonna hafta git married, too. Ah hate that mess-hall cookin'."

"What kind of husband would you be," Damianos asked, "running five miles a day, sounding off all the time?"

Sophie stood up. "I forgot the salt and pepper."

"You know, Duane"—Damianos leaned toward Jacks—"women don't ever talk about sex. They pretend it don't exist. They talk about this man not knowing how to dress, about that one who looks so lonely, about another who seems sweet, and a guy thinks: all women are somebody's sister. Yet all they ever think about is getting into bed with a man and biting his ear."

"No foolin'? How come you know so much an' Ah know so little?"

"I'm just trying to tell you, in a poetic way, that the broad I see you out with occasionally—the one you was with at the NCO club, not that Dorene bitch—would not be bad at all. How come you don't ask her to marry you?"

" 'Cause she's already married."

"Oh," Damianos said.

Sophie returned with the salt and pepper. "Gus, you haven't told me . . . will you be out in the field all the time Razor Blade is on or will they let you come back every now and then?"

"Why?" He winked at Jacks. "You got plans for when I'm gone?"

"You know better than that!"

"A man nowadays don't know anything except he's got good friends, which is one commodity I'm blessed with. Excuse the expression." He turned to Sophie to see that she was coloring slightly. "I might be back every now and then. I'll be a guerrilla, and no one'll know where I'll be with my team except a captain who just come into the unit and don't know too much about guerrilla warfare. I guess I might be able to escape and evade for a day and a half. Why?"

"It just seems like a long time, that's all."

"They'll give us a few administrative breaks, I guess; but it'll be tough taking off over the Appalachians every time they give us twenty-four hours to get ready for the next phase."

"You know," Sergeant Jacks said, when Damianos and Sophie finished their brief conversation, "Ah was wonderin' this mornin' as Ah was runnin' with mah platoon 'bout the name of Pisgah forest. That don't sound like no American word. What's Pisgah come from? The name, Ah mean."

"I looked that up," said Damianos. "I was wondering myself."

"That's a mountain, isn't it?" Sophie asked. "A mountain near Jerusalem."

"That's the mountain"—Damianos spoke authoritatively—

"where Moses was standing when he saw the Promised Land."

"No foolin'?" Jacks cut a bit of steak and held his fork in the air momentarily. "Those old-time pioneers must of really knowed their Bible."

"That's what gets me mad sometimes. Everything means something else." Damianos shook some salt on his steak. "Almost nobody's got the courage to make up his own name for something or someone. They always say, 'Let's call the boy John for my father' or 'Let's call the area Pisgah 'cause it means the mountain where Moses saw the Promised Land.' No matter what you do, no matter where you go, you're always carrying the past with you. What should of been forgotten long ago. Whether you know it or not, you're always carrying a sack of bones on your back—the bones of your ancestors."

"That's an original handle you got there, Gus. Can't say as your name means anythin'." Jack smiled.

Damianos snorted. "That's where you're wrong. Cosma and Damian were Orthodox saints who traveled around with ten others. I forget their names. They were all doctors and went through the countryside healing the sick and not wanting to get paid. They're called the Holy Unmercenaries." He smiled. "So, with what I get paid, I guess I'm one of them wholly unmercenaries myself." He took a sip of wine and stared ahead. "Everything means something else. You try and grab hold of it, and it changes before you get a good grip. For years and years people been living, and nothing's been changed. Not even the names."

He thought of the doe staring at him placidly, then bending her graceful neck to chew on the grass. Why did he go berserk? Why did he kill her? Was he hungry? Had the doe done anything to him? Nothing: the act was senseless, completely without reason. And, granting the fact that slaying the deer was meaningless, a random bit of madness, why did the memory of it remain with him? Why did he always recall the doe in the same way he saw her, suddenly, abruptly, seeing her always as he did for the first time? Damianos tried to work back into his thoughts, tried to follow the deer's spoor in the terrain of his memory, to decide what idea, what word could have triggered the tableau that had been a fairly consistent one since the slaying. Pisgah? Ancestors? Holy Unmercenaries? The fact that everything meant something else? The fact that nothing had changed? What did these have to do with his slaying of the doe, as helpless and harmless as the victim was? The eagle's scream? Or was it all just a puny, human device to justify his feeling of uneasiness, of guilt?

Sophie turned to him. "Gus, I've known you for a long time, but I've never heard you talk like his before."

"You've either seen me cold sober or dead drunk." He lifted his glass. "When I drink wine, I get melancholy and philosophical."

"Yes, fine; but you're really depressed about something."

"When I'm happy," Damianos said, "I'm always depressed. Here I am, about to get married to a woman I should of married as soon as I set eyes on her. A guy who has been a friend of mine for years is gonna be a witness for me tomorrow, and my best man in a couple of months, and all I can think about is that a man can't really change anything. I mean, he wants what he didn't think he wanted. And that, for some reason, he don't want what he wanted all along." He turned to Sophie. "I don't know why I didn't ask you to marry me a long time ago. But I held off. It would of been the best thing for me—to marry, settle down right away. But I didn't ask. Why? Why didn't I ask? When I'd of been happier than I ever would be alone, with nothing. Nothing! This is what I'm getting at. Everything means something. Something important. This is why I'm depressed. 'Cause I don't know what it means." He emptied his wineglass.

"Like right now—I may as well say it. I feel peculiar about Razor Blade. It's like a night jump when you ain't jumped at night for a couple of months. You know the ground is down there. You know where the door is. You can hear the roaring of the airplane. You know your parachute is gonna open, and if it don't, you know you're gonna be fast enough and alert enough to pull your reserve in time, and yet you don't feel comfortable. What can happen? I ask myself. What can happen that ain't happened in every maneuver the U. S. Army's been on since World War Two?" He shrugged his shoulders. "All right!" A wave of the hand. "Five guys will die. One'll get hung up on a tree. Another guy'll fall from a Deuce-and-a-Half and break his neck. Something else'll happen to the others. Five guys will die—let's say that. But there's something more."

Damianos felt an intensity gripping him. *Something more. This time I'll get it.* He leaned his back against the wall and propped his right shoe on the booth's opposite seat. "Something more. I feel like I'm going into combat. I've been in enough of those jumps to remember what it felt like. The adrenalin is always there, pumping away. Always." He stared at the wall. *I'll die,* he thought. *I know I'll die. It's my turn.*

He filled his glass with wine. "Goddamn it, why didn't you stop me? How long was I talking like this? This is supposed to be some kind of half-assed bachelor party. Sergeant Jacks, how come you're not talking? Sophie, what did you put in my drink?"

"Ah'll tell you, Gus. Ah heard a couple NCOs talkin' 'bout Razor Blade like that, wonderin' 'bout it. Ah ain't had that much time to think, bein' mainly with the Jump School. But it's jest a long one, that's all. It's a long maneuver, longer than any Ah remember. Guys start worryin' 'bout bein' out in the field for more than a month, 'cause a lot can happen back home in a month. That's what those men were worryin' 'bout, Ah'm perty sure."

"What can happen back home?" Sophie asked.

"Well," Damianos began, "you see, Sophie, when about twenty to twenty-five thousand guys go away for a long maneuver, their wives have the cars and so forth. . . ." He waved his hand inconclusively. "They drive around a lot, like going to the NCO Clubs, the Officers' Clubs, Von Steuben. They call up old friends, and so forth. It happens every year. The place really starts hopping. The ratio is almost equal."

"Is that really what happens?" Sophie glanced from Damianos to Jacks. "You mean the women can't be without their men for as long as a month without driving around to find someone?"

"That's right, Sophie," Damianos said. "And it ain't only a few. It's most of them. From corporals' wives clear on up to colonels' wives. For a single man, it's the time of plenty."

"But . . . what happens?" She stared at Damianos intensely. "What happens when the men come back?"

"Well"—Damianos shrugged his shoulders and rested a square elbow on the booth—"most of the guys don't care by this time, but a few of them get pretty jealous and they beat up on the woman and then maybe go out and look for the guy." He glanced at her with a slight smile. "What's the matter? Don't you read the papers?"

"This is horrible! It must be terrible for the soldiers!"

"It ain't that bad. It gets worse during the war."

"I don't think women should be that way." Sophie shook her head. "I don't agree. I don't like it. A woman's got to have loyalty to her husband." She pushed her plate away. "How can men fight a war"—she hesitated—"when they know that . . . back home . . .?"

"That's why sergeants was invented," Jacks said.

Damianos put his arms around Sophie. "What's the matter? Why are you disturbed?"

"I just never thought of it, that's all. I mean, I knew things like that happened, but I always assumed that they happened individually, that one woman just weakened and thought she'd feel better if she took a walk. Then she met someone who was nice and polite, and they had dinner together. Then after a few days they kissed and she wasn't as strict as before. I just assumed that it happened this way and not the other—not thousands of women doing the same thing. Somehow it cheapens it, makes it filthy, ugly, hateful."

"Hey, stop this." Damianos squeezed her arm.

"No, I just wanted you to know how I felt about this. I just wanted you to know that I won't do it . . . ever. I just want you to feel confident and to trust me completely."

"Stop it, stop it! I never doubted you." He turned to Jacks. "What the hell did you bring this up for, anyhow?"

Sophie rose to go into the kitchen, and Damianos excused himself to Jacks and followed her. Since the dishwasher was working at the back sink, Damianos leaned Sophie against the nearer wall and took her gently by the wrists. "Now look, Sophie, you're old enough to know all about this. I'm sure you saw the same things happening in Germany. I'm sure the same things happen all over the world, wherever people exist. The reason I think you're so disturbed is 'cause you think I'll be wondering about you. Stop right this minute. I'll trust you. I trust you right now."

"I feel miserable, Gus. I feel terrible."

"But why? Why do you feel terrible? Didn't we have a nice meal? Didn't our good friend Duane show up and say he wanted—felt honored—to be a witness tomorrow and to be a best man in January? Didn't he say that?"

"I feel terrible, Gus, because I allowed myself to give you everything I could offer you as a wife before we got married. I can give you nothing more." She became quiet. "I was not a virgin when you met me. I couldn't be, coming from Germany after the war."

"I know all about it. You told me before. I don't care."

"I want you to listen!" She pawed a few tears from her face. "I was a good girl once. *No, let me finish!* I was a good girl, not because I didn't do anything bad, but because I wasn't satisfied with the good I had done. I wanted to do more. I wanted to get married, to have children, bring them up right. *Let me finish!* But everything wrong happened. I didn't have

a chance to do what I wanted to do. I became a tramp, and that's what I was when I met my first husband. That's how I came to the United States. That's how I became a citizen." She leaned against the wall and sobbed, her hands shielding her face from him. "I can't give you anything more than I've already given you and others. And if you don't trust me, I can't blame you."

Too proud to burrow herself in his embrace, she waited for him to reach over and draw her to him, hoped for his heavy hands to rest on her shoulders, paused for the comfort of their weight, for the inarticulate forgiveness of flesh and bone. "I know everything about you 'cause you told me. The likes of me don't deserve a virgin. I'm not sure I'd want one. I don't think I'd of asked you to marry me if you wasn't pregnant. That's how stupid I am. But it don't matter." He shrugged his shoulders. "It don't matter 'cause I finally asked you to marry me. You'll make a good wife. I don't think I love you"—he felt her stiffen—"but I respect you. I think you'll make a good mother for my children. . . ." He stopped. "For the baby." He chuckled warmly. "Here I got a family all planned. You'll make a good wife. I don't know about love. I don't think I ever was in what people call love. So I'm suspicious of the word. It might be a big hoax. All I can say is I'm pretty sure it'll work out. After all, we're both in our thirties. We're not kids. We're getting married for a good reason. We know each other a long time. We *like* each other. I don't think I'll get in a fist fight 'cause someone stared at you. I might even decide to compliment him on his taste. I mean, we're getting married 'cause we *like* each other, 'cause you're having a baby, and 'cause I don't want it killed or growing up as a bastard, and 'cause I don't want the law to have too much to do with us. Just give us the permit to live together. Outside of that, I want them off my back. Otherwise, with you a mother, I'll have cops stopping around asking me if I gave you money and so forth."

He pulled a handkerchief from his back pocket and patted the tears from her face. "Does it hurt you very much that I said I don't love you, Sophie?"

She looked at him steadily, calculating her response. "No," she said simply. "No, Gus, I'm not angry with you, if that's what you mean. I think we pretty well agree with each other. It'll be a good marriage, I'm sure. I like you, too. I don't love you, but I like you very much."

She returned his handkerchief. "I'm going upstairs to wash

my face and put some makeup on. I look a mess. I'll be down in about five minutes."

Damianos saw her walking away from him to the stairs leading to the upstairs apartment. Even when she had climbed up to the next floor, he continued staring. *Don't love me!* he thought. *Likes me!* He felt hurt that she would say that to him, that she would admit marrying him only because she was pregnant and did not want to bring a bastard into the world. It was as if a knife had been pushed into his heart. *The world's so screwed up. Here a guy asks a woman to marry him 'cause she's pregnant, and right to his face she tells him she don't love him!*

He walked out into the bar to see Sergeant Jacks standing up, ready to walk out. "Look, Gus, Ah gotta be goin' back to the barracks to see how mah boys're makin' out. And Ah got the 'Long Run' tomorrow."

"Thanks a lot for stopping by, Duane. Can you make it around seven tomorrow night? We'll go to the Justice of the Peace and get squared away."

"Sure, sure. How's Sophie?"

"She's OK, I guess. She's been touchy lately. I don't know what it is. Probably be all right once we get married."

After Jacks had left, a group of six men came in and sat at a booth. Since it was a round robin affair, one man getting up each time for the beers, all Damianos had to do was draw the tap beers or pry open the caps of the bottles and ring up the money on the register. The men had had three rounds, four more groups had entered the Green Light, and a brief fist fight had started across the street before Sophie came down from the apartment. She and Damianos did not look at each other but worked behind the bar, limiting conversation to the necessary talk of business. "Ring this up," he would say, and she would depress the keys of the register. "Open these," she would say, and he would pry open the caps of the beer bottles. And in this manner the two worked until closing time—that is, until Damianos decided it was time to close and turned off the neon sign.

"I'm gonna get someone to run the place starting tomorrow," Damianos said when the last person left the Green Light.

"Do whatever you want to do."

"I wanna get you out of the tavern after tomorrow."

"What's the matter—don't you trust me?"

Damianos looked at her steadily. She was drying off a few glasses and faced away from him. His face was a mask, his eyes were steady, his hands were motionless. "Sophie," he said gently, evenly. She continued polishing the glasses, her nervousness and anger obvious in the workings of her head. "Sophie," Damianos called again.

Reluctantly, she turned. Damianos slapped her backhanded across the face, a sharp crack of bone striking soft, white skin. Her eyes opened wide, the glass she held in her hand dropped to the board-meshed floor and shattered, and she remained, holding the dish towel in front of her body with her left hand, staring at him.

"I want you to stop this, *you hear?*" Damianos shouted at her. "I don't know what's come over you, but, whatever it is, I don't like it." He grasped her by the wrists. "I want you out of here by tomorrow 'cause you'll be Mrs. Damianos then. Not because I'm afraid you'll put horns on my head. *Do you hear?* A couple hours ago I said we were old enough and mature enough not to care too much about what the kids care about. I know you're not a virgin, Sophie. I told you that. I know your life story. You know mine. I'm looking forward to tomorrow when you'll be my wife." He pulled her to him, cold, inert, a stiff mannequin. "I told you I don't know what love is." She stiffened even more. "But if I knew what it was," he continued, "I'd of said I do love you." *You stupid fool,* he thought; *too obvious, too obvious.* "Because every now and then I find myself always thinking about you, wanting to be near you." He stared at the wall mirror across from them to see Sophie as she burrowed into his embrace. Damianos frowned into the mirror. "I think I love you, Sophie." At that moment he felt her hands reach across his back and press him tenderly. *Women are silly,* he thought. *Silly . . . and they know it.*

"I love you, too, Gus."

"Let's go upstairs and have coffee."

CHAPTER 20

He and Sophie had spent the afternoon looking for an apartment located between Fort Mosby and Von Steuben, but because most of the available quarters were either in trailer courts or too near the highway, they had decided to keep the apartment above the Green Light until Damianos returned from the maneuver. The cabins and trailers lining Mosby Boulevard had repelled him, reminding him as they did of women like Esperanza, of the rootless, ephemeral existence he had been satisfied with several weeks before. Oppression had seized him whenever they entered a cold, dark cabin or were asked to inspect a narrow trailer. He could not breathe. This was the life he had rejected when he married Sophie; he would not confuse the Damianos he was now with the other self he had known. It was to be a clean start; he would be a new man.

Since this was to be his last evening with his wife, Damianos decided to have dinner in one of the better restaurants and see a film. Halfway through the movie, realizing that he would not be spending the night with her—since Colonel Simms had ordered the Special Troops into the field several days early—he told her to take her coat: they were leaving. In the car, on their way to the Green Light, she teased him, saying she had a headache, she felt tired, she was ill; he had detected a smile on her face, however, and ignored her vague protests.

On entering the tavern, he noticed the girl he had seen walking in Von Steuben. She was sitting alone in a booth. Damianos checked a momentary feeling of frustration; no more city strolls, no more chases: this was a stage he had passed. As attractive and available as she was, he would ignore her. But Sophie stopped at the booth. They knew one another.

"Gus"—Sophie turned to him—"this is a friend of mine. She's been stopping by occasionally. I think you know her husband. I'm sorry"—she appeared embarrassed—"I don't remember your last name, Nikki."

"Clarke." The girl smiled at Damianos. "Barrett and I were in here one evening together. We weren't introduced, but he spoke to you, I think."

Damianos nodded. "He's the guy who's in Jump School right now, ain't he?" He had wanted to go upstairs with Sophie, for they had only a few hours left to be together, but the girl interested him. An hour would not make much difference. He looked Nikki over carefully, preserving the fiction that he was hurried because he did not want to appear too obvious. "How's he doing?"

Sophie broke in: "Let's sit down for a moment."

Damianos held back for an instant. "OK." He pretended to relent and took a seat in the booth. "But I gotta get some equipment ready tonight."

"I haven't seen Barrett for two weeks. He hasn't called me, so I guess the training is taking up most of his time."

Damianos was puzzled. *What's going on here?* he wondered. *Hasn't called her?*

"You mean you ain't talked to him since he left for Airborne training?"

"I'm home all day. I go to the movies, usually after eight o'clock, and come back around eleven. And he hasn't called."

"What d'you think—he's free all the time? He's in Jump School. He's probably got about fifteen minutes to make his call. If he don't get you then, he goes back to his barracks and waits another day."

"Oh," said Nikki, "I thought—"

"You thought *what?* That he's got one of them white telephones next to his bunk? He's gotta call from the orderly room. And them sergeants ain't too easygoin'." Damianos was amazed. *What a stupid ginch,* he thought.

"Do you want a beer, Gus?"

"Naw, that's all right, Sophie. I gotta get ready to leave."

"You've got plenty of time. You don't leave for hours yet."

Damianos angered briefly. He knew when he was being teased. The husband-wife struggle was beginning already, evidently. If this was the case, he knew how to handle the situation. "Okay, get us three beers." He was going to say that he had nothing important to do, but that would have been too obvious. "I could go for a drink."

When he sensed Sophie returning with the bottles, he offered Nikki a cigarette and lighted it for her, gratified that she glanced at him briefly before leaning back in her seat.

"Is he going on the maneuver?" He poured the beers into their glasses without thanking his wife.

"Who?"

"Your husband." He thought: *What a zero.*

"Yes, but that won't be for a week yet. I mean a week after he gets back."

"Don't be too sure." Damianos rested his elbows on the table and hunched his shoulders over them. The table moved slightly. "We weren't going out for a week either, but Colonel Simms told us yesterday that we should be ready to move out this morning."

"You mean Barrett won't have a chance to make his novice jumps before he's sent out in the field?"

"He'll make his jumps. Unless he washes out of Jump School, of course. He'll make his jumps with the men in his cycle. The only thing that'll happen is that right after he makes his five jumps and graduates, he'll be pulled right into the maneuver. That means he won't see you for another month."

"That's not fair!" Nikki stared at him. "That's not fair at all!"

Damianos shrugged his shoulders. He had already determined that Nikki was a rather silly girl, but this last outburst proved it to him. Anyone who said the Army was unfair needed more than a course in logic. The Army did not operate on principles of ethics; Damianos had learned early that it operated on rules and regulations that changed only when those "up top" decided a change was necessary. How could the Army be unfair when all its rules could be found written in stacks of unreadable volumes? Simms had nothing to do with their orders. The Army in this area was General Aarons, who said that everyone will go on maneuver early. Clarke is considered part of the Army. Therefore, Clarke will go on maneuver early. No fair or unfair about it.

Nikki continued complaining about the Army, and Damianos, nodding his head occasionally, appeared to be in agreement with her. Actually, he was not listening. Sophie was getting restless, obviously beginning to wonder when Damianos would mention that he had some equipment to pack so that she could agree with him. But Damianos continued nodding, pretending a great interest in what Nikki was saying. *This'll learn her,* he thought. But Nikki did not seem to tire of talking. She had spoken about California, told Damianos and Sophie about her husband's problems with his family, retold the plot of the film she had just seen, touched briefly on the "ghastly" succession of airline crashes, and admitted her confusion at the numerous riots occurring throughout the world.

"You have some equipment to pack, don't you?" Sophie asked.

"Yeah."

"I really must be going." Nikki paused. "It *is* getting late."

"Hold on," Damianos said. He knew he was behaving stupidly, but this was a lesson Sophie would need to be taught well. "We'll drive you home. There's no percentage in you walking in the streets this late." He patted Sophie on the thigh, signifying that she was to stand up.

The stars blinked silently in the cold night sky. His hands were shoved in his coat pockets, and, balancing on his toes, Damianos breathed deeply. Nikki glanced at him before sliding into the car. After slamming the door shut, Damianos gazed at the sky. He shivered, but whether from the cold or from an impression that had teased him briefly he did not know. For some reason, he dreaded the maneuver. Just that. No more.

"I got a feeling about Razor Blade," he said as he entered the car and turned the ignition key. "I got a feeling in my bones there's gonna be a big snafu."

Sophie, next to him, was silent.

"What do you mean?" Nikki asked. "What's a snafu?"

Sophie shrugged when he looked to her for guidance. He did not like to be vulgar in the company of women, not even his wife. "You look like you been around." He hesitated. "It means situation normal, all fouled up. Only it ain't *fouled* up, if you know what I mean."

"You mean fucked up?"

"That's right," Damianos said uncomfortably. "That's what it means."

Nikki directed him through the city streets until she pointed the house out to him. The clothing store he had stopped at was across the street. Damianos pursed his lips. He had married at the wrong time. Perhaps a week with Nikki would have made him eager to settle down to married life; it was ironic, however, that he would meet her now that he was committed. But his duty was clear-cut, and the experience of his life proved to him that only one's duty was important.

Nikki smiled at him warmly. "Thank you very much for the ride. Good night."

"Stop by the Green Light occasionally," Sophie said. "I'll be upstairs now that we've got someone to take care of the bar. If you get lonely, just visit."

"Thanks. I'll do that."

When Nikki had closed the door and run to her apartment, Sophie turned to Damianos. "I thought you had some equipment you wanted to pack."

"Yeah, that's *all* I got time to do now."

They drove back to the Green Light in silence. She made coffee as he pretended to be working on his equipment. But he had completed his packing that morning. It was merely his excuse to get her out of the theater and back to their apartment. The Clarke woman had ruined all his plans.

The fragrance of coffee made itself evident in the living room while he made a last-minute inspection of his equipment. All that remained for him to do was to get into his fatigue uniform.

He could hear the *glug* of the percolator in the kitchen and the mild clatter of the cups and saucers as Sophie prepared the tray. He shivered pleasurably. For a moment, he was content. He knew, moreover, how heavily this contentment rested on factors that were totally irrational. It was dark and cold outside; within it was warm and lighted. His woman was in the kitchen making coffee and readying herself to bring the doughnuts, which he had seen earlier were stale but which he would eat anyway, pretending not to notice. And he was about to get dressed in his fatigues and have his wife drive him to Fort Mosby, fifteen miles away, not to see her again for a month. Why did everything this moment seem so sweet? Even after their misunderstanding. Even after the first conflict of wills. Perhaps because it was not new, perhaps because it had happened to so many men so many times, this scene, the scene of parting, had been engraved on the human memory—sweet because universal, sweet because elemental, sweet because universally and elementally bitter.

He went into their bedroom and undressed. The shades on the window were not drawn and the light was off, so as he pulled off his trousers and shorts and replaced them with his long underwear and the fatigue uniform he could view the empty, darkened intersection—its shiny cobblestones now reddish-hued, now amber, now green—and see a crumpled newspaper page rolling aimlessly down the street and a man hurrying by, stopping under a streetlamp, lighting a cigarette, and hurrying off again. Damianos sat down and pulled on his boots. "Clodhoppers" they were called in western Pennsylvania. Only there the boots would not have been so high. A mere four or five hooks, not twelve holes.

But it was all the same. Only a few of the incidental props were changed; the plot was unvaried, universal. Warm homes, cold outside; man dressing in the darkness, woman in the kitchen near a bubbling coffeepot (wife, mother, daughter, sister—it did not matter what—a woman). And, outside, night, cold, and eventually, dawn and the unknown. It was all the same. Nothing ever changed. Only the unknown seemed to change. It was unknown, and as soon as it occurred to a man it appeared strange, different from anything he had ever seen. But after he had lived with the unknown, after he had struggled with it, and after he had stored it in those cellar trunks that were his memory, he knew it was not really different, for nothing strange could happen: it was all inevitable. And when he looked to his past, he could not distinguish between one maneuver and the next, between one strike and another, between his first war and his second.

Damianos pulled on his boots strings, not enough to tighten the tongue at the joint and pinch his skin, but enough to permit his foot to feel sheltered and tightened. *Shelter,* he thought; *that's the word.* That is why he shivered a moment ago. He was sheltered, and yet he knew he would be out in the cold again. Everyone felt that, he thought—everyone. Even—or, perhaps, especially—General Aarons and Colonel Simms. He had shivered because he was warm and comfortable and did not want to leave but had to leave because, otherwise, he would be AWOL and be punished by court-martial.

But Aarons is just as unfree as Damianos, he thought. There was really very little difference: Aarons merely had general orders commanding him to call a maneuver within a certain period, while Damianos had specific orders commanding him to be present at a certain place at a certain time. Aarons was at this exact moment probably searching under his bed for his other boot, saying to himself: "Life is a miserable joke. Why did I ever want to be a goddamn Army officer?" It was all the same, Damianos knew. At three o'clock in the morning all men were brothers because all were tired. It was only dawn that alienated them from each other, forcing them to wear different uniforms—some to order, the rest to be ordered.

Damianos stood up to feel his boots comfortably encasing his feet. *Even the Russians,* he thought; *even the damn Russians feel the same at three in the morning. But they know we're up at three, so they set their alarms at the same time. They don't want to get up at three, but they set the alarms before hitting the sack, when they are still full of the sun's moonshine*—he snorted and rubbed his eyes—*when they're full of the daytime's lies. And at three we all get up and say to ourselves: Life is so boring; life is so tiresome. Why can't we all stay in bed?*

"Gus!" Sophie called from the kitchen.

"OK, OK, I'm coming."

He tightened the belt buckle and smoothed the metal-tipped end of the cloth belt into the left belt loop. As he walked from the bedroom he stepped over the binocular case which he had set on the living-room floor. He almost bumped into Sophie as he entered the kitchen.

"I thought we'd have our coffee and doughnuts in the living room," she said.

"I got my stuff all over the floor. Let's drink it here."

She set the tray on the kitchen table.

"I'm going to miss you, Gus."

"Let's not start that. I know you'll miss me. Let's have our coffee and pretend I'm going away for a weekend."

"A lot can happen in a month, Gus."

"Like what?" He glanced at her sharply.

"You can begin wondering why you ever decided to marry me."

"That's been on my mind since you told me the news. I don't see what a month in the field will do to the question."

"You might decide you . . . well . . . you don't want to be married to me anymore."

"But I can't decide that! I already made my decision. I already married you. You're my wife. You're carrying my kid." He blew on the hot coffee. "That's very important to me. I want to be a father." He looked at her meaningfully, debating whether he should tell her of his fears. "I'll be a good husband to you. I'm sure I will."

"I wouldn't want you to feel that I've tied you down."

"But I am tied down! Just 'cause I'm a man I'm tied down. I can't be otherwise. As soon as I was born, things started happening to me. Just 'cause I married you don't mean anything's gonna be different. I'm glad I married you. You'll be good for me. You done me a lot of good so far."

"I saw the way you looked at her."

"At who?"

"At that Clarke girl."

"You mean that tramp? What way did I look at her? How could I help looking at her? She was sitting across from me." He set his cup in the saucer ring. "Look, let's get this straight. I don't wanna argue with you before leaving. I wanna have a nice, quiet conversation. We're two mature people and we oughta be able to get along with each other without fighting all the time. You weren't like this before you told me about the kid. Everything was fine with you then. Well, look, just 'cause you're having my baby don't mean you're gonna try controlling me. And another thing—I don't like that woman's looks. She's a tramp. I forbid you having anything to do with her."

"What makes you think she's a tramp?" But Sophie changed the direction of the talk; perhaps she saw more possibilities along another line. "Just because I'm having your baby.

Well, just because I'm having your baby is no reason for you trying to control *me.*" She stopped there, the momentum of her accusation quivering in abrupt arrest.

"Well, I am. I am, and the sooner you know about it, the better. I forbid you to go out of your way to see her. If she comes into the bar to talk to you, all right, then you talk to her. But you don't go to her apartment. You don't go to the movies with her. You don't go out to dinner with her. Understand?" Damianos groped through his pockets, looking for his cigarettes. "Any broad that goes into a bar dressed up like some goddamn jitterbug, like some Hollywood clown, while her husband's away in Jump School, and drinks beer like it was water, and tells all her business to strangers—and blasphemes—ain't gonna have nothing to do with *my* wife." Then he saw that Sophie was smiling at him.

"What's so funny?"

"Nothing." She tried to cover her smile, but her eyes betrayed her, for they shone. "Say that word again, Gus."

"What word?" He stared at her.

"Forbid. Say you forbid me to see her again."

"Why?" His eyes narrowed.

"Nothing. I just want to hear it."

He repeated the statement as if by rote. "I forbid you to see her again."

"All right, Gus. I won't see her. Since you say so."

"What's the matter? What's going on here?"

Sophie reached over and took his hand. "I just want to tell you that that's a beautiful word—forbid—a beautiful word for a husband to use to his wife." Damianos said nothing, staring at her all the time. "It means he loves her when he says 'I forbid you.' " Her eyes shone. "It means he loves her."

"I love you," Damianos said argumentatively. "I do. I can say it without feeling stupid now. I love you."

Sophie stood up and walked to him. He pulled her down and set her on his lap. "My Gus," she said; "my husband." She placed her left arm around his shoulder and, smiling, ran her index finger gently down his profile. His calloused hand caressed her soft abdomen, rubbing it warmly. A pleasureable shiver seized her. She kissed him on the cheek and rested her temple against the column of his neck.

"Take care of yourself," he said. "Go to the Army doctors right away. If anything happens, contact the Special Troops' Headquarters. They'll know where I'll be."

Her hands stole behind him and interlaced at the back of his neck. "I'll be lonely."

"I know, I know," he murmured. He nipped at the lobe of her ear. "Loneliness ain't bad when you know it'll end."

Her hand caressed his back aimlessly, traveling in wayward half circles across the powerful and hard surface of its muscled ridges. "Do we have time?" she asked.

"Time for what? We got no time whatsoever. You and that Halloween clown took care of that." But he crushed his anger. "What kind of clothes was she wearing? Was that black underwear?"

"No," she murmured. "Those were leotards."

"Crazy goddamn kids."

He pushed Sophie away gently—he was beginning to feel aroused—but quickly pulled her to himself again. His hand cupped her breast. "We'll have plenty of time later." If there was to be a later, he cautioned himself. But the hand which so recently had tried to part them was now caressing her again. "We should be leaving." He spoke halfheartedly, as much to himself as to her. "We keep this up and I'm gonna be late." He rested a hand, which he hoped would remain paternal, on her knee.

"We should be leaving," he said again.

They parted immediately, she to go into the bedroom to get her coat and he to heave the rucksack on his back and get his jump helmet from the sofa. His beret was on the coffee table, and he placed it on his head, tilted rakishly above his right ear.

"I'll carry your binoculars," she shouted from the bedroom. She was drying her eyes when she came out. "Did you forget anything?"

Damianos shook his head.

Sophie drove in silence toward Fort Mosby. The streets were empty and dry. As they passed beneath large trees, the swaying branches striped the windshield with shades of darkness and light. When they reached Mosby Boulevard, the road stretched from horizon to horizon. The primeval stillness and emptiness were punctured only by the blinking amber lights at lonely intersections. The stars were out, the moon was on its way to a nightly oblivion, but the ridge of hazy light that meant dawn was ascending from the east was yet to surmount the horizon that imprisoned it. A car had overturned on the side of the road, its wheels groping stubbily and helplessly toward a salvation that would come with a tow truck after dawn. A mile beyond the overturned car, the carcass of a rabbit lay flattened on the road.

Damianos' cigarette traveled to and from his lips, the

lighted coal glowing, then flaring abruptly in the darkness. Damianos turned to look at her while she stared ahead at the road and knew that she turned to look at him as soon as he took his eyes from her. It was a game two grown people played because they did not want to permit themselves to communicate an affection that both recognized, that both expected. They had nothing to say. She could not very well tell him to be careful, to do nothing rash, for his job demanded that he be careful while performing a rash act. All she could do was to drive him to his destination carefully and to take care of herself, because in her body, at this moment, a small sac was forming that would soon contain a human being, distinguished from the thousands of others born on earth within the same hour by the last name, Damianos, and by the fact that it would represent both parents somehow—whichever way the mysterious rules of nature had ordained. Neither he nor she would know how this happened, but it had happened before and it would happen again, perhaps into eternity, and he knew that she accepted this with the same equanimity, perhaps with the same joy, with which she accepted his forbidding her friendship with Nikki. There were certain rules a woman had to follow when she was loved, and she would exhibit her own love, he was certain, by following these rules, arbitrary or not.

A ridge of pine trees loomed ahead of them. Fort Mosby came into view. The sign of the paratrooper's wings was spotlighted, and, with blocked red and black letters, THE XXIV AIRBORNE CORPS blazed its greetings to a deserted highway. Sophie took a left turn beyond the sign and drove between empty fields until she reached another intersection. A blinking red light stopped her at the crossroads, and she waited long enough to convince the waiting, occupied military-police sedan that she had looked in both directions. Within a few minutes she pulled into the Special Troops' area, now fully lighted, busy with hundreds of men rushing back and forth to the idling Deuce-and-a-Halves. She disengaged the gears of the car, idled the motor, and pulled the emergency brake. And waited.

Damianos opened the door of the car and set his equipment on the ground. Then he turned to her, kissed her quickly on the lips, and stepped out. "Go home right away," he said. "Don't stop for anyone." He slung his rucksack on his back, hung his helmet on the crook of his elbow, and adjusted his beret. "Take care of yourself. I'll phone you as soon as I can." He closed the door and walked away into the darkness of the predawn night. Only when she had lost his figure among the many others, he knew, would she permit herself the luxury of crying.

CHAPTER 21

McIlhenny's name was on the bulletin board. He was to report to the orderly room with fifteen others and—in the two hours remaining to the company before it was to leave for Operation Razor Blade—was to police the lawns and drill field surrounding the company barracks.

There was a certain feeling of ease in McIlhenny now. He had arranged most of his affairs. He had not seen Esperanza since he wrote her the letter and, by not meeting her, had not confronted any of the objects he possessed when he was Captain McIlhenny. It was as if his old self, his old identity, had disappeared and only the recent McIlhenny, this Corporal McIlhenny, had ever existed.

He had, moreover, succeeded in keeping himself out of trouble. Sleep was still difficult for him, but a few cans of PX beer usually aided in putting him in the proper frame of mind for uninterrupted slumber. Peculiar dreams visited him, but only one woke him—a baffling dream. He had been sitting on soil that had evidently been softened by rain. McIlhenny did not recall what his age was in the dream and whether or not he was wearing fatigues; all he remembered about himself at that point was that the world seemed to sparkle. This, in fact, was the reason the question of his age came up when he tried to decipher the dream the following day.

He was sitting on the ground; the earth around him was lucent. Everything, in fact, seemed to reflect light: the dewdrops coating the trees' leaves; small, colorful pebbles; the sun's rays piercing a dark forest to his right, sending poles of golden light to the turf. And he was sitting on the ground cutting pictures out of what appeared to be a magazine or a newspaper's rotogravure section, not with a pair of scissors, but with a straight razor. After tracing the sharp blade around the head and body of a figure, he would set the razor down and free the image with his fingers. Occasionally he would glance about to see that he was situated in a great, flat valley bordered by mountain ranges. It was an area he had never seen before, an area that appealed to him greatly.

He had cut out three figures, all resembling himself, and set them on the ground. As McIlhenny sat still, looking at the images he had freed, he saw them disintegrate from the dampness of the earth. He glanced up, disturbed that this should be the reward to such painstaking labor, and noticed the straight razor falling toward him, uncontrolled and uncontrollable, revolving of its own accord. Perhaps it had been thrown by someone, for it appeared to be aimed; its revolving fall was in slow motion. Sitting on the ground, Indian fashion, he could not get up immediately. He fell back. The straight razor neared him, like a propeller blade revolving in slow motion. He woke up.

The world to which McIlhenny wakened, however, was the one that was counted by the calendars, that was reckoned by men. And it was this world that forced itself on him, its great weight pressing itself down on his chest, choking him, crushing him. After making his bunk, he would lift his footlocker, place it on the bed, and sweep his area with the broom. If that week his platoon was responsible for sweeping the center aisle, he would perform the work on the day assigned him by the sergeant; or if the detail was to clean the latrine, McIlhenny would brush at the toilet bowls, wipe off the mirrors, and scour the washbasins, never permitting himself to remember the days when it was his duty to inspect latrines cleaned by other men. And he cleaned the latrines and swept the floors the way he wanted them done, spending time that could have been spent on something else, something personal. But McIlhenny had nothing else to do. He had lost interest in everything else.

What did he care about politics? The Communist menace did not threaten *him*. What were a hundred million puny human beings to him—to him who was surrounded and attacked by a greater force, the great, looked-forward-to menace? Something frightful approached him, and McIlhenny looked forward to it, whatever it was. Gone were his questions about God, about history; he had no need to study and wonder. He knew, and with this knowledge came not power, not fear, but acceptance, even willingness.

The sixteen soldiers stretched across the drill field, finger to finger, and began walking toward the other end, bending over to pick up candy-bar wrappers, cigarette packs wet with dew, and slips of paper blown about by an aimed and dedicated wind. The long rank of men, not straight now, ruffled like the advancing wave of the sea on a hard-packed beach, walked toward the limit of their responsibility, and policed the area, clearing it of the flecks of white hidden in the general mass of green.

It was cold, but because they were troopers of the 43rd Airborne Division, they would not think of raising the collars of their fatigue jackets. They walked stiffly, arms slightly bent at the elbows, sloping at the shoulders, never moving an inch unnecessarily, not giving the inquisitive wind the opportunity to sneak up through the sleeves and into the chest and back.

The troopers were fully dressed for the field; steel helmets were secured to heads by airborne chin straps. The long winter underwear beneath the fatigue suits made the men look thirty pounds heavier, and because of it they walked stiff-legged across the drill field until, finally, they arrived at the farthest boundary. After returning to the barracks for their field packs, McIlhenny and the others were instructed to march to the airfield. His rifle company had evidently been chosen for an immediate mission; it was to be flown to the area of operations.

The trucks were lined up in company formation. Units of the 43rd had been pulling out all day and all night. Most of the five rifle companies were still on Post, and it was only the support groups, the signal battalions, the division engineers, and some of the command and control battalions that had gone earlier to organize the base of operations. Of the 12,093 officers and men in the 43rd Airborne Division, approximately half had arrived at the operational base, located somewhere in western North Carolina; the other half would be there the following day.

Only a man who had led a secluded life by his own choice, in order not to be thrown into the temptations and tensions he feared, could know the excitement McIlhenny experienced at this moment. This was to be his great opportunity to leave the Post without involving himself in the same routine, without having his loneliness, his apathy, his confusion made obvious to him when he saw a woman's smile, when he heard the tap-tap-tap of a woman's heel on the pavement, and when he encountered the never-ending occasions for weakening.

The rifle company marched along the highway. Ahead of him, McIlhenny could see the great arched hangars of the airfield and, on the runways, the waiting C-119s. In fifteen minutes, he reasoned, they would be there. They would stand at ease near the aircraft and wait. No one would know why; they would merely wait. In a chaotic world, waiting was the only constant factor. As long as men were permitted or were forced to wait, no chaos would seem new to them. As he marched along, McIlhenny took deep breaths. He did not feel as cold as he did previously. In fact, something—some idea—had made him feel at ease with the world. *That's right,* he recalled. *The dream . . . the razor dream . . . pleasant, a pleasant dream. I can see the horizon,* he thought.

When the columns arrived at the airstrip, the men were given at-ease and the sergeant permitted them to light cigarettes. Most of the troopers had returned to the maneuver pattern: a lighted cigarette was never thrown away. The lighted coal was pinched off and the butt was stuffed in the pocket, to be extracted when the light-up signal was given again. No one knew how long the men would be waiting in front of the C-119 before they would be given permission to enter—it could be ten minutes or it could be enough time to take three drags on a cigarette—and this was the most practical way of smoking.

It was cold now that the troopers had stopped. The quick march had succeded in warming them considerably, but the wait permitted the cold to seep into their bodies again. It was not pleasant, this wait; it may have made McIlhenny feel intellectually or philosophically secure, but it chilled him physically.

"Hey, Sarge," someone shouted, "how long we gonna wait here?"

The sergeant angered. "You don't see no fly-boys here, do ya? What the hell d'you want me to do—complain to the janitor?"

"I'm freezing my nuggets off," the voice said.

"You ain't got no nuggets to speak of." When the sergeant stopped, he heard a mutter from the direction of the voice, "Then why're you a soprano?" he asked. There was a laugh, and the troopers settled down to wait again.

"Hurry up an' wait; hurry up an' wait. Lord, Ah don' know about this U-nited States Ahmy."

McIlhenny shivered. No one seemed to be coming.

A nervous, grating voice next to McIlhenny spoke. "What this fucken Army needs is a time-and-motion-study man. All we got here is time and no motion." The speaker shivered and sucked in air. "Jesus, I'm freezin'."

"All right," said the NCO. "Let's double-time in place."

He called them to attention and gave the command. They

began running in place, pumping their arms as much as possible to warm themselves. After three minutes, the NCO called a halt.

"Here they come," someone said, and the company looked up to see five Air Force men walking toward the C-119.

"Man, I shoulda joined the Air Force," the man next to McIlhenny said. "They got themselves the *real* life."

The paratroopers waited in the cold until the sergeant received permission from the pilot to bring the men in. The NCO called the troopers to attention and marched them in two files toward the Flying Boxcar. They carried their equipment into the aircraft on their arms and, after arriving at the canvas bucket seats they were to sit in, sat down and placed their combat packs and rifles between their legs. It was just as cold within the fuselage as it was outside, for the doors had been open for quite some time, and all the men could do was huddle close to each other, hoping that the pilot would decide quickly to tell his crewmen to close the doors.

McIlhenny felt a momentary tremor pass through his body but quickly reminded himself that they were not going to jump today, that they were merely flying to western North Carolina and to Operation Razor Blade. By this time in McIlhenny's paratroop career, although he seemed as fearless as the other paratroopers, he had developed a permanent dread of the surroundings: the perpetual cold; the gray murkiness of the aircraft's metal womb; the forced, subway-like intimacy of the interior; the studied nonchalance of pre-flight conversation; and the quorum of cigarettes on the drag. Even now—when he did not wear a parachute, did not have a reserve hanging from his chest—McIlhenny found it difficult to persuade himself that he was going to land with the craft, that at some point the red light would not flash, the sergeant's stentorian voice would not blare out a *"Stand up!"* and the sticks of paratroopers would not all, to a man, leap up, eager and expectant, to near the screaming door and see the carpet of the earth below.

The propellers began with a roar, a roar so loud as to be painful, a roar to which no one could accustom himself no matter how often he sat in a canvas bucket seat and pretended to be thinking of something else. The Air Force crewmen, who seemed to have accustomed themselves nicely to the roar, moved through the aisles with the nonchalance of men who wore parachutes only for the sense of security they offered and not as daily implements to their lives, implements that were used every time they were worn. They went to the doors and closed them. The roar of the engines became more furious than ever.

McIlhenny, looking past the drab, grayish world of the aircraft, stared at the small window and saw the landscaped green and the concrete gray of the runways drifting past the windows. The pilot had evidently completed his taxiing to the boundaries of his strip and began turning the craft and pointing its nose. The roar increased until it became more than a punishment for the ears, until its effects were felt by the nervous system. Then, with a climactic rush that was merely a preface, it sprinted, gained speed and momentum, and charged down the airstrip. When the horizon lowered, Corporal McIlhenny knew the C-119's wheels had left the ground. In a matter of seconds the craft was hundreds of feet above the earth, banking over Fort Mosby. He saw the great water tower; the blocklike company barracks of the 43rd; the roads, now virtually empty of traffic; the deserted motor pools; and the pine forests that seemed like landscaped grass, fearfully brimming at the confines the engineers had imposed on them.

The aircraft straightened and winged its way eastward. Corporal McIlhenny closed his eyes. By now he had accustomed himself to the enjoyable feeling that he would not be jarred awake by the preparatory shuffling of boots, by the shout of the NCO, by the flashing red light, and by the green light that promised a quick, cold exit into propeller blast and noise. It was good; it was comfortable. Things were going according to plan. There was order. He was permitted the luxury of waiting, and he had grown accustomed to waiting. Waiting was the only sure thing in the world. That and death. It was gratifying to know that life had not changed that much, that when all else had failed, a man could put his trust in two eternal verities and have all his life to prepare for both. His head bowed, and McIlhenny slept soundly, a nap—sweet because undeserved—in the middle of the day.

He woke gradually when he felt the airplane bank to the left. Looking out of the window, which at this angle was now below him, he saw a thin path—a highway. A string of small, insectlike vehicles crept, motionless, in what McIlhenny realized were thirty-yard intervals: a convoy of Deuce-and-a-Halves driving to the 43rd Airborne Division Maneuver Headquarters. When the pilot banked his craft to the right, McIlhenny saw the entire panorama of a highway covered from horizon to horizon with military trucks and jeeps, proceeding gradually, without haste, to western North Carolina.

Operation Razor Blade will soon begin, he thought. His mind was blank. All the fears and hopes he had expressed to himself or to others concerning the maneuver seemed to have been washed clean. His mind possessed an objectivity, a clarity that amazed him. Somehow, in his sleep, his mind had divorced itself from the turmoils, the chaos that churned and battled in his heart. He was merely a man sitting in a canvas bucket seat in a C-119, flying toward Maneuver Headquarters. During the next few weeks he would merely act. Gone was the feeling that he would encounter his destiny in western North Carolina. The sleep had done him good, evidently. Midday sleep was always good, for in afternoon naps a man saw pleasant dreams, and even if he could not remember these gracious dreams, he was nevertheless rested. His mind was clear, and life, when a man is rested, when his mind is clear, is itself a pleasant dream.

He dozed off again, to wake up when, with a quick jolt, the aircraft's wheels touched the runway in western North Carolina.

CHAPTER 22

With numbers taped to their steel helmets, the trainees stood at attention while Sergeant Jacks inspected the ranks. The day was calm. Across the field, a large red banner leaned against its staff. If airfields are noisy with roars and screeches that threaten Airborne Trainees, Rickenbacker Air Force Base—because of the maneuver—was a quiet retreat this early Monday morning. The comforting silence permitted the soldiers to ignore the test they would soon endure. A high winter sun had cleared the fuzzy clouds of dawn, and the world about them, flat with alternating blocks of grass and concrete, seemed gentle and peaceful.

This morning was the first time Barrett Clarke had not run since he had entered Jump School; he felt amiable. The blood and muscles which would have been throbbing from his exertion were now drowsy; no further tests would be imposed on them.

His body had not dishonored him. It had proved to be the willing instrument of his mind, a mind that had willingly abdicated its role as controller of the body when Clarke had judged that the sergeants knew better than he how to train. Now, in this calm, lazy morning, as noiseless and empty as a suburban Sunday, the body's obligations had been fulfilled. It was now up to his mind and will to complete the chore that had first punished and disciplined his compliant flesh: he must jump from an airplane in flight. But he did not want to think about this too much. Better to ignore the finale of the day and consider, instead, the sequence of events that had prepared him for the finale.

The trainees had put their parachutes on earlier. The heavy T-10 chute, attached to Clarke's back by means of harness straps, had been secured on him by a quick-release assembly located over his solar plexus. Having slipped his arms through the sleeve loops and squatted to adjust the harness' saddle under his buttocks, Clarke had straightened out the two chest and two leg straps and pushed the metal lug of his right chest strap into the quick-release. The release mechanism was permanently attached to his left chest strap. An aviator's kit bag had been placed between the leg straps and his groin for protection, so that the straps, brought under his crotch and passed through their respective rings, would not pinch his testicles during the descent.

His parachute was now locked on his body. When his jump would be completed, or if the worst happened and he needed to get out of his harness immediately, he would merely turn the button on the quick-release and strike it hard with the flat of his hand. The chest and leg straps would fall limp. He would be free of his harness within seconds.

Over the T-10 he had attached the clasps on the back of his reserve chute to the two metal rings of his chest harness. Finally, Clarke had secured himself by passing the harness belt through the reserve and tightening it around his waist. He stood now, easily, at parade rest and thought of the sequence of events that would begin once he moved his boots from the area they now occupied.

"Number 182, how's your ringworm today?"

"It still itches, Sergeant!"

"You gonna feel relieved up there, Number 182. All that cool air whippin' 'round you's gonna refresh you."

"I hope so, Sergeant!"

The NCO stepped back to inspect the trainee. "Number

182, why ain't your fatigue trousers got their customary knife crease in 'em?"

Number 182 looked down. "But, Sergeant . . ."

"Now, Ah diden tell you to look, did Ah?" Jacks grinned. "For not havin' confidence in yourself when you was certain your fatigues was knife-creased . . . git down an' give me ten!"

The sound of Jacks' voice, the good-natured bantering, the grunts of Number 182—who, because he was wearing his parachute harness, did squat jumps instead of push-ups—helped Clarke in his fight against a terror that up to this moment had not been able to frighten him.

The most disturbing part of the day was the anticipated but never experienced event. The silence, previously comforting, was now oppressive. He knew, however, that the great noise of airplanes taxiing back and forth would be much more intimidating. Clarke stared ahead, forgetting for minutes the fact that Sergeant Jacks inspected his rank, and thought only of the moment when he would be dancing toward the open door.

It was curious that he never feared the split second he would stand in the door—only the dancing to it. Once he stood in the door, he would be committed to jumping out of the airplane.

Whenever his mind rebelled, whenever he refused to think about something he would be required to do, he quickly forced himself to return to that point and dissect it as thoroughly as possible. Rehearsing his fears, bringing them to sunlight, he knew, was the best way to render them harmless.

"Number 220, how come you got your chin strap on backwards?"

Clarke, his face still frozen to the front, realized that Sergeant Jacks had worked his way up the rank so quietly that he had not noticed it. The sergeant was inspecting the man next to him; six trainees had dropped out between Clarke and 220 since the beginning of the training course. More than fifteen had quit from the sixty originally in Jacks' platoon.

"I didn't know it was on backwards, sir!"

"Don't call me sir!" Jacks shouted, as Clarke knew he would. "Ah *work* for a livin'." His hands on his hips, Jacks stepped back a pace. "Oh, Ah'm sorry"—he mimicked the trainee—"how could you know your strap was on backwards when it was already on your cotton-pickin' chin? What's the matter, Number 220? Don' you dress yourself in the mornin'?"

"No excuse, Sergeant!"

"Git down an' give me ten."

Number 220 squatted and did two squat jumps before Jacks stood in front of Clarke. Number 227 snapped to attention. Jacks bobbed his head right and left, checking every loop, every strap, every juncture in Clarke's dress. He pulled at the harness, glanced at the chin strap, and checked the quick-release box.

"Number 227?" Jacks spoke softly.

"Yes, Sergeant!"

"Where did you go to school?"

"In California, Sergeant!"

"An' how high was the highes' classroom in that school, Number 227?"

Clarke hesitated. "I don't understand, Sergeant!"

"How high, in floors, was the highes' classroom you ever sat in?"

Clarke was confused. "Two stories, I guess, Sergeant!"

"You guess! You guess! An' you wanna be an airborne paratrooper! Git down an' give me ten!"

One, two. Jacks remained impassive. *Three, four.* He stepped back and glanced down the rank. *Seven, eight.* He looked both right and left. *Ten, eleven.*

"Now . . . how high was your highes' classroom?"

"Two stories, Sergeant!"

"That's not too high, is it, Number 227?"

"No, Sergeant!"

"You gonna be much higher today, ain't you, Number 227?"

"Yes, Sergeant!"

"You gonna be in the *highes'* classroom in the U-nited States today, Number 227." Then he added patriotically: "An' that means the world, don' it, *Number 227?"*

"Yes, Sergeant!"

"Git down an' give me ten. Jest on principle."

Clarke squatted and gave him ten more squat jumps and one more for the airborne. By this time Jacks had gone to the next man and stood before him, moving his head, rooster-like, looking for errors.

Clarke's body was slowly recuperating from the exhaustion of the past two weeks. He felt stronger than he had ever felt before, stronger and more manly. This was a paradox. No matter how they treated him, no matter how juvenile he felt, performing push-ups and squat jumps for punishment, all these exercises, these tests, enabled him to feel more confident and manly. He thought he had known the limits to his endurance, but the vague, thrilling insight that there were no limits to a man's endurance was slowly changing his mind. He had burned calories he had not replaced with food, and he felt stronger; he had run for miles after he thought he would not be able to throw his foot out another step; he had done sets of "correctional push-ups" when he thought he could do no more. And this was all a foretaste of what he could do, of the forces he had within him.

Life was puzzling: that a finite, reasonable human being, convinced of his finitude and his ability to reason, could punish himself and strain himself until, unwittingly, he had surpassed the limits that he, himself, consciously or unconsciously, had established as limits.

There are no limits to the body if it is a disciplined instrument . . . obeying a mind that has . . . He stopped, frightened. He was about to think something, and though he was interested in its consequences, he still feared them. For they were fearful. He began again: *There are no limits to the body if it is a disciplined instrument . . . that obeys a mind that has abdicated its function and succumbs to the authority of fear and of force.*

He could not have run, he realized, the distance and at the speed he had run last Saturday, on that horrendous ten-mile dash over sand and forest trails to the airfield and the marshaling area, if he had personally decided to do it. *My will is not that strong. I'd have convinced myself that I should stop, that I was serving no useful purpose in overextending myself that way.* And yet, the past Saturday, he had run ten miles, dissecting in the process his motives for not dropping out and discovering that they were primarily ones of anger, of hatred. He did not drop out of the run because he felt certain this was what the sergeants, and particularly Jacks, wanted him to do. If Jacks could have run that far and that fast, Clarke had thought, there was no reason he could not do the same.

He had also toyed with the idea that Jacks might collapse on the way, might suffer a stitch in his side and fall in front of Clarke, and that he, ordinarily a civilized man, of a good Philadelphia family, would have taken the most ferocious delight in running over the sergeant's body—would, in fact, have taken his time about running over Jacks, perhaps by turning and twisting on his bootheels.

"Parade . . . rest!" Sergeant Jacks' voice broke the stillness of the morning. Keeping his right boot in place, Clarke raised his left and slammed it to the concrete, toes pointed out in a forty-five-degree angle. A C-119 taxied past the waiting ranks of trainees and continued to the end of the runway. There, far out of sight, it turned and approached the soldiers.

His knees felt weak as he walked to the metal ladder and climbed into the long, hollow fuselage of the plane. In a daze, his hands still and sure but his heart throbbing wildly, Clarke walked down the aisle. Golden light poured into the area where he was to sit, but for the moment Clarke did not notice it: he was preoccupied with fastening his seat belt across the girth of his reserve parachute. When he had succeeded in securing his safety belt, he looked around him, shivering slightly from the cold that whipped up through the open doors, and wondered what to do with his hands. They seemed to stare up at him, idle and white and cold. He tried to ignore them by placing them on his thighs.

He felt light, inadequate, as if the slightest breeze would be strong enough to blow him away, as if the shortest fall would be great enough to splinter every bone in his body. His only consolation was that he was a number, 227, and that everyone else in the aircraft (with the exception of the cadre, who were, admittedly, of a different breed of men) was in the same predicament. *If they can do it, so can I.* Besides, he was not to be the first, or the last, to jump from an airplane. *What about the thousands upon thousands of men—many younger than I—who had jumped from airplanes into combat, jumping to kill or be killed?* Although this was well reasoned for a man in his situation, Clarke realized, it still did not comfort him.

With every roar and scream of the engines, his heart pounded harder. He needed a cigarette. He needed one desperately. The man next to him was pulling out a pack, and Clarke, in the roar that prohibited communication, tapped him on the knee and motioned with two outstretched fingers that he wanted one.

Many of the trainees were smoking, but most of the soldiers stared ahead, the skin of their faces pulled tight after weeks of rugged training, fighting within them a mounting dread that seemed to etch itself permanently into their personalities.

Will they ever forget what it is to fear, Clarke wondered, *and to fight this fear . . . now that they have been trained to ignore it?*

The C-119 lifted off the ground after a great running start. Within a few minutes it had summed the height from which the trainees were to jump. The earth below moved slowly, casually, as if nothing different, nothing extraordinary was occurring. The earth was a patchwork quilt, an abstract painting. Geometric shapes of different colors wedged in against each other, separated by ridges that were probably hobbles or wooden fences or steep, soil-packed mounds. Contours flowed freely, like meandering, lustrous rivers, in alternating browns of plowed earth and greens of alfalfa or timothy. The earth rotated onward, following seasons that man had surmounted and ignored, resting in the winter while man had taught himself, cleverly, not to require rest. Narrow rivers flowed over indentations of the earth and, reflecting the slanting rays of the winter sun, appeared metallic at the craft's lonely height. Small tufts of clouds, scattered indiscriminately throughout the blue sky, seemed forlorn and useless. The black shadow of the aircraft was still, fishlike, over level land, with hardly a ruffle disturbing its outline. Then, approaching a fence, a farm divide, a river's scar, a wedge of pine forest, it fluttered, sank and rose, then steadied itself as soon as it attained another flatness in the placid earth.

The red light flashed on.

The NCOs called the trainees to their feet. The soldiers struggled erect, lost balance momentarily, then righted themselves.

"Hook up!"

Clarke reached up to the static line and tried to fasten his hook to the wire. He had done it so often in practice, but now something was wrong! Now that he had to do it quickly, his fingers would not respond! There! He had done it! He should have felt relieved, but he did not.

"Check static lines!"

The trainees pulled and released the static lines. Clarke saw that his was secure.

"Sound off for equipment check!"

"Twenty OK." . . . "Nineteen OK." . . . "Fourteen OK."

"Ten OK." . . . "Five OK." . . . And, finally, Clarke felt the tap on his buttocks and shouted: "One OK!"

"Stand in the door!"

Clarke was first in his stick of paratroopers. He danced to the door, right foot extended, left foot in drag, his left hand raised above his shoulder, gripping his static line. *"One-two-three,"* and he was at the door, at the threshold to the sky. This was the end, the culmination of a series of events. Clarke was now more conscious of fate, of the irrevocability of decision, than at any other time in his life. Whatever he had done in his history had led him eventually to this open door, to the cold propeller blast that raced through his opened, booted, shivering legs. Below him was the earth, occasionally obscured by small, delicate clouds, and above it, standing in an open door, was Barrett Clarke, ready to jump.

His hands were outstretched to the wind-buffeted jambs. His knees were slightly bent—the right knee angled at forty-five degrees, the left closer to the threshold. He was ready to leap. Staring ahead to the thin line of the horizon, ridged by a few low clouds, he realized that life was a series of doors, each promising escape but each fulfilling what every man wanted deeply: freedom, self-knowledge, and, finally, death, the end of doors, the end of leaping.

Sergeant Jacks was standing above him, to his left. "Er you scared, Number 227?" he shouted.

"No, Sergeant!" Clarke said, as mildly as he could in the roar.

"Ah diden think you'd be." Clarke, staring at the horizon, did not look up to see Jacks' expression. "Tell me, Number 227. What do you see down there below you?"

"I see a pine forest, Sergeant."

"That's good. It's good to know it's still there." He paused. "Er you nervous now, Number 227?"

"No, Sergeant!"

"What do you see now, Number 227?"

"I see a stream, Sergeant!"

"We call 'em things rivers down South, Number 227. What do you see now?"

"I see a road, Sergeant!"

"That's Patterson Road, Number 227. That's the end of the line for you!"

The green light flashed. Clarke felt a powerful, stinging slap on his buttocks.

"Go!"

He jumped.

Crouched like a babe, his hardened hands tenderly holding his reserve parachute, Clarke fell through the sky. *One thousand*. The propeller wash, as soon as he had exited, had turned him to the left abruptly, and as he dropped the fifteen feet before his parachute cord was broken, the wash roared inside his steel helmet. *Two thousand*. His eyes had not closed. Below his boots, the patchwork earth waited for him. *Three thousand.* Far to his left, at the horizon, at the boundaries of his peripheral vision, the speck of the sun's reflection on an auto's windshield glared at him. *Four thousand.* The canopy of his parachute blossomed, and Clarke felt a gentle tug. The aircraft and its roaring gone, he looked above him to a silent sky.

But he did not fall. He seemed suspended in the air, a plaything of the winds. Hands outstretched above him, clutching risers, booted feet dangling below him aimlessly, he glanced at an empty, silent world, and if at that moment a dinosaur had roared at him from one of the clearings, he would not have been shocked. For the world was new again to him. Another birth, another door, the snapping of another cord, and he was free and weightless again.

His eyes adjusted to the approaching earth in stages; at first it seemed that he had not fallen, that he was held, suspended, and gazed on a world he had never seen before. But then, as his body fell toward the earth, he became conscious of the differing focuses, the quickly enlarging dimensions that seemed to freeze for an instant, then to enlarge again once he had passed another stage. The silence was overwhelming. Never had his eyes worked so much, his ears so little. The drop zone below him had not changed; it was still a sandy, tannish platform without indentations, without shadows or shade. But the forest that surrounded it had been transformed from a green carpet of pine trees to individual trees of varying heights, to spires and clearings, to firebreaks and beige dirt paths ribboning through the green trees.

And ahead of him, dark and toylike, he saw his shadow enlarging on the hard-packed earth. He brought his boots and knees together, raised his eyes to a horizon higher than he and spiked by treetops, and, in the seconds that remained to him, repeated a personal litany of relaxation: *Relax, r-e-l-a-x.*

The earth touched his toes.

His legs bent like disciplined springs; his hands pulled down on his risers until they were over his face; his elbows scraped against his chest. Falling, he struck his calf, his thigh, his buttocks; and, turning, he rolled upon the earth, hard and unyielding but friendly. In a heartbeat he was up, erect, the collapsed canopy hugging the sand of the drop zone. He turned the button and struck his quick-release. The straps fell limp.

As he stuffed the parachute into his aviator's kit bag, he

smiled. It was a beautiful day. Over the drop zone's platform, blobs of camouflaged canopies lay collapsed and men were pulling them into bundles and stuffing them into their bags. A cool wind caressed his forehead, now damp from perspiration that, politely, had not announced itself to him before. He attached the handles of the kit bag to the clasps of the reserve chute and threw the bag over his shoulders. His head passed between the bag's handles and the reserve that rested across his collarbone.

Mild, dull sounds broke the preternatural silence of the drop zone. And then, as he was marching toward the assembly point where he would return his used parachute and get into the Deuce-and-a-Half to return to the airfield, he heard the chirping of a bird. Like an old lady, it seemed to be singing in silence, attempting to recapture in its loneliness the feeling of a bird community that at the moment did not exist.

Clarke marched happily over the sand, which gave slightly to the pressure of his booted feet. If he had not been weighted down by his equipment, he would have liked to run to the assembly area, leaping over an occasional stump in his way.

The men stood in files, in their particular stick order, and waited for the sergeants to arrive with their clipboards to check them. When the roll call had been completed, they marched past two trucks and gave their used and reserve chutes to men on detail. They walked to the waiting trucks, jumped on, lighted cigarettes, and talked excitedly to one another about their jumps. Two eighteen-year-olds across from Clarke were planning to go into Von Steuben when all their jumps were completed and "beat up on" a few straightlegs. That ten minutes ago they too had been straightlegs did not seem to enter their minds. Agreed between themselves, they tried to persuade a third trooper to go with them, but he held back. "I don't know 'bout that," he said. "I seen some pretty tough legs in my lifetime."

Clarke borrowed another cigarette and dragged on it slowly. The truck lumbered its way from the drop zone to a dirt road that led to the highway and to Rickenbacker. The day was still mild, there was little wind, but the instructors wanted to get in as many jumps as possible so that, if the weather changed, if the wind picked up—as there were indications—the trainees would have most of their novice jumping completed.

Clarke did not speak. He sat back and looked about him at the trainees, at the world outside the open truck, and tried to control a mounting feeling of exultation. Like an adolescent after first love, he found it difficult to believe that parachuting was not new, that many men before him had done it. In this was the grandeur of the ancient earth: there was always some new pleasure to be found in unexpected places, in unlooked-for acts. Fear, when studied, ceased to be fearful; terror, when confronted unswervingly, ceased to be terrible; life was clear and certain, and the threshold to the sky could be attained by the use of quiet reason. Barrett Clarke sighed happily. *It's good to be alive.*

They took new parachutes, entered the waiting C-119s again, attached their safety belts, roared up into the sky, and received the "get ready" signal from the red light.

On his second jump Clarke looked up to check his canopy and saw that he had a malfunction. A sharp, exquisite pain tore into his chest, but his mind was alert. The canopy, he saw, was beginning to invert around the skirt on his right side. The skirt had blown inward through a pair of suspension lines that were attached to the risers above his shoulders.

For a moment, he hesitated. His mind, quick enough to detect the malfunction, did not recall the method for repairing it. The skirt was forming a secondary lobe, a large pimple, and air filled it in at the expense of the rest of the canopy. He dangled in the air, thinking about what to do, ignoring the ecstatic impression he had received on his first jump. He realized, logically, that, though quiet and still, the malfunction occurring above him was a life-and-death matter. He looked down to the earth briefly. He was still far enough away to be able to pull his reserve if the situation worsened. And yet he did not want to panic and pull the rip cord now, for it might be a more serious mistake: the two parachutes, incompletely inflated, could begin revolving, each taking the other's air, each growing smaller and smaller with every revolution, until one or two hundred feet from the drop zone both would collapse and he would plunge to his death.

Clarke blinked. The bubble was getting larger. Whatever would happen would happen soon. He must make a decision. He shook his right riser once, again, then again, and finally, with the blood pounding in his temples, he shook it violently back and forth, only the methodical jerking of his right hand showing that he did it with a plan and not in panic. His arm worked feverishly, back and forth; his eyes strained on the bubble. And slowly, effortlessly, the skirt smoothed over, and Clarke looked down to see that the earth was approaching.

His hand shook uncontrollably as he tried to stuff the canopy into his kit bag.

The third was like the first, remarkable only in that the pleasure Clarke had experienced on the initial jump was doubled because nothing untoward had happened to excite him.

The fourth and fifth jumps were to be accomplished with full field equipment and weapons' packs. The first three jumps were always "Hollywood" jumps, not weighted down with necessary baggage, not ungainly, utilitarian exercises.

The men returned to the areas where they had left their field packs, with the horseshoe blanket rolls and their M1s in padded weapons' containers, and put them on. Now they weighed one hundred pounds more than usual. They walked stiff-legged and ducklike to the C-119s, struggled up the ladders into the fuselages, and lumbered to the bucket seats. The sergeants had told them that all five jumps were to be performed that day because high winds were coming up from the south; if all the jumping was not completed today, the trainees' graduation might be postponed until the following Saturday, with morning runs reinstituted to keep the men in the proper physical condition.

"Is that understood?" the sergeants asked. The trainees roared their approval.

Clarke was first in his stick again for the fourth jump. Sergeant Jacks looked out of the open door to the markers on the drop zone's surface. Clarke glanced at Jacks and saw the powerful 120-mile-an-hour prop blast take the skin on the sergeant's face and push it back, molding it against the bony structure of his skull.

"Number 227!" Jacks shouted in Clarke's ear. "Was that you that almost met your Maker on the secon' jump?"

"Yes, Sergeant!"

"Be careful on this here one. Winds er gettin' stronger. Stay on the drop zone."

"Yes, Sergeant!"

The green light flashed.

"Go!"

His canopy was intact and taut. Paratroopers above and to Clarke's right slipped away from the forest, toward which the gentle but insistent wind drove them, and directed themselves to the drop zone. A few jumpers were permitting themselves to be taken dangerously near the dirt path that divided the DZ and the forest, but Clarke had tired of adventure and sought only to complete his required five jumps without any more excitement. He was falling faster now, he knew; the extra weight was telling. As he neared the earth he felt the wind pulling him, realizing that what seemed to be a gentle wind ceased being gentle when it pushed against a canopy of thirty-five feet diameter. He landed hard, on his right side this time, for his left was splinted with his weapons' pack. The parachute dragged him.

After getting to his feet, he ran behind the canopy, trying to sprint around it before another gust made this impossible. Finally, breathing heavily, he succeeded in collapsing his chute. As he was stuffing it into the kit bag, he saw a colored boy being dragged across the hard-packed earth. Clarke dropped what he was doing and sprinted to help. When he was returning to his parachute, another jumper was dragged about fifty yards away from him. Clarke ran to help again.

By the fifth jump the wind was steady, coming in from the south and east at twelve knots per hour, not strong enough to warrant calling off the jump but steady enough to call for extra precautions. Clarke was sixth in his stick. In the air, he struggled fiercely against the wind. He landed near the trees and, after a short dash, collapsed his canopy. The five novice jumps were over. It was still Monday. He would be home in two hours.

«««»»»

Allowing his car to warm up, Clarke permitted himself the luxury of listening to music over the radio, for in the barracks the sergeants forbade radios or record players. He was evidently still nervous: as he reached over to flick a cigarette ash into the tray on the dashboard, he managed to get it only halfway before the shaking of his hand knocked it off. A newscaster broke into the music to say that another airliner, with sixty aboard, had gone down in the Mediterranean; NATO planes were searching for survivors. Clarke turned off the radio and concentrated on his driving.

His nervousness, he thought, might be explained because of his expectancy; after all, he had not seen Nikki, had not spent a night with her for three weeks. *Then, again. . . . No, it couldn't be! It couldn't be that business with the parachute.* He had forgotten it as soon as he had hit the ground on the second jump. And even if he was shaken up by the partial malfunction, the following three jumps were good ones—ideal, in fact—to help wipe away any unfortunate memories. That was the reason generals ordered new jumps immediately when anything went wrong on a mass jump. For the unit's morale. *An excellent idea,* Clarke thought. There was no reason to permit fear to work its way into a man or a unit. Suppose the partial malfunction had occurred on his fifth and final jump? And suppose he was not due to parachute for another month after his novice jumps? This would mean one entire month to think about malfunctions, to think about the terrible moment when a paratrooper glances up to see a ripped gore; a cigarette roll, with the skirt unaccountably rolling up toward the apex; a semi- or complete inversion, with the nylon suspension lines and the canopy slowly grinding at each other, burning into each other, then dissolving at the great heat. And then the helpless, chilling drop.

No, it was much better that the generals called jumps immediately after a disaster, after a few deaths. Fear should be stopped immediately. And only reason—calm, quiet reason, holy where nothing else holy had survived—only reason could combat fear.

He pulled into his street. The lights at that moment were turned on throughout Von Steuben. Clarke smiled expectantly when he slowed at his curb and saw Nikki standing in front of the kitchen window. She was making dinner.

He ran up the stairs. *The old landladies be damned,* he thought. Clarke pounded on the door, then managed to locate his keys. He opened the door to see Nikki standing, frightened, in the kitchen, her hands in the elbow-length rubber gloves she wore when she washed the dishes.

She smiled happily and ran to him. They embraced. "You washed out!" She glanced up. "You didn't jump! Oh, I'm so glad!"

He laughed. "What do you mean—washed out? What do you think I am?"

"But this is only Monday!"

"That's right. We jumped five times today. I'm a paratrooper." He placed his hands on her shoulders and took on a stern appearance. "What's been happening here? I must have called ten times. Did you write to . . . ?"

"I'll have to put more lamb chops on," Nikki said. Then she looked at him. "I've been so lonely. You have no idea what it's like to stay cooped up in this dump for weeks. All I did was read and drink coffee. And coffee only made me nervous, so I had a hell of a time sleeping. I'd stay up till three in the morning, worrying and worrying, wondering what you did the day before, what they'd have you doing that day." They went into the kitchen. "These past few days it hasn't been so bad. Sophie and I—you know . . . the blond woman at the Green Light? Well, she and I have been going out to the movies or visiting one another. But before—oh, God—it was horrible!"

"Sophie? What do you have to do with her?"

"Sophie, the woman at the Green Light. Well, she's married to Sergeant Damianos now. You wouldn't know. You've been away at that silly Jump School. She and Damianos—you know *him?*—got married a week ago, and now that he's been away on the maneuver she's as lonely as I. By the way"—she paused momentarily—"when will you have to leave for the maneuver?"

"My orders say that after Jump School graduation I'm to report back to the unit. The ceremonies will be tomorrow afternoon, if the weather holds up, so I guess I'll go back on Wednesday. There'd be no reason to go back right after graduation because it'll be four in the afternoon by then and the new CO will be gone for the day. If all goes well, I might not leave for Razor Blade until the following Monday."

"I hope not. You have no idea how lonely it gets here. Particularly before I started seeing Sophie. No one would call . . ."

"Well, I called every two—three evenings, whenever I'd get a chance."

"I was probably out for a walk. About eight o'clock I'd just give up waiting for your call and just take a walk. Why didn't you call earlier?"

"I had certain things to do before asking the sergeant's permission to use his telephone. Things like polish my boots, shine my brass, and get ready for the next day."

"That's what Sophie's husband said."

He was about to scold her for not being in the apartment on the nights he had called but then remembered the letter he had received from his family. "I got a letter from home."

Their eyes met. "What . . . what did it say?"

"When did you write, Nikki? I thought I had said we wouldn't communicate with them."

"I just wanted to tell your family. After all, they should know."

"Well"—he shrugged—"it doesn't matter. My father wrote. 'What's all this nonsense,' he asked, 'about Jump School?' They're ready to accept you." Nikki still appeared tense. "We're invited to Philadelphia." She was impassive. "But we're not going yet. We'll take our time."

"Are you . . ." She hesitated. "Are you sure that's all he said?"

"What else could he say?" Clarke showed his irritation. "I'm my own man now."

"How about . . ." Nikki paused. A quick smile played on her lips. "How about your birthright? Your father still has that."

"No, he doesn't. The birthright I meant has nothing to do with law or money."

Nikki touched his face. "What's happened to your skin? It's chapped."

"From the prop blast, I guess."

She kissed him on the lips. "I missed you."

"I'm glad." He unbuttoned his OD jacket. "How about those chops? The ones you promised me."

"You must be famished." She noticed the scabs on Clarke's arms as he unbuttoned his shirt sleeves. "What happened here?"

"Nothing. From the wind machine."

"You mean you got hurt?"

"Well, what do you expect? The training was pretty tough."

"Was it that tough?" She looked up. "Oh!" she shouted, having just remembered. "Tell me about the jumps!"

"Later," he said, moving toward their bedroom, "after we eat." He chuckled to himself as he dressed. Such a flighty girl occasionally. She chattered on about her loneliness when he had faced death that same morning.

Re-entering the kitchen, he saw that Nikki had set the table and was pouring wine into juice glasses. "We'll probably be able to afford some table service in a few months."

Nikki did not respond; she was trying not to spill any wine on the tablecloth, which Clarke saw was their only damask. When she pulled the bottle back, she noticed that a drop had fallen on the white cloth. "Damn it!"

"Don't worry about that," Clarke said. "It doesn't matter that much. We'll soon be able to afford a few more things."

Nikki glanced up at him. Her expression was serious. "You don't have to buy me things, Barrett. We can get along with what we have for now."

He watched her bend over to place the wine bottle on the bottom shelf of the cupboard. When she had returned to the table, wondering what she had forgotten, he pulled her to him and kissed her hard on the mouth, his hands traveling down her back. "You know what . . . ?"

"Hmmmmm?" She had closed her eyes.

"I'm not hungry any more. Not for chops, anyway."

"Oh, no! No, you don't!" She giggled and pulled back. "They're in the broiler and we've got to eat them." She slapped him playfully on the cheek. "We have all night for what you have in mind. And I don't want you getting tired."

"And not pleasing you . . . ?"

"You always please me. I wouldn't be in Von Steuben waiting for you, all alone, if you didn't please me."

"Are you sure?" He lifted her off the floor and cradled her in his arms. "Are you sure? You know . . . I have my doubts about you. Where were you every night I called?"

"Oh, that! I was out making love with all the Hollywood stars. Sophie and I. She's a lovely woman, but an awful drag, you know. All the men know she's married to Damianos and steer clear of her."

"That's not very likely."

"You ought to try picking her up sometime, then. The trouble with males is that they think happily married women are as available as happily married men." She mussed his hair. "When are you going to put me down, love? You can't get close to me when I'm up in the air, you know."

"So you're in good hands with her?"

"If I'm in no hands, I'm in good hands; is that what you mean?"

"That's about it."

"Oh, Barrett. You're such a prude." She tweaked his ear. "You're still very bourgeois, you know."

"Just selfish. I want you all to myself."

"And here I thought I had liberated you from all that."

"Any liberating to be done"—Clarke answered mildly as he lowered her to the floor—"will be done by me." Nikki went to the stove and looked in the broiler at the chops. They were ready. "Oh, well, I suppose we'll have to eat," he said.

"Yes, we'll have to eat. That way, we won't have to eat again until tomorrow morning." She exaggerated her wink.

He slapped her hard on the buttocks. "Sometimes, Nikki, I think I've married a shameless hussy."

"Not shameless." She burned her fingers transferring the chops from the broiling tray to their plates. "Oh, hell!" she muttered, licking her fingertips. "Not shameless, Mr. Clarke of the Philadelphia Clarkes. Just healthy."

They raised their glasses for a toast.

"Airborne," she remarked dramatically.

"All the way."

She leaned her head back and drank the wine. "You mean," she said, tapping her lips with the napkin, "you mean they actually talk like that? It's as juvenile as that?"

"It's kids' stuff, all right. Particularly on the ten-mile run. You'd be surprised at the things I said and thought when we had reached the last mile."

"Tell me all about it. Any brutality?"

"Oh, Nikki." He grinned. "You'd love to hear about brutality, wouldn't you?"

"I mean, was it like the Foreign Legion? Whippings and things?"

"Not too much. There was some . . . torture, you could call it. But everyone was involved, so no one was discriminated against. Actually, they were pretty rough on *me*."

"You don't matter, though, Barrett." She fought a smile as she served the salad. "You're white, Protestant, and Anglo-Saxon. I can't get any of *my* friends interested in *your* plight."

"Well, then, I'm sorry. That about does it."

"Tell me about the jumps, then."

He spoke with his mouth full. "Not too bad. Some risk, but only from the wind." He decided not to tell her about the malfunction. "It's exhilarating."

"Like sex?"

"Unfortunately, no. You descend too gradually. There isn't the titillation you get in an elevator, for instance."

"That's a pity."

"Yes and no. I'd like to get my sex without a harness."

She smiled. "Tonight you will. It's the right time. The moon, et cetera, et cetera."

"You *are* shameless." He finished his wine.

"How about dessert, Barrett?"

"That's been on my mind for three weeks now."

"Well! Is that all you think I am?" And she began telling him how one-tracked she thought men's minds were, how inconsiderate men were of the feelings of their spouses. "Spices?" She had drunk too much wine. "Spooses?"

Clarke sat back, taken with her charm, her enthusiasm, her mannerisms, the little shrugs of her shoulders, the grimaces he had forgotten, the quick smiles and quicker wit he had done without for three weeks while in the company of stolid men who faced the tests of body and will with a monomaniacal obsession with the youthful, and perhaps juvenile, questions of courage and death. He leaned back and listened to Nikki, glad that he was back home, for home, he now understood, was where she was.

At ten o'clock, after more wine, they went to the bedroom, leaving the dishes as they were. He lay in bed, waiting for her to undress, completely forgetting the fact that he had almost fallen to the earth with a usless parachute on his second jump.

Since they had left one of the lamps on in the parlor, Clarke could see his wife as she approached the bed and stood before it. Her slender, firm body seemed to glow as the light behind her caught her shoulders and back.

He pulled her to him and kissed her when she lay on the bed. How could he have forgotten her body? It was absurd. He had not forgotten it; it was as flexible, as soft, as smooth as he had known it to be three weeks before. Pearlike breasts, long-nippled, firm; a round, smooth belly; long, tapered legs —she was part of himself. Making love to her, caressing her warm body, was like encountering another reflection of himself after three weeks.

He lost consciousness of himself as he became aroused, and, feeling her soft, cool hands caressing his shoulders, he entered her. She uttered a sharp initial squeal, then kissed him passionately, sweeping his back with her cunning, knowing hands. The mounting tension they both felt reached its acme, throbbed, then ebbed with each heartbeat. Clarke was drained of energy. He rolled over and slowly drifted off into a deep slumber, not feeling the blanket she drew over him.

Nikki was asleep when he awoke, terrified. He had dreamed, a dream both strange and familiar. A dream of falling through the sky, turning over and over, head over feet, in silence, in slow motion, into the caverns of a city, into the dark, cool shadows of skyscrapers, past the pointed spires of churches.

He stared at the ceiling for a moment; then, hearing her gentle breathing next to him, he lay back in bed. *Why the same dream?* Why did not the day's events destroy the terror that had hidden itself so well from the daylight? It was the inner man again, the inner Clarke. The one who made all the decisions.

When will I ever know who this one is? How can I ever know myself when I am two selves?

The windowpanes rattled. The wind was picking up. Another storm was coming. If it rained, the graduation exercises would be postponed: another free day. Before he fell asleep, he heard the first raindrops of the storm striking the windowpanes and sill. Just as a giant wave carried him into sleep again, the rain became a steady wash.

PART THREE

This is the earth, the bloody arena of man's soul; we fight our heavy god that, whether he will or not, he may assume a face as full of light as ours.

—NIKOS KAZANTZAKIS,
The Odyssey: A Modern Sequel

CHAPTER 23

The truck sped along the rutted dirt road, its tires rolling in the grooves created by vehicles that had recently passed. The driver occasionally swerved the wheels to miss an obstacle, and the Deuce-and-a-Half bounced over the center mound, raising, then dropping Corporal McIlhenny, with a crash, to the wooden bench on which he sat. The M1 rifle, its stock wedged between his muddy boots, served as a support for his tired shoulders; gripping the weapon at the front handguard, he leaned on it and stared ahead blankly.

There was little for him to see; he felt he had reached a point in his life where the world outside was not so interesting and, therefore, not so challenging as the chaotic world within himself. Maneuvers, those charades of war, and war itself, the charade of man's internal conflict, were merely stages in his life that helped him grow to maturity. That which interested him more than anything else now was the meaning of all these vast expenditures of energy, thought, and wealth. The individual pattern he had followed was unmistakable. Instead of Army maneuvers preparing him for war, actual combat, it seemed, had prepared him for Operation Razor Blade.

McIlhenny snapped out of his reverie and noticed the new sergeant watching him. The corporal glanced to his right, to the dirt road over which the Deuce-and-a-Half raised a cloud of brown dust.

Sergeant Jacks seemed to be a quiet, competent NCO. He was tough on McIlhenny, but also fair, and somehow the corporal had the feeling that Jacks knew he had been riffed, for within the sergeant's institutional harshness he sensed a tenderness toward him, a desire to shield him from certain unpleasant duties.

McIlhenny glanced back to the sergeant, who shifted his eyes. The truck lurched to a stop.

"OK . . . men . . . on your feet," Jacks whispered. The tail gate was let down quietly; the antiguerrilla paratroopers jumped to the road, their weapons at port arms, and followed Jacks' order to form a skirmish line at the forest's edge. They advanced slowly toward the interior, bending to evade the clutching limbs of low trees, setting their boots carefully on the needle- and cone-covered turf.

McIlhenny detested the steel helmet he was forced to wear. After being in the Special Troops and having accustomed himself to the practical light beret, he found himself tired and irritated by the very weight of the steel pot. He stopped abruptly on seeing a metallic glint near a tree. It was a clip of eight blanks, possibly dropped by a guerrilla. He raised his hand and signaled Jacks. When the sergeant came over, McIlhenny gave him the clip. Jacks nodded.

All my life, McIlhenny thought, *all my life I've been doing this . . . living by stealth . . . living tightly . . . as if danger and death would come to me from my negligence.* He walked gently on the earth, setting his heel down first, then slowly lowering his boot and rolling up from his toes. Even in play, the rules of the foolish game must be carried out consistently and carefully, and McIlhenny knew that, for all the dreamlike absurdity of his life, he should not permit himself the full awareness of his behavior. For, as a full-grown man, to cease participating in the fantasies that had been his career would mean to cut himself off from the only life he, and the human race of which he was a part, could possibly know—would be, in other words, to cease living. *Only with death . . . with someone touching us, shouting "You're It," does the game stop . . . and we wake up from our dreams. . . .*

There was a stream ahead. The guerrillas, who were almost certain to be in the sector, would choose the general area beyond the small river to make their camp. A costly ambush of a Divison convoy the night before had proved that the Special Troops, after two weeks of heavy fighting, still occupied the forested areas of central North Carolina. The order came that morning to clear the region around Base Headquarters, Eleutheria, of the partisans, for it was intolerable that small pockets of Aggressor resistance be allowed to threaten the equanimity of the United States Army in what was now—according to the scenario timetable—rear area. Following the convoy ambush, the Aggressor guerrillas probably marched all night, and they were now—if partisan doctrine were applied—asleep, with a fair percentage of the Troopers standing guard. A reconnaissance helicopter pilot had spotted their green berets and special Aggressor uniforms in this vicinity a few hours after sunrise.

Jacks motioned for the line to spread. Then, after sending

two soldiers across the stream to make a cursory inspection of the other side, he gave the unit the order to cross.

McIlhenny slipped on the bank and made some noise entering the freezing water. Sergeant Jacks glared at him briefly, then turned away. The water reached above his knees, and McIlhenny shuddered with the cold as he walked on the pebble-covered floor. The opposite bank, steeper than the one he had just left, provided him with a momentary cover. He stretched his arm, set his M1 on the bank, and struggled to pull himself out of the stream. A slight *squoosh, squoosh* threatened to betray him as he walked on numbed legs toward a hill directly in front of the skirmish line.

With the realization that the Aggressor guerrillas for whom the paratroopers had been searching all morning were definitely ahead of him now came the hope—which McIlhenny understood immediately as a pathetic wish almost certain to prove violated—that he would not be recognized by any of them. Somehow, the idea of meeting people whom he had known when he was Captain McIlhenny had curiously never crossed his mind. *Yes . . . yes . . . I've seen* . . . But he could not recall the man's name. *In a PX once . . .*

It was paradoxical that, after the turmoil and despair he had gone through with his reduction in grade, he should still be conscious of other men's attitudes toward his loss of status. It was ridiculous that he should care about the opinions of others toward something that had changed his entire life. *I'm absurd,* he realized. *It's as if I were careful to comb my hair or pronounce my name properly before I die . . . as if what other people think is important to my existence* . . . Then, in what appeared to be a moment of clarity, he realized: *This can't be me! I must be dreaming!*

The platoon lay on the earth as Sergeant Jacks and a colored soldier, Private Boyd, advanced to make sure of the guerrilla camp's existence. The line advanced to Jacks' wave, crawling over the turf.

McIlhenny rubbed the earth with a strange feeling of licentiousness, briefly recalling Esperanza under him. No, he would forget her. He would forget his books, his records, everything that had to do with the long-dead Captain McIlhenny; he would forget his body and hers; he would accept the role he now played in the drama chosen for him by forces beyond his control; and, if at all possible, he would lose himself in the role he now acted. He would continue to dream.

The paratroopers now had the guerrillas contained within a semicircle. Behind the partisans rose a hill, conveniently denuded of trees, with only a few rocks promising a shelter that the guerrillas would be fortunate, but unlikely, to attain. Between the narrow trunks of the pine trees, McIlhenny noticed the oval darkness of a cave, probably the behind-the-lines supply cache for the Aggressor. Approximately twenty-five men, lying in their sleeping bags, were stretched under the trees. Then he observed a guard sitting near the lip of the cave, resting his back against a cardboard box of C rations. The sentry appeared to be dozing.

A burst of shots from Jacks' submachine gun broke the stillness and was answered by the cross fire of the M1s. The guerrillas, caught unawares, lurched out of their bags and scurried for cover. After a moment of aimlessness, shattered constantly by the enfilade of the skirmish line, the Aggressor partisans were convinced of their capture.

They raised their hands sheepishly and waited for Jacks and Boyd to reach them. The sergeant entered the cave, inspected it for evaders, and herded the guerrillas into a small clearing away from their camp. The United States paratroopers began a systematic search of the cache and confiscated the Aggressor weapons.

"Who's in charge here?" Jacks questioned a partisan. He did not receive an answer. The sergeant then approached the largest man in the group and shot a vicious jab into the man's abdomen. The soldier collapsed to the turf and held his stomach. "Who's in charge here?" Jacks repeated the question without changing the tone of his voice. Again there was no answer. Jacks straddled the fallen man and readied himself to slap his face.

"I am." A partisan stepped forward.

"Your name?"

"Captain Trombeaux."

"Well, Captain, you took your time, diden you?" He stared at the partisan. "For that, Captain, you're gonna tote a little more than your share of the crap you got here." He turned to the man lying on the ground. "On your feet, blubber-gut!" The man stood painfully. Jacks glared at him. "How come lard-asses like you git into the *Special* Troops?" He did not wait for an answer. "Pick up that stuff!" He commanded. "Git. . . . Git . . . !" He pushed them toward the stream. "We ain't got all day. *Git!*" Several guerrillas, jumping from the abrupt bank, fell into the stream and twisted their ankles, but Jacks rushed them to the other side.

As they marched toward the truck, McIlhenny suspected that many of the partisans had recognized him. Unlike the Special Troopers, who were allowed to go unshaven during maneuvers and had, consequently, a two-week growth of beard, McIlhenny, as a member of the Division, was forced to shave every morning. It was unfortunate. He would have been able to hide behind a beard. As it was, however, his face was the face everyone who knew him as a captain would remember. And the name tape on his fatigues carried the designation of his identity. *How pleasant it would be* he considered bitterly, *if I could disguise myself and hide the shame of my past.* He turned his back to the partisans, hoping that by hiding his features he would attain the anonymity he sought.

"Ah never seen so many beards . . . on so many *boys* . . . in all mah life. Ah'll bet you're all Yankees. Ain't that right, now? *Git!*" A few men stumbled on the underbrush. "Believe me . . . Mister Beards . . . gentlemen . . . when we git to Base Headquarters, Eleutheria, you're gonna tell me all you know. Ah'm gonna put you in a little room and learn all 'bout what you ain't suppose to tell me. That goes for you, too, Captain!"

When the men arrived at the truck, Jacks ordered them to put the supplies and confiscated weapons in the van, then told the driver to return to camp. The distance to Eleutheria was approximately ten miles. McIlhenny knew it was to be a forced march, because the guerrillas had not recovered from the night's trek and would be much easier to question in their state of exhaustion.

"All right! Form up, now!" The guerrillas were pushed into a single file on the center mound. Jacks took the coils of rope he had thrown down from the trucks's van and told Boyd and McIlhenny to pass the cord through the partisans' belts and string them together. The sergeant who had been struck by Jacks winked at McIlhenny as the corporal tied him.

"You're a plant, aren't you, Captain?"

"Yes, yes," McIlhenny agreed quietly.

"I knew we had agents planted in the Division. You'll help us escape, won't you, sir?"

McIlhenny tightened the rope around the man's midsection. "Of course," he whispered. "What do you think I'm here for?"

Captain Trombeaux, an acquaintance of his, pretended not to have noticed McIlhenny and stared down at his boots self-consciously.

"Now," Jacks shouted, "er all these here bearded *gorillas* secure? We don' want any of 'em to try an' escape an' make *real* enemies of us when we git 'em back to camp, do we?" He paused. "For-ard . . . *march!*" The march began, and, as the time passed, the exhaustion of the partisans became more obvious, for some of them fell, dragging down their neighbors with them. *"Git!"* Jacks shouted. "Ah never seen such pansy paratroopers in all mah life. *Git!*"

When the prisoners were herded into the fenced compound at Eleutheria, Sergeant Jacks called McIlhenny over to the gate, where he was checking off the guerrillas on a clip-board. "Ah'm sorry 'bout askin' you to tie up them partisans, Corporal. Ah forgot you'd of probably knowed some of the men from when you was in the Troops. Ah shoulda had someone else give Boyd a hand with the tyin'."

"That's all right, Sergeant Jacks." McIlhenny shrugged his shoulders. "That's just something else I've got to accustom myself to."

CHAPTER 24

The fact that Operation Razor Blade had passed the halfway point made Clarke feel vaguely dissatisfied. He had done nothing but sit around in the tent provided for the psychological warfare personnel, occasionally working on a leaflet text; read novels he had previously disguised with tan field-manual covers marked FM 21-76, *Survival;* and drink coffee. If he were to believe all he had heard, great battles between Aggressor guerrillas and United States forces were being waged in a mythical land called Okcidenta Carolina in Esperanto, the Aggressor native tongue.

According to the maneuver scenario, Okcidenta Carolina was a vast, mountainous region, vaguely triangular in shape, flanked by South Carolina and Georgia to the south, Tennessee to the north and west, and the general line Bristol–Hickory–Gastonia to the east. This triangle was merely another wedge of conquest Aggressor had supposedly made on the continental United States; the nations of Florida, Georgia, Alabama, and South Carolina had previously been subjugated, and, according to the timetable of conquest, the five nation-states were to be merged within the next five years.

During Stage One of Operation Razor Blade, the first penetration of the United States forces had been made through the boundary defenses of the general line Mount Airy–Winston-Salem–Kannapolis–Charlotte, approximately thirty-five miles east of the Okcidenta Carolina border. Aggressor, primarily composed of loosely coordinated guerrilla bands, fought back with no real desire to meet the American Army in the relative flatness of central North Carolina. The bands retreated in an orderly fashion, leaving in their wake small teams, whose duty it was to create pockets of resistance within the American rear area.

Stage Two of the maneuver saw the American Army rolling over the borders of Okcidenta Carolina, easily crushing the hasty defenses Aggressor threw up at the general line Bristol–Hickory–Gastonia. United States Base Headquarters, Eleutheria, was established near a large airfield, and the mopping up of the partisans was now under way.

The third stage was to begin in two days with a mass drop on a place called Crossroads Drop Zone, supposedly bounded on all sides by mountains and forests. The drop zone's name did not appeal to Clarke; it sounded pompous, the sort of term unimaginative military leaders invariably chose so that their exploits would appear more imposing. There would be a day of heavy fighting near Crossroads, for the guerrillas would be there to meet the falling paratroopers. Then, after two or three days of antiguerrilla activity on the part of the Division, Aggressor would capitulate; Stage Four, the demobilization phase, would be introduced; the rucksacks would be stuffed; the tents would be taken down; the charts would be rolled up; and everyone would go back home.

To Barrett Clarke, Operation Razor Blade was one of the most absurdly expensive camping trips he had ever been on. It was ludicrous how seriously everyone took the maneuver. Like a child's game, it was "us" against "them" again: the Special Troops, alias Aggressor, fought against the 43rd Airborne Division, alias the United States Defender Army. Razor Blade seemed to offer everyone concerned with it the opportunity to pretend, to play at war, and to leave the Post, home, wife, and responsibilities.

It was surprising to him, moreover, how in fewer than twenty days he had forgotten the rigorous discipline he had undergone in Jump School and resumed his old, casual attitudes. The daily, agonizing tests of Jump School seemed far away—another life, virtually—and Clarke's old habits had returned. Certain commands, which during airborne training would not have been at all disturbing, now irritated him excessively, and the absurdity of military life, with its regimentation of every minute in the day, became to him an oppressive burden.

He was occupied now in writing the text of a propaganda leaflet for the maneuver. Since much of the psychological warfare material was necessarily antimilitary, Clarke could do good work without feeling that he was violating his integrity. But he knew that eventually, after the leaflets had been scattered and the loudspeaker announcements had been made, this type of warfare demanded that someone, some soldier, think about the proposals offered to him by the enemy and act on these proposals. Thought, therefore, was not enough. Thought without action was valueless. Action, therefore, was the only criterion. And in this subtle but sharply defined area, Clarke detected another challenge to himself, another test. For he was a hypocrite. He was a hired man. In trying to convince the "enemy" soldiers to defect, he assumed in them a valor that he was too cowardly to duplicate.

The hidden FTAs he would leave to the others, to Winters and to Martin. Clarke would not be forced into a petty defiance of military authority and thus exhibit to himself and this authority his own pettiness. His rebellion, if and when it occurred, would need to be a more responsible, a more manly revolt. If he was dissatisfied with a world in arms; if he was sickened by his inability to say farewell to this hostile, fully armed, and frightened world; if he hated every hypocritical government which had skillfully identified itself with the cause of freedom—then he would be forced, eventually, to stop being satisfied with rebellious thoughts and to commit himself to a course of action that duplicated the decision the leaflet he now worked on would demand of the individual "enemy" soldier.

Fortunately, however, there was a great deal of work to keep him occupied. There were details to perform, commands to fulfill, leaflets and propaganda speeches to write, and he could lose himself in his work. Perhaps he allowed himself to be irritated by the daily vexations of military life so that he could ignore the greater challenge, the greater task. Perhaps he was secretly grateful for the minute-by-minute irritations because they obscured from him the horror of his inactivity.

His time was well occupied. He now looked forward to a coffee break. Later in the day, Winters, Battaglia, and Martin would arrive from Fort Mosby for the final phases of Operation Razor Blade. Within the next few days, Clarke would fly over this curiosity, this Crossroads Drop Zone, in an L-20 Beaver and throw out the leaflets that would be chosen by Colonel Simms. All in all, Clarke was forced to admit, exacting labor was comforting. He could lose himself in work, lose himself so well that there was no fear that he would ever find himself again. He looked at his wrist-watch. It was time to leave the tent.

Before leaving for his regular coffee break, Barrett Clarke glanced at the four leaflets from which Colonel Simms would choose the one he thought most appropriate. The first showed a man being kicked by a brutal-looking soldier. The legend, in Esperanto and English, read: "We fight for the right to say *no* to tyranny." On the second, a woman, sitting half naked on a bed, was putting on a pair of nylons: "What is *she* doing while you are away?" The third showed a pair of Division paratroopers, both dead, lying on the earth: "Both fought for what they were told was freedom. Which one is free?" And the last was illustrated with the Statue of Liberty: "What have *you* been doing while she's been away?"

Clarke frowned. It was all so idiotic, this thinking up of bogus issues for a game played by supposedly mature men. He placed the four leaflets on the desk and set a clip of blank ammunition, as a paperweight, on each.

Colonel Simms' voice came to him from outside the tent. The officer's monologue seemed to involve the poor toilet facilities at Libereco, a fact also noticed by Clarke. Most of the men at this point, the voice went on, were not overly busy. A detail should be assigned to dig a few deep trenches further away from camp so that the pits already in existence would not be so overcrowded. And, Colonel Simms continued, a screen should be erected around the officers' latrine, for a soldier's respect toward officers was undoubtedly lowered when he saw the officer sitting reflectively over a latrine pit with his trousers pulled down to his knees.

Clarke rose from his chair quietly, put on his green beret, and walked toward the tent flap. Sergeant Dobbin, or whomever Colonel Simms was speaking to, would certainly enter the tent soon with a clipboard and a shovel. The direction from which the voice came was unchanged. He exited quickly and strode to the field mess with a concentration that clearly indicated to whoever saw him that PFC Clarke was carrying out an important mission. It was only when he stood before the coffee urns that he realized he had forgotten to bring his canteen cup. Clarke did not want to hear the cook's curses when he asked him if he could have one of the plastic cups reserved for officers' use. Turning to leave the tent, trying to think of an alternative, he heard a Deuce-and-a-Half screech to a stop. A team of men, bearded, unkempt, and dusty, jumped out of the van. Clarke recognized the features of Sergeant Damianos behind a luxuriant black beard. The NCO appeared to be angry.

Damianos' team members moved quickly, emptying the truck of their equipment so efficiently that he was unable to shout at them to hurry up the process. It appeared that they were trying to frustrate him by anticipating his moods. The sergeant glared at the men around him, stamped his boots to shake the dust from them, and brushed off his trousers, all actions appearing to be parts of a formula designed to give him something to do while he brooded.

Clarke wondered if he should greet the sergeant, then, realizing that Damianos would not be in a mood to be interested in the pleasantries, decided to forgo his greeting. He would ask the cook for a cup instead. As Clarke turned to enter the mess tent again, Damianos swerved toward him.

"Hello, Sergeant," Clarke was caught by surprise.

Damianos stared at him, recalled who he was, and nodded his head curtly. Since the sergeant preceded him into the tent, Clarke felt squeamish, not wanting Damianos to think he was being followed. He went ahead, however, hesitating near Damianos as the sergeant filled his canteen with water.

Every conversational opening Clarke considered was either strained or obvious. Damianos would have thought it silly to be told that it seemed as if he had just come back from a long mission, that he was probably glad to be back at Libereco, that he needed a shave. Then Clarke remembered. "Congratulations!"

Damianos did not look up. "What about?"

"I heard you got married."

"That's right."

Clarke was committed now. He could not very well drop the conversation at this point, and before he could leave he had to put his opening remarks in some kind of context. "I heard it from my wife when I finished Jump School."

"Yeah," Damianos grunted. "I met her one night."

This was as good a point as any to abandon the conversation. Clarke stepped back a pace, maintaining his silence, and decided quickly that he would permit Damianos to make the first move in leaving.

The sergeant capped his canteen and straightened up. "You wanna know something?" The brown pupils of his eyes fixed on Clarke. "You're gonna see something in the next few days that you'll never forget." He turned and walked to his rucksack, lying on the path, now empty of trucks; swung it on his back with his free arm; and walked slowly toward the reserve area where the team was to rest.

Clarke had not moved since Damianos had spoken to him. He did not know what to think about what he had just been told, whether he should feel embarrassment or affront. At that moment, a paper airplane, sailing between his outstretched legs, diverted his attention.

"What d'ya say, Blue Eyes?" It was Battaglia, wearing a baggy, misshapen suit of fatigues, a cap that was sizes too large for his head, and the merest hint of a mustache.

"I was wondering where you guys were. How about Winters and Martin? Have you come together?"

"Come on over, Daddy. We just arrived. I no sooner got settled with my personnel records and stuff when some jughead sergeant comes up and tells me that they're gonna have a detail for us in an hour. What can it be, I figure. There ain't no latrines to clean up here, are there?"

"There are latrines to dig!"

"Kiss me again!" Battaglia's lips puckered. "Is that all the goddamn officer-duds think about? Wait'll Winters hears about *this!*"

The artists had been looking for the psywar tent. Not knowing where it was located, the driver told them to unload their supplies from the Deuce-and-a-Half because he was needed elsewhere. Winters, Clarke noticed from the distance, was attempting to grow a small beard.

"What's up, Barrett?" Winters asked. "Good to see you. Even with the green beanie." Battaglia laughed. "It looks avant-garde, though. Do you mind?" He reached up and took it from Clarke's head. "Nice material."

"Felt," Clarke contributed. "Only you can't wear it"—he mimicked the Jump School cadre—" 'cause you're jest a straightleg."

Battaglia laughed. "Any broken bones, smart money?"

"No. They were good jumps." He looked around at the art equipment. "You made good time from Mosby."

"Yeah. Drove straight through." Winters pulled out a cigarette. "None for you, Battaglia. What d'you think I am—a cigarette factory?" Battaglia hissed something. "Hey . . ." Winters continued. "What d'you think about this Esperanto jazz? You'd be surprised at how many FTAs Martin and I've been sneaking into our leaflets." He paused. "How have you been making out?"

"Bored stiff"

"I mean with the FTAs."

"I haven't given the problem much thought." Winters' expression was confused and possibly hurt. "I mean, Simms is right over me and I don't want to try anything."

"They had old Moser going nuts," Battaglia interrupted.

"Let *me* tell it." Winters glared at the personnel clerk. "It's *my* story." He continued: "We had Moser going batty trying to find *eftan* in the Esperanto handbook. 'It should be,' he kept saying, 'it should be between *efikelo,* efficiency, and *ekflugo,* an aircraft's takeoff. What's it mean?' he kept asking. 'What's *eftan* mean?' Well, Martin told him he studied Esperanto in school, like it was a progressive school, and *eftan* meant effortless! The fight for freedom will never be effortless. *La batalo por libereco neniam estos eftan.* 'I can't find it in my dictionary,' Moser kept saying. 'Well,' Martin said, 'that's an Esperanto dialect.' We sweated that one out, you know, wondering when Moser would find out that Esperanto was used to get rid of dialects and national languages. . . . Do you know what Moser said?"

Clarke shook his head.

"He blinked his eyes and said: 'It must be wonderful being a college man!' "

Clarke laughed. "That's all you've been doing recently? Just fooling around with Moser?"

"Well . . . we had the goddamn IG while you were gone. And we tried to take it as easy as possible. Battaglia and me, anyhow. We're short-timers, you know. Battaglia has about five days before he's a 90-day loss, and I got approximately 172 days left." He frowned. "Counting this morning, I guess you can say it's just 171 and a half. That's not including half-day Saturdays, Sundays, Christmas, and New Year's Day. I mean, it's an honest, hard count."

The three men walked toward the truck, where Clarke told the driver he would direct him to the psywar tent. Clarke glanced at Winters. "There must be a word in Esperanto for effortless. You'll have Simms over you all the time, and he's out to find FTAs. You should have an airtight defense."

"Hey, Martin!" Winters shouted. A mutter answered him. "Come the hell over here and see Clarke. We know where the tent is now." Winters turned to Clarke. "He'll give you the whole business. In the two weeks after the IG and before we left for here, Martin became an authority on Esperanto. He's even talking it."

Martin appeared from behind the van. "Hiya, Barrett. How's everything? This maneuver keeping you busy?"

"Clarke here wants to know what the word for effortless is in Esperanto."

"Well, I chouldn't find it in the dictionary they gave us with the maneuver field manual. I did find the word for effort, though. It's *klopodo*. Now . . . I figure . . . they usually attach a negative to effort, making it *noklopodo*. But my alibi for not using it is that it sounds like hell."

"That's fair enough. I think Simms will catch it, though. At least he'll catch *eftan*."

"How's Nikki?" Winters asked. "We were thinking of calling her before we left, but one thing and another came up and we didn't get the time."

"She's fine. I got a letter two days ago. You know . . . counting the time I was in Jump School, I haven't spent more than a few days with her in about five-six weeks. She's got a friend, though. A girl friend," he added quickly. "And she isn't too lonely that way."

"It must be hell being a girl like Nikki in an Army town." Winters leaned against the truck fender. "Take off!" he said to the muttering driver. "What're you . . . a company man?"

"Hey," Battaglia interrupted. "What's that town we passed through about twenty-five miles back? Do you guys ever go there? I mean, has it got any fluff? Is it off limits?"

"I haven't gone in, but some of the troopers go in every night." Clarke spoke to the personnel clerk. "It's supposedly under enemy occupation, but it's pretty easy to slip past the MPs if you have civilian clothes with you."

"What happens if they catch you?"

"They toss you in jail and cross-examine you. You don't want to get caught, though. Not that they play rough, although I've heard some pretty rugged stories. It's just that, up here in the mountains, as guerrillas, we lead a relatively free life. Down there, you're in the conventional Army again. You're back in garrison. It's not so bad up here, really. The simple fact that you don't have to shave if you don't want to is a pretty good indication that being on a maneuver with the Troops is a relief to some of these guys, the Regular Army types." He pulled a C-ration pack of cigarettes out of his pocket and offered them around. Battaglia accepted quickly. Clarke smiled, both at Battaglia's agility and at a thought he had just remembered.

"In a few days you'll be working on a leaflet that should be ready to go to the presses after the mass jump." He turned to Winters and Martin. "You'll be told to do the artwork, mainly the copying of surrender forms. This came out in conversation. Simms wasn't too satisfied with the leaflet ideas that had been used in past maneuvers. I brought the whole file with me from Mosby, and after about an hour of searching through the stack he decided they weren't realistic enough. It was propaganda used during World War Two. So he said to me: 'Why can't the Special Troops make up a leaflet, include a surrender form on it that can be cut across the perforations, stating that this is an authentic surrender pass guaranteeing the bearer good treatment, hot food, a comfortable bunk, no hardships and manure like mock torture, and signed'—this is the gimmick—'signed by General Aarons himself?' Forged, of course. I asked him: 'Can't this have repercussions, sir?' 'This is a maneuver, after all,' Simms said, 'and, according to the scenario, I'm not Colonel Simms. My name is Simmsjac!' "

The artists were interested. Battaglia pushed his glasses in place with his index finger.

"So I forged General Aarons' signature from an old mimeographed *Post Bulletin* that was lying around. It looks like the real thing. I wrote up the text, and Simms has already narrowed the audience for the leaflet pass. It would be useless to drop these on the paratroopers under Aarons, because they're too disciplined to accept it. Their sergeants would be all over them in a minute. He's going to drop this on the companies our intelligence unit has determined are composed of from sixty to ninety percent draftees and nonjumpers."

Battaglia laughed. "You know what that means? It means you'll be dropping the surrender passes on the Division's own propaganda unit."

"Yeah," Martin agreed. "A regular paper war. It sounds like fun, though. I wouldn't mind working on stuff like that. What else does he have up his sleeve?"

Clarke looked at Battaglia briefly. "Keep this quiet. I've seen a team of guerrillas running back and forth on one of the clearings recently. I guess they've been training as quick-change artists, because one minute they're Special Troopers, partisans, and the next they're military police. They exchange road signs, traffic markers; they mess up the traffic lights; they've got MP jeeps . . . the works."

"Aarons is going to flip his lid when he sees what's happening." Winters smiled. "Simms is heading for trouble."

"No skin off my ass, as the man says," Battaglia added. "Let 'em court-martial each other. Who gives a diddly-squat?"

They jumped into the truck and rode through Camp Libereco to the psywar tent, noticing that the guerrilla encampment was beginning to have a holiday atmosphere. The Special Troopers, who had composed the marauding bands that performed hit-and-run missions and ambuscades in the eastern portions of Okcidenta Carolina, were returning to Libereco for the two days prior to Stage Three. Clarke and the others saw the bearded men flanking the dirt path, stripped to the waist, washing themselves in what must have been near-freezing water.

Colonel Simms was in the tent when they arrived.

"Oh . . ." He noticed Winters and Martin. "You're here, are you? Good. . . . We'll put you to work right away. Clarke here knows all about the surrender leaflet I've planned. He will tell you what I want. And . . . by the way, Clarke, I've decided to use this one." He pointed to a leaflet on the desk. "The one with the two dead paratroopers lying on the ground." He nodded and walked toward the tent flap. "Before I forget . . . I've given Sergeant Dobbin a detail to dig an officers' latrine. He should be coming through this area for volunteers. If he should ask you to help him, you can consider yourselves available." He ducked under the opening. "A few more things. One: I'd like to see some preliminary work on the surrender leaflet by dawn tomorrow. And two: Clarke, I've thrown the books you've been amusing yourself with—on Army time, I might add—into one of the latrine pits you'll fill up soon. How many times have I told you that you should think of nothing else but Operation Razor Blade while you're here?"

When Colonel Simms had left the tent, during the silent embarrassment of the others, Clarke spoke in a quiet, angry voice. "There must be some way I can stop saying yes to all of them. There must be a way I can repay them all for being what they are."

CHAPTER 25

Damianos cursed as he rinsed the lather off his smooth-shaved face. He wiped the razor blade on his underwear sleeve. After two weeks in the field, marching every night and sleeping a few hours during the day, covering an estimated distance of four hundred miles, interspersed with five ambushes to make the trek interesting, he assumed that he would be allowed a two-day rest between Stages Two and Three. But it seemed that Colonel Simms and Major Zoltan had other ideas. With the beard, perspiration, filth, and mud of two weeks still on him, he had been called to Major Zoltan's tent and briefed about a mission he would be sent on that night. *Gotta get sleep somehow . . .* His fingers trembled as he looked for the razor-blade dispenser. *Why me . . . all the time?*

Duty was duty, however, and orders were binding. The fact that there was no precedent for this mission in the American Army, at any rate not during a maneuver, made him feel uneasy, not for his career as an NCO, but for Colonel Simms and the Special Troops. *Things like this can screw up the whole Troops.*

Operation Razor Blade was designed to show how quickly an airborne division could crush a guerrilla revolution, and as far as Damianos could determine, since this was a relatively uncontrolled maneuver, Simms had every right to show the conventional staffs that this was not as easy as everyone supposed. If truth were important, and if, as everyone was quick to admit, truth was painful, then there was every reason to show the conventional staffs, the Pentagon, and Congress that the task before the Western armies was not as comfortable as the newspapers said it was. Operation Razor Blade was the ideal instrument to cut through the pretenses and illusions people carried around within themselves.

Damianos stripped to the skin. After cupping his hand under the canteen's spout, he washed himself with the cold water. This would have to do; he did not have the time for a better bath. He put on a clean, dry pair of socks; slid into his spare suit of long underwear, stepping on the green Aggressor coveralls when he lost his balance momentarily, quickly—for the cold shook him; got into a thick OG shirt; then put on the fatigue suit on which one of his teammates had stitched the 43rd arm patch over the one of the Special Troops. After lacing his boots tightly, he slapped the dust from his green beret, rolled it up in his dirty clothes, and stuffed the bundle into his rucksack.

A master sergeant, leaning against a nearby tree, evidently wanted to talk, but Damianos ignored him; he was not in a talking mood, and there was no time. This was not solely because of his exhaustion. He had been taciturn for the past two weeks, speaking only when he gave orders. On his second day in the field, almost thirty-six hours after having left Sophie in the car, he had been overwhelmed by a feeling of loss, of alienation toward what he had for most of his mature life considered his only function.

This confused him. Nothing actual had gone wrong. The men were all attentive to the instructions. The ambuscades went off as planned. The Maneuver Observers accompanying them were all impressed with the team's performance. But something had happened to Damianos. Suddenly he was overcome by the futility, by the mock seriousness, the simulation of the maneuver. Whatever this doubt was, it forced him to question his entire life. And this feeling of having lost his total orientation toward the Army was something he would never be able to communicate to anyone, particularly not to Sophie; she would misinterpret this, he knew, flattering herself that she had softened him, had civilized the violence still hiding beneath the surface of his deceptively calm, authoritative equanimity.

All his life Damianos had fought against, and eventually accepted, someone else's guidance; because he had survived the violence that had started in his youth and had never stopped, he was rewarded with relative comfort and security. It was ironical, for his was the most tested generation in American history; in the thirty-four years of his existence, Damianos had relived the war history of man, battling first with fists, with stones, with clubs, and then with rifles—and now, if the scientists were to be believed, he would battle with weapons even more frightening. But he had never fought to defend *himself* from harm or pillage, perhaps because he had never had anything worth taking; it seemed that he had always warred to protect one of the intangibles skillfully explained by those who rarely fought for them.

Damianos was mute about this to everyone. No one imagined his venom on seeing an elder statesman, appearing on television, who could barely walk to the rostrum without support, swinging a fist in a generally eastern direction, threatening the "hordes" with sudden death. For Damianos knew that if the old man's challenge was ever accepted, he would be off again to provide stirring battlefield copy for a newer generation of war correspondents. It seemed to him that men were destined to become old before certain intangibles became important enough to fight and die for. The irony, of course, was that by the time men discovered this truth, they were too old to fight and concerned themselves, philosophically, with preparations to meet an awaited, and natural, death.

Now he dreaded the remaining years before he would be free of the Army. Four years to a questionable freedom, a freedom that would be canceled as soon as old men throughout the world decided it was time to shake their impotent fists again.

But we never started a war . . . He checked himself. *But then . . . how come I'm always fighting?*

He would be thirty-eight years old upon retirement. What had he accomplished with his life? Nothing. He had fought other people's battles for them: a stud, a warrior without the necessary brains to be a mercenary, as if mercenaries had a place in a world where the most important thing seemed to be money, a fact skillfully camouflaged by ideals the world's old men passed on to youth in order to perpetuate the slavery they termed the fight for freedom.

Damianos walked on the dirt path swinging his steel helmet by its airborne chin strap. Guerrillas were sitting before bonfires, scooping out food from ration cans, talking languorously in the late afternoon. A few were crawling into their sleeping bags. Damianos nodded to those who waved at him.

What have I been thinking? I'm tired . . . exhausted . . . losing my self-control. . . . Other people's battles *had* been his battles. He was always too willing to destroy his articles of faith point by point until he arrived at nothing to believe in, nothing to hope for, expecting that by cutting himself free of all his supports he would be offered the dubious freedom of falling unsupported. Perhaps this was one of the few freedoms man had. *Can't let myself go too far. . . . Need some sleep. . . .* His jaw muscles twitched.

"Afternoon, sir." He saluted Major Zoltan. "Are we all here?"

"The MPs have gone ahead. It's about a two-hour drive.

We'll give them an hour, then move out for Eleutheria."

"Fine, sir." Damianos glanced at the half-ton truck. "Is this what we're gonna use?"

"Yes. We'll put him in back."

"I'll sit in the van, sir. If it's all right with you."

"Certainly. Get some sleep. You need it."

Damianos scaled the tail gate and sat in the cold darkness of the canvas-covered interior. He rested his chin in his hands, trying to combat the great bitterness that surged through him. *The world's screwed up, somehow,* he thought. *People are never satisfied . . . never comfortable on this earth.* . . . He rubbed his eyes.

Was this what his child was going to live through? Without asking to be born? Just as he had never asked to be born? And because Damianos had been born at a certain time, he had been destined to go hungry, to beg, to drag his wagon to the relief trucks for food, to wear the government-offered blue denim shirts, dungarees, black ankle boots—the uniform before the other one, the Army uniform. Then the strikes. Then the war and its brutality. Then the captivity of peace and the comfort of the opened cage of civilian freedom that had almost destroyed him. Then the Army again.

Damianos rolled his heavy hand into a fist. If there were only something to strike at, something to slug. If he could only force the steel-like knuckles into something, to watch whatever it is reel back, to see confusion on *its* face!

Damianos stretched out on the bench. *If a man can just be satisfied with what he's gotta do day by day, week by week . . . he'd be OK . . .* The sergeant felt light. *Good . . . good.* Sleep was coming on. Get two hours of shut-eye. *If a man can stop himself from thinking about things that can never be solved . . . depressing things . . . he'd be OK . . .* His father had a word for it: *Ataraxia . . . that's it.* That was the word. *Maybe the world's not screwed up.* Maybe man *does it. Maybe . . .*

The truck was motionless. Damianos opened his eyes briefly to see the driver lashing the loose tarpaulin near his shoulder to the van's framework. He heard the major ask the driver "Is he still sleeping?" and then chuckle. The truck started again.

When he woke up, the silence was deadening; the van was in complete darkness. He lurched to his feet, felt the blood throbbing in his head, and climbed out of the back. The major and driver were still in their seats.

"General Aarons isn't back yet. He went to Mosby by helicopter for the afternoon and evening. By the way, we've just located the man you're replacing on this mission. He's in the POW compound in Eleutheria . . . taken prisoner yesterday." Zoltan glanced at his watch. "Go back and catch up on your sleep. I'll call you when it's time."

"Thank you, sir." Damianos' voice was thick. "Couple more winks and I'll be all right."

Tiresome, he thought, resting on the plank again. *Tiresome being a man . . . beating your head against a wall you can't see.* But he stopped thinking.

It was deep night when they woke him. Within ten minutes his head had cleared and Damianos felt refreshed. No need to rub his eyes now; he was rested. It felt good: being in reality again. Fortunately, he had shaved. Made him feel more like himself, more like the Damianos he knew so well. What on earth had he been thinking? *Can't remember. . . . Can't remember a thing. Whatever it was . . . I was pretty mad about something.* He smiled in the darkness. *What does a guy expect . . . with no sleep? Must of mumbled all the way from camp, griping about wars and strikes and what all. . . .* He ran the tips of his fingers over his smooth face. *Good thing I shaved. . . . Feel like myself again. . . . Feel civilized. . . .*

"Well, Sergeant." Major Zoltan approached Damianos. "How do you feel now?"

"I'm all rested, sir. Is this Eleutheria?"

"On the other side of the hill. Where all the lights are." He took Damianos' arm. "Let's run through this once more. When we go in, you'll know why I requested you even though I knew you'd be just about dead on your feet."

"We drive right into camp," Damianos whispered. "The general's tent is situated on a mound of earth. About seventy feet away there's a bulletin board. The Provost Marshal's headquarters is near the board, facing the general's tent. We drive through the entrance, check with our MP about who's in the tent with the general. Then he knows the mission's on and signals the other partisans to start diverting attention. If he tells us everything is OK, we walk into the tent. If the guard holds us up, I drop him. We go in, tell General Aarons he's our prisoner, and hustle him into the truck. By that time, the other MPs are in the prisoners' compound freeing the partisans. They steal a Deuce-and-a-Half, drive it out of Eleutheria, and wait on one of the side roads. We drive straight out. If there's a chase, the Deuce-and-a-Half leads them off our trail. The area's a labyrinth anyhow by this time, 'cause all the road markers are turned around. Our

MPs are screwing up traffic. By 0200 hours we're back in Libereco, after taking the long way home."

"Good. OK . . . hop in front."

They consulted their wristwatches.

The rutted road twisted violently. Every one hundred yards a white arrow, with BASE HQS–ELEUTHERIA printed in black, pointed in the direction from which they had just come.

They were in Base Headquarters now. The sounds of voices coming over loudspeakers blared in the flatness of Eleutheria. The road swerved to the right. An MP waved a flashlight's beam, calling the truck to a halt. He looked past the driver, speaking to Major Zoltan.

General Aarons was alone in his tent. Within a half hour a colonel in charge of the Public Information Office was expected in to receive orders concerning the handling of news about the mass drop on Crossroads. Reporters and photographers were arriving tomorrow.

Damianos ignored the rest. Ahead of the truck he could see the mound of earth and, on that mound, the tent. The MP saluted Zoltan, and the truck drove slowly through Eleutheria.

There was only one guard at the tent. When the truck halted approximately ten feet from the flap, Damianos noticed several MPs gathering around the bulletin board. He did not bother to wonder if they were imposters or actual military police. He shouldered the door and held it open for Zoltan. The major led the way, walking confidently toward the tent flap. Damianos followed by three feet, the pupils of his eyes swinging from right to left. The guard presented arms smartly and stared ahead. Zoltan entered the tent. Out of the corner of his eye Damianos saw the guard turning to glance at him.

General Aarons was standing before a chart. Compared to the outside cold, the tent was overheated. A thin, gold-rimmed pair of glasses was perched on the general's nose. Damianos noticed the inverted triangle of graying hair between Aarons' neck and the top button of his heavy undershirt.

"What's the meaning of this?" He stared at the major. Zoltan faltered momentarily.

"Sir . . ." He hesitated. "Sir . . . you're under arrest."

"What?" The overhead light shone on the general's bald head. As Aarons' mouth opened to shout something, Damianos lunged and gagged him with his hand. Then he lifted a handkerchief out of the general's back pocket and stuffed it into his mouth. Taking his wrists, Damianos twisted them quickly and manacled them with the handcuffs Major Zoltan held out. Then after throwing the overcoat over the general's shoulders, the two men buttoned it as adequately as possible at the midsection, where the manacled hands protruded.

Damianos tapped Zoltan, who seemed a little worried by the general's attitude, and nodded toward the tent flap.

"Guard!" Zoltan shouted.

By the time the guard had entered, Damianos was at the tent's side. He swung at his midsection, and the soldier fell to the ground.

When the three men left the tent, Damianos observed a crowd near the bulletin board. Some Division paratroopers were arguing with the military police, who were trying to disperse them. A violent discussion broke out between two of the police, and the crowd, losing interest in the bulletin board, surged around the bogus MPs.

Damianos and Zoltan helped the general into the truck, and the half-ton began moving off before the two officers had sat down. Damianos curtained the back of the van and looked out at the rapidly moving terrain. The ride was bumpy. As they passed the MP with the flashlight, Damianos saw, to his left, the red brake lights of the Deuce-and-a-Half, which drove off in the opposite direction. Within five minutes, after numerous turns, the road behind them was black with night.

"We're not being chased," Damianos said. "They probably went the other way . . . that is, if they know about it yet." Major Zoltan might have nodded, but it was too dark within the truck for the sergeant to tell.

When the gag was extracted, General Aarons' voice was icy. "Tell me, Major: what does Simms hope to get out of this little maneuver? A star?"

"I don't know, sir."

"Shut up!"

Silence.

"This is the most unheard of thing I ever heard of. Indefensible! Doesn't he know there's a maneuver on?"

Damianos chuckled silently.

"Sir . . . I was just following orders."

"Shut up!"

It was quiet again in the van.

"This is more . . ." The truck went over a series of bumps. The chassis' tight springs bounced the three men violently.

"This is more than just ordinary stupidity. More than"—they bounced again—"more than looking for . . . newspaper glory. . . . This is *criminal!*"

Damianos listened pleasantly as Zoltan tried to justify the fact that he followed orders well. At times, it was convenient being a mere sergeant. NCOs were rarely presented with the problem of explaining their actions to generals. He fought a chuckle in the darkness. Anonymity was a blessing sometimes. As far as General Aarons was concerned, only two men were responsible for his humiliation: Colonel Simms, the man who conceived and ordered the mission, and Major Zoltan, the man in charge of its execution. He ignored the fact that Sergeant Damianos had gagged and manacled him, had shoved him toward the tent flap, and had pushed him down on the truck's bench. When a sergeant did something unpleasant under orders, he was a good NCO, a "hard nut." When an officer was instrumental in humiliating a three-star general, he was irresponsible.

"What's your name, Major?"

"Zoltan, sir."

"I'll remember that, Major. You haven't heard the last of this."

"Sir . . . I was just—"

"Shut up!"

Damianos went to the canvas again and looked out at the road. Empty and dark again.

"Who are you?"

"Sergeant Damianos, sir."

He waited in the darkness for a reply.

"You're the big moose who handcuffed me, are you? And slugged my guard?"

"Yes, sir."

"Take these handcuffs off me."

"Sir?" Damianos hesitated. "You're a prisoner, sir."

"I'm still a general. Now take them off. . . ."

"Major Zoltan, I . . ."

The major seemed preoccupied. Damianos was answered by silence.

"C'mon, Sergeant; take them off."

Damianos groped for the key and unlocked the manacles.

"These goddamn things are too tight. You may sit down, Sergeant. I'm not about to go anywhere. Not with you around."

"Yes, sir." Damianos gave a low, relieved laugh.

"What was your name again?"

"Zoltan, sir."

"You shut up. I'll attend to you later. I'm talking to the sergeant here."

"Damianos, sir."

"Greek name, huh?"

"Yes, sir. So I'm told."

"First woman I ever laid was a Greek." There was a pause. "Best screw I ever had. They're supposed to be very passionate. I didn't know it at the time." A moment of silence followed. "Must be the sesame seeds they bake in the bread."

Damianos did not know how to respond. Should he thank the general? He sat back in the darkness and smiled.

"Her old man owned a grocery store. Back home in Virginia. Don't remember the name. Not very long, like most Greek names. Can't remember the face either."

"It's hard to remember the names and faces of women you went to bed with, sir. It's easier to remember the ones you wanted to plank but couldn't."

"Yes," General Aarons agreed. "That's true."

What in the hell are we talking about? Damianos wondered.

"There's one name I'll remember, though."

"What's that, sir?"

"Zoltan!"

Damianos could not see the general, but he was certain the name passed through Aarons' clenched teeth.

"Zoltan *and* Simms *and* the Special Troops." There was a pause. "It's preposterous!"

"Yes, sir."

They rode in silence back to Libereco. *It's not so bad . . . my life,* Damianos considered. *Won't be able to make a living at anything else. . . .* He smiled. *Wonder what Zoltan's thinking now?*

CHAPTER 26

Two Army helicopters, their twin rotors swirling tandem, hovered above Crossroads, then parted, each whirring toward its own corner of the drop zone's northern flank. Damianos watched them from the rise of a hill. They appeared sway-backed, like bananas, with the rounded portion toward the earth, a rotor churning from each tip. He fixed the binoculars to his eyes and trained them on he open door at the front of the nearer craft. A bulky figure—at that distance a mere spe k—dropped from the door, followed by another, then another. The second helicopter began dropping its team on the far side of the drop zone.

The paratroopers, under the blossomed canopies, drifted lazily to the drop-zone sand. Then, when the container bundles were pushed through the open doors, Sergeant Damianos looked at his wristwatch. It was 0800 hours. The two pathfinder teams would probably precede the main personnel drop by from twenty to thirty minutes.

The teams rushed the fluorescent panels to the northern center of Crossroads and fixed four of them, long axes pointing north and south, to the earth in what became, a few minutes later, the stem of a gigantic, blazing T. Four panels, axes east and west, completed the crossbar of the T, each sheet divorced from the one next to it by an empty distance of two panel lengths. Three long fluorescent sheets, on each flank of the crossbar, running parallel to the stem, completed the T. A ground radio was established at each flank, an air-ground radio was at the junction of the stem and crossbar, and two homing beacons were on opposite sides of the stem.

Damianos snorted. Several pathfinders were rushing toward clearings—on both sides of Crossroads' approximate center—that his team had prepared for them, knowing they would be chosen as assembly points. Aggressor guerrillas were lying in wait a hundred yards from the clearings. They would not be very effective against the Division, but they would succeed in marring the excellence of the spectacular mass jump. Aggressor would capitulate, according to plan; the United States would win, as usual; and Operation Razor Blade would be over. The boys would be back home a week before Christmas; this, it seemed, would be the only precedent establishd.

The sergeant tried to estimate a few of the factors known to the pathfinders. The aircraft would fly in V's, along the stem of the T. The pilots, unable to see the crossbar as they passed over it, would guide themselves on the flank panels. If the pathfinders knew Aggressor was nearby, they would have marked only the left flank, the one easier for the pilots to see; evidently, since they had marked both panels, they expected no difficulty.

As each pilot, then, flew over the crossbar, he would give

the jumpmaster the green light. The troops would jump, drifting according to the velocity of the wind, trying to slip as close as possible to the assembly-point panels. And as each Flying Boxcar crossed the T, the paratroopers would tumble from the doors.

Damianos felt a twinge of jealousy. He would have liked to jump with them, but since this was impossible, he satisfied himself with waiting for the airplanes' humming engines. As often as he had parachuted, he had not surmounted the feeling of exultation implicit in the commonplace of the mass jump. Tiny men, like microscopic motes, exercising fierce wills and contempt for life, leaping—disciplined and confident for all their minor fears—to the earth. *Like the fire gods,* he thought, recalling the Greek lessons his mother had forced him to study. Like the fire gods, all contemptuous of the fact that God punished those whom He feared. All struck down in fury, hurtling to an awaiting earth (one to be chained to a rock); all imitated by men; all airborne; none avenged.

A smoke grenade was thrown near the crossbar, and the black cloud ascended slowly. Damianos sighted it with his glasses. The smoke drifted to the far side, the south, of Crossroads.

Damianos realized that he recalled his mother at the most curious times. The unwitting woman, teaching him the language and the grammar of his ancestors, was shocked to find that, en route, he understood the meaning of their myths, the challenge of the human fist upraised, the pride and valor, the knowledge of certain punishment, and, yet, the eternal *yes* to the workings of fate, as if, in accepting fate, men would exhaust it.

Several men were talking excitedly next to him. As Damianos turned to caution them, he followed their pointing fingers to the treetops. Lost in his thoughts, he had heard nothing. Gusts of wind tossed the slender pines. He scanned the drop zone to see the black smoke being scattered across the heights of Crossroads; then, after each gust had spent itself, the blackness resumed its placid pace. Someone whispered in his ear. "Do you think the jump will be called off?"

"Don't think so. Wind's too irregular." He pointed to the surface. "Pathfinders probably think it's OK on the ground." He stood up, moving his heavy shoulders to relieve the back muscles he had strained as he lay prone, his elbows spiked into the turf. "They got all the facts and equipment down there. They got anemometers you ain't even seen yet." He stretched out prone again, following the antlike movements of the pathfinders.

He thought briefly of Clarke, sorry he had been so curt with him on his return from the ambush. It was peculiar how the strangest people would be attracted to parachuting. There was no pattern in the characteristics of the volunteer. But once they were in, they were in all the way. Courage was a strange quality, unnatural and often punished. *Yes . . . punished. . . .* He glanced at his watch: 0820 hours.

Another gust of wind shook the trees. The forest, recovering from the blast of air, hummed like the beach near a retreating surf. There may be danger in the drop. *Shouldn't of kidnapped Aarons. . . . He should be with his men today. . . .* Damianos fixed the binoculars to his eyes; the pathfinders did not seem concerned. He looked at his watch again. *The airplanes should be nearing Crossroads,* he thought. Every second that passed forged another link in the causal chain. Only an emergency could halt the juggernaut now. The necessary decisions had been made, and the sequence of events was rooted in destiny.

He turned his head abruptly, trying to distinguish with his keen hearing the swaying wash of the forest from the low hum, which seemed to grow louder. The droning noise approached, nearing the vast tannish platform, which someone, over a topographic map, had called Crossroads. Again, Damianos was intrigued by the name. Deep in the luxuriance and mystery of the past, lost in the vast terrain of time and human memory, the name—Crossroads—had worked a mystic incantation. The anticipated would be encountered, it seemed to say; the final link in the chain of contingency would be confronted; the destiny in which men existed and subsisted would be concluded—and from that encounter men would, perhaps, commence a new life. And Damianos, listening to the aircrafts' drone become a shattering roar, wondered if the meeting with which destiny threatened him was what he needed, coming to him in the guise of what he feared.

The flight of V's in trail formation burst upon Crossroads Drop Zone like a swarm of maddened bees. Each V of three aircraft, as not quite interlocking arrowheads, spanned the sky from horizon to horizon. The point triangle sped above the junction of the T; the second roared over it, then the third, the fourth, the fifth; and from each one cocoonlike dots streamed out of open doors, then blossomed with nylon wings. The sixth V blazed across, the seventh, the eighth, the ninth—the sky was filled with opened canopies—the tenth, and then the last. To the surface of the vast Crossroads, the camouflaged nylon parachutes, dangling men, descended in various altitudes, in every stage of opening, from those approaching the ground fully inflated, the first to leap, preparing themselves for the impact, to those who had just jumped, tumbling unsupported through space, their twisting nylon and suspension lines still embryonic tails.

Damianos heard the surflike wash again, saw the swaying pine tops shudder, stop, then dance again to the push of the gust. He stared at the surface of Crossroads, transfixed; he saw the first paratroopers falling, their unseen toes stretched to the waiting earth.

Damianos rose to his feet, the horror catching in his throat. *"The wind,"* he shouted. *"The wind! Gonna drag 'em!"* He began sprinting, bull-like, through the scrub, under stately, towering trees that ascended like cathedral spires to the sky; ran tripping over exposed roots, blundering into intertwined branches and vines, and lurching into saplings that bent at the impact of his great weight. *"Gonna drag 'em!"* he bellowed. By the time he rushed into the flat barrenness of Crossroads, the first men, too far from him to be tackled, had landed on the drop zone. He could see them struggling with the wind, wrestling with their billowing canopies, being dragged across the hard-packed earth.

A few had managed to free themselves of their harnesses, and Damianos, waiting for a trio of descending paratroopers, expected those who released themselves to help those nearest them. He looked up at the leaden sky, both great hands hanging tense at the seams of his trousers.

The three paratroopers landed around him within one second of each other; Damianos, standing helplessly, felt rooted to the earth, unable to choose which one to save, until the man to his right cried out for help. He flung his bearish body through the air, caught the man at the shoulders, tugged at the taut, vibrating risers of the chute, and slowly battered the parabola empty of air. He sprinted to the second man, now being dragged across the frozen earth, and leaped upon the nylon canopy. The distance between Damianos and the third paratrooper was too great, and the sergeant saw him briefly, struggling with the brimmed air-full chute and then collapsing lifelessly, a human burden hauled across the ruts and stones of Crossroads.

He swerved his head and, in a moment's blaze, beheld the immense drop zone coming alive. It seemed unreal, the measured pace with which the thousand canopies puffed from right to left, drifting like a sea of brown-green sails across an immobile platform, like a migrating flight of mallards at the point of takeoff from the oily stillness of a lake.

The Aggressor guerrillas had rushed to the drop zone, collapsing chutes, sprinting after struggling bodies, they too, advancing right to left, like sandpipers after a retreating surf. The green-bereted specks of men advanced, and, with an equally stately pace, the billowing canopies withdrew.

Damianos was in the midst of parachutes, throwing his great bulk on hard canopies that constantly surprised him with their impregnability, a cumbersomeness that maddened him enough to crush them finally with battering blocks. Off balance, he was knocked flat by the stiffness of a wind-filled parachute that struck him from behind. By instinct, his fingers clutched the slender nylon shroud lines and pulled the canopy around. It shuddered, partially emptied of the driven wind, and writhed, exhausted, on the surface of the earth.

Damianos raised the palms of his hands to his sight. The nylon lines had burned into his hand; vicious red streaks had cut his skin. Licking the singed flesh with his tongue, he stopped, ashamed. Would he pamper himself while men were in danger?

By now the east side of the drop zone had been cleared. The cries for *help* and *medic* had lessened. The wall of puffed canopies was retreating again, and all Sergeant Damianos could do was begin a steady jog, certain he could no longer manage a sprint, pacing himself though his tumultuous heart and racing mind cried out for him to spend whatever energy remained. His thick chest heaved; he staggered and fell, exhausted and shaken by the leaps and jarrings he had taken to save the dragged paratroopers.

A man lay on his side, fighting his canopy. For a second Damianos hesitated. The man was in a state of shock. His buckled arms and legs seemed rooted to the ground. He raised his pleading eyes to the sergeant. *The doe,* Damianos recalled. *The doe!* With just these eyes it had looked at him, hurt, uncomprehending. And he had killed it for no reason. The sergeant rushed to the straining canopy, swung it around against the wind, and stood, legs trembling under him.

He raced the wind again, forgetting his depleted reserves, springing against a canopy that dragged the bouncing body of a man. Boot by boot, he neared the man, now prone, now supine, now on his side. Damianos' legs quivered. He flung himself into the air, arched his body, and grasped the man by the shoulders. Then, touching earth again, he grappled with the chute, fist by fist pinning it, lifeless, to the ground.

Damianos staggered erect; forced his exhausted body to respond, to run; and, falling, shuddering, spitting out soil that clogged his mouth, raised himself again on trembling legs and challenged the billowing, stately canopies again, sprinting with them, drawing on nonexistent reserves, battling the wind until *it* tired, until *it* flagged, falling on scalding, slicing nylon lines that ripped at his hands and wrists with taut, vibrating wires and gripping them no matter how hot they became, clutching and pulling them toward him with hands afire, defeating the shuddering canopy, offended that men could be puppets on strings, although he knew this to be so.

Tears streamed from his eyes. He coughed and spat and trembled and fell, only to get up again, to be thrown to the ground again by the collapse of his rubbery legs, and then to crawl, remembering only that men needed aid, that men treasured life (though he did not), that men wanted to live (though disasters were part of every life-span), that men abhorred death (though it meant an end to dancing to the wishes of a fickle wind). And so he crawled—for he could no longer run—dragging his inert body to a vibrating canopy whose bottom skirt skimmed the surface of the earth and quivered, taut and stationary, with the force of the wind. Damianos crept to it, elbows scraped and bleeding, knees as frozen and insensitive as the soil they hobbled upon, and struggled with the stiff canopy, wrestling it to the earth. His knees wobbling, he stood up to help the paratrooper out of his harness, only to find the man lying prone, wedged against a jagged tree stump, his helmeted head resting loosely in the hollow of his shoulder blades and the airborne chin strap framing the pulp of a face whose features no longer existed. The name tape identified him as Brixter.

There were few cries for help now, and those that sounded came from the forest, from men hung up on trees. Sergeant Damianos eased himself to the earth, his mucles twitching wildly from the intense exertion; he rolled to his back, lulled somewhat by the new-found silence of the drop zone. The wind still blew, but, without the billowing canopies, it seemed to lack conviction, humming mournfully, merely rearranging grains of sand on the platform of Crossroads.

He rose to his trembling legs. There was nothing to do but wait for the ambulance trucks and helicopters to arrive with the stretchers, the doctors, and the graves registrars. How many fatalities there were he could not estimate, but, judging from the groans and cries he had heard off toward the forest, there were at least five, excluding the faceless man wedged into the tree stump. The decision would come after the doctors and the graves registrars—as if the great decision had not been made when the wind gusts dragged the first man to his death; as if the seed of the second mass jump could not be found in the failure of the first. General Aarons would be freed from one imprisonment to assume the manacles of another.

Snafu, he thought; *snafu.* He stumbled on the hard-packed sand. He had forgotten. *Snafu!* He had intuited somehow that there would be a mix-up, a disaster, in Razor Blade. Did he foretell *this? A snafu,* he had said. *I feel it in my bones.* But why? *Why would I of felt this way?*

It's all nonsense! A wind came, as winds do, and encountered paratroopers falling to earth, as men must, and dragged them, as could have been expected. Most were saved . . . but some died. As is natural.

Deep in the south flank of Crossroads, where the flatness of the drop zone imperceptibly shadowed into the ascending bluish-purple of the mountain range, Damianos saw a mass of paratroopers, possibly of regimental size, forming around the red-and-white dot of an ambulance truck. As if hesitating above the troopers who rushed into formation, a small airplane droned and banked slightly to its right.

CHAPTER 27

"Something's wrong," the pilot said.

Clarke did not hear the flier's comment; the wind was stiff at that altitude, and the door of the small Beaver was open for him to throw out the leaflets. He was amazed to see the drop zone crowded with men wandering indiscriminately over the broad platform, as if Aggressor had been defeated and the operation was over. As the small, one-engined aircraft approached the large gathering, he knew he had found his audience. Clarke tapped the pilot on the shoulder. "Would you bank over this way, sir?" he shouted. "I'd like to drop the leaflets on this group."

The L-20 banked to its right, and Clarke, braced by the loose safety belt, leaned painfully toward the door, dropping stacks of unbound leaflets over the dense crowd. The steel helmets of the men on the ground moved up and back, and pale faces peered up at him; their skin seemed drained of blood, and their protuberant steel pots appeared liable to shift and cover their stubby bodies and shortened, distorted legs.

The leaflets fluttered and folded wildly as Clarke's hand passed the open door. Free at last, the paper sheets were caught in the propeller wash and thrashed, like snow swirls, about the crowd of men on the drop zone's surface. They were then blown steadily to the west flank of Crossroads.

Clarke frowned. The dispersal pattern of the leaflets was good, but evidently there was a slight breeze on the DZ's surface of which he was not aware; the leaflets were dropping far away from the center of the crowd.

The pilot was shouting at him. Clarke had difficulty understanding the warrant officer. Stopping his leaflet broadcasting momentarily, he pulled himself near the flier's seat. *"Disaster,"* he heard. It was confusing. Clarke stared stupidly at the back of the man's neck. *"There's been a disaster."* He glanced to the earth again to see the white leaflets scattering across the drop zone. The Beaver was at an altitude of about two hundred feet now. Directly below him, Clarke saw two men lying stiffly on the brownish-green nylon of an extended canopy. A leaflet was embedded between the two figures.

The earth seemed closer to Clarke's open door. He glanced at the pilot to see, over the man's shoulders, the flat, tannish sand of Crossroads through the silvery haze of the propeller's circle. He was about to ask what the pilot was doing, but, realizing that to call for the man's attention at the moment he needed it most might have proved dangerous, he maintained his silence, readying himself for an abrupt jolt by tightening his safety belt. He leaned back and braced for the landing.

His eyes searching the approaching terrain for bumps and hollows, Clarke was relieved to see a primitive, seldom-used landing strip declining toward him like a grass-ridged conveyor belt. The Beaver's stationary wheels touched earth and spun. The pilot slowed the craft, turned it against the straining wind, and taxied waywardly across the drop zone. The craft turned with a flourish, and the propeller's transparent globe became opaque, obscuring a circle of forest across from Clarke with its slowing blades, then revealing instantly masked slices of forest green and earth brown—eighths, quarters, and halves; finally, with a sputter, the propeller's shaft swung erect. Clarke and the warrant officer removed their safety belts and jumped to the platform of Crossroads Drop Zone.

"Any injured here?" the warrant officer asked a nearby PFC, whose eyes appeared glazed.

The trooper did not understand the question and responded by staring dully at the pilot and Clarke, as if trying to determine whether or not they here hostile. The WO repeated the question. "One injured, sir," the PFC replied, "and one dead."

"Ovah heah!" Clarke swerved to his left. *"Ovah heah!"*

He saw a Negro sergeant waving at them; then a medical vehicle stopped between him and Clarke. The pilot jogged toward it. Clarke, left alone with the dull-eyed PFC, began walking away self-consciously. The back doors of the truck opened, as if of their own accord, and a man leaped out, turning immediately and leaning into the van to pull out two empty stretchers. A medical officer appeared suddenly from the shielded side of the truck, following—by a second—the slam of a door.

"We can take a couple back by air," the pilot said.

The medical officer, a captain, ignored the comment. He rushed to a canopy, stretched on the ground, on which two figures lay, and glanced at the leaflet that had settled between them. "The bastards," he muttered, and crumpled it. The captain froze for a moment. "What's this knife doing here?" It was a short, narrow hunting knife. "What's been going on?"

"That's *his* knife, suh," the colored sergeant explained. "Ah figure he was tryin' to cut hisself loose from bein' drag, but he juss 'bout got the shiv from his boot when he hit a rock or somethin' and got turn ovah. Slashed at his hip," he added unnecessarily, for the blood had soaked the man's fatigues from the groin to the rib box. The knife was bloodied and flaked by fine grains of sand. The sergeant had evidently saved the man, released him from his harness, loosened his belt, taken off his helmet, and unstrapped his combat and weapons' packs.

Clarke watched the doctor open a sharp penknife and slit the fatigues open, examining the slash the man had inflicted on himself. The soldier groaned. "Is this all?" the doctor asked. "Is this all?" He leaned toward the injured man's lips. "The foot, too?" He touched the left boot. "This one?" The man was silent. "This one?" he inquired, touching the right boot. The paratrooper screamed. "Just the foot?" He began feeling above the knee and worked down. "Hurt here? Hurt here?" The soldier said nothing.

The doctor looked up to the pilot. "Can you take off without too many bumps?"

"Yes, sir. It's a pretty good strip. There's hardly any wind left."

"Fine. Is the cargo compartment clear?" The answer was negative. "OK, then jettison the seat and equipment. I'm going to give these men first aid and put them on stretchers. You should be in the main field hospital within twenty minutes. The one here is a little crowded and disorganized." He rose briefly and kneeled beside the next soldier. "This man's dead," he said to the sergeant. *"He has no face!"* The doctor was horrified; his features were twisted in nausea.

"Yesh, suh. Ah don' reckanize the name Brixter, suh. He musta be drag into that tree stump."

"Him, too," the captain said. "Take him along. And, Sergeant"—the doctor's tone was mild—"next time—cover up the corpses."

"Yes, suh."

Clarke and the pilot rushed to the Beaver, threw out the remaining bundles of leaflets, and unbolted the seats. Clarke estimated that the cargo compartment of the L-20 was approximately seven feet long and five feet wide. The two stretchers would fit easily, with one man's shoulders next to the other's boots. When he and the WO had cleared the compartment, Clarke turned to see the stretcher-bearers approaching the plane.

"You . . . Clarke." The doctor had glanced at his name tape. "Sit in back and don't let the stretchers move around. It'll take too long to brace them to the floor. Got it?"

"Yes, sir."

"And be careful of this one." The captain did not specify.

Clarke climbed into the compartment after the WO and sat on the floor with a makeshift safety belt strapped around him and the pilot's seat. His legs were flanked by the man delicately poised between life and death and the other one, the already committed, already cold, faceless one.

The propeller sputtered. Moving under the open door slowly, then faster, the tannish earth dropped, and the men on it, formerly proportional and erect, now appeared dwarfed again, with enormous heads and helmets resting precariously on stunted bodies. The corpse stirred briefly as the Beaver banked to the left, toward the main field hospital, and Clarke, struggling to concentrate on the living man, wondered how much blood was left.

This was the third time he had confronted death. The Clarke family had gathered when the grandmother, the matriarch, had perished, cinematically, with the same small nod she gave when recognizing acquaintances. Then he had strained to hear a bachelor uncle's last words, only to comprehend much later that his father's brother had made a feverish attempt to sing that it was he "who broke the bank at Monte Carlo" and to feel a mixed pathos and embarrassment toward his uncle's last moments, revealing, as they did, so much of the man: a man who took responsibility too seriously; a man too shy with women; a man too devoted to his widowed, possessive mother. But these details had been denouements of lives consistently and safely spent, finales that were necessary because death was unavoidable, conclusions that were meaningful because even he, a young Clarke, could understand them as a necessary part of life.

The L-20 hit a small air pocket, and Clarke's knee bounced against the corpse's thigh. He felt chilled, as if he had nudged a mannequin. Clarke drew his legs closer to himself.

The injured man groaned; his lips fluttered briefly. (Was he trying to sing about Monte Carlo? To call his Mum or his wife? To utter, feverishly, wordless sounds somehow concerned with love? To ask for water?) Then, becoming still again, he returned to his coma.

When a man nears death, Clarke thought, *even war must seem defensible.* For if a man is ready to perish, he would like to know that others have died and will continue to die, just as meaninglessly as he will; that everyone will eventually share in his terror and anguish. In peacetime the world moves on, people are too busy to care, and men grow cold in rooms warmed by surviving members of the family to make, ironically, the dying person's last moments comfortable.

When the wheels touched the runway at Eleutheria and taxied to a stop, Clarke stepped over the covered corpse with a feeling of revulsion. He jumped to the ground. As he and the pilot lifted the stretcher out of the L-20 and set it under the wing of the plane in order to rush the wounded man to the surgeon's tent, Clarke held it tightly, hoping the stretcher would not slip out of his hand: for that would have meant devoting extra attention to something he wanted to forget about as quickly as possible.

CHAPTER 28

"Hey, you! Corporal! Come here!"

"Yes, sir!" McIlhenny jogged toward his company's executive officer, snapped to attention, and saluted. It was important that he change the early impressions the officer had of him since he had arrived in the Division, he knew, for his numerous trips to the dispensary, the two times he had been caught in his bunk asleep when he should have been viewing training films, and the general lack of interest he had displayed on several occasions disposed the executive officer unfavorably toward him.

The captain ignored the greeting. "Leave your equipment where it is. Get those six privates"—he motioned to the group of men with whom McIlhenny had been standing—"and double-time to that area." He swerved to his right, pointing to the forest. "A couple of canopies have been sighted in the trees. Send one of the men to report any injuries and come back here when you're through."

"Yes, sir." McIlhenny hesitated.

The captain looked at him carefully; then, in a cold voice, he said: "Get your ass moving, Corporal!"

"Yes, sir!" McIlhenny, hurt by the rebuke, jogged back to the group, the ever-present feeling of anxiety worrying into him. His loosely fisted hands, pumping at his sides, trembled slightly, but Corporal McIlhenny knew better than to assign all the blame to the struggle with his wind-inflated canopy a half hour before. He asked for the attention of the six men, finding it difficult to meet the arrogant and quizzical stare of the new transfer, a Private Sueños, who had recently become Regular Army from the Puerto Rican National Guard.

Four of the soldiers—Lennox, a blond farm boy from Ohio; Williams, a slender man in his early twenties; Boyd, a sturdy Negro from the North; and Cotter, a heavy-drinking ex-sergeant—had been in the company before McIlhenny was transferred into the Division, and he addressed himself to them. Although the corporal had not welcomed the conversations in which they had tried to involve him when the Division was still garrisoned, he found himself developing a nodding acquaintance with the four, strengthened somewhat by the obvious respect they exhibited toward him when they asked for help in writing letters or in settling disputes when none of them wanted to consult the encyclopedias in the Post Library.

The two other men were new to the 43rd, fresh out of Jump School. Acorn seemed to be a shy, uncommunicative boy, but McIlhenny could understand his reserve, for the private was too recent an arrival to have made any close friends. Sueños, however, rattled the corporal. His swarthy face, falling short of genuine beauty, as it did, because of thin, distorted lips, displayed an acquisitive, probing, disrespectful attitude. McIlhenny felt uneasy under Private Sueños' stare, as if everything about himself, his whole life, his myriad weaknesses lay exposed.

"A few parachutes have been spotted in the forest," he began, "and we've been detailed to see if the men are still in them injured." *That was awkwardly put,* he thought. *Can't even speak English anymore.* He talked to the four men with whom he was on familiar terms, feeling nervous and uncomfortable whenever he glanced at Sueños.

"I don' know why we s'ould do eet."

McIlhenny glanced at the dark boy apprehensively; something about Private Sueños destroyed what little equanimity he had left. "Things are very disorganized," the corporal said, looking furtively at the thin, cruel mouth, then shifting his sight quickly, as if catching himself in something reprehensible. "The drop zone is in chaos and the pathfinders have their hands full. I think . . ."

Lennox fidgeted nervously. McIlhenny saw a slight frown beginning to form on his face, possibly due to an irritation at McIlhenny's finding it necessary to apologize for a command.

Sueños interrupted. "I don' wan' to go."

"Shut your ugly mouth," Lennox muttered, "and do what he tells you."

"Chinga tu madre," Sueños snapped.

"All right, now; all right." McIlhenny tried to check the potential fracas, knowing that if it started, he would be impotent to part the two; that if they were seen fighting by any officer, he, the NCO in charge, would be held responsible, since it would be a virtual admission that he was unable to maintain discipline among his men. "All right, now," he said. "Right *face!*" He realized immediately, with Sueños' snicker and Lennox's bewildered glance, that he had not called them to attention yet. "Ten-*hup!*" he barked, feeling as he shouted the command that he appeared ridiculous to them. His eyebrow twitched, but he fought the impulse to rub it. "Right *face!*" His fingers drummed excitedly on his thigh. "For-ard . . . *harch!*" The file of six men marched toward the forest. He had almost forgotten the captain's desire for speed. "Double-time . . . *harch!*"

The jog began, and McIlhenny permitted the file to gain on him, at least to the point where he was behind Sueños, for running where he knew the private could watch his movements was sure to fill him with a curious feeling of tension.

Two paratroopers on McIlhenny's right were sitting on a mound of earth, their forearms resting on spread knees. Shoulders hunched and helmeted heads lowered, they appeared to be staring at the drop-zone earth in despair. The soldiers did not speak to each other and ignored the heavy thudding of the runners' boots nearby.

Corporal McIlhenny was about to shout at them, asking them if they were injured, for they looked to be in a state of shock, but then he reconsidered: he was no officer; it was none of *his* business. As the file of paratroopers double-timed within twenty feet of the two soldiers, McIlhenny saw the nearer man casually spit out a great clot of blood. *Poor man,* he thought, and ran on.

When the file left the flatness of Crossroads and entered the scrub pines that surrounded the drop zone, McIlhenny saw the earth covered with what appeared to be white pages torn from a large notebook. Jogging over several sheets of paper, the corporal realized they were leaflets. He picked one off a snag of a broken tree limb, folded it into quarters as he ran, and slid it into his trouser pocket.

They were double-timing now under tall trees, and McIlhenny racked his mind for the proper command to halt the file. His memory was blank, and the frustration and terror of being caught helpless, of exhibiting his incompetence to lead the six privates, virtually brought tears to his eyes. *They were right,* he thought. *They were right to take my commission.* After all, what kind of soldier was he, not to remember the commands every NCO could recite in his sleep? The primitive trail disappeared fifty feet away; he had less than half a minute to recall the command. It was impossible. Lennox, at the lead, was jerking his head around at every step, waiting for the order to stop jogging. Finally, in desperation, McIlhenny blurted out, "OK, let's march," and was stung to hear the vicious, knowing laugh of Private Sueños. He pretended not to notice the dismayed looks Williams, Boyd, and Lennox gave him as he walked before them. Cotter was smiling disagreeably.

They began walking aimlessly toward the west, and with each pace McIlhenny glanced in anguish at the treetops. There were no canopies. If there were, he could not find them. But the captain had told him some had been sighted here! Then it was his—McIlhenny's—fault that the men would not be able to perform their mission. And now human lives depended on him. *Oh, no . . . they were right when they took my captaincy. . . . They knew what they were doing.*

The corporal stopped momentarily to squint his eyes at a far-off treetop, and the file marched past him.

"How far are we gonna walk?" Cotter asked.

So the ex-sergeant had turned on him, too? Even Cotter, who should know what it is like to be demoted, had joined Sueños against him. *Why couldn't he have approached me away from the others and asked that question?* McIlhenny wondered. *They all want to make a laughingstock out of me.*

"Just a little further down." Corporal McIlhenny spoke authoritatively. "The path ends down there, near a stream. I remember the area," he lied, but diabolically forced the burden of proof on the path. If it did not correspond to his description of it, then it acted in bad faith by making him appear ludicrous and impotent in the eyes of the very people whose respect he should command. If the path did not conform to his lie, then everything that had happened to him recently was a deliberate, coordinated undermining of his sanity. He checked an urge to rush ahead.

Oh God, he thought. *Oh, God!* The path disappeared into a chaotic area of saplings, ferns, and crisscrossing limbs.

Cotter smiled disagreeably in McIlhenny's face. *He should know better than to hurt me this way,* the corporal thought. *He was reduced himself*. Boyd, Lennox, and Williams stared down at the ground in embarrassment. McIlhenny knew what they were trying to do to him. *What do they think I am?* he wondered. *There's a word in the English language for what they're trying to do to me,* he realized. *Intimidate! Who do they think they are?*

"Here," McIlhenny said angrily. *"I'll* get in front. We won't get lost that way." He glared at Lennox. "We won't take any *wrong turns* that way!" Jostling between the privates, who, it seemed to McIlhenny, were becoming purposefully unhurried and awkward, he assumed the lead of the file and began marching quickly and steadily back to where they had stopped double-timing.

"I theenk I see somethenn."

McIlhenny turned abruptly. For the briefness of an insane, taut moment, he hoped Sueños had made an error. Then, following the private's pointing finger, he saw the unmistakable, mottled parachute nylon poured over a tree. Why hadn't he seen it? Why had the others maintained their silence? *They're in league with him,* McIlhenny decided. *They're against me!*

Three men were hung up on trees in the same area. Swaying gently, one of the paratroopers appeared to be unconscious, with arms and legs which dangled heavily toward the matted earth of the forest. The soles of the man's boots swung a few inches above the turf, and McIlhenny, although not so tall as Lennox or Cotter, stretched up on tiptoe to feel the man's pulse. It was weak. He placed the palm of his hand under the trooper's harness, flat against the abdominal pressure point. *Thank God . . . he's alive. I've not failed him.*

He bent over and probed for the small hunting knife he had sheathed between his left boot and the inside of his calf. It was not there. *Of course!* He recalled the incident. He had lost it somewhere on Crossroads.

McIlhenny straightened up. "Let's cut him down. Who has a knife?"

He heard a *whulick* behind him. Sueños held a long, thin switchblade in his hand.

"We can get him out of his harness without using a knife," Cotter said. "Just turn his quick-release."

"Yes, yes, of course," McIlhenny agreed. "That's right." The command was gradually slipping through his fingers; he realized this objectively, as if it were occurring to someone else.

"Why don't three of us get this guy down and the rest try to help one of the others?" Lennox contributed. "This way we're wasting time."

Everyone but McIlhenny seemed to agree with the last statement, but the corporal was unable to explain his reasons for not being in accordance with what had been said. In the few seconds during which he considered Lennox's suggestion, however, he found himself concurring with the rest. It was a valid, practical insight. He was chagrined not to have thought of it himself. *They despise me,* he thought, *and I deserve it.*

"All right," McIlhenny said, "that's what we'll do. Boyd, Sueños, Williams, and Cotter will go to that man over there and get him down." He threw his shoulders back and raised his voice authoritatively. "Lennox." McIlhenny glanced at the next man's name tape. "Lennox, Acorn, and I will work on this one. When we finish, we'll come over and help you."

"I wan' to stay here," Private Sueños said.

"No, you'll go with Cotter, Williams, and Boyd." McIlhenny's voice was severe.

"No, I will stay here."

"You heard him." Lennox glared at Sueños.

"You wan' to make sometheen out of eet?" Sueños' upper lip curled into a taunt.

"Don't fight!" McIlhenny shouted, staring at the dark boy's beautiful, cruel face. *"Don't fight!"*

"Who's fighting?" Lennox looked at McIlhenny placidly. "You fight your own battles, Corporal." A cool smile appeared on the blond soldier's face.

Was it necessary that he say it in that way? McIlhenny wondered helplessly. *He's turning against me.* The corporal swallowed. "OK!" he said belligerently. "OK! I'll go with them." And he walked ahead of the three, pressing his hands against the seams of his trousers to keep them from shaking.

"Hey . . . buddy! You OK?" Cotter shouted up to the paratrooper. It was obvious to the four men standing under the hanging soldier that he was conscious; but it was also understood that only an inexplicable, momentary panic was strong enough to outweight the painful stab of the harness juncture at the man's groin and to keep him aloft. Approximately thirty feet separated the man's boots from the earth's surface —certainly not long enough to prohibit using his reserve canopy as an escape ladder.

"Yeah," the parachutist replied. "I'm OK. How's yourself?"

Corporal McIlhenny had been standing behind Boyd and Williams, gnawing at himself for his deadening, relentless feeling of impotence. He could not lead, he knew; he had lost the ability to consider himself infallible. An uncertain leader could never mask his self-doubt. At any rate, not to those he was supposed to control. Before a man could conquer the world—he recalled the military axiom—or even govern as small a portion of it as the wills of six men, he would need to have conquered himself or, at least, to be aware of the direction of his own will. But, McIlhenny knew, even if he could not do this, he should make an attempt to salvage his self-respect; his conscience, his self-esteem demanded that he assume the authority the Army had given him. And Corporal McIlhenny was never more aware of the ludicrous nature of himself (this failure who once believed he had been created in the image of God), never more privy to the insight of how allied self-ridicule and the degeneration into ineffectuality actually were than at this moment. Four men were looking up, one man was looking down, and he who should have made the decisions and given the orders was standing behind everyone, as if in hiding, staring morosely at the dangling paratrooper and witnessing only his personal deterioration.

He felt the flush of blood warm his face. *"I order you!"* he screeched. *"Come down this instant!"*

The paratrooper gazed down at him reflectively. "Screw you, big nose," he said.

McIlhenny's senses, as if perfectly attuned to his decline, discriminated among all the wayward impressions he was open to and selected only that which exhibited to him his own debasement. His ears ignored the whisper of the wind, the rustling of the canopy against the branches, and registered only the stifled laughter of the three privates ahead of him; the sound of ridicule came to him with exaggerated volume. His knees wobbled, and the suffocating bitterness mounted in his chest with every heartthrob. *I am weak,* he thought, *and everyone hates me. I am vulnerable, and everyone attacks me.*

As if he were less important than the youngest, lowest-ranked man there, McIlhenny was paid the unforgivable courtesy of being ignored. Over his mourning, the self-keening man heard the sure, confident commands that Private Cotter, so recently sergeant, was giving Boyd and Williams; each authoritative order rescued the corporal from the failure of his mission while exhibiting to him the hopelessness of his decay.

Just as Boyd and Williams were halfway up a nearby tree, working their way toward a substantial limb from which they would have reached him, the soldier gathered his courage. McIlhenny saw the man pull the rip cord of his reserve chute and play out the canopy until the nylon barely touched the turf. The paratroopers paused at the crotch of a limb and observed. The soldier, glancing at them, felt the intimidation in their stares. He turned the dial of his quick-release box, grasped the webbing of the harness above his head, and struck the button. The straps of the harness parted, and the webbing flung loose; the two chutes were linked together at the midsection. He hesitated briefly; then, already committed, the paratrooper began descending, hand under hand, sliding painfully down the nylon shroud lines with burning hands. He clutched desperately at the nylon canopy. From there, it was a small drop to the earth. Landing on his toes, the soldier glanced at Cotter while cooling his palms with spittle. He ignored McIlhenny.

"You straightleg motherless son of a bitch," Cotter said. "We wasted time getting to you. We got another man hung up."

"That one?" He nodded toward the tattered canopy on a nearby tree. The name tape on his jacket read Herrold. "That one's dead." Herrold smiled nervously.

McIlhenny stared at him. He did not say anything, for it was none of the corporal's affair. This was between Cotter and Herrold.

"You mean you knew the guy was dying and you didn't do a goddamn thing?"

Herrold shrugged his shoulders. "I heard him moaning. Then when he stopped I figured he was dead and there was nothing I could do."

"Didja hear that, Corporal?" Cotter looked at McIlhenny, then turned to Herrold again. "Your ass has had it, buster. That's a court-martial for sure."

When Williams and Boyd had climbed down, Cotter sent them both up to determine if the man was actually dead. He was. With McIlhenny watching helplessly, as in a nightmare, they cut him down; the paratrooper thudded to the hard-packed earth, where he flopped and twitched briefly, like a scarecrow in a heavy wind.

It doesn't matter, McIlhenny thought. *The man is dead.*

The corpse's features had frozen in pain; a horrible bruise mark across his temple showed that he had probably died of a brain concussion. No one knew who he was—not even the man who had dangled next to him for almost an hour. Try as they did, they could locate neither his dog tags nor the name tape that had been ripped from the breast of his jacket.

Cotter took Sueños' switchblade and cut up the available canopies into stretchers. Acorn, Boyd, Lennox, and Williams began carrying the injured man towards Crossroads. Cotter told McIlhenny to grasp the right rear of the canopy on which the corpse was placed; Sueños held the right front, and Herrold was ordered to take the left front, so that he could be watched. In case he tried to flee, he would be between the ex-sergeant at the left rear and Sueños; one of the two would stop him first.

McIlhenny was happy to be doing something, glad that he was needed. It was pleasant to follow orders, for in being governed a man still preserved the sanctity of the thoughts to which he could return unmolested. But the lithe form of Private Sueños disturbed him. Slender and strong, the dark boy strode ahead of McIlhenny effortlessly, as if he knew the corporal stared at his beauty; he seemed to exaggerate the movements of his walk.

The stretcher parties left the scrub pines and entered the flatness of Crossroads. The wind had ceased. Vague human sounds came to McIlhenny from the far side of the drop zone, like mothers' voices waking boys from childhood dreams. The vast platform was virtually empty. Crossroads, he perceived, must have been, for ages, as vacant and as silent as it now appeared; for at least a decade it had lain still, unknown, host perhaps to a small hunting party, to a solitary woodsman, to deer, to bears, to raccoons—a great sandy carpet forgotten by the human mind. And only today, when men arrived, did the unrecorded, random violence—which doubtless was a daily fact—achieve a human meaning.

Crossroads, McIlhenny thought. *Crossroads was here and I didn't know it . . . and it won't disappear when I leave.* . . . He slipped and lost his footing briefly. As his grip on the nylon loosened, the corpse slid stiffly, headfirst, to the earth. Cotter muttered something. The men, reshifting the body on the primitive stretcher, picked up the corners again. They were far behind the party carrying the wounded man, and the corporal descried them walking in the distance, minute, trivial, under the vaulting canvas of the sky.

The boy doesn't understand, he realized, looking ahead at the confident Sueños. *He doesn't see Crossroads as I do!* McIlhenny smiled mysteriously. *To him, Crossroads is just another drop zone. He's living in a dreamworld.*

The corporal changed his grip on the canopy and, glancing to his left, encountered Cotter's irritated glare. He paid no attention to the ex-sergeant. *Dreamworld,* he thought. *Youth lives in a dreamworld.* Then his face flushed and a tremor passed through him. He remembered the casual interest he had once taken in Spanish and a play (or was it a poem?) that he had read and forgotten. *Por toda la vida es sueño, y los sueños sueños son.*

Corporal McIlhenny stared at the back of the dark boy's head. *For all life is a dream, and the dreams themselves are dreams.* He gazed, as if drugged, and walked mechanically. *Sueños signifies dreams! . . . Is this,* he wondered, *that has been happening to me all a dream?* He saw nothing, stumbling as he walked on the sand. *Oh, vast God . . . make it all a nightmare and have me wake up soon. Yes,* he realized, *it's all a dream. Everything. People dream themselves into existence and then wake up.* And occasionally, he continued, perhaps from boredom, they play tricks on their dreaming selves; they tease themselves with the truth that life is a dream, a dream whose rule is to lie as deliberately and consistently as possible, to believe that life is real.

Corporal McIlhenny stifled an excited laugh. He snorted noiselessly through his nostrils. *How clever.* He smiled. *How clever of me. . . . Private Sueños. The idea! . . . And I thought I had forgotten my Spanish.* A happy surge worked into him. "I'll wake up soon," he thought aloud. "I'll wake up soon. I'm tired of these lies."

Cotter turned to him. "Who's a liar? Don't give me none of your fruity crap."

"I didn't call you a liar!"

"You best not."

Private Sueños glanced over his shoulder, first at McIlhenny, then at Cotter. He smiled conspiratorially, although the corporal was not sure to whom. The boy's dark eyes and twisted mouth put McIlhenny into an agitated state. For some peculiar reason, he wanted to touch the private's shoulder. *He's a good lad,* he thought. *Young . . . believes in dreams.* Then he stared at his dusty, scraped boots. *I'll wake up soon.*

«««««»»»»

In the late afternoon, the 43rd Airborne Division stood in unit formation on the east flank of Crossroads Drop Zone, between the forest and the giant T stretched on the ground. The NCOs and officers were busy determining how many of the men were present or accounted for. By twilight the company roll calls had been checked and the initial suspicions confirmed. Ten men had been killed, and thirty-two had received disabling injuries, ranging from severely sprained ankles and wrists through lacerated thighs and chests to fractured legs, arms, and spines. Those with serious internal injuries were gradually being transferred from the hastily established field hospital on the north side of Crossroads to the well-equipped hospital at Base Headquarters, Eleutheria.

The men had not eaten yet. At five o'clock, the formation

was disbanded and small fires were started on the drop zone. As the wintry darkness descended on Crossroads, platoons of men hurrying with firewood from the forest lighted their bonfires. One by one, just like the stars which glimmered in the sky, the pinpoint flames blossomed in the vast, black silence. When the men had eaten and were leaning back to talk of what had happened, the blaze on the drop-zone surface appeared to be reflected in the constellations of the universe above them.

Following dinner, McIlhenny overheard two sergeants saying that the Division would stay there overnight. General Aarons had been released by the Special Troops. The maneuver scenario had been abandoned until further word. Later, McIlhenny listened to the younger paratroopers talking about the disaster; reliving it in their descriptions; recounting what they did, what they felt; laughing tensely at their own fears. They stated their decisions for wanting to jump again as quickly as possible: they were uncertain of their confidence. They admitted it. They had nothing to hide from other paratroopers, did they? They wanted to jump again tomorrow, because jumping immediately after a disaster was a paratrooper tradition, and a good one, too. Showed they weren't afraid, right?

Corporal McIlhenny was lost in his thoughts. He listened to the young men; he had been here before, here where they were now. He knew all about these things. Youth, eternal youth, always making its decisions. He knew that all decisions but the small ones were out of his hands and that uncertainty was the only sure, stable attitude a reasonable man could have. Corporal McIlhenny could be certain only of the small things: eating, sleeping, being confused, and following orders. He had eaten, his entire life was one confusion after another, the orders were postponed until the following morning, and all that remained for him to do was sleep. He went to his combat pack and unrolled his blanket and waterproof cover.

«««««»»»»

He dreamed of an oily-calm river and himself in a sleek, narrow craft, a felucca or a caïque, with a gorgeous lateen sail, crimson with black dots, like a one-winged monarch butterfly, bending in a mild breeze and stooping sideways, as if trying to touch the tip of its mast, its one wing, with that of its reflection in the still waters. Like a felucca on the

Nile, fluttering toward the source of the river, deep, deep, to regions that no man remembers, to the source, the spring. To the Golden Islands.

Private Sueños was on board with him, and they lay together naked under the sun. The time for their playful wrestling had evidently ceased, for the two embraced passionately; the beautiful lad's cruel, smiling lips retreated from McIlhenny's until Sueños, exhausted from the petulant teasing, rested his dark head against the deck. McIlhenny caressed the firm, tawny body and closed his eyes over a deep, throbbing kiss, moaning deliciously as an unlooked-for breeze cooled his fevered skin. It was a glorious day. . . .

The craft slowly flapped its way to the source, to home, where one day he had fallen asleep and dreamed himself into exile. No more lies. No more loneliness. He was going home. The black dots on the crimson sail were enlarging, filling out. The sail was crimson and black, then black with crimson dots. The timeless sand on both banks was silent, and the lateen sail, now totally black, kissed its watery reflection and fluttered softly, like a butterfly, winging toward the source. . . .

CHAPTER 29

The truck convoy's head lamps pierced the darkness of the pre-dawn night. Twin light shafts fixed the moving road with a corridor of radiance, plunging the highway's shoulders and the nearby forest into deeper black. Vague specks of snow flaked downward from the uppermost curve of the penumbra, disappeared briefly in the brightness of the headlight's glare, then settled softly on the freezing road.

Clarke was suspended midway between slumber and consciousness. Two hours before, he had felt a hurried boot nudge him into wakefulness and had learned that he was to get out of his sleeping bag. *Antiguerrilla attack,* he had thought immediately. *But all the lights are on?* The sergeant had briefed the men: they were due in Eleutheria by dawn. A radio message had just been decoded: "All airborne qualified personnel will report to Base Headquarters, Eleutheria. Signed, General Aarons." That was all the message had said.

Barrett Clarke, although still groggy, had suspected something else. It would be more than curious—it would amount to indefensible stupidity—to devote all the time and energy necessary for the development of a realistic maneuver between two opposing forces if, toward the end of the war play, all the Aggressor guerrillas were driven to the Headquarters of the United States forces for what was merely no more than a military social call. *No . . . there is something more involved,* Clarke had realized. *Something more threatening.*

On an occasional open curve of the highway, he saw the head lamps of the convoy trucks, like luminous jewels of a necklace, and realized that the line of Deuce-and-a-Halves continued for miles. They had started out with five trucks. During his helpless, intermittent naps in the van, he understood, the other partisan units had made contact with the original five Special Troops trucks. They were now trailing them to Eleutheria. The faraway shafts of lights, probing the flatness of the asphalt, shot up occasionally and glared directly ahead, as if it were they that shunned a bump in the road and not the springs of the trucks' chassis.

Clarke covered his face, for his not quite rested eyes were still unaccustomed to the harsh black-and-whiteness that he saw. He sat on the cold, metal floor, flanked by two rows of paratroopers on the benches. His shoulders were pressed by the men on either side, and his knees touched the spine of the soldier in front of him. The truck was filled to capacity. The men were huddled, motionless, in the cold, like wax dummies in a closed museum. Only the inevitable flaring hole of a cigarette punctured the dark. The gray-blue smoke, clouding placidly out of the van's open end, veered and whirled toward the approaching light poles of the follow-truck's head lamps, then gyrated into the night sky.

The daily fulfillment of the scenario's calendar and terrain objectives had been disrupted by the heavy drop-zone winds. General Aarons had been released. *We are driving to Eleutheria!* PFC Clarke, with a rush of comprehension, understood what the dawn would bring: the Special Troops would jump into Crossroads with the Division! With this insight came the realization that every silent, half-asleep paratrooper in the truck with him had known immediately on opening his eyes the reason for being shaken from his slumber. *This must be Aarons' punishment of us. . . .*

Clarke did not want to jump. His brief love of parachuting had perished soon after completing his five novice drops. *Am I afraid?* he wondered, and quickly negated his own accusation. *Not fear,* he allowed. *Not fear . . . concern.* He judged concern a better word, a more precise word than fear, more fair. Concern was merely the intelligent man's hesitation when confronting the unknown.

There was something illogical, moreover, about the command to embark for Eleutheria that offended Clarke. He did not want to participate in a mass jump merely to prove that he was not afraid. Concerned, yes; afraid, no.

And, yet, Clarke was forced to admit that calling for a mass jump immediately after a paratroop disaster was an astute tactic. To a man causally involved. . . . The word interested him: causally! (How curious that he would have thought this word!) To a man involved in the first jump, he continued, the commitment to an Army career of parachuting, and the coexistent fear of it, particularly when time worked it into something more oppressive, might have become greater than some men would be able to live with. An immediate second jump would still any suspicions a man might have about his courage to jump again; it would, at the outset, stifle any potential terror. If only twenty-four hours separated tragedy from a man's feeling that he need not fear it, he would then exonerate himself from his ephemeral encounter with an unmanly fear. It would be a gift to offer a man the opportunity of re-encountering the object of his terror and of exposing its fraudulence in a moment of valor.

Clarke's truck turned into a narrow, declining road. The open end of the van was now cloaked in darkness. Only the bouncing of the follow-truck sent probing shafts of light washing on the macadam of the road perpendicular to the one Clarke was traveling on now. The poles of light hesitated at the turn. The nearer head lamp, a mere splinter, ovaled briefly, then, like an amoeba, fissioned into paired globes. The follow-truck had turned into the narrow road, lighting up the intervening sightlessness, spotlighting into prominence the flat, sandy earth on the shoulders of the highway.

The morale of the units, Clarke supposed, as ironic as it may have appeared, was more important than any momentary discomfort and any transient concern an individual soldier might feel. In fact, the silent paratroopers surrounding him in the dark van were probably looking forward to exhibiting their fearlessness, because they knew this reservoir of unhesitating valor was expected of them by their commanding officers, by the other paratroopers, and especially by themselves.

But for me . . . all this is meaningless, Clarke thought. *Why should I be called to demonstrate my discipline and courage because ten men from another unit were killed on a jump that should have been called off at the last minute? What were the pathfinders doing all that time? Wasn't it obvious that winds were building up on the drop-zone surface? This disaster doesn't challenge me.* Why should he be forced to jump gratuitously, he questioned, when he would not re-encounter the object of his terror, because, in his case, it did not exist?

But there was nothing he could do. He was committed. By volunteering for the paratroops, he had signed away his final right to remain grounded. A year before, he had abdicated his right to the control of his destiny when he took the step forward and raised his hand to the flag on his induction into the Army. *What would have happened if I had refused?* Commitments he had made in good faith (*Marriage, too?* he taunted himself.) had a way of going bad once he accepted them. His whole life appeared to be a series of choices between alternatives for which yes to one would have made him patriotic and brave and good and committed and no to the same would have made him treasonous and cowardly and antisocial and uncommitted.

There was only one comfort left to him now: he did not fear as many things as he thought he would after a lifetime of retreats. He did not fear parachuting—and, more important, he did not fear not parachuting. *There is a point,* he thought, *beyond which I will not be pushed.*

Clarke shut his eyes briefly. The soothing darkness and the relatively good road the truck was traveling on now lulled him. His head lowered slowly until it stopped near his knees; his interlaced fingers, containing his folded legs, relaxed; and he was carried by the rumbling of the tires into another nap: He heard Nikki's laughter and looked up. She gripped him tightly by both wrists and kissed him wetly on the mouth. From outside the house, he heard the chilling scrape of lock chains. Then a steel platform clanged against the back of a truck. "What's that?" Nikki asked. "What would men be doing out on a night like this?" He shrugged his shoulders. "I don't know. Sounds like the garbage truck. I'll see. . . ."

"On your feet!"

The elbow of the man next to him nudged Clarke in the ribs. His eyes opened. The men on the floor were moving about.

"On your feet!"

Clarke lurched up. The rumble of boots on the resounding truck floor was steady. Clarke shuffled toward the open end of the van; when he came to the edge of the truck, he hesitated momentarily, then jumped into the grayness of the dawn. He could not see what was below him, but he landed well, on his toes, and then ran off in the bitter-cold twilight, following the group of men he had been wedged against in the truck.

A dark, triangular shape loomed up in the darkness to his right. It appeared to be a tent. Aside from that and the men getting in formation with him, Clarke could see nothing, even with the light poles of the turning trucks swerving behind him.

"Gentlemen, may I have your attention?"

Clarke recognized the voice of Colonel Simms.

"I doubt if I'm telling you anything new. Many of you have been paratroopers as long as I have—and that's about fifteen years. All of you know what happens when there's an airborne disaster. It is unwritten policy that the unit makes another jump."

Although it was still too dark to see, Clarke raised his hand. He was nervous; his heart pounded rapidly. "Sir . . . !" The colonel ignored the interruption.

A sergeant stalked quickly through the ranks and halted before Clarke. "Was that you?"

"Yes."

"You keep your mouth shut, candy-ass. Soldiers don't interrupt Full Birds." The man paused. "What's your name?"

"PFC Clarke, Sergeant."

"I'll forget about this, Clarke," the NCO said after a moment's pause. "I'd of thought you knew better."

"Now," Colonel Simms continued, "the reason we, of the Special Troops, are jumping into Crossroads with the Division, even though we had nothing to do with the disaster, can be explained. First of all, we're all paratroopers and involved in the same maneuver as the men of the 43rd. Secondly, we witnessed the disaster. We were all there, and, in fact, if it was not for us, there would have been many more casualties and fatalities than there were."

Why, why, why, why? The question churned in Clarke. *Why me? Why must I risk because others failed? Why must I risk my life before I've learned who and what I am?*

"And there's something else you men should know," Simms went on. "Two nights ago a group of Special Troopers dressed as MPs kidnapped General Aarons. The mission was successful. It was a brilliant maneuver, something the Special Troops can justly be proud of, catching, as it were, the entire Division off guard. . . ."

The sentence was stopped there. Clarke expected the colonel to explain himself further, but Simms evidently had abandoned the thought.

"However you consider this command," he continued, "every man here will get his jump in within six hours of daybreak. If everything goes well, we'll have finished the reprise jumps by tonight." He cleared his throat. "Stay at Crossroads and continue Operation Razor Blade where it left off."

Clarke was able to distinguish the colonel's features now; he stood tall and straight, his eyes glancing over the assembled ranks of men.

"The jumps will commence at 0900 hours. Make sure your name, rank, and serial number are on the manifest so you'll be given credit for the jump. Gather at the East Crossroads Assembly Area after your particular drop." Simms stopped and nodded to his right. "Sergeant!"

"Yes, sir!"

From the corner of his eye, Clarke saw Sergeant Damianos walk along the first rank and salute the colonel. When Simms had left, Damianos did an about-face and confronted the formation.

"I'm going to read off the names of the jumpmasters. The men who are called off will report to the tent and draw up their manifests." He consulted his clipboard. "Bernard, Bianchi, Brown, Condom"—Damianos glanced up and smiled—"Constant, myself, Foster, Gilpin, Henry, Jackson, Krapp . . ." He hesitated briefly, then read off the remaining names without a pause. "The above men will report immediately to Captain Trombeaux in the tent. Are there any questions?"

"Sergeant!" Clarke raised his hand and noticed a quick frown on Damianos' face. "Could you clear up something for me?"

Sergeant Damianos stared at him. "Maybe I can," he said slowly.

"Was the command for the 43rd to jump again given before our order to jump with them? I mean"—Clarke suspected he was not being very clear—"was there a time—an hour or two, say—when the men of the 43rd knew they were to jump a second time and no one knew that the Special Troops were to jump with them?"

Damianos was clear and quick. "The 43rd knew it was gonna jump again as soon as the first pair of boots hit the drop-zone sand and the trooper was dragged. I don't know when we got the command to make this jump . . . but I'm pretty sure it was after General Aarons returned to his command tent . . . after . . ." He stopped.

"Sergeant . . ." Clarke knew he was being overinsistent, but his sense of helplessness seemed to be making him desperate.

"You're out of order," the sergeant snapped. "Hold your questions." Damianos squared his shoulders. *"Is everybody gonna jump?"*

"Yes, Sergeant!" The formation shouted.

"Dis-missed!"

Clarke thought of running after Damianos and asking him what happened if a man refused, on principle, to jump, but he realized immediately that his question would be misinterpreted by the sergeant. Damianos would see fear where Clarke would be showing only an internal debate. There was nothing more intimidating, he now understood, than military law, for it required less personal courage to follow an order than it did to refuse to follow it. The mutinous man, in revolting against authority, destroyed the moral power this authority had over him and, thereby, created two enemies for himself: those whose role it was to lead him and those against whom he was to be led. Both enemies would demand his punishment. *I'm in the West. . . . I'm a Westerner,* Clarke realized, *and I have no freedom of choice. . . .*

I'll jump, he thought. *I'll jump . . . and abdicate again. It's nothing new for me.* To refuse the command would be interpreted as cowardice; this had already been determined. *I'm not afraid of jumping.* Yet he taunted himself: *But I'm afraid of not jumping.*

The crowd of paratroopers dispersed toward a large tent, where the coffee urns had been established. Clarke followed them. *What motive do I have for refusing to jump? I'm just irritated that I must pay for being in a unit that inflicted an indignity on a commanding general, that's all.*

He found a clean plastic cup and sipped the strong, vile coffee. *I'm not courageous enough to be called a coward and not care.* He gnawed at himself. *Another abdication.* Clarke stared across the airfield to the mountain ranges in the west. *But there's a point beyond which I won't be pushed.*

The sun, when it rose, provided the day with little warmth. Its slanting, wintry rays lighted the earth with a frosty glare, and the earth reciprocated with silence. It was this quiet which stunned Clarke as he tried to warm himself by double-timing in place. The surrounding forest was completely still, as if no birds existed there, as if they had all migrated from

Eleutheria. Aside from several low-pitched conversations and the rhythmic thud of the parachute harnesses in Deuce-and-a-Halves being readied by the rigging detachment, the area was abysmally silent, with hardly a vagrant breeze rustling the scrub pines nearby. A thin cover of snow, now trampled, lay on the hard-packed earth.

A chill went through Clarke's body. *It'll be freezing in the airplane,* he thought. *Particularly at the open door.*

In the intimate obscurity of twilight, Damianos had felt lulled; when the day grew lighter, however, he saw the sector of Eleutheria for what it was. Thousands of men, dismissed briefly from their unit formations, stood about on the skirts of the airfield or sat on small hills that rose gradually beyond the strips, using the square, bulky combat packs as protection from the frozen earth. The sight displayed the magnitude of the operation. At least five thousand paratroopers, in inadvertent terraces along the slope of the hills—like layers of a contour map—waited for commands to board the Flying Boxcars. *The dawn of an important battle,* he thought. *The second assault on Crossroads.*

Leaving the tent after drawing up their manifests, Sergeants Damianos and Gilpin, the jumpmasters of their aircraft, walked toward the coffee tent.

"You're new in the Troops, ain't you?"

Gilpin looked directly ahead. "Yeah, I transferred from the Division three weeks before Razor Blade." He chuckled. "I wanted to get out of all that chicken-shit before the maneuver."

Damianos smiled at the irony. "Well, you're out of it now, ain't you?"

A major from the 43rd walked past them. The two NCOs saluted.

"They're all kids, you know. There ain't many of the old-time paratroopers left. All teen-agers outa Jump School. And I wanted no more part in that." He reached into his jacket pocket, withdrew his OD woolen glove shells, and put them on. "I had a feeling something like this'd happen. It sounds crazy, but I sorta felt it in my bones."

"Oh, yeah?" Damianos asked with little interest.

"I said to myself, There ain't been a fuck-up for at least three years. We're gonna have ourselves one soon."

"I know what you mean," Damianos allowed. "So you wanted to get out of the Division before it happened?" He did not turn to Gilpin.

"I didn't say *that,*" Gilpin replied quickly. "Look, Sarge, I didn't say *that!*" They bent slightly to enter the darkened tent. "I'll get the cups," Gilpin said.

"OK." Sergeant Damianos stamped his boots on the hard-packed floor of the tent and, one at a time, wiped the rounded toes on his calf at the back of his trousers. *Candy-ass,* he thought.

Gilpin returned. "No sugar left."

"Don't sweat the sugar," Damianos said. "No sweat whatsoever." As he blew on the coffee, he saw a figure to his right move toward the tent flap. It was Clarke. "Hey, Private," he snapped. Clarke turned to him. Damianos nodded his head, motioning him over.

"What's this manure about wanting explanations?"

"Well, Sergeant—"

"You're a paratrooper now," Damianos cut in. "You're wearing the green beret. Jacks told me all about you. All about how you were beginning to shape up . . ."

He was interrupted by Gilpin. "You mean Duane Jacks? From the Division?"

Damianos paused briefly, without turning to Gilpin or responding to his question. Then he continued. "I'm your jumpmaster today, and I don't like to answer questions. So don't ask me any."

Clarke was motionless. Damianos noticed this, observing the color rise to the PFC's face. "You'll know as much about the jump as I will when we're on the plane," he continued, "so don't crowd me." Clarke was about to say something, and Damianos, not wanting to push the man too far, softened the tone of his remarks. "You embarrassed me in front of the colonel this morning. No sergeant likes that. It's a good thing it happened to me, 'cause I know you're no wise guy. If it happened to an NCO who was really chicken-shit, he'd of written your tail up."

The change in the sergeant's attitude was evidently felt by Clarke, who relaxed slightly. "I know, Sergeant, but I got a little irritated at being forced to pay because of someone's brainchild mission."

"Shut up!" Damianos snapped. "Where do you think you are—in some bar in Von Steuben? You're in a tent at Eleutheria. There might be officers around with you shooting your mouth off!" He stopped immediately, recalling the fact that he owned a tavern. "You got a lot to learn about the Army."

"I'm not interested in learning." Clarke's voice was restrained.

"Well, Clarke . . ." Damianos managed to grin so that his smile became an almost aggressive act. "You're gonna learn, interest or no interest. I suggest you straighten up." He spoke as if Sergeant Gilpin was not a third man in the group. "These days are gonna be rough for all of us, and some sergeants and officers don't take a PFC's opinions lightly. They *think* about 'em, especially in maneuvers and in wartime. They consider them carefully. You don't wanna go to the stockade for the duration of the Cold War, do you?"

"No."

"Fine. . . . Another thing." Damianos sipped his coffee, then wiped his lips with the cuff of a sleeve. "This is your cherry jump, ain't it?"

"No. I've already had five novice jumps."

Sergeant Gilpin chuckled. Damianos did not turn to him but frowned slightly. "A cherry jump," he explained, "is the first unit jump a trooper makes after graduating Airborne School. It's one of the toughest. In school you're prepared for parachuting, but when you get out, you don't have the pattern right yet. You're back in life as you knew it as a straightleg. Then you find out you gotta make a jump. And the guys around you are old-timers at it. They're making jokes and you're thinking you're about to get your legs busted or die on the DZ." Damianos squared his shoulders and blew on his coffee. *Disgraceful,* he thought, *how I'm showing concern for this candy-ass.* PFC Clarke looked at him carefully. "So I got you down as first on the stick," Damianos continued. "You'll be at the door when the green light flashes. It's better that way."

"I'll jump anyhow," Clarke said, "but thank you. It's very fairminded."

"No fair or unfair about it. I'm the jumpmaster." He glanced at his wristwatch. "Time to be getting back to formation."

Clarke backed up. "I'll see you back there, Sergeant."

Damianos nodded. *Peculiar guy,* he thought. *Don't look frightened . . . and probably ain't. Just an old latrine lawyer.* Damianos recalled what Jacks had told him about Clarke and wondered if his friend was correct about the PFC's not having the usual fears about jumping. If Clarke's fears were conventional, he would cover them up in the same way the others did—in bravado.

Whenever an act or mood caused the sergeant to wonder

about a man, it was automatically underlined in his mind. Particularly before a mass jump, any strangeness in a paratrooper's behavior or speech became an important factor to Damianos. He was going to keep an eye on Clarke. *Something curious there . . .*

By placing the PFC first on the stick, Damianos had given himself, as jumpmaster, a feeling of control over any possible weak link. Being first at the door tricks a man into thinking he has prepared himself for the jump, that he is his own master, making his decision to leap, struggling with his own fears until, when the green light flashes and those fears are under control, he parachutes of his own accord. In reality, however, all the paratroopers behind the first man are eager to complete their jump, and these troopers, when the light is flashed, begin to push. The man at the open door has one second's grace to leap from the aircraft of his own free will. Otherwise, he is pushed by the second man and the jumpmaster. After one second, the freedom of choice is quickly revealed to be only the freedom to say yes willingly.

Damianos pursued his thoughts: And each man in the stick thinks he initiates the pushing, but he, too, is wrong. Being pushed from behind, a paratrooper immediately assumes that the line has slowed down somewhere, and, in order to maintain the one-second intervals, he pushes the man ahead of him. This continues until the trooper reaches the open door, where the jumpmaster maintains the proper spacing between men. *But who starts the sequence?* Damianos removed the clipboard from under his arm. *The last man. . . .* The creature of the system. *The pusher.*

"You know"—Sergeant Gilpin broke into Damianos' thought—"the newspapers have been giving the maneuver a big play." He appeared to wait for a response. There was none. "There's been a helluva lot of reporters right here in Eleutheria writing articles about Operation Razor Blade."

"Oh, yeah?"

"Yeah. You know what they call us?"

"Who?"

"Us! The paratroopers."

"No, what?"

"The newspapers call us the American Freedom Fighters."

"That's nice," Damianos said. He thought, *There is no freedom for man,* but quickly crushed his desire to speak aloud. Gilpin would not understand.

As Damianos and Gilpin walked back to the Special Troops' area, weaving between paratroopers seated on their packs and walking around stalled trucks loaded with parachute harnesses, they glanced to their left, toward Eleutheria airfield, whenever a silvery C-119 loaded with soldiers roared to its takeoff. One Boxcar after another sprinted to the center of the strip and assumed flight.

Damianos thought someone was calling his name. "Yes, sir?" he shouted. A captain was approaching the two NCOs, talking rapidly, heedless than an airplane's takeoff drowned out his voice. Damianos raised his hand and walked to meet him. "Yes, sir?"

"There's a possibility of putting an extra Boxcar on the second flight. Your men are to prepare themselves for moving to the marshaling area."

"Fine, sir." Damianos threw him a salute. "Let's go, Sergeant," he said without turning to Gilpin. "We gotta hustle. I'd like to get my jumping in early." The two NCOs hurried to the Special Troops' section.

"OK, men." Damianos assumed that all the paratroopers had read the bulletin on the board near the tent and knew on whose manifest they were listed. "All those who are to jump on the Sergeants Damianos and Gilpin aircraft . . . *on your feet!* We got a chance to get on the second flight in about an hour."

Most of the paratroopers approved of their good fortune. They ran into formation, performed a left face, and marched toward the marshaling area. Eleutheria was now as silent as it had been at dawn; the Flying Boxcars had completed their takeoffs, their cruising about in the sky waiting to assume a V formation, and had streaked, like migrating birds, to the west and Crossroads. Only the thud of harnesses being readied on the truck's metal floors and the *hup, two, three, four* of Damianos' count broke the quiet.

The flights were organized efficiently. Deuce-and-a-Halves, in a giant semicircle near the field, loaded with main and reserve chutes, were waiting for the planeloads of troopers to arrive and take their harnesses. Damianos, walking through the standing ranks of men, checked off the names of those present on the manifest with a chewed pencil stub. He glanced at the red wind banner to see it hanging limp against the mast. *No sweat on the wind,* he thought; *less than five knots.* But they were to jump at capacity—forty-two soldiers per Boxcar. *No sweat . . . just so nothing else happens.*

Damianos' main concern was whether the Boxcars would be able to take the strain of almost continual use. The average peacetime flight tempo of the Military Air Transport

Service was about five flight hours daily per craft. With maneuvers as large as Razor Blade, this tempo was increased to nine and ten flight hours a day. The maintenance men and ground crews were required to work twelve hours a day, seven days a week. Any weak points in an aircraft's construction, any points of stress that went unchallenged in periods of ease, could snap when unrelieved pressure was applied to them. This was, after all, the purpose of maneuvers: to determine the weak points in strategy or tactics, to expose any existing lack of training, to test the men's discipline, and to exhibit any structural defects in equipment which might prove disastrous in actual war.

Damianos paused before Clarke and looked at him sternly. After glancing at the PFC's name tape, then at his clipboard, he attached an E after the K in the name and moved on. *Each door would drop twenty-one parachutists.* He continued his thoughts. *Easy drop . . . no wind . . . plenty of time.* An aircraft traveling 120 miles per hour would cover Crossroads from north to south in two minutes—120 seconds. Taking into consideration the approach to the crossbar of the T and the slight wind velocity, the twenty-one men at each door, requiring only one second per man to exit, would empty the fuselage in much less than a minute. *A no-sweat operation.*

He double-checked himself, folding over a page of the manifest sheet. *Forty-two paratroopers per aircraft . . . times . . . . thirty-three Boxcars in eleven V's of three . . . equals 1,386 paratroopers per convoy of V's in trail formation. All dropping in the air above the DZ within two minutes.*

"*At* ease!" Damianos shouted. He briefed them concerning the information he and Gilpin had received in the tent, repeating Colonel Simms' order that they assemble on the East Crossroads DZ point. Then, commanding them to a right face, he directed the planeload to a pair of Deuce-and-a-Halves, where the harnesses were waiting for them. Gilpin went to the truck full of reserve chutes, and Damianos, the clipboard in his large hand, checked off those who had taken main harnesses. Returning to their particular marshaling area, Damianos and Gilpin retired, permitting the men to strap themselves into their equipment.

The two jumpmasters did not wear Army parachute harnesses; they were to be given Air Force hand-operated chutes on entering the Boxcar. They had, consequently, to concern themselves only with seeing that the planeload of men for whom they were responsible was correctly harnessed.

Without Damianos noticing it—so preoccupied was he with inspecting his ranks—the roar of returning Boxcars had begun again and had sustained itself for a quarter of an hour. When he stood before Clarke, Damianos inspected the PFC's harness thoroughly, speaking to him briefly above the engines' noise, as was his manner, more in the interest of learning how the soldier was taking the tension of waiting than in the desire to exchange incidental information. Clarke's answers were short, revealing little more than his preference to be left alone. Damianos was displeased to find Clarke's harness perfectly comfortable for him and, being left with nothing else to do, gave the straps around his groin a hard, gratuitous tug.

A C-119 taxied to a stop fifty yards away from Damianos; responding to his command, the planeload of troopers walked stiffly toward the twin-boomed aircraft. Corporal Whittaker, Damianos' pusher, disassociated himself from the line and went to the rear. A metal ladder, organic to the Boxcar, was lowered by an Air Force crewman from the craft's metal door, whose threshold stood about five feet from the ground surface, and Clarke, the first man, lumbered up the steel rungs into the fuselage. The others followed. They sat in bucket seats according to their stick orders, strapped on their safety belts, and waited while the pilot revved the engines.

Damianos and Gilpin got into their Air Force chutes, checked with the pilot for any last-minute instructions—there were no extra Boxcars on the flight—left the pilot's compartment, and advanced toward the C-119's tail, briefly inspecting each man's belt on their respective sides of the aircraft. Damianos strapped himself into his seat, glanced at the somber faces of his men within the shadowed interior, and felt the airplane move forward.

The C-119's titanic resources were still chained, still unextended, but the tremendous shaking had lessened. Then, its engines' energies channeled, the Boxcar picked up speed, sprinted down the airstrip, bobbed into the air momentarily with every indication that it would touch earth again . . . but did not drop . . . stayed up an inch, two inches, four inches, then pulled up powerfully, airborne now, within seconds surpassing the treetops, then debasing them even more, higher and higher, until, at 1,200 feet, it met two other Boxcars and merged into its triangular destiny, an arrowhead among arrowheads.

Damianos undid his safety belt and stood up, feeling below him the quivering metal floor. He went to the screaming door; his two powerful hands gripping the steel jambs, he looked out to the green of the pines framed by the white of the snow and saw his Boxcar's sibling craft, directly across from the open door. Ahead of him, viewed through the swirling, circular propeller haze, the V in trail formation flew as on an invisible platform.

His heart pounded with pride and regret—pride that he belonged to something as vast and as epic as this and regret that the vision he now witnessed would last no more than thirty minutes. A transient glory, this vast carpet of steel a thousand feet above the earth. The V in trail, eleven interlocked arrowheads, laid tip to end, end to tip, in one straight line, flew from Eleutheria to Crossroads, sprung from the bowstring of necessity.

McIlhenny shivered in the cold fuselage. Outside, through the dusty window at his right shoulder, the picture-postcard world glistened whitely in the morning sun's glare. *Sleigh bells ring . . .* He groped through his memory, the present's refuge in the refuse of the past—*are ya list'nin'*—for an idea or a recollection to give him the courage he was sure he had lost. *In the lane . . . snow is glist'nin' . . .* Self-consciously, he studied the faces of those across from him, hoping to discover in them the turmoils and doubts which churned within him. *A beautiful sight. . . . We're happy tonight . . .*

He sat between Sueños, at his right, and Cotter, the pusher, at his left. McIlhenny felt embarrassed that Private Cotter had been selected as pusher while he, a corporal, had been placed beside the ex-sergeant. *They know,* he realized. *They know all about me. They suspect my fears. They think they can see them in my face.* As if his face could tell them anything, he proceeded; as if a man's face had anything to do with his self; as if a human being's features had anything to do with his spirit; as if accidents could betray the secrets of the essence. But in a world of externals, McIlhenny supposed, the externals were crowned as rulers by default. In a world of dreams, the greatest dreamers assumed the royal purple.

Before and behind his aircraft, McIlhenny knew, the entire V in trail formation roared toward the mountain ranges. But that was unimportant; he was cold. The penetration at that altitude had grown progressively more intense. His Boxcar, one of the first aloft, had idled in the air some time before the V's in trail had formed; the chill had seeped into his bones, imprisoned as he was in his bucket seat. He went through stages, believing first that it was the open door that was responsible for his discomfort, permitting as it did the wind to whip through the fuselage. Later, he recalled that the doors had probably not been closed for days. *But what does this have to do with it? The temperature must be fifteen degrees above zero. It will be cold no matter where I go.* Even with the doors shut tight, therefore, he realized, the temperature would be below freezing. *There's nothing to do, then,* he thought; *nothing . . . just wait.* He began looking forward to leaping out of the Flying Boxcar into the much colder air of the sky, as if it would be an alleviation of his suffering. *Curious world . . . that there don't seem to be solutions . . . only change. . . .*

And to think that all his life, as recently as a few months ago, he desired to know his destiny. *Folly,* he understood; *it's all folly. That dream . . . that dream . . .* McIlhenny shuddered. *With my arms around him. This, too?* He shut his eyes. *This, too, is me? Shameless . . . shameless . . . the depths in him man hides!*

The Flying Boxcar staggered, bucked, then quickly plunged into calm air again. Corporal McIlhenny turned to look out of the dirty window. The bony, snow-covered ridge of mountains, surmounted now, drifted back toward the aircraft's double tails. The C-119, although maintaining the same altitude, seemed to be climbing now that the mountains sloped toward the flatland. Coniferous trees spiked through the thin snow cover, and McIlhenny knew that, beyond this brief, forested tract, lay—in certain, silent waiting—the bloody arena that was Crossroads.

Why didn't I die, he wondered, *before I knew what and who I was? Why was it my destiny to learn the truth about myself?* He could think this now, for he intuited that more was waiting to be uncovered. *I want to wake up . . . from my dreams. . . . I don't want to dream more dreams. . . .*

"Stand up!"

He heard the jumpmaster bellow in the darkened cavern and moved forward, only to be met by the restraint of his safety belt. His gloved hands, stiff from the cold, groped for the lock. The other soldiers were up; the command *"Get ready!"* had been given earlier, and he, lost in his thoughts, had not heard it.

"Hook up!"

"Back here!" Private Cotter waved to the jumpmaster. "Back here!"

Sergeant Jacks blasted his way through the standing paratroops and stood, his face screwed up with anger, above the trapped corporal. "Sit still, goddamn you!"

McIlhenny leaned back helplessly, watching the NCO undo his safety belt; he was hauled to his feet, and his line was hooked to the static wire. The sergeant rushed back to the open door.

"Check static lines!" The almost priestly intonation was answered by a metallic clatter.

"Check equipment!" McIlhenny went through the pretense of inspecting his harness, his straps, the reserve chute, the small knife in his left boot, which he knew existed no longer. *Not being saved,* he admitted, *might save me yet.* He plucked half-heartedly at his airborne chin strap.

"Count down for equipment check!"

He heard the shout from Cotter, felt the slap on his buttocks, and yelled his own number, following it with the necessary "OK." He patted Sueños on the hams. *Shameless,* he thought, for he realized that he had held his palm too long against the boy's body. *When will it end . . . this hateful knowledge of myself?*

Suddenly, everyone began milling and shouting. *Someone at the door doesn't want to jump,* McIlhenny reasoned. Cotter's shoulder rammed against his back, shoving him forward with a lurch. The noise in the fuselage was deafening. Men were screaming and pushing each other. Sueños, his elbows working frantically, waded through the stick. McIlhenny watched, in a dream, as Cotter charged past him and dragged Private Sueños back into the stick order.

Then the corporal understood. His knees wobbled. He no longer felt the cold boring into him, no longer viewed the world about him as a dreamer's lie. "The aircraft must not be my coffin," he muttered. *No, no, no, no, no. . . . THE LONG BELL THE LONG BELL mustgetout mustgetout EMERGENCY EMERGENCY THE LONG BELL EMERGENCY mustgetout mustgetout!* His hands trembled. *Something went wrong. Oh, God, something went wrong!*

The aircraft bucked and shuddered. The paratroopers still left inside were thrown against the fuselage walls.

Brokenpiston? flashed through his mind. *Mustgetout intothesky intothesky mustmust. Brokenconnectingrod? ESCAPE mustget ESCAPE! Pushpushpush. . . .*

There was chaos in the aircraft; the paratroopers, no longer in line, shoved their way toward the open door, leaping with no regard to spacing. The metal floor of the Boxcar shivered. *This must not be my coffin!* He fell to his knees at the door. *My name is Kinnard McIlhenny. . . . My name is . . .* In his exhaustion and terror, his body had lost all coordination. The *gong* of his helmet's impact against the steel jamb sounded through his head. Cotter leaped over him into the sky. McIlhenny's hands slammed painfully on the floor and were stepped on by the jumpmaster. The two wrestled at the opening. Then, simultaneously, he felt the frigid welcome of the prop blast and the square of Sergeant Jacks' boot on his hams. He was free from death. Battered by the swirling air, his parachute still on his back, unopened, McIlhenny dropped from the parent craft. His beating heart betrayed another truth: *Afraid to die . . . afraid to die . . . both love . . . and hate . . . my dreams . . .*

His canopy became a frightful streamer. He was hurled toward the earth, each second gaining speed, each second closer to the morning of awakening. *Afraid to die . . .* He sobbed and, with bruised, stepped-on fingers, pulled his rip cord. The T-7 pilot chute sprang out, dragging with itself the canopy of his reserve; the parabola filled with air and bounced him violently against his harness straps. He drifted placidly, now saved from death, toward the drop zone.

With the woolen OG shirt between his long underwear and fatigue and field jackets, the bearlike Sergeant Damianos appeared even more formidable. Unhurried and deliberate, he seemed unaffected by the frigid, swirling wind. He stared at Clarke briefly. *A little tense, that's all,* he thought. *What the hell. . . . It's his cherry jump.* But there was something about Clarke that puzzled the sergeant. There seemed to be a lack of certainty in the young man. Perhaps this uncertainty existed in the sergeant's own ideas about Clarke. In a vague, confused manner, Damianos had intuited that the problem lay in the man's attitude toward jumping. To leap from a flying airplane was not the challenge for him that it was for the other paratroopers. The challenge Clarke accepted, the risk he took, was somewhere else, and the fact that Damianos could only grope and stumble about for a solution irritated him.

The light directly above the sergeant's left shoulder had been red for several minutes. *Must be close to Crossroads by now,* he estimated. *Better take a look.*

Damianos grasped the steel doors with heavy hands and leaned out. The view of the forest, which stretched from horizon to horizon, terminated at the giant silvery wing of the C-119. Beyond it lay Crossroads Drop Zone. The whipping of the prop blast, drawing his skin to the left side of his face, had become unbearable. He pulled himself back into the fuselage. He glanced at Clarke for a moment, then permitted his eyes to stray down the waiting stick of paratroopers. *"Stand in the door!"* he intoned.

Clarke, clutching his static line, stamped his boots in the paratrooper's dance to the open, screaming door.

Damianos watched carefully as Clarke swerved and confronted the earth below, the sky above, and the mountainous horizon that fused the two. *His form is pretty good,* Damianos admitted. The man's gloved hands grasped the frozen steel jambs, and his legs were bent slightly at the knees for the leap into the sky. The toe of his right boot extended over the bucking metal floor, poised midway between the sky and threshold.

The jumpmaster of Damianos' sibling craft leaned out of his door to determine the distance from the T's crossbar. At the lateral distance that separated the two base points of the V, the man looked minute but proportional; Damianos knew that to his opposite number he appeared as small.

But men were only specks of matter. Only a minor distance was enough to remind Damianos of this axiom. And all of these specks—mere men—were readied to burst upon Crossroads with only one intent: to make contact with and destroy the enemy. Which was themselves . . . their fear of death . . . their dread of fear . . . their helplessness in destiny's flow.

Clarke stirred at the door, obviously feeling intimidated by the nearness of the jumpmaster and the second man on the stick. *Probably making his decision to jump right now.* Damianos chuckled silently. *I'll give him a second to make up his mind,* he thought. *Then he'll get my boot.* The PFC's face was tense. *He'd like to be home right now, in the saddle, probably.* Damianos' face felt raw from the prop blast. *Nikki . . . that's her name.* He drew his woolen gloves across his lips. *Colder than hell,* he thought. *Dry, too.* The day was sparkling outside. *Be a hard impact.* He wondered: *Tell him to watch his landing?* Then his jaw muscle twitched. *Screw him. Told him enough already. Can't befriend candy-asses.*

The jumpmaster of the plane across from Damianos ducked into the door quickly. Paratroopers seemed to be milling around. He squinted to see what was happening. *Something funny going on there.* Then he gasped. *Who's off? Who's off? Us? . . . Them?* The plane across from his was getting farther away, but Damianos could not determine which craft, his own or the sibling, was going off course.

The green light flashed as the fluorescent panels of the T slowly drifted under his booted feet. Damianos leaped across the door and grasped, with powerful hands, the jamb nearer Clarke. The PFC was struggling, trying to jump. *Can't let him go yet. Gotta find out what happened!* The entire line was shoving now, like frightened cattle, pushing toward the open door. Damianos looked at the sibling craft. *It's them! They're off!* He pushed the line, almost toppling out of the door; pushed Clarke back into the craft with his shoulder; then returned to his own side of the door.

Clarke leaped into the sky and the stick followed him. Corporal Whittaker hesitated at the door, and Damianos booted him out, realizing immediately that the pusher merely wanted to ask him what had happened. He smiled, then squinted at the faraway plane, its silveriness outlined against the mountain's dark bulk. *Jesus, what's gonna happen now?*

Gilpin walked up and stood next to him. Damianos pointed to the trail of canopies, like a wild animal's spoor, that tracked the Boxcar as it flew into the mountain's side.

One thousand. Clarke leaped into the sky, his legs taut, his hands hugging the reserve. *Two thousand.* The prop blast turned him to his side. *Three thousand.* Things were happening above and behind him; cord was stretching and pulling, remaining where he had been, grasping the air he had passed. *Four thousand.* His canopy blossomed. He looked: a fine opening. He glanced around the drop zone. The T was to his right. He decided not to guide himself to it, for the sky seemed to be less crowded where he was.

What happened up there? In the plane? The incident was confusing. *He went for me! That man must hate me . . . for something.* Clarke fell toward the waiting earth. *What's he trying to do? Make me out to be a coward? He's crazy! Thought I was frightened. Thought I jumped because I had to.* Clarke was glad he had fought with Damianos at the door. *I showed him that I jumped because I wanted to, not because he told me I must.*

The mountain-bounded immensity of Crossroads cupped below, and, landing on its surface, blobs of green-brown canopies flattened themselves on the thin coat of snow. Tiny figures ran about. In the depths of the arena that was Crossroads, backdropped by the mountain shields, he viewed the paratroopers falling. *It was my choice. . . . I chose to jump. He tried to stop me.*

There was still time before the drop zone's impact. *Strange* . . . He sighted a silvery Boxcar flying directly to a darkness in a mountain, followed by a trail of canopies. The aircraft was dangerously near the treetops. *My perspective is wrong,* he realized. *Why would a plane be diving into a mountain?*

He followed its career. First to his sight, then to his comprehension—the unexpected inevitability occurred. A pillared flame flung itself from the shadowed mountainside and tongued into the sky. Oh . . . no, he beseeched. Oh . . . no . . . again . . . ? *Again . . . ?*

The flame leaped mutely in the mountain's bosom. Then came the explosion. Damianos' plane was flying over the wreck slowly. He stared down at the burning, crackling pines. *This is it,* he thought. *We're in the box.* A smile, appreciative yet bitter, curled on his lips. *And Aarons is in it with us. There's no way out now. . . .* He snorted. It was too good. Too fitting. *We fell for the bait, and the mousetrap closed.*

The C-119 turned gradually and made another pass over the wreckage, flying slowly above the circle of fire. Damianos followed Gilpin's pointing finger. Two hundred feet below, in a small clearing surrounded by burning trees, Damianos saw an antlered buck, stretched out. Dead. A great metal fragment was embedded in its flank.

CHAPTER 30

Sunday followed the second disaster. Sergeant Damianos, lying in his bag under the trees, stared at the dark sky intently for a half hour.

After convincing himself to get up, he began a search for firewood. The 7-shaped flashlight, lost in his large hand, probed the forest's turf for kindling. It was obvious to him that there would be none, for 13,000 men had bivouacked in the Crossroads area for days. The sergeant decided to steal some of the wood the other teams had stored near their sacks as they slept.

Damianos had a fire going within a few moments and succeeded in warming a helmetful of water. He washed his face and, with a shaving brush, swirled lather over the beard stubble. Since his old razor blade was dull, he returned to the rucksack, found the dispenser, and slid a fresh one out, aware of the fact that a new razor blade always cuts into the skin. A mingling of pampered luxury, daily boredom, and pain: shaving was only a minor vexing action rooted in one's manhood. But today Damianos considered it highly important; today the act of shaving assumed the dignity of the essential.

Beginning at the hairline, he pulled the razor down along his jawbone, barely missing the softness of his ear. A mirror, if he had one, would have proved useless, for the world was still dark. But he had shaved thousands of times before; he knew what his face looked like: it was an ancestral face.

The razor tore authoritatively at the Damianos-bristles, as if, having shaved the sergeant hundreds of times, it knew as much about the face as there was to know. In the darkness, the fingers traced the bones; touched the hollows, the cleft; felt the nose, the lips; guided the razor here; raised it there; and cleared the face of the cover behind which it tries to mask itself.

Death, if death came for Damianos today, must find him clean-shaven—must find him with a face free of disguises, of ambiguities, of camouflage. After all, that was what razor blades were for: to bare the faces that men carried with them, on which were to be found the daily tended features which otherwise would have been ignored—the features whose blood ties, whose meaning, men fought against, but whose truth it became vital for men to accept. A man's name and a man's face *were* important, and even if, throughout his life, a man rejected them, changed them, manipulated them, now, at the moment when death approached, he was forced, for truth's sake, to bare what he was to the world. *My name is Cosmas Damianos,* he thought, *and my face is a Damianos face. I am only what I was meant to be.*

He rinsed off the lather and spilled the dirty water under a pine tree. Combing his hair quickly, he felt, with the tips of his fingers, the small bald spot at his crown: a Damianos bald spot. *There is no freedom.* He smiled bitterly. *We even grow old in the same way.*

When he had finished his morning's preparations, he sat cross-legged on his bag and lighted the day's first cigarette. The bonfire's embers still glowed, and he could barely see the tobacco smoke ascending into the quiet sky. Off to the east, the sun had still not shaken itself free of the earth's great bulk.

His poor mother had tried to teach him Greek, forcing him to learn from the simple, coverless books the complexities of his ancestral language. But he did not learn the grammar: he learned only the hopelessness, only the enslavement of man to forces he does not comprehend. This was the reason man became the measure of all things: each man could find comfort in the amount of truth he could bear. And, since man was the measure, too little was measured. *If only I could grapple with God,* he thought, beyond horror now, beyond restraint, beyond the point of measuring his ideas. *If we could only wrestle . . . like athletes . . . with olive oil on our bodies . . . I would give Him what He deserves. I'd make Him suffer, too.*

But He was too wily, Damianos knew. He confused men. The sergeant was bewildered. *Is God Man's enemy . . . or is man's enemy moira—his fate, himself?*

Damianos heard an electronic *pop* and then the scratching noises of a cracked record. The system of loudspeakers that had been established throughout Crossroads responded with the wayward, indefinite notes of a bugle calling the men to the beginning of a new day.

"OK, you guys: on your feet!" Damianos bellowed. "Rise and shine, now!" He snorted at the irony, the brief good nature that had overcome him, that had almost changed his mood. "Rise and shine, boys," he muttered to himself. "Get set to meet the Black Cavalier; get set to meet Father Death."

The paratroopers scurried out of their sacks. Damianos stretched, leaped to his feet, and squatted a few times, ridding himself of the stiffness that had come over his crossed legs. The sky was grayish.

One hour after the wavering bugle notes had called them into the day, the men had accomplished most of their busywork. The police call, an almost touching reminder of garrison life, had been completed; the men had eaten; and now the thousands of paratroopers sat around on their packs, near their unit groupings, watching the day grow lighter, seeing the horizon stretch out to its limits of clarity, waiting for the orders to make their slow, painful way, link by link, down the chain of command.

Evidently the commands had arrived, for Damianos was told to give the men calisthenics. *No jump today?* he wondered. Then Sergeant Damianos smiled. It was curious how generals, whose only reason for existence was to give orders, invariably deliberated when they became aware of the risks lurking behind the performance of their commands. Human lives, the axiom stated, are important—especially American lives. As if, this very hour, thousands of women from coast to coast were not giving birth. The image of Sophie carrying his child intruded into his thoughts, but he erased it quickly.

The only command Aarons and maneuver directors could possibly give was the command that they will be forced to give, the inexorable order. (Could an honest logician betray a valid major and minor premise with a fraudulent conclusion?) Men could only explain events—not change them. The paratroopers would jump a third time. That much was certain—was, in fact, almost history. And if a disaster occurred on the third jump, they would jump a fourth, a fifth, a sixth time. (Unless, of course, the paratroopers would admit to cowardice; unless, of course, Aarons would be intimidated by that meaningless, unmilitary word: fate.) Aarons would delay, certainly, but the sequence had begun. The irony was too good to fight, and so Damianos smiled, delaying for a moment his approach to the Special Troopers who awaited his speech.

"Seems like certain people ain't too sure what we should be doing today," Damianos began. To his surprise, his statement received a laugh. The men were evidently in a good mood. "Those of us who been in the Army since Christ was a corporal know what we're gonna be doing tomorrow. Or, at least, what we *should* be doing tomorrow." A few paratroopers, NCOs in their thirties and forties, leaned over, spat between their boots reflectively, and glanced at Damianos with amused grins. "Well," he continued, "I been given a very interesting project today." He heard a few moans and raised his hand abruptly, as if to silence the men. "It's no detail . . . so don't sweat it."

The sergeant threw back his shoulders and smiled. "I been told to give you apes calisthenics." Grinning, he waited until the group stopped laughing. "That's right. I guess they figure we're getting soft and wanna make he-men out of us. Today is workout day, so this is what I propose: we're gonna do our daily dozen first. A couple of the jockstraps are gonna lead us, and one of them is gonna call out the numbers. Then we'll form up and go on a jog around Crossroads."

A great deal of noise broke out in the rear of the group. Damianos' voice became stern. "Everyone is going on this jog. If any candy-ass has to drop out, he will drop out when we get beyond the first turn of the DZ. That's two miles from here. Those who have nothing better to do this Sunday, namely me, will continue the jog. *I'd appreciate it if I have some company on the return trip.*" He paused for a moment. "We'll be back in plenty of time for the religious services. Those of you who feel you need a little bit of religion will get yours when we return." Stepping back a pace, Damianos realized that his last sentence might be misinterpreted. He scanned the group. *Screw it,* he thought. "I'll lead the run, and we'll probably need about four sergeants to keep everyone in step." His jaw moved as the tip of his tongue probed at some food matter caught between his teeth. "OK . . . let's form up. I want two jocks to volunteer for the PT."

To the exercise leader's command, Damianos performed his squat jumps, his push-ups, and his abdominal exercises, carefully conserving his strength for the long jog he was to lead. The physical training lasted for twenty minutes, and when the twelfth and final exercise had been completed, Damianos gave the men a five-minute break and went off a few paces, alone, to have a quiet smoke. He squatted—his toes the only contacts with the earth—and rested his upper body's weight on his forearms, braced against his hard, wide thighs.

The sergeant frowned. Trouble was coming. Clarke, occasionally glancing at the sergeant to make sure he was still alone and in the same place, worked his way through the paratroopers who had grouped themselves in the PT area.

"Hello, Sergeant." Clarke squatted beside Damianos.

"What can I do for you, Clarke?" The sergeant's tone was flat.

"I just wanted to ask you how long this was going to keep up."

Damianos was happy to have found a weak point in Clarke's statement. He pretended ignorance. "How long is *what* gonna keep up?"

"This stupidity of jumping into the same place just to prove a point." Clarke shifted his position, evidently finding it difficult to maintain his equilibrium. Possibly his legs were tightening up, also. Damianos fought a pleased smile. Clarke continued. "You're only the fourth person so far this morning to say that we'll probably be ordered to jump again because of yesterday's crash."

"I didn't say *probably,* Clarke." Damianos was beginning to feel the tension and pain in his legs, but he deliberately remained motionless. *Can't have Clarke think my legs are tightening,* he thought, realizing immediately how irrationally he was behaving. "I guess jumping tomorrow is the surest thing you and me will ever know."

"Why? What's General Aarons trying to prove? Who's he trying to intimidate?"

What's he mean—intimidate? Damianos wondered.

Clarke stood up briefly and stretched his legs. Damianos did not shift his position, did not even glance up at Clarke. The sergeant looked straight ahead at the drop zone and thought: *You wanna talk to me, candy-ass? Then get down here where I am!*

"He ain't trying to prove anything." Damianos spoke when Clarke returned to the hunkering position. "He's got nothing to prove. Sure . . . there are a lot of teen-agers in the Division . . . but just 'cause they weren't in the war don't mean they're any less tough than guys in their thirties. Mature men, that is. All Aarons wants to do is get his maneuver over with. You realize, of course"—Damianos lowered his voice, wondering immediately why he had done this, yet not wanting to speak louder again, since it would appear that his voice was wavering—"you realize that this maneuver would of been over by now if these disasters didn't start happening. He's minding his own business . . . then everything happens. Winds start blowing and a plane crashes. What else can he do?"

He stared at the PFC. "Clarke . . . do you know what kind of a guy Aarons is?" The PFC shook his head. "Aarons is a man who likes to do first things first. He ain't trying to prove nothing. All he wants to do is get this maneuver over with. And these accidents won't let him. He's not gonna ignore the fact that something has been happening on both mass jumps on Crossroads, and he ain't the man to back down from a challenge." Damianos noticed Clarke's surprised expression. *Did I have to say challenge?* he wondered. "That's right! Challenge." Since the word had come to him as it had, he decided to use it as an offensive tool. "Don't you look at these reprise jumps as challenges to your pride, your manhood?"

"It never occurred to me, Sergeant. Challenge! You talk as if there's some great force looking down and forcing you to keep jumping. To me, this is no challenge! Two accidents have happened in the last three days, that's all." He stopped, gazing intently at Damianos. There was tension in the PFC's face. "Don't you understand, Sergeant? Out there, whatever happens has no meaning, no pattern! Nothing connects one accident with another. Nothing! It would be very comforting to believe what you do." He smiled, but to Damianos it was more of a grimace. "I'm afraid, Sergeant, that there's *no one* in charge out there." He paused for a moment. "This much I'll grant you. Perhaps . . . I said *perhaps* . . . the ten men who were dragged to death died inevitably. But the five

Air Force crewmen who were burned to death yesterday burned to death just to prove a point for Aarons. The point is, I think, that men aren't—or shouldn't be—afraid to die."

Damianos interrupted. "Don't forget, Clarke . . . Aarons jumps every time you jump. And most of the time he jumps fifteen to twenty minutes before the Division to make sure the wind ain't too stiff. Don't think he's some chairborne, Pentagon son of a bitch with a fat gut."

"I didn't say that. All I said was that the five men who were burned yesterday died because Aarons was too much of a coward to call off the second mass jump. . . . And they weren't even paratroopers!"

Damianos did not want to continue the discussion, yet he refused to take the easy way out by calling Clarke to order and telling him to get back to the unit. "You know," he said, "it ain't only Aarons who is doing this. There's the maneuver director; there's the commanding general of the tactical air support wing; there's Aarons' staff. Sure . . . he's the big mahatma . . . but don't forget . . . if all these guys under him don't want him to do something . . . it's their responsibility to give him plenty of good reasons for not doing whatever he wants to do. Like jumping. Maybe that's what they're talking about today. This much is certain, though. We're dropping tomorrow."

"Then they're all afraid. Aarons and everyone else involved in Razor Blade. . . . They're all afraid of defending a position that will make them look bad . . . cowardly." To Damianos, Clarke's smile seemed almost like a taunt. "I find it very amusing, Sergeant, that the United States Army—which should be the last outpost of the brave man—is full of moral cowards who are afraid to contradict a superior."

Damianos' jaw muscle twitched. He was about to yell at Clarke, but he hesitated. "You may not believe it, Clarke"—he spoke carefully and slowly—"but it takes a lot of courage to carry out an unpleasant order. It also takes a brave man to give an unpleasant command, especially when the man who does the ordering has gotta be the first to do what he's asking of his people."

A small plane droned over Crossroads Drop Zone. Damianos glanced at it, then consulted his wristwatch. "Take a look at that, Clarke. You know who's up there?"

"Haven't the slightest idea."

"Two to one says it's General Aarons. Two to one says he's gonna jump."

"It doesn't matter if you're right or wrong. What matters

is that you and all the older NCOs are sure there's going to be another jump tomorrow and that you . . . all of you . . . half expect another disaster."

Damianos betrayed a slight smile. "You may be right." He shifted his legs slightly. The intense pain had stopped.

"And two to one says that none of you refuse to jump." Clarke stared at the sergeant. "Two to one says you've got it rationalized before it happens. That you can jump daily, now till Christmas . . . till New Year's . . . and get knocked off one by one, and you'll continue jumping."

Damianos smiled. *He's got a good mind . . . a good straightleg mind.* He shifted his position again. "That won't happen. The disasters'll stop before we do. Now . . . we're looking for only a big bust, one that takes five or six men. Otherwise . . . one dead ass hung up on a tree won't make much difference. That won't be a challenge. When five or six clowns get it, then it's a threat. Then we'll jump. You're just too sensitive, Clarke. Sergeant Jacks told me all about you." Damianos paused. He fixed the PFC with a steady, taunting stare. "Two to one, Clarke. Two to one says you're too much of a coward to refuse to jump."

Clarke frowned and stood up abruptly. For a moment Damianos thought the PFC was going to stalk away, but then he saw Clarke stretching his legs painfully. The position was beginning to tell, but Clarke was either too polite or careful to ask Damianos to stand with him. *If he wants to talk to me,* the sergeant thought, *he'll have to get down here where I am.*

"Maybe you're right," Clarke said when he returned to the hunkering position. This was not spoken in a defeated tone. "Maybe you're right. But this much I'll tell you. . . . The man who refuses to jump tomorrow will be the most courageous of the lot of us. He'll be the freest." He clasped his hands, palm to palm, and joined his wrists. "We're all like this, Sergeant. Crossroads has manacled us. Whoever refuses to jump will be free."

"Don't give me that manure about freedom, Clarke. The only freedom we got in the Airborne is that of doing our duty. Whatever it is. Whoever assigns it. Freedom is for dreamy philosophers and civilian candy-asses and slaves. To be a real man is to know that you'll always be enslaved but to do your duty 'cause you wanna do it, not because you have to. Men shouldn't get carried away by tinsel and trinkets like freedom. I hate that word, Clarke. I hate that word. . . . Do you know why? 'Cause I hear organ music in the background whenever someone says it. It's for Fourth of July mother-humpers with potbellies and American Legion buttons. It's for headquarters boys and personnel boys and quartermaster depot boys. It's a parader's word!"

Clarke, squatting motionlessly, stared at Damianos. If he was uncomfortable in the hunkering position, he did not betray the fact to the sergeant. At the outset he appeared to regard Damianos quizzically, but as the sergeant continued speaking, Clarke's face registered dismay.

"OK," Clarke stated quickly, "maybe it doesn't exist. But if it does, you aren't going to find it by risking your life just to prove that it can be found in duty."

Clarke stopped. As if whispered, Damianos heard: "I pity you." The two men looked at each other.

Damianos laughed. It was not an unpleasant laugh but one that seemed, for all its brevity, to cut through Clarke's statement. "We gotta jump, don't you understand? We gotta jump . . . 'cause . . . what's the world the newspapers call free to do without meatheads like us who're ready to fight for the freedom everyone believes in but no one has?"

Clarke tried to interrupt, but Damianos did not pause. "You see, Clarke, I can't afford lies. No matter how much I like to believe them, no matter how comfortable they are, I can't do it. Operation Razor Blade is gonna cut through a lotta lies. It's gonna cut right down to the bone. I used to lie to myself, but now I'm through. Now I'm a man. I gotta live in truth. Man don't have freedom." He mimicked Clarke's action, placing the palms together, touching wrist to wrist. "So when people talk about freedom . . . you know they all got manacles on their wrists . . . only they can't see them."

He stood up. The pain in his legs was excruciating. As his muscles and tendons eased and stretched, the torment reached its peak, lingered, then slowly subsided. "I like the Army, Clarke, 'cause when General Aarons talks about freedom, I know or I hope he knows it's just so much manure. When Radio Moscow and Voice of America talk about freedom, I know it's just so much manure, though they may not. There ain't any. You see? That's the big joke!" Damianos laughed. "There ain't any. All there is is duty. That's all! There's no patriotism, except back home during bond rallies. There's only duty."

Clarke stared at him incredulously. "Then . . . then you can't believe that a man . . . all men . . . have dignity!"

Damianos laughed again. For a moment he wanted to put his arm affectionately on the PFC's shoulder. *He's just a boy,*

Damianos realized. *Just a kid*. But then, his hand almost at Clarke's elbow, the sergeant let it fall again.

"OK, you guys!" He shouted to the paratroopers, who were waiting for a command. "On your feet! Let's form up. We gotta get our jogging in."

CHAPTER 31

The unit of Special Troops began double-timing. In four files, the eighty men jogged from the forested clearing into the tableland of the drop zone. They ran parallel to the high wall of pines which, with the mountain ranges in the background, formed the second enclosure of Crossroads. Their booted feet thudded on the dirt path skirting the vast, barren rectangle.

Barrett Clarke was in the extreme left file, having managed to find a position in the rear of the unit. The pace was a leisurely one, and Clarke, with each light step, gradually understood that the others around him did not consider this run a chore; it was an outing. Damianos, farther ahead of Clarke, was a powerful, burly, slightly bowlegged scoutmaster, and he and the others were the cubs. *A Sunday morning at Crossroads*. Clarke smiled.

The day *was* pleasant. Monday, of course, would be horrible; that much he knew. Each passing hour brought the following day's threat closer. But now, each step warming his body, each left, each right boot raised from the path's surface made him aware, on this quiet Sunday morning, of how much he would risk on Monday. *My life has been aimless . . . and will probably continue to be. . . .* Yet, glancing at the harsh, aloof mountain ranges, still spotted with virginal snow, he did not seek for the end of this aimlessness, this confusion. The bed of eighty green berets, vivid against the dull greenery of the coniferous trees, almost impertinently colorful, bobbed slightly above the spiked spires and below the mountain peaks. Clarke breathed in the piny fragrance. *Life's good,* he thought. A man could not evaluate life properly until he had witnessed more of it, Clarke knew, but what he had known was, in retrospect, good, aimless though he felt it to be. *Sunday morning!* he wondered. *What am I doing here?*

"Lord, Lord, what'll I do . . . ?"

Free of the feeling that the sergeants were waiting for him to make an error, to break discipline (this was, after all, a Sunday outing!) Clarke turned his head and saw the great stretch of Crossroads Drop Zone loom before him and, by this time, to his rear, a gigantic tan canvas, full of dips and mounds, completely barren of vegetation.

"Why ain't I a straightleg just like You . . . ?"

Damianos swerved to determine who had just sung. Clarke wondered why he had done this, then realized that perhaps the Jody rhyme was a new one, even to Damianos—for he himself had never heard it during his course at Jump School —and that Damianos possibly wanted to determine who had improvised his own chant. Damianos began clapping his hands; the unit followed suit immediately.

"Wings are fine and the money's handy. . . ."

A different voice chanted this time. It was a sequence then, Clarke realized, with each of the lead NCOs devising his own airborne chant, thus adding to the storehouse of Jody rhymes, the paratroopers' liturgy, which permitted them to face their never-ending dread with irony.

"But being a straightleg would be dandy. . . ."

The men in the unit laughed. Clarke puzzled over this. *They should hate this reminder,* he thought. *Why do they laugh . . . when they're only laughing at themselves . . . at their impotence?* The clapping began again and Clarke joined in, both palms sounding when a boot struck the earth. The Jody rhyme was a common language but one he still could not understand. It was not enough to know the words, for he knew what each word meant. He could not laugh with the other paratroopers, and this meant that he did not understand the chants as they did. *Perhaps the doubts of a man,* he wondered, *can only be reflected in his songs.*

"Ah don' hafta wash mah socks. . . ."

Clarke sang along with the unit this time, hoping that by joining them he might understand.

"Ah can't wear them in mah box. . . ."

The others laughed again. *Sepulchral . . . gallows humor. For them,* Clarke thought, *death is just the day when the hazardous-duty money is held up at Post Finance.*

The eighty paratroopers clip-clapped again. *I don't want to die, and I can't laugh death off . . . but I'm free to make my own choice.* And then, as he heard the deep and clear voice of Sergeant Damianos sing the first line of his chant,

Clarke thought: *But nothing will happen tomorrow. We'll jump . . . and nothing will happen.*

"Airborne sergeant went to heav'n. . . ."

The files repeated the first line.

"Never cussed and had no lovin'. . . ."

A few men in the group chuckled at Damianos' primitive sense of poetry. *There's more,* Clarke realized. *It's probably a quatrain.*

"When he didn't see God nowhere . . ."

Another one about God! They're about either God, death, money, or women. . . . But then . . . what else is there? The final line interrupted his thoughts. It was a bellow, a challenge.

"He said: Sound off, Lord, like you got a pair!"

The paratroopers shouted the fourth line loudly and then laughed again. Clarke was shocked. *They want another disaster!* Clip-clapping in unison with the others, synchronizing with their steps the thud of his boots on the complaisant earth, as if he had completely merged his individuality into the group, Clarke thought, amazed: *He's daring God to a third disaster. He's offering a challenge!*

The unit rounded the first corner of the Crossroads tableland, and now, to Clarke's left, the four-mile plateau stretched out. On the far side, the tents that stood triangled on the earth and the men who moved between them could barely be discerned. Regardless of the mounds and hollows on the drop zone, the troopers kept an even, rhythmic pace, initiating, on their own, the clip-clapping whenever they seemed to be losing their pattern. *It's an outing,* Clarke realized again. *As long as they jog . . . they can't think.* It was significant to Clarke that no one dropped out of the run, although they had passed the point Damianos had mentioned. But it was too easy, too necessary for him to feel superior to the other paratroopers. *After all,* he thought, *they don't seem as afraid to die as I do . . . and since we can't really know anything about anything . . . the appearance of not caring about death is just as important as the reality of not caring about it.* He stared at the beret of the man ahead of him. *I don't want to die. . . . Death has no meaning.*

As they turned the other corner, Clarke saw the small L-20 droning over Crossroads, far ahead of the jogging unit. It must have been at the approximate altitude of four thousand feet. A parachute blossomed in the blueness of the sky and fell, placidly, without wavering, without oscillating, down to the flatness of the drop zone.

"Ah don' fear the Lord our God. . . ."

An older lead sergeant jogging next to Clarke chanted. The canopy, under which the toylike man hanged, descended toward the barren tableland of Crossroads.

"Ah jest fears ol' Aarons' rod."

The paratroopers laughed again. Clarke felt a shiver run through him. *They're mad. . . . They're crazy.* And, although he knew that he was being illogical, that there was nothing and no one *out there,* that the first and second disasters had no causal connection and thus did not presuppose a third, he experienced a sharp uncertainty, a dread. *They're taunting Him!* And today was Sunday. *But God doesn't exist.* He checked himself. But tomorrow was Monday, the beginning of another week, the day of the third jump, which, by now, Clarke had accepted as mandatory, as an almost historical event.

CHAPTER 32

Corporal McIlhenny woke in the middle of the night. Monday morning. Something had upset him, but he could not recall what it was. Perhaps it was the cold that seeped into his blanket? No, it could not be that: the bag was still comfortable. That which had come to him at night was sweet, like a long-forgotten melody, like the hurdy-gurdy music rising to the second floor from cobblestone streets, like band music for a circus trapeze act. Sweet and faintly remembered. Yes. Yes. The Sunday comic pages again. *That's it!* He was sitting down. Reading them? No, he was doing something else. Cutting them out! Yes. Cutting them out with a straight razor and placing them on the damp ground. *Oh, yes.* He remembered. *That's an old dream. Very familiar.*

He glanced at his wristwatch. The luminous dial swam up to him in the darkness of the night, green and indefinite, like a neon sign's reflection in a rain puddle. It was three o'clock. *Good. Good. I have time,* he thought pleasantly. *Time for more sleep.* It was two hours before he would be jarred awake. Two hours yet before Monday came upon him. And he was unprepared.

I'll sleep. Yes. *I'll sleep,* he thought, and curled up in his blankets.

He dreamed: He was running down a street, frantically. The cobblestones twisted his ankles and shocked the muscles of his legs. A frightening roar followed him. Then his legs would no longer function. He turned to face whatever it was that chased him. A police whistle blew. *What will I do? Where can I go?* The whistle pierced the stillness again.

He woke up, startled. *It was a dream, thank God!* Men were stirring. Had they, then, the same dream? He heard the whistle again. "OK, men!" a sergeant to his right shouted. "On your feet! It's wake-up time!"

McIlhenny saw gnomelike figures rising from the ground near him, getting out of their sacks. He stared at his wristwatch. *There must be some mistake. . . . I just woke up. It's only three.*

But it was five. He had slept. Two hours had passed. Yes, it was time. Monday was here. He stirred himself, but it was cold outside. The harsh voices kept at him, forcing him into Monday.

His legs trembled from the cold; it was Monday, and he was unprepared. But, then, no one is prepared for Monday. How could he have prepared? Monday was the day of unpreparedness. He knew that. Monday was the day he went to school and knew he did not belong there, the day for which he had not studied, the day when no one knew his lessons and the whole class brazened it out, each one hoping the others would be called on to recite, to do fractions, to conjugate the Latin verbs.

And it did not surprise Corporal McIlhenny (although his wayward heart behaved as if the news was unexpected) that, since today was Monday, the paratroopers would ready themselves to make their third mass jump. But he had wasted all of Sunday! He had listened to the sermon, trying to concentrate on the priest's words, but had seen only a small boy, himself, reading the Sunday comics on the parlor floor; closing the front door of his row house, hopping down the three white steps, passing closed taverns, running for the rickety green trolley car that would take him to mass; and coming out of a movie house in the evening, glancing sideways, self-consciously, at the reflection of himself (confident but lonely—yes, lonely) in the lobby's gilt-edged mirror.

These images, projected before him clearly, like the green and red bottles in pharmacy displays, had seized his mind as he half listened to the priest speaking about fortitude and

God's plan. *How touching,* he had thought. *Man is always trying to explain his own destruction . . . as if he wants to take credit for it.* Second by second, transfixed before the screening of his past, he had almost recovered the paradise he had lost on becoming a man, then had discovered with a thrill that he had not lost it, because it would always be remembered.

He rushed to dress himself. It was Monday and he was unprepared again! He must hurry. The cook, when McIlhenny arrived at the field mess, complained to him about his lateness, but the corporal merely opened his kit and saw a lump of scrambled eggs drop into the tin. He filled his canteen cup with coffee, opened a pound cake, and tried to concentrate on eating. But the scraping of his fork on the mess kit sickened him. His stomach was nervous and reacted to every bit of food he took; each time, however, he checked this by taking a sip of the bitter coffee. *No, no, I must relearn to discipline myself.* The coffee helped. *This is fine . . . fine. . . . I feel much better. . . .*

McIlhenny walked to the large stainless-steel tub filled with soapy water and washed his mess kit and utensils; then, after moving to the next can, filled with clear water, he rinsed them off. Not bothering to dry anything, he placed his silverware in the mess kit, capped it, and stuffed it into his combat pack. The whistles would soon blow, he knew. He must hurry to the latrine. It was Monday, after all, and there was never enough time on Monday. The rusty machinery of life, quiet and motionless during Sunday, always sounded louder on Monday than it did the previous week. That was why no one could prepare for Monday: Monday was everything people expected it to be.

The whistles blew as he returned to his area, and McIlhenny, following the others, double-timed into the harshly lighted clearing. The paratroopers fell into formation. In the blackness beyond the perimeter of the lights, hundreds of whistles shrieked. *Yes . . . I forgot. . . . We are a whole division. . . .* And then he hesitated. *Can all this be my dream?*

A captain began speaking to the formation, and as he concluded his remarks the sky's blackness was streaked with gray. Dawn was near. *It's wake-up time,* Corporal McIlhenny mused. He had not listened to the briefing, had merely caught phrases. "Airplanes thoroughly inspected." "Best mechanical condition." "No combat or weapons' packs on jump." There was plenty of time to ask the others what had been said. It was Monday, after all, and the only preparation a man could make was to assume the worst would happen. Or the best. McIlhenny, in the grayness of dawn, smiled a secret smile. *It's wake-up time.*

He snapped to attention at the command and performed a right face. A long file of trucks with their headlights glaring stood motionless a distance away. *Back to Eleutheria. . . . Peculiar word,* he wondered. *What on earth can it mean?*

CHAPTER 33

Thirty-three shiny aircraft, eleven V's in trail formation, glinted in the harshness of the wintry sun and roared from Eleutheria to Crossroads. Silvery white, they seemed stabilized over an earth that rolled and tossed from the central flatness to the mountain ranges of the west. Under the crafts' cold abdomens, the earth lay placid, unshaded by fluffs of clouds, reflecting in its brilliance the clarity of the choice each paratrooper faced.

General Aarons had parachuted into Crossroads fifteen minutes before the flight of C-119s had blazed over the Eleutherian pines. In loneliness and grace, he had dropped safely to the DZ sand with hardly a breeze marring his canopy's descent. And now, the wind conditions tested and found ideal for the mass exercise, his command was radioed throughout the region, was heard in the commo shacks at Eleutheria and in each of the thirty-three Flying Boxcars winging their way toward their now-familiar meeting place, the Crossroads tableland.

"The jump is on!"

"The jump is on!"

"THE JUMP IS ON!"

And the order came as no surprise to paratroopers trussed in harnesses and strapped to bucket seats—facing each other in darkened fuselages like men staring at reflections of themselves in full-length mirrors—that they would perform what they had spent years of their lives preparing for, that they would act out what was to them inviolable duty, that they would further define themselves in what months of indoctrination had proved to them to be their only definition: paratroopers.

Corporal McIlhenny was first at the door of his Boxcar, the

left base aircraft of the second V. Jacks was again the jumpmaster for the flight. The corporal was not antagonistic toward the squarejawed sergeant for what he had done to him on the second jump; Jacks had only done his duty. After all, they were both old-time paratroopers. Jacks had done him a favor. *I almost shamed myself . . . but he saved me.*

In the screaming of the open door that prohibited conversation, the two men acted out the roles demanded of them by the task to which they—by a disciplined silence—had given their soldierly assent. Occasionally, Corporal McIlhenny would feel Sergeant Jacks' eyes rest momentarily on him, and, giving the sergeant a few seconds to study his features, McIlhenny would pretend to be lost in his own thoughts.

He had only one thought now: to leap from the door without being pushed. To salvage something of his reputation. To permit no fear to destroy a life of devotion and of dedication to the airborne. To die, if die he must, without the taint of cowardice. Life had leveled him into many definitions. To Kinnard McIlhenny, words such as apostate, pervert, failure, madman could be applied as qualifying terms; coward must never be, for he had devoted his life, his manhood, to the service of his country, and if he were to die, he would die as he had lived—bravely.

Jacks turned to him. *"Stand in the door!"*

Corporal McIlhenny stamped his feet on the metal floor, swerved to the sky, and stood poised at the threshold.

Sergeant Damianos was pusher for his stick. In the cavern of the fuselage, standing motionless, his left arm raised to the static line, he waited for the command to advance to the door before pushing the man ahead of him and emptying the front portion of the twin-boomed craft. Sixteen men separated him from PFC Barrett Clarke. He recalled the conversation he and the young man had had the day before. *Don't know what's happening. . . . Don't know what started with the first disaster. . . . Been a candy-ass all his life.* Damianos felt restless. *Let's get this stick moving.* His right boot, bull-like, pawed the floor. *Gotta get out into the sky.*

Clarke, fifth man from the door, felt oppressed. Before and behind him, he felt the bulky intimidation of the other paratroopers. *This is the last time I choose to jump. I'm not afraid . . . but there's a point beyond which I won't be pushed. . . . Last time. . . .* His left arm, raised to the static line, felt strained. He permitted it to hang, supported by the stretched wire. *I must find myself . . . must make my stand. . . . It's all a man can do . . . know himself. So far I'm nothing. . . .*

"Stand in the door!"

The stick of paratroopers advanced several feet nearer the screaming door.

Behind the second V where Corporal McIlhenny waited at the open door of the left base aircraft, behind the point craft of the fifth V where Damianos and Clarke waited for the green light, the right base Boxcar on the ninth V detached itself from the rigid confines of the formation and slowly lost altitude. The pilot glanced at the dials, saw a rise in his oil temperature, a drop in the pressure, and observed a high cylinder-head temperature. He feathered the propeller and turned off his left engine, hoping to stall for time until his personnel load, to whom he had just given the long bell, would be able to clear the airplane in time. The giant left propeller, swirling colorlessly—a quatrefoil, with each lobe a razor—gradually lost its transparency, became thickly opaque, assumed the sun's hue, then, as each moment passed, became more definitely yellow. It stopped revolving.

Destiny offered the pilot five seconds to decide what to do.

To bank to the right would mean to drop his paratroopers over the forest and to make a fatal crash dive into the mountain's side. Saturday's crash was doubtlessly vivid in his mind. His other alternative was to swerve to the left, release his stick loads on the drop zone, and attempt a crash landing on the tableland of Crossroads.

He banked to the left. Half of his forty-two paratroopers had by this time exited from the craft. Then he saw, directly in the path from which he was powerless to move, the paratroopers of the preceding V's descending placidly, gracefully, confident that this was to be their final jump—only, as human beings, unaware of the irony with which destiny would look upon their hopes. The sky was filled with canopies, like dandelion fluffs scattered by a breeze.

The soldier first at the door of the craft Clarke and Damianos were on had bent down, waiting for the green light to flash above his left shoulder so that he could leap into the sky. But when the light flashed on, and when the jumpmaster slapped him, shouting *"go,"* he braced himself at the jambs. His paratroop boots flattened against the metal floor.

Clarke, several paces behind the man at the door, heard him shouting: "Screams. . . . I hear screams!" But then he felt a push against his back. *I make a choice to jump,* he thought. *I won't be pushed.* Clarke did the next best thing. He pushed.

Damianos, at the rear of the line, could not see or suspect what was happening. All he knew was that the green light had been given by the pilot and that pilots were not often wrong. The *go* signal had been flashed and the line had not moved. Obviously, someone had refused to jump. Someone, permitting himself to be terrified by the jump, had frozen at the door; his hands had stuck on the jambs with the awesome power of a panicked man and could not be budged by the jumpmaster.

And the stick was motionless. Damianos looked down the straight line; no one moved. "Push!" he shouted. "Push him out!" He bellowed at the challenge. "Push!" And every man in the line, restless after seconds of delay, knew that—large as Crossroads Drop Zone was—it was not endless and began pushing forward. Within two seconds the movement of the stick toward the door became a stampede. The man at the door had been struck by the momentous shock; his hands gave way, his boots kicked out from under him, and he fell into the path of the onrushing disabled Boxcar.

He landed under the tip of the aircraft's nose and bounced off inertly. The second man was impaled on the rigid propeller blade; the third soldier's body thudded on the narrow point of the aircraft's main-central fuselage; the fourth man dropped safely through the space between the airplane's twin booms; and Clarke, fifth on the stick, barely missed scraping off his arm on the scythe-like tail connecting the two booms. After Clarke, each paratrooper fell safely into the untroubled air. But the disabled Boxcar had just begun its destructive career.

McIlhenny was first into the sky. He dropped for a three thousand count, felt the comforting tug as his T-10 chute opened, and, in the incredible silence the sky always possesses after the rumbling of the paratrooper's mother craft has passed, he looked down to the snow-spotted earth. There was no need to guide himself, to slip to the right, to the left. Everything seemed in perfect order. All dreams cannot be bad.

He heard shouts. *Youth,* he marveled. *Exuberant youth . . .*

all dreamers . . . shouting their battle cries. . . . On second thought, the noises he heard may have been screams. A frightening roar seemed to follow him. *I've had that dream,* he considered peevishly. *I've already dreamed that . . . the cobblestones and the police whistles. . . .* the roar grew louder. "Go away!" he shouted. "I've had that dream!" But then he heard thuds, like large stones striking corrugated roofs. He swung himself around.

To his right he saw the stationary propeller, yellowish gold, like a Greek cross; directly ahead, coming toward him, he saw the swirling, silvery haze. McIlhenny gasped for a moment, then recovered. He smiled nervously and tried to hold himself stable. He faced the propeller of the oncoming aircraft.

"My name is Kinnard McIlhenny!" he shouted, but immediately perceived: *That's unimportant.* He sobbed happily. *Everything is unimportant: my name . . . my face . . . my past. . . .* A thrill shook him. *I was confused,* he realized. *Life is a dream. . . . It's not a dream. . . . I was confused. But I knew this was coming. . . .* It was not unfair. He had known it would be like this. "Beloved God," he shouted, "to think . . . to think . . . I doubted You! You warned me . . . but I could not prepare." The swirling propeller roared nearer. He would wake up soon. "There's order," he exulted. "There's order. . . . There's a plan!" He smiled. He sobbed. His body trembled: it was, after all, the instrument on which God played. There was nothing he could do. There was never anything he could do. He was trapped in the sky. God was vast and great and all-knowing. God loved man enough to waken him from lies, from dreams. God loved man. . . . McIlhenny waited now, suspended. The circle of haze grew larger. The noise became deafening. "Beloved God," he shouted, "I worship You. . . ."

And at that moment the propeller sliced into his body with a whoosh, like finely honed blades of a lawn mower rushing through luxuriant grass; and in a second all that remained of McIlhenny were the bits of flesh, of bone, of cloth which were broadcast, like confetti, throughout the sky above Crossroads Drop Zone.

Before the aircraft crashed, it tore through one more cluster of paratroopers; many of the soldiers could not turn around to see what was to take their lives. It threshed through four canopies, struck one man across the soft midsection with an epic sweep of its wings, and guillotined another. The stationary propeller, like a bull's horn, already burdened with one victim, hooked into another's canopy and dragged him with the aircraft for a hundred yards before the impact of the Boxcar's pull wore off and the trooper recovered. He was groping for his left boot to draw the knife and cut himself free when the soles of his boots touched, then scraped, then bounced along the pine tree's spires. He had cut one riser free when the aircraft erupted into the flames which soon engulfed him.

CHAPTER 34

Damianos surveyed the craft's descent and pillared blaze from his swaying, silent height. He had heard the shouts, the screams, the infinitesimal muting of the propeller's roar as it whirred through falling bodies, and the sudden thud of boots and helmets against its metallic skin. Whatever interpretation the men who lived through this disaster might choose to give it, he knew, there was only one way it should be viewed: it was another challenge.

Readying himself for the landing, Damianos felt the impact on his toes, collapsed to his right calf, his thigh, his hams, rolled on his back, and, in a second, was erect. He freed himself from the harness tentacles, then rolled his chute methodically. *The world's to blame,* he thought, *but so are we.* Stuffing the canopy into his bag, he frowned. *I must fight. . . . And when there is no war . . . I gotta find one.* He hesitated, groggy from his idea. *For the past week I been standing before a mirror . . . sparring with my reflection. I'm the aggressor. My enemy . . . myself . . . the counter-puncher. . . . My gloves meet head on.*

Jogging over the mounds and hollows of Crossroads, heading for the Assembly Area, he ignored the groans he heard. The time for the wounded would come. Things must first be organized. Otherwise, everyone would be rushing about frantically, accomplishing nothing.

Scores of paratroopers had quietly gathered on the sand, hundreds of yards from the assembly area, looking with glazed eyes across the drop zone. Lost in a stupor so uncharacteristic of them, the soldiers appeared to the sergeant to be cowed.

Scared! Damianos thought, flushing with anger. *Scared . . . like a bunch of goddamn rabbits. . . .* He sprinted, his legs galloping across the sand that separated him from them, his hardened fists, like ax heads, swinging tautly at his sides. He rushed into the group, pushing, elbowing, fisting the men across the shoulders, the arms, throwing body blocks on them, trying to get them moving toward the Assembly Area where they belonged. One man, his face gray and intense, as if in deep narcosis, turned to the sergeant and struck him without anger. The blow jarred Damianos and forced him back a few inches, but, responding immediately, he clubbed the man's face with his right fist, following through with a slam of his massive shoulder. The man went down, his eyes wide open, and fell back on the ground, still staring at his attacker.

Damianos swerved to the others: they were all the same. Then he understood. The paratroopers were in a state of shock. *They did not know they were safe. They thought they were still in the air.* Something so vast and horrible had happened to them in the sky that they would never forget it. And now, regardless of what they stared at, they only relived again and again the horror they had witnessed.

Damianos heard the faraway shouts for medic and the deep animal groans breaking the brimming, unreal silence of Crossroads. He studied his hands in awe. *I've gone mad,* he thought. *I've lost my reason. I hit him . . . but I wanted to kill myself. . . . What am I? A slavemaster? A savage? All this hatred in me . . . when I only want to worship. . . .* He sighed heavily. *I'll never be free.* Lifting his eyes to the mountain ranges, he scanned the treeless peaks. *This is all I remember of my life . . . this earth . . . this sky . . . those mountains . . . death. . . .* At that moment, as he stood rooted to the drop-zone sand, a moment of panic came over him: he wondered if it were a dream that he had a wife, Sophie by name, and would soon have a child—so much had Crossroads Drop Zone become his native land.

Someone was calling him, but Damianos continued to stare across the barren plateau. "Sergeant!" A pathfinder captain grasped him by the elbow. "Sergeant, gather all these men and march them down to the T at the north end. We're going to need everyone in an hour . . . for a police call."

Damianos turned to him slowly, moment by moment trying to reconstruct the features of the officer's face and assemble them into a recognizable whole. He regarded the captain stolidly. "Yes, sir," he said quietly, then comprehended.

"Yes, sir. . . . Police call. . . . Yes, sir!" He turned to the paratroopers.

"All right," he shouted. "Fall in!" His voice seemed far away. Was he shouting in an echo chamber? Was this his voice? The voice of Sergeant Damianos, whom he knew so well, yet not at all? The husband of Sophie? "Ten-*hup!*" This sergeant, over whose shoulder he seemed to be looking, had just called them to attention. "For-ard . . . *harch!*" The soldiers had heard him. "Double-tiiime . . . *harch!*" They jogged comfortably over the drop-zone earth.

He called for a half right, for he had discerned something ahead of the formation. He knew what it was, of course—an ordinary boot, a paratrooper's boot, laced tightly, as if in preparation for a mock inspection. In solitude, it stood erect on the DZ, insignficant on the vast expanse. The top was flaked with blood. "Look straight ahead," he ordered the men, but disobeyed his own command. Brimming with blood, the boot contained someone's halved leg, the fibula severed evenly, like a sawed-off tree trunk.

Damianos heard a sobbing in formation and turned abruptly. It was a young boy, a teen-ager. "Stop blubbering," he snapped. "What're you—a paratrooper or a candy-ass?"

Scores of soldiers were waiting at the T when Damianos and the unit in his charge arrived. No one there knew what to do. Officers and enlisted men stood in clusters or sat on the ground, their eyes immobile, their faces masked of any emotion.

Sergeant Damianos groped in the side pocket of his field jacket for his pack, found a cigarette, and drew it to his lips with trembling hands. *What's this?* he thought. *What's this? . . . Me too?* The match flame teased the cigarette's tip, and Damianos was forced to brace his elbows on his sides. *It's getting to me. . . . It's working on me. . . .* The sergeant's facial muscles twitched, and he pawed the drop zone with heavy boots. *I'm not afraid to die. . . . I'm not afraid,* he maintained as a horrible thought blossomed in his mind. *Suppose I break . . . disgrace myself . . . ?* He drew a few short breaths. *I'll suicide first. . . .*

"What's going to happen now, Sergeant?"

He turned to the voice. A second lieutenant in his early twenties stood near him, his eyes focused somewhere over Damianos' shoulder, his lower lip trembling.

"Sir?"

"What's going to happen now?"

Damianos' lungs felt oppressed. *Been breathing too fast, too hard.* He sighed. "Well, sir"—he looked at the slender boy—"our dead can't lie on the DZ overnight. . . . We're waiting for the ambulance trucks to finish with the wounded. . . . Then we're gonna . . . gonna have a police call, Lieutenant . . . to pick up the bodies." Damianos stopped. *And the parts thereof,* he thought.

The officer's expression did not change. He nodded his head absentmindedly, stepped back a few paces, and sat on the ground.

The short talk with the lieutenant made Damianos feel much better. *Others are worse off than me. . . . That's good. . . . That's good. I can hide myself this way. . . .* He took a deep breath, then saw that trouble was coming. Clarke was limping toward him. Sergeant Damianos, for a brief insane moment, wanted to laugh. Clarke, the gadfly, was coming.

"Well, Sergeant." The PFC's voice was harsh. "I suppose this means we'll have to jump again."

Damianos looked at him steadily. *Tough nut. . . . A bad limp is all he's got from this.* A nervous smile he could not fight came over the sergeant's face. "We don't *have* to jump unless we're ordered to. . . ."

"But someone will find it necessary to order us to jump, won't he? He can't have us being challenged and not responding—isn't that so, Sergeant?" Clarke's lips were thin and colorless. "After all, what would happen to paratroop tradition, to morale, if we let a little thing like this scare us?"

The wayward, irresponsible smile appeared on Damianos' face again. *Tough monkey,* he considered, almost proudly. "That's right, Clarke. And you'll be dropping right along with me, jump for jump."

"That's where you're wrong, Sergeant. I've had it. No more jumps for me." Clarke stared at him. "I'm no one's slave. I won't be condemned to heroism."

There was no way Damianos could stop his capricious smile. "You're just griping, Clarke. Only good soldiers gripe."

"Well . . . I'm a bad soldier . . . and I'm griping just the same. What do you think of that?"

The young lieutenant had been listening to the conversation; when Damianos turned to him abruptly, the officer, uncomfortable and embarrassed, pretended an interest in his fingernails.

"I'm not jumping, Sergeant Damianos. I want to tell you right now . . . so you can report me to whoever is still alive. . . . And I won't change my mind."

"Look, you!" Damianos leaned over to Clarke. "I don't

wanna hear any more of your candy-ass bitching—you hear? I don't give a fuck what you wanna do or what you don't wanna do. You volunteered for the airborne . . . and you're gonna follow orders." His fist was cocked and Damianos was ready to swing, but he hesitated because the lieutenant was nearby. "Sir"—Damianos spoke to the officer gruffly—"would you leave us for a while?" A moment passed before the lieutenant realized what had been said to him. When he understood, he rose to his feet and wandered toward another cluster of paratroopers.

"I know what you think about freedom"—Clarke spoke quickly—"and I know what they'll say when we're ordered to jump again. They'll give us all that manure about the Free World. Well . . . I'll have no part of it. Don't you understand, Sergeant? Freedom *does* exist! But not in duty!"

Damianos could not grasp what had been said. Hatred toward Clarke, confusion at what the PFC had said, and then despair churned within him. *What's he mean? Have I lied to myself? Is this all a dream? What's he mean?*

"You're a slave to duty. You'll never be free." Clarke straightened his shoulders and pulled apart the wrists he had, a moment before, joined. "I'm free . . . because I'm through playing other people's games. I won't jump. *I'm free!"*

"Shut up! Shut up! Shut up!" Damianos yelled. "You make me sick!"

"You're afraid, Sergeant. You're afraid to do what you think is right. You're afraid to be free." Clarke shot his hand up to his neck abruptly. "I'm up to here with lies, with—"

But that was all he managed to say. Damianos caught him with a heavy right cross and drove Clarke to the ground ten feet from where he had been standing.

"On your feet!" Damianos shouted. "You make me sick. You're a disgrace—"

Clarke picked himself up and stared at the sergeant. "Well, Sergeant, you make me even sicker. You're such a coward—such a *moral* coward—and such a hypocrite!"

"Keep talking like that, punk, and you'll find your candy-ass in a sling."

"And . . . next time . . . hit me when I'm looking." Clarke, from his distance, glared at Damianos. "I'm not afraid of you. You only hit me because you know I'm right." He smiled bitterly. "You disgust me."

"Are you looking?"

Clarke stared at him without comprehending.

Sergeant Damianos moved in. His fists were up and his boots stepped heavily on the earth. Clarke waited for him, his eyes fixed on the sergeant's legs. When Damianos was three feet away, Clarke flung himself and threw a body slam against the sergeant's knees. Damianos, before he toppled forward, managed to graze Clarke's chin with his knotted knuckles. They wrestled on the sand, Clarke above the sergeant. Damianos was grateful for this. He wrapped his legs in a scissors around Clarke's waist and hooked his booted feet. Then, straightening out his heavy, muscular limbs, he pleased himself with each gradual pressure he applied to his ankles. Clarke's face registered pain, but his lips were clenched tightly. His hands sought out the sergeant's, and Damianos smiled at another of his opponent's mistakes. He bent Clarke's hands back to the wrists and held him aloft. Then, after he heard Clarke's moans leave his throat unashamedly, he released him, flinging him loosely to the ground.

Damianos stood above Clarke. "Get your ass back to one of the formations. That was insubordination. . . . It was a lot of things." The sergeant brushed himself off. "But I'll forget about it."

He walked away, dissatisfied, for there was a feeling within him that he had somehow acted dishonorably. A harsh voice from a nearby loudspeaker interrupted his thoughts.

CHAPTER 35

"Attention in the area. Attention in the area."

Clarke, lying on the earth, took several deep breaths and probed his sore rib box with aching fingers. He struggled against the tears that welled in his eyes and trickled to his earlobes.

"All men will report to Major Tatum regardless of parent unit."

He should have known better than to become involved in a fight with an NCO. All sergeants were alike. *It was my fault . . . thinking he was better than the rest.*

"Report to Major Tatum at the crossbar of the T."

More important than any other impression Clarke had about Operation Razor Blade was the feeling that he had somehow been violated, that outrage following outrage succeeded in divorcing him from the other soldiers. Great undertakings were supposed to bring a human being closer to his fellowman. Clarke never felt more alone. The paratroopers were essentially preparing to fight for what amounted to Clarke's freedom and individual dignity (and their own); because, however, Clarke had the misfortune to be with the paratroops while they were training to fight for these worthy objectives, it was assumed that he considered his freedoms unimportant enough not to complain when they were taken from him without his permission. The maneuver had made unmistakable only what he had known before: in the gigantic, impersonal institutions dedicated to defending his value and beliefs, his value and beliefs were considered too cumbersome to be respected.

He stood up. The monotonous voices coming over the public-address system served to remind him that commands still existed. If he wanted to rebel, to refuse an order, he would be forced to act now, and act, moreover, in a way that could be interpreted only as irresponsible. For this order, coming to him at the time he was prepared to make his first refusal, only frustrated Clarke. Unknowingly, he had complied with it before it had been given. He was already at the T.

Stop right now, he cautioned himself. *I'm not going to refuse any order just to get myself into useless trouble. I'm not rebelling against reasonable command or the necessity of subordination.* He dug into his back pocket for a handkerchief and wiped his eyes, glancing about to see if anyone was watching. The men were still groggy. *No . . . I won't refuse any order just because it's an order. I'll just retain within myself the final authority on whether a particular order is acceptable to me or not.* He would give to the military authorities the support they deserved, but, in giving them his loyalty, he would retain from them only that which was his to decide, that which had been given in trust to him by neither his parents nor the state nor the Army.

The order to advance to the T was a proper order. He was already there. In fighting this proper command, therefore, he would be forced to act irresponsibly. He would comply with this order by remaining where he was. *At every point in the path of my life I've been offered a choice. If I didn't take this choice consciously, I've no one to blame but myself. From now on, each fork, each intersection, each crossroads . . .* He paused. *Each crossroads in this path will give me an opportunity to choose. I'll always have a yes and a no. In using my freedom of choice, I'll maintain my freedom of action. I will not jump again!* This was his choice, and the combined forces of the military and civilian powers in America would not be capable of bending his will into doing what he considered wrong. *I will not jump again!*

Glancing deep into the flatness of Crossroads as hundreds of men, small in comparison to the mountains and the vault of the sky, jogged toward the stretched panels of the T, Clarke felt a great emotion sweep through him. *I know myself. I know myself! What power I have!* His hands trembled slightly. "Barrett Clarke." He spoke his name. "So this is Barrett Clarke!" *At last I'm free. . . . I know what free choice is. . . . I possess it. . . . I'm free. . . . My wrists are unshackled. . . .*

"Will the men still on their way please double-time. What we must do requires daylight, and the sun will be setting soon."

Clarke decided that the request was a reasonable one. If he were still on his way, he would double-time without feeling any qualms about violating his personal integrity. *What's the detail?* he wondered. *No matter. I'll soon learn.* He immediately recalled his personal declaration of independence and felt a certain fear. *I'm heading for trouble. I'm going to get involved.* But then he realized: *I am involved! I'm involved in organized insanity. I'd rather follow my own madness . . . than that of someone else.*

"In a few moments, gentlemen, several Deuce-and-a-Halves will drive into the drop zone."

Clarke searched about for the loudspeaker so that, in facing it, he would feel that he confronted the man giving the orders.

"The detail we are going to perform today is one that you'll never forget. It is a detail that must be completed within two hours."

Clarke began walking toward the loudspeaker, for a few words had sounded vague and muffled.

"All the wounded have been located and transferred to field hospitals. But there are buddies of ours, men we've known for years, who are lying on the drop-zone sand, dead and disfigured."

Clarke stopped short. What? What? His nervous system appeared to have understood what had been said before his mind did. *What? What kind of detail?*

"We cannot allow their bodies to remain on the ground

overnight. Before darkness comes, we should have the bodies of our comrades, our buddies, assembled and identified."

His eyes frantic, Clarke glanced to the right, to the left, staring at the paratroopers. It could not be what he was thinking! It could not be as horrible as that!

"Will all the NCOs assemble at the juncture of the stem and crossbar?"

Men double-timed past him. Soon afterward, the whistles began screeching, and the NCOs, waiting at the crossbar of the T, herded the paratroopers into formations. Squads of soldiers were detailed to comb the forested areas surrounding Crossroads. Three ranks of men—staggered to cover every inch of sand—stood fingertip to fingertip across the width of the drop-zone tableland, confronting the vast corridor of Crossroads.

Clarke, his arms raised winglike at his sides, wondered what he would encounter in the sandy mounds and hollows beyond his sight. The command was a proper one. It would be irresponsible—it would be cowardly—of him to refuse to follow it. No, he had chosen to act honorably, and his individual honor demanded that he submit to this, for the dead must be assembled and identified. If he refused to do this, then every man in the Division and the Special Troops would be morally justified in refusing. His heart throbbing, Clarke glanced quickly to the right and left to see the rank he was part of stringing out. Two ranks behind him did likewise; each rank totaled about a thousand men. The NCOs followed the third rank, and behind them the convoy of Deuce-and-a-Halves made the gradual turn from the forest-skirting dirt path, whimpered upon changing gears, and assumed their positions.

The public-address system sputtered again.

"For-ard . . . harch!"

The first rank advanced. Clarke stared ahead, attempting to blot out the fantasies his mind threatened him with. There were still a few hours of daylight. By the time they would arrive at the south end of Crossroads, Clarke knew, the twilight would be well advanced, for the task demanded of them required a slow, measured pace.

Clarke stopped his racing mind. *I will not think. I will not anticipate!* But the images crowded into the horrified arena of his mind. He saw mangled, bleeding stumps of hands. *No . . . No!* He would stop. He would force everything out of his mind. He would recognize the dreaded object only when he encountered it, and afterward he would force himself to forget. He would destroy its memory.

To his left, Clarke saw something lying still, an object that did not belong to the flatness of Crossroads. *It's a steel helmet, an ordinary steel helmet.* Clarke felt elated. *Just a steel pot . . . Someone will pick it up.* Then, as the first rank advanced toward the helmet, a series of shocks throbbed through Clarke's body. His eyes were fixed hypnotically on the round object. Someone's head was still in the helmet, and the face—frozen in death—contemplated the drop zone with an enviable serenity.

Clarke stumbled on, trying to ignore what he had seen, struggling to focus his sight on his immediate lane. He felt alternately chilled and heated. An object on his right disturbed him even more. *Good,* he thought. *Good. . . . It's on the right . . . not my lane . . . I won't look. . . .* He would not glance that way. He had no interest in what it was. But the rank was turning gradually. Clarke tried to walk straight ahead and bumped into the soldier to his left. The entire rank was turning, making a perceptible readjustment to the right.

"You. . . . You . . . !" He heard a voice behind him. "Get back in your lane!"

Whatever it was lay ahead of him now. In his lane. Mechanically, he threw one foot ahead of the other. His eyes were focused on the toes of his boots. But something ahead of him disturbed the barrenness of the sand. He stopped. Two hands, clutching risers which had been shorn off three inches above the closed fists, protruded from the ground. Midway between the two hands, Clarke saw the rounded dome of a steel helmet. Two men in the rank behind him and one from the third stopped next to the PFC and stared at the paratrooper whose canopy had been cut by the propeller. Not having realized he was unsupported, the chutist had not pulled his reserve and had been driven into the earth with the velocity of his fall.

Sergeant Damianos double-timed to the gathering. He stopped abruptly when he saw the helmet and the blindly stretched hands, waved to the follow-truck, and shouted for entrenching tools.

Clarke continued to stare at the helmet. A small shovel was placed in his hands. He glanced up to see Damianos regarding him almost tenderly.

"C'mon, there . . . let's go."

The five men began digging the corpse out of the hole it

had created with its own momentum. The shovel's blade wobbled back and forth continually, and each time Clarke tried to slice it into the earth, the blade folded uselessly. Damianos took the entrenching tool from Clarke's hands, straightened the blade, and tightened the nut connecting the metal flatness and the wooden pole. Clarke began digging again, looking at the covered man only by accident, only when he forgot, when he permitted his eyes to stray.

"Grab him under the armpit," Damianos said when the earth around the man's body was cleared away. "Drag him up." He glared at Clarke. "I mean *up,* goddamn it. That's right. . . . Slide your hand under his armpit. . . . That's right. . . . Drag him up. . . . What's the matter? . . . You afraid of death?"

Clarke had difficulty breathing. His arms trembled with the strain. He felt as if he were about to vomit, for the man's legs were shortened, like a dwarf's legs: the bones, smashed into each other from the force of the fall, had telescoped into his bulging boots. The limbs retained the position he had assumed when he had prepared to land. His arms were raised; his hands clutched risers that did not exist three inches above the fists; his body was postured for the impact—the boots and knees together, his toes still anticipating the earth that had become his self-dug grave.

"Poor bastard," Damianos muttered off to Clarke's right. He waved his arm. Clarke heard a truck drive up. "Didn't feel the prop cut him loose. Clarke. . . . Clarke. . . . Come the hell back here!"

"Under the arm again," Damianos ordered when Clarke returned to the pit. "That's right. . . . Now . . . lift . . . *lift!*"

Two men rushed over with a stretcher. Clarke and Damianos rolled the corpse on it roughly. "Probably wondered why he was coming down so fast. . . ." Clarke did not attend to the sergeant's conversation. "Figured he hit someone's airstream. . . . Probably tried to slip. . . . Wonder if he looked down at all."

Clarke stumbled up to the three moving columns. To his left, a violent argument was in progress. Words were exchanged loudly. Glancing over, Clarke saw three men. One was a sergeant. They were fighting to determine whose duty it was to pick up a severed arm that lay between them.

Every five steps, Clarke raised his eyes to the horizon, trying to estimate how many paces were left. The first rank, of which, because of Damianos' coaxing, he was again a part, was now halfway across the drop zone. Clarke muttered a curse. If he had only remembered how many paces he had taken to the midpoint, he would know how many were left. He had been fortunate, though. He had not encountered anything in his lane since digging the man out of his self-made pit. He stumbled ahead, and, in surveying the distance, observed what appeared to be bits of paper, like confetti, flaked over the area before him. He stopped to inspect the bits and then realized what they were: small tatters of nylon cloth, blood-impregnated bits of fatigue uniform, and worms of flesh. Clarke's head seemed to sway, his knees buckled, and he crumpled to the earth.

"Jesus Lord . . . Jesus Lord," someone muttered. Clarke heard, as in a dream, Damianos' voice asking for a white sheet. Then, the sheet stretched out on the snow-spotted gray sand, the group of men stooped over and began picking up the shreds and tatters of a man they might have known, of a man they might have been. The slices of flesh gave between their fingers with the softness of ground meat.

When the area was picked clean, the men were ordered to their feet. They marched toward the south. The day was becoming dark, and, finding nothing, the paratroopers walked toward the forest that loomed before them. The southern flank was unmarred by death and dismemberment. The police call seemed to be over, but Clarke and the others were too stunned to experience any relief. The three thousand men gathered at the darkened forest's edge and sat on the earth, facing the glaring headlights of the Deuce-and-a-Halves ranked before them. The stars were not yet out in the vast ocean of the sky.

Clark could not sleep that night. Much as he tried to bar the second-by-second review of the day's events, those events proceeded before his helpless mind, focused as it was only on the moments of threat and violence. All through the night the screen of his mind was bathed in a projector's light, and with photographic precision the logic of events was resumed, following inevitably, image by image, sequence by sequence, like an unwinding film clip—the open door; the panic of the leap; the heavy silence and the *whoosh* of the passing, barely missed aircraft tail; the severed head; the overstuffed paratroop boots; the stumpy, dwarf's legs; the wobbly shovel; and the scattered fragments of a man sown over the barrenness of Crossroads.

In the darkness of the forest under siege of night, Clarke saw hundreds of flashlights turned on and heard, as though in a dream, the mumbled litanies of soldiers reading their pocket Bibles. With eyes that did not see the universe above them, the men read, whispering sibilant prayers in the night, inviting the God called all-powerful to combat the evil that seemed beyond His grasp.

The Lord is my shepherd; I shall not want. The prayers rose up to the silent twinkling ocean of the sky; each star, it seemed, reflected a white flashlight's hole in the darkened drop zone. *He maketh me to lie down in green pastures; he leadeth me beside the still waters.* Clarke relived his moments of horror again. The film clip began, and the images tumbled one after the other, each time as terrifying as the last. He could not saturate himself and thus cast off the recurring fears that inundated him. *He restoreth my soul . . .*

Clarke moaned. *No . . . no. . . .* But the reel started again: he swerved at the open door; he fell into the sky; the scythelike aircraft tail swept past him with a horrendous *whoosh;* and then he picked up the stunted body and the flakes of clotted flesh.

Yeah, though I walk. . . . Valley of the shadow of death . . . fear no . . . No . . . no . . . no. . . . He turned to the screaming door again, braced himself at the bucking threshold, fell into the screaming sky, and felt the menace of the Boxcar's bladed tail. . . .

Clarke sobbed. He was defenseless. For the first time in his life he had encountered death, his death, his annihilation. Before Crossroads, no matter what had happened, no matter what he had done, he had always felt secure. A circle of light and safety had existed around him, like an impregnable shield of some familial god which protected him from that which slew others. Whenever a fire broke out, an auto crash occurred, a crazed killer roamed, an airplane spun toward earth, he, Barrett Clarke, would be elsewhere, with a newspaper before him, reading about the annihilation of others. Barrett Clarke, he had thought, would die in bed. But now death was intimate; it seemed to have taken a personal interest in him. And he had managed, very cleverly, not to wonder where the casualties went in air crashes, who was detailed to remove the torn and gouged bodies forced through the windshields of destroyed autos, who carried out the charred corpses in tenement fires. But now he realized death was everywhere. He had ignored death all his life, but death had waited, biding its time, certain of its eventual triumph.

I will not jump! Repeating that comforting sentence was

now difficult, for the rebellious words were fused with fear. He could no longer stand proudly and state that he did not fear his death, that he refused to jump on principle. If he did not parachute once more, he would be rejecting the order to jump because he was afraid to die. The line between personal honor and fear of authority had now lost its definition. Everything was blurred, confused. Before the police call, Clarke could have stated that he, Barrett Clarke, was more important than any command, logical with a consistent madness though it might be. For, after all, that is what they were supposedly fighting for: the preservation of individual dignity. But now he was afraid, and fear had destroyed his certitude. Now he no longer cared about dignity; now he was fighting for his life, for a frightened, unmanly awareness of the only world which existed for him, the only world he could ever know. He did not want to jump, but now he feared both jumping and not jumping, for he doubted himself and his manhood.

He could exonerate himself in only one way, Clarke knew. He could rewin his courage and clarity in only one way. He could crush this overwhelming fear in only one way. He would jump one more time so that he could refuse to jump when he would be certain of his valor.

CHAPTER 36

The whistles screamed in the darkness. Damianos lunged out of his sleeping bag and stared ahead, his muscles tense and his hands fisted for protection. Within a few heartbeats his mind had cleared; he remembered where he was. *Yes,* he thought, *today is Tuesday. Yesterday was Monday.* He looked about. It had snowed during the night.

Pulling on his boots, he was surprised at the feeling of decision, of anger, that existed within him. While on Operation Razor Blade, he had waited for each dawn with a curious disinterest, like an ironic, uncommitted viewer at the spectacle that fate presented to him, forcing him, disaster by disaster, to recognize the power it always held over him. Up to this morning, whatever he may have said, he had felt humbled by his weakness, his helplessness before a force that made pathetic the dreams of freedom he entertained. Now all this was changed. Now he was furious with a slow, crafty fury, not at himself for being such a pawn or at people like Clarke who taunted him with an easier path to the freedom he desired and which, up to now, he suspected he may have betrayed. Today he was angry at the fate that tempted him to doubt everything on which he had based his life.

He was too old to change. Damianos he was born. . . . Damianos he would die. This was all he could do. It was all any man could do. *How simple I must be,* he thought, *for a guy like Clarke to know how to taunt me. I'm free, he told me. Free! And he spread his arms!* Damianos' hands shook as he tried to thread the bootlaces through the openings. *I should of said: You're not free. No one gets his freedom except by fighting his fate, by overextending it, by exhausting it, by outlasting it. That's what I should of said. You don't win freedom by running away.*

He tied the laces and stood up, frowning as he recalled his anger and behavior yesterday, fighting Clarke like some streetcorner bum. *I should of said: Do you think you're free by fearing death?* But no . . . like some hoodlum . . . some stupid animal . . . he had fought the only man he was certain understood what was involved in the sequence of the three disasters. The other soldiers merely waited for orders. He and Clarke approached this problem as a moral one, for it had long ago ceased to be military.

Damianos felt the tight comfort of his boots encase his feet. *How free I feel,* he thought. *Loose boots slow up a man, tire him out. A tight fit makes him feel free . . . light.* Why was it that he had good ideas only when he was alone? When he attempted to speak to others about matters that really counted, he felt frustrated and was forced to resort to his fists. He quickly slid the fatigue jacket over the heavy OG shirt he had worn in the bag and tucked it into his trousers. He put on the field jacket next, felt the tapered comfort around his waist, and tightened the inside cords at his hard abdomen and hips. Luckily, he had shaved the night before, because he knew Tuesday would begin with a vengeance. He combed his hair quickly. He was ready for anything now, ready for the death his ancestors called the Black Cavalier.

Damianos admitted that Clarke's attitude was a reasonable one—reasonable but incorrect. Clarke's error was that he did not consider himself challenged. The boy was still looking around for himself, still fighting the burden of having gone to school where the teachers evidently spent all their time telling the students how unique and different everyone was. How could he, then, be expected to view the past week as anything other than human stupidity?

And he had been wrong to pull his rank on the boy, Damianos realized. He should have told Clarke that the U.S. Army was in western North Carolina for one reason: to prepare itself to defend the West and Western freedoms. Once the boy granted him that premise, Damianos would have continued: *How can Western freedoms be defended unless certain men are willing to give their lives? Freedoms are threatened every day—whether in peace or war—and men must be courageous enough to defend these liberties, must be ready to give up their freedom in order to fight. What about the men at Thermopylae? Were they free?* Damianos felt a thrill stir through him, wondering how those stories, the unforgotten ancestral tales, still had such power to move him and direct his life with their logic. *The Three Hundred were freer than free: they were heroic. And heroes are never free. Only the brave can't afford to think of freedom, for only the brave accept duties willingly.*

This is what he should have told Clarke. He should have said that a man need not know what he is fighting for in order to be a hero, because in fighting he merely does what he can, hoping that others will come along to find a reason for his death. But now, this still-darkened morning, Damianos understood the reason for the death he expected. Might it not come to him as an unmerited gift for his devotion to freedom?

These are some of the things he should have told Clarke, instead of fighting with him like some corner hoodlum. He should have said that although the paratroopers were forced to continue jumping (in doing so, giving up what little freedom they had) and although they were ostensibly preparing to defend the Free World and all the individual freedoms everyone seemed to talk about, it was up to them, a perhaps undeserved gift, up to the paratroopers to show that men, especially ignorant men like Damianos, could fight their fate and squash it with their heavy but still human fists.

In line for coffee, Damianos nodded his head gravely when the news passed through the NCO grapevine that General Aarons was going to speak to the troops after chow. This was it, he knew: *A rousing, gutty speech . . . and into the airplanes again.* Damianos hoped the general would say what he hadn't the ability to tell Clarke. *Men,* he should say, *this is what we are fighting for today: we're fighting for freedom, human freedom. Because if we, the brave, don't have the courage to fight our fate, what would the others do who need us to defend them? It is our duty to jump again!* And then every whoreson of a paratrooper would fight to be first in an airplane. *Only the brave are never free,* he thought, proud of this conception, fated and grand as it was. Nothing would ever be accomplished on this earth without men who willingly gave up their ideas of freedom so others might possess the illusion that it existed.

Damianos recalled the steel-mill strike he had been on as a teen-ager. It was the same pattern. As long as he remained inside the mill, suffering, battling, and doing without, only so long was he free. His only freedom came when he was besieged. And the war? No one could tell him differently about the war. All the pacifists and neutrals during that war gnawed at their insides, hoping that the wrong side did not win. And it was just as true today. *There is no freedom—not for the brave.*

He held his canteen cup before the man pouring coffee. Smiling to himself, Damianos recalled the times he had waited for bread and coffee with stubble on his chin, with bloodshot eyes; the times he had sung hymns at Salvation Army missions, swallowing his pride and being herded by those militant (but those who, nevertheless, rarely stood poised at an aircraft's door), pasty-faced, vengeful Christians. *Fuck them,* he thought. *They don't know and never will know what it is to be a hero, what it is to have a real mission.* To soar in the sky and know that by a simple act of defiance, of fearlessness toward death, a man, even a failure like himself, could show that freedom should exist, even though, if it did, he would know that he could never share in it. Freedom existed only in duty. And duty was a slavish task accepted willingly. This is what he should have told Clarke. *To accept slavery willingly . . . that's freedom. To do your duty . . . that's freedom.* Everything else was tampering with failure, and with failure came the singing of Salvation Army hymns, came the shuffling of feet, came bitter impotence, came greasy, hypocritical charity forcing you to sing for your supper and making you despise the very food you required.

When he had finished drinking his coffee, Damianos glanced up into the grayness of twilight and noticed Clarke standing several yards away. He inched toward the PFC and cleared his throat. He pretended to blow on his coffee, as though he had some left. Raising the cup to his lips, he made a painful, sucking noise, as if it burned him. Clarke stared ahead. "Hi, Clarke," Damianos began. "Sorry about yesterday." He tried to make his voice seem genuinely apologetic, but it left his lips sounding gruff, almost threatening. "We both blew our tops."

Clarke confronted him. "What's going to happen today? Is it what I expect?"

Damianos became conscious of his displeasure at moving closer to Clarke and adopting a conspiratorial tone, as if the PFC were a longtime sergeant and it was important what he thought. "The grapevine has it that the Old Man is gonna make a speech today." Damianos felt that he was groveling. He was about to blow on his nonexistent coffee again, but the hypocrisy weighed on him; he turned the cup upside down and shook the few black drops out of it.

"I've been thinking about what happened yesterday. The conversation, I mean. What I wanted to say was . . ." And he groped, trying to resurrect the ideas that had seized his mind when he woke up. But all the words had scattered and the thoughts appeared confused. He raised his shoulders, like a boxer, as if he wanted to protect his chin. "I mean . . . only the brave are not free." He realized the inadequacy of the statement as soon as he uttered it. "You said yesterday that the Free World wasn't free. That you don't like being forced to do what you don't wanna do. I go along with that. I *do,*" he insisted. "But it's gotta be protected." He was floundering. Nothing he wanted to say was coming out properly. "Freedom is important and it's gotta be defended—"

"Even though it doesn't exist?"

Damianos stopped. In the depths of his admitted ignorance, he saw himself as a pathetic man trying to convince another of his sanity.

"I don't hold anything against you, Sergeant."

Damianos stared at his boots, surrounded as they were by the snow's whiteness.

"After the police call yesterday, I wasn't sure of myself. I thought: I'm afraid for my life. But now . . . now I'm not."

Damianos raised his eyes.

"I'm not afraid now, Sergeant. I'm not convinced that I should jump again because a general is going to tell me to. I'm up against it, Sergeant. I didn't sleep last night. I've been thinking about this, and just a few moments ago, when the dawn came, I knew what I had to do." He raised his cup, then brought it down again. "You see . . . if I'm afraid to jump, then I'm a coward. I'm a discredit to people like you. I'm a discredit to myself. But if I'm afraid to say that I refuse to jump, then I'm a moral weakling, a discredit to the things I believe in. I become a discredit to myself again."

The two men stared at each other. The light, powdery snow that had fallen in the night's darkness was now trampled under their boots.

"I'm not very military, Sergeant, and I'm pretty sure you're aware of that. I volunteered for the paratroops for a number of reasons—bankruptcy, mainly . . . more than one kind, perhaps—but I knew very well that I'd be required to jump when I would rather not. That's OK, I thought. It's what I volunteered for. But this is insane! It's madness, Sergeant. We aren't defending anything or anyone. We're obstinately jumping to prove a point." Clarke sighed. "Yesterday, when we had the fight, I wasn't afraid of parachuting. Maybe it was too close to the disaster. But afterward, on police call, I was never so sick and terrified in all my life." Clarke's hands trembled. "You see, if I hadn't gone on police call, I wouldn't have faced the dilemma I struggled with last night. I'd be more certain, more convinced, that I was true to myself. Now . . . I'm not as sure as I should be. I don't want to jump, *and I won't;* and I don't want to be afraid not to jump . . . but I probably will."

"That's it." Damianos spoke quickly. "That's it. I like the way you put that. Let me give you some advice, Clarke. I'm older than you. I'll talk to you like an uncle. Jump, is my advice. Jump . . . and then wonder if you did the right thing. But jump. You see . . . we're talking about freedom . . . but it don't . . . it don't . . ." He hesitated. "Freedom is only something you give up. But you only give it up for an hour. You get into your harness; you enter the plane; you're in the air—and you jump. Then it's all over. This way . . . by refusing to jump . . . you're refusing a legitimate command. That's a court-martial offense, Clarke. You won't be free in the Post Stockade."

Damianos glanced down at Clarke's hands. The PFC was pulling them apart, touching the insides of the wrists, then drawing them out again. "I'm free, Sergeant! I've made up my mind! I refuse to jump! I'm free!"

"Attention in the area. Attention in the area. Fall into your unit formations. Fall into your unit formations."

"That's it," Damianos said. Clarke's face had gone white. On the PFC's lower lip Damianos discerned a momentary quiver. The sergeant turned away, for he felt like an intruder. "Take my advice, Clarke." He looked across the drop zone to the mountains in the west. "Don't refuse to jump. I warned you what will happen otherwise."

He was gruff with Clarke when the Special Troops began assembling. With the other paratroopers he was jovial, and they, although the morning found them grumbling and cross, responded with wisecracks of their own. Team by team, the provisional companies were formed, and the Special Troops, with Colonel Simms at the lead, marched from the bivouac area to the gigantic, earth-fastened T, their green berets tilted jauntily on their heads.

Sergeant Damianos breathed deeply. He had forgotten Clarke and Clarke's problems. Marching in the senior NCOs' file to the left of the massed soldiers, his arms swinging freely, his boots falling in unison with the thousand others, Damianos felt the unmistakable rhythm of the pace. If Colonel Simms had not led the formation, he would have attempted a Jody rhyme, one he had just conceived. *Fine group of men,* he thought. Bedraggled and footsore, exhausted and unwashed, they looked not like soldiers but like refugees. *This is how men are tested. Not in ease, in contentment, but in adversity.*

Time seemed to stop; the past and future were forgotten, and only the present contained any meaning, for it became an unending arena of sacrifice and combat. This was Damianos' native land. He hummed the Jody tune, trying to rid himself of the surfeit of emotion that began flooding him as, boot by boot, the paratroopers marched across the gray plateau to the faraway T.

From all sides of Crossroads, solid blocks of men marched to the same destination. The thin cover of snow on the surface was darkened with the moving squares of paratroopers. They were too far away for Damianos to hear the Division sergeants' commands, but he observed them marching, puppetlike, turning smartly to the right, to the left, keeping their spacing as commendably as if they were on parade. He glanced to his right, at his own men. They were faultless.

This is what it means to be a soldier, he thought. To be so exhausted and terrified that the slightest bit of rest would permit all the nightmares to come bubbling to the surface, and to keep everything inside yourself; to express yourself only by saying yes to every command, by singing a Jody rhyme, by making an occasional wisecrack to keep your sanity, and by showing your steadfastness only by the precision with which you marched. To challenge everything you can possibly challenge; to bear everything you can possibly bear; to endure privation, terror, shock, and fear of death—yes, even death—and, with the yes, with the wisecrack or the Jody rhyme, with the neatly executed right turn, to thumb your nose at all these threats; to follow orders (which means to do what must be done) to the point where you are just an automaton, marching in formation with others, but to accept this dehumanization and, in accepting it, to perform what no machine ever could; to survive without the pampering a machine requires, to outlast steel and concrete, saying: If this what the befucked and bemired world demands for aggrandizement and defense, then this is what we will be. As long as we live, we will be the eternal reminders of mankind's hypocrisies. This is all . . . beyond the beautiful words and sentiments humanity feeds itself with . . . this is all it needs: dehumanized men, robots, to keep it from crashing. And this is what we will be, and, in being what is demanded of us, we will show in our silent, ignorant, cloddish way another human grandeur.

"Hup, two, three, four. . . ."

"Hup, two, three, four. . . ."

Damianos could not bear to maintain silence while his heart soared; while his blood, always volatile, throbbed more violently than ever before; while chilling tremors passed across his arms and back.

"Hup, two, three, four. . . ."

"Hup, two, three, four. . . ."

Each boot count, falling as it did in the empty, hostile silence of Crossroads Drop Zone and matched simultaneously by the tread of a thousand answering boots, provided the beat for the nonexistent chant which, by its very absence, called attention to itself.

"Hup, two, three, four. . . ."

"Hup, two, three, four. . . ."

He glanced to his right. The paratroopers were dissatisfied with merely marching to the T. They wanted to sing; they wanted to soar. Sergeant Damianos' voice roared through the heavy silence.

"On Crossroads sand our blood was shed. . . ."

The Special Troops responded within two beats.

"On Crossroads sand our blood was shed. . . ."

Damianos' eyes burned.

"And if we live—we'll be four times dead."

"And if we live—we'll be four times dead."

The cadence count was resumed. The paratroopers, now halfway across the drop-zone tableland, could see the other units forming at the paneled T area. Clarke, Damianos noticed, was still pale; his lips were thin and drained of color. *The boy's up against it,* he thought. Within minutes the formation would reach the T, would stop, would listen to the general's speech, and then would prepare to jump. *He'd better not refuse. He'd better make it easy for himself.*

Damianos' company was the last to arrive. After forming themselves, facing the stand, which was set on the juncture of the T's crossbar and stem, the Division and Special Troops stood at attention and waited for General Aarons to ascend the platform. The day's cold penetrated the soldiers now that they had stopped. Damianos, far to the rear, standing motionless in the snow, viewed the empty wooden stage. A distant blur between ranks moved abruptly toward the clearing, climbed the steps, and marched to the platform's center.

Aarons cleared his throat at the microphone. "We've run into a lot of problems on this goddamn maneuver," he began. "The way Lady Luck has been behaving to us, you'd think we were in combat. And I've heard many of you men saying how much like combat Operation Razor Blade seems." The general paused, surveying the 13,000 men standing rigidly around him in the snow. "But I'll tell you one thing, men. We've been tested, and that's important. Because it is us who are going to have to fight for freedom. And any fruit who thinks the paratroopers have gone soft will change his mind when he learns that during a certain week in December, in Operation Razor Blade, the men of the airborne ran into every disaster in the book and not only kept jumping but were steadfast, full of piss and vinegar, just as they were in North Africa, in Sicily, in Normandy, and at the Bulge. Let me tell you this, men. Every pansy straightleg unit is watching what we do today. They hate us. They hate the airborne. They think we're loudmouths . . . braggarts. They say: 'Sure the paratroops did a lot in the big war; but who the fuck is in the Division today? A bunch of mamma's boys. A bunch of teen-agers. The old-timers are gone,' they say. 'The only paratroopers in this man's game ready to defend Western freedoms and the dignity of man are last year's high-school graduating class.' That's what they're saying, men. And they're watching us to see what we do today."

Damianos stared at the general. A feeling of uneasiness, of resentment, had come over him. The general was not talking to him, was not saying what he should have said, was not stating what Damianos thought should be expressed about himself and the men of the airborne. The general was talking to the youngsters in the Division, bringing up arguments for them to continue jumping when Damianos would have said: *OK, simmer down. The line forms to the right. Whoever makes it first to the airplane gets two jumps today.* The others stood stiffly at attention, staring ahead blankly. Their impressions, Damianos judged, were similar to his.

Barrett Clarke was ahead of him and to the right. Sergeant Damianos was deeply embarrassed. All his aspirations, all his ideas were being corrupted, perverted, so that men less tenacious than he would be persuaded to jump again. At that moment he hated Aarons more than he had ever hated anyone. The general had outraged his self-respect. *Aarons ain't saying the right things.* Damianos felt insulted in being told that he must jump because a pack of straightlegs was watching to see if he would or not.

"So I'm going to have to ask you men to jump again," the general continued. "We're going to prove that we're just as good as we were in the big war. We're going to show them just who the paratroopers are!" He snapped to attention and jerked his head back. *"Is everybody gonna jump?"*

A roaring *Yes!* went up from the formations—not just one yes but a chain of them. "Yes," they shouted. "Yes." Damianos added his own voice, but not enthusiastically, because he would have wanted a more simple speech without references to nonjumpers. "Yes," he shouted. Yes, this was paratroopers' business. Yes, the others had better keep out of it. Yes.

But then the chant continued, and Damianos realized with a great surge of emotion that the men, pent up all this time, staring ahead at the man who had unintentionally trampled on their ideals, on their visions of themselves (*Enlisted men have ideals, too,* Damianos thought, and they were inviolate, unexpressed, pure, lost somewhere in the mud and beer and re-enlistment bonuses), listening to all their ideals being cheapened and lowered by an officer who would never understand them, had expressed themselves in the only way they knew how, with the only meaningful word in a soldier's vocabulary: yes. Yes. Yes. The chant rolled: Yes, yes, yes—short, clipped, with as much hatred in it as love. Yes, yes, yes—challenging not only themselves to endanger their lives again, not only the others who supposedly watched to see how they would behave, but even the God Himself; raising their thousandfold voices up to the heavens they would soon surmount. Yes, yes, yes—insulting fate by not fearing it, threatening death with death. Yes, yes, yes.

Damianos brushed a wayward tear from his cheek. "Yes," he shouted. *"Yes."* They would storm the very gates of heaven.

Yes, yes, yes. . . .

CHAPTER 37

Clarke had anticipated the question, for he had heard the same one from sergeants who were not expected to know any better. He was shocked, nevertheless, when he realized that the commanding general of the entire Airborne Corps was using the same diction. But that was only a minor shock compared to the one he experienced when the continual affirmatives, fully one minute after the question, still roared on Crossroads.

He wanted to withdraw. He had nothing in common with these men. They repelled him, for they were manipulated and would, to the end of their days, be manipulated by every idea and word that flattered their manhood. They did not deserve to be considered part of the West they were preparing themselves to defend. What they would war upon would have more appeal to them.

Westerner, he thought, *free thyself.* Their individual reactions, their selves, did not matter, even to them, and they presumed, by chanting "yes, yes, yes," to protect the abstract right of valuing what they themselves did not.

He turned in anguish to the men near him. For all their precise formation, they were a mob, and in their faces, their straining necks, their rooted feet, their fisted hands, he saw that this was what a civilization needed to defend itself with: the malcontents—those who defended values they themselves did not respect.

"Yes," the drop zone echoed. "Yes," the air around Crossroads throbbed. "Yes."

Clarke churned with anger. There must be some way to halt this continual abdication from himself, some means to check his falling, some path to his liberation. *No. I will not jump,* he thought, and was ashamed of his timidity. When will he not jump? When will he refuse to jump? When he would wear a parachute on his back? In the airplane? In the sky? At the open door? And be considered a coward?

"Yes, yes, yes." The chant roared on.

Clarke reached to his green beret and pulled it off. Frightened, his hands shaking, his knees wobbling, he stamped his boots in the powdery snow. *This is the crossroads,* he realized. *If I don't refuse now, I'll never refuse. If I say yes now, I'll always say yes. Even if I say nothing, I'm saying yes.*

As if preoccupied, Clarke stepped out of formation. A small white square, blank with snow, shone in the vast darkened area covered by the 13,000 assembled paratroopers. A few sergeants eyed him, amazed.

"No!" Clarke shouted. "No!" For the first time in his life Clarke felt whole. "No!" he shouted. "No!" He will not jump. "No!" He did not fear anything they would do to him. "No!" Somewhere in all that mob there should be a man who feared nothing and no one, who was fearless, not only toward death and injury, but toward the punishment of other men. "No!" he shouted, and while the juggernaut chugged on—yes, yes, yes—sweeping everything in its path, Clarke shouted, "No, no, no!" with more certitude than he had ever possessed, a no that grew louder and more hoarse as the yeses began to wear. And after every yes his no would follow.

Then he saw them coming after him, and at their lead, for he was nearby, ran Damianos. The sergeant leaped on him to gag his mouth. Clarke shot a hard jab into the sergeant's abdomen.

"You've shamed the Troops," someone muttered.

"I'm free of you all," Clarke shouted. *"I will not jump!"*

Another grasped his shoulders, and the two men wrestled on the ground.

I'm free, Clarke thought. "No!" he shouted. "No!" And then, as he leaped to his feet, he saw Damianos bearing down on him again. A great fist traveled toward him. Clarke ducked, but Damianos had feigned and caught him with a massive right to the jaw. The moving earth blacked out, and in the velvet backdrop of his mind, black but luminous with star punctures, the constellations of the sky went on a hasty dance.

Look down, he thought. *Look down.* And there below him, as always, was the city, its great beehive buildings jutting into the heavens that were only sky. He did not fear the beehive city now. He would not despair. He would not panic. There would be a solution to his fall. And then, below him, he saw the solution. A cornice projected from the building. He clutched at it confidently, feeling the razor-sharp edge slice into his wrists. His fingers strained at the molding. *Up. . . . I'll pull myself up. . . .* He began to chin and, as his face passed the cornice, he scraped the flesh against the concrete. *It will heal,* he knew. *My face will heal.* The pain was excruciating, but he could endure it.

He neared the ledge now, trying desperately to raise himself high enough so that he could rest with the greater weight of his upper body over the point of balance. He fell forward and rested, breathing heavily from his exertion. His face was alive with pain. But the pain had value, for it would help remold the face he had rejected when he fell.

He looked down again, confidently, to observe—miles away—the caverns of the skyscraper city beneath him. Church spires were lost in the shadows of the commercial buildings, whose towers neared the sky much more than did the Gothic spires and were rooted more certainly on the rock foundations under the ground. He would have learned nothing by falling. And less from the fall. He dreaded the fall no longer, for he had saved himself.

After pulling himself into a room, he raised his violated wrists to see that they were scraped raw. The red blood throbbed wildly over the blueness of the damaged skin. A woman neared him. It was Nikki. She touched his face. "You look different," she said. "It's as if I'm seeing you for the first time. Your face . . . your face is . . . beautiful. . . ."

When he regained consciousness, Clarke found himself manacled. The cuffs were tight on his wrists, and his ankles were chained to the metal legs of the jeep's front seat. A Negro MP sat next to him. Clarke opened his mouth to speak but felt a dull, consistent pain on his lips. Raising his manacled wrists, he probed the face he discovered to be swollen.

"He knocked a couple of your teeth out, too, man." The MP chuckled good-naturedly. "That sergeant is a *bad* ass, whoever he is."

Clarke said nothing.

"You *that* scared of jumping?"

Clarke shook his head. "I don't think so," he replied softly. "I jumped twice this week."

"Why'd you refuse then? Your ass is in a sling, man. Colonel said he's gonna throw the book at you."

Clarke shrugged his shoulders. *Why did they have to clamp the cuffs so tightly on my wrists?* he wondered.

"You're gonna be in the Stockade a long time, man. You embarrassed hell outa the colonel. An' General Aarons heard you saying no. I'll be long gone out of this Army by the time you get out."

Clarke fought his tears. He was slowly realizing that this person sitting in the jeep with handcuffs imprisoning his wrists was himself and that, truly, the jeep would take him to the Post Stockade. How easy it would have been to chant yes with the others, to chant nothing if he did not want to, but to jump with the rest, fighting constantly (for a mere hour, as Damianos had said) the sense of shame and guilt that would come with the knowledge that he was too insignificant and unimportant to be the master of his own destiny. But, it seemed, he was master of nothing, and everything—fate, his personal history, generals, colonels, sergeants, MPs, handcuffs—everything mastered him.

Now the statement—"No, I will not jump"—appeared silly, irrational, immature. It lost the vehemence, the importance it had had previously. Perhaps he should have jumped. Perhaps the idea that he was master of himself was just an illusion, a necessary and useful fiction, a falsehood that in times of peace, of ease, became an undisputed truth. *And now,* he thought. *Am I free now?* He sighed and touched his swollen lips again. *I was a fool to take myself so seriously.*

Another MP hopped into the jeep and started the motor. He looked over his shoulder. "Is the prisoner secure?"

"There's only one place he's going . . . and that's the Post Stockade. Isn't that right, now?"

"Where're you going when we get back to Mosby?" the driver asked.

"Going home for a while," the MP said, "and get in the saddle a bit."

The two soldiers laughed as the jeep lurched over ruts and managed to attain the dirt path that skirted Crossroads Drop Zone. The driver made a sharp left turn and sped into the pine forest. An hour later, just as the jeep was about to enter a paved road, Clarke heard the droning engines of the first flight of aircraft, flying V's in trail formation.

CHAPTER 38

The marshaling area of the field swarmed with men awaiting the command to strap on their equipment and enter the aircraft. Near the runway, a contingent of Special Troopers, Damianos included, was placed on the manifest and permitted to ascend with the second flight. After the main chutes and reserves were issued to them, the men helped each other into the harnesses with trembling hands.

They were performing the commonplace airborne chores again, concentrating on the familiar tasks, knowing that they were the only ones within their power, that the major decisions—whether they would live or die, whether or not the fourth would be the final jump—were not theirs to make. They passed their arms through sleeve loops, squatted slightly to fix the harness saddles under their buttocks, and straightened out the chest and leg straps as they had done countless times before. They snapped the right strap's metal lug into the quick-release mechanism. (How comforting it was to follow old patterns while death lurked above.) They placed the aviator's kit bag between their groins and the leg straps and clicked the two final straps into their respective notches. They had almost completed their preparations. (What would they do if they were forced to wait, to think, to smoke cigarette after cigarette?) Over the T-10 main chute they attached the clasps of the reserve to the two metal rings of the chest harness. Finally they slung the harness belt through the reserve and tightened it around their waists. They were ready now; they were standing tall. Another link in another chain had been forged again.

"Is everybody gonna jump?" a jumpmaster asked the planeload of men for whom he was responsible.

His question carried in the stillness of Eleutheria, and the thousand voices of the second flight roared: *"Yes, Sergeant!"*

Commands calling the assembled men to attention bounced from the field like syncopated echoes. *Teeeeeen-ten-teeeeeeeen-ten-hup!* And the men stood as straight as possible in their harnesses. *Parade . . . Parade-rade . . . paraaaade rest!* The jumpmasters went through the ranks checking the troopers' equipment.

Because Damianos had been chosen as pusher for the jump, he was inspected first. When he felt the tap on his buttocks, he stepped out of the formation and helped the jumpmaster by checking the rear of the rank and advancing along with the sergeant, man by man. He talked to the troopers in a low voice, forcing himself to banter with them. "Watch that leg strap," he said to one man. "Don't want your family tree to stop with you, do you?" And he immediately censored the thought that the man's family tree might have stopped as soon as he had shouted yes from Crossroads. "Your boot strings are loose," he observed to a young man. "What's the matter, Smiley? Can't you bend over with that big ol' reserve in your gut?" Damianos winked at the jumpmaster. "Well, now you know what it feels like to be pregnant." (Why did that thought, that word, leap to his mind?) "Lift your boot, candy-ass." The neighboring paratroopers laughed as Damianos leaned over and tightened the man's laces. He returned to the rear of the rank and continued testing straps. *What's Sophie doing? Is she beginning to feel her burden? Does she get dizzy spells yet?* "You're OK." He slapped a trooper on the hams and stepped behind another. "All set." Then to the next, asking himself how many men would perish before the destructive fate in which they found themselves came to an end. *It will stop. . . . It's gotta stop.* But how satanic it all was: to be outfoxed, led slowly and cleverly into a trap for which their own strength was the lure, the paratroopers' own discipline the cage, progressing—dilemma by dilemma—into a labyrinthine maze of precise alternatives, each one as reasonable as the last, yet each one, by degrees, calling for a deeper retrogression into madness.

And what about Clarke . . . that shameless man? He's out of it, the bastard! What did he mean—he is free? Shameless, Damianos insisted. *He's shameless.* He was comforted somewhat in the knowledge that Clarke was to be imprisoned for some time. *What do they mean—the dignity of man? How can we have dignity if we're not free?*

When he had completed his inspection of the stick of paratroopers, Sergeant Damianos scanned the faces of the men, interested in how many were harboring doubts similar to Clarke's, wondering if he would have to aid the jumpmaster in battling with someone at the door.

They were called to attention again and marched to an open space on the runway, where they would wait to board their particular aircraft. Another planeload of paratroopers marched toward a C-119 about a hundred feet away. At the rear of a file a man struggled to keep his legs straight. They wobbled out of control, however, and kicked apart, dropping the man on the runway. He was unnoticed as the open door of the Flying Boxcar gradually swallowed his file. Damianos rushed to the fallen private and helped him up.

"Sarge, Sarge, Sarge," the soldier moaned. "Help me. My legs don't work. I can't get 'em to walk for me. Help me up the ladder."

"Yes, yes," Damianos said reassuringly. "Don't worry. I'll help you." He wondered: *To your death?*

"I don't wanna shame my name."

And Sergeant Damianos, himself burdened with fifty pounds of equipment, raised the young man as a nurse would an invalid, grasped him under the main harness, and half carried him to the aircraft.

"Thank you, Sarge, thank you," the private murmured. "I don't wanna shame myself."

Damianos and the jumpmasters of the C-119 raised the man up to the aircraft's floor.

Courage, Damianos considered as he walked back to his stick of paratroopers, *is greater than the muscles and nerves of the puny body . . . part of the human soul . . . immortal . . . strengthened by being tested. . . .* He assumed his position at the end of the file. The planeload of men was given a left face, a forward march, and, with a *hup, two, three, four,* the paratroopers were led to the open door of the waiting Boxcar. Damianos leaned forward and climbed into the rounded darkness of the fuselage.

He lumbered down the aisle. Walking directly to the last seat of the row, he snapped open the catch and let the surface fall parallel to the floor. Lowering himself into the bucket seat, Damianos stared, seeing nothing.

"Is everybody gonna jump?"

"Yes, Sergeant!" The roar in the fuselage was deafening.

Clarke is in chains! Damianos thought. He, himself, had subdued him and held his wrists for the manacles. The sergeant glanced about at the silent paratroopers in the harness burdens. *We are free in the only way men can be free—performing our duty. Yes,* Damianos thought, *performing our duty.* And what of the facts that the safety belts imprisoned him and the others into bucket seats from which they would all rise at the shout of *stand up* and that, in unison, to each precise command, they would respond with a well-trained subservience? What of it, if they winged their way to a thrice-encountered Crossroads, where they had gained nothing but the wisdom that they must encounter it again and again?

Damianos felt the spine-shattering roar of the propellers. *Yes,* he thought as the aircraft taxied to its strip and charged toward the sky. *Yes . . . this is the only freedom I have.* For out there, in chains, like Clarke, rooted in the certain, secure world, he would be anything but free. *There is no choice.* Each alternative was slavery—only one enslavement was more manly than the other. *Yes,* he thought, *manly. . . . Yes . . . more manly.* Freedom did not exist. *Only candy-asses can think they're free. What did Clarke mean—he's free?* All Damianos had known history to be was the mere exchange of one set of manacles for another, and the only free men were those who had accustomed themselves to the metallic bite of their chains. *I have no dignity. . . . What do they mean—the dignity of man?*

The aircraft bucked wildly for a moment, then came to rest in quiet air. In the roaring fuselage, Damianos, unwatched, sang silently to himself, mournfully, knowing with the first line of the Jody rhyme the inevitability of the last. *"Snow fell on the drop-zone sand. . . ."* He saw the mud caked on his fatigue trousers and absentmindedly tried to pick it off. *"Set upon my bleeding hand. . . ."* He raised his head and stared at the man across from him as, lips fluttering, the trooper recited the beads of his rosary. *"Snow and sand and blood will fly. . . ."* Damianos sighed deeply, checking a surge of emotion which threatened his equanimity. *"Who'd of knowed that I passed by?"*

Yes. Who would have known that he had passed by? Sophie? *Yes, Sophie.* His unborn son? *Yes, him too.* But they would have known that a man like Cosmas Damianos existed only as he himself knew that his mother and father had lived, had passed by. Their sufferings, their travail, would have been forgotten, for those cannot be inherited by the race. Only heroic stories and ancestral chains are immortal. Not men.

"Get ready!"

Sergeant Damianos loosened his safety belt and shifted his boots.

"Stand up!"

The men in the stick lumbered to their feet. Damianos looked down the long line of paratroopers: the file of helmets pointed true, then stopped a few feet from its goal, the open door. Steel helmets, Damianos had been told—then grew to accept as obvious truth—encased and protected the most precious possession of man: his mind. But when it needed the steel bubble's protection, was man's mind his most precious possession? He crushed his thought. He would not permit a sniveling doubt to shake the strength of his conviction.

"Hook up!"

The paratroopers hooked up.

"Check static lines!"

The wire running from front to back in the fuselage was jerked several times.

"Check equipment!"

Damianos inspected his harness; felt the tightness of a few straps; examined, with little interest, the position of his quick-release; and looked down the file of helmets again.

"Count down for equipment check!"

Sergeant Damianos shouted his number and the OK and slapped the buttocks of the man ahead. He heard the numbers being counted off as they neared the jumpmaster at the open door.

There was a pause. Damianos observed the jumpmaster leaning out of the screaming door, knowing the vicious pull of the prop blast on the face, recalling the necessary squint of the eyes to see the junction of the stem and crossbar.

"Stand in the door!"

The stick of paratroopers danced forward three paces. Sergeant Damianos neared the man ahead of him, readying his shoulder to apply the forward pressure on the man's back.

The electrifying moment came.

"Go!"

The line moved, dancing with boots in unison, stamping on the ringing metal floor, pressing forward inexorably, Damianos pushing from behind, the point men advancing second by second to the open door, turning, and kicking out, not needing the pusher's force, second by second dropping from the screaming door to the silent earth below.

Yes, Damianos muttered. In this was his freedom. In this act his manhood. This brief second, his immortality. His shoulder pressed against the man before him. His feet danced forward, the enslaving boots slamming on the metal floor. Second by second he neared the door, staring at the jumpmaster. His hands gripping the cold steel jambs, he swerved at the door and confronted the horizon. This was his freedom. This was his fate. He bent his knees at the threshold and vaulted into the sky.